I0603497

ALWAYS A FAE

ETANI BOOK 3

N. MALONE

MORE FROM THE AUTHOR:

Etani

Trapped Princess

A special thanks to the Arthur family. I have never known a more beautiful,
supportive family, and I will never forget everything you have done for me.
Not only with my books, but for my entire life.
I love you all.

Thank you.

No part of this book may be reproduced, scanned or distributed in any form or by any means electronic or otherwise without the prior written permission from the Author unless for a brief use of quotations in a review.
If you are reading this book and did not purchase it, or it was not purchased for your use only, then this copy must be destroyed.
This is a work of fiction. Names, characters, businesses, events and incidents are the products of the author's imagination. Any resemblance to actual persons, living or dead, or actual events is purely coincidental.

Copyright © 2020 N Malone
All rights reserved.

Cover Design by DAZED designs www.dazed-designs.com
Rear Cover Design by Cecilia G.F. @ThanatosOfNicte

ALWAYS A FAE

1

LET THE GAMES BEGIN

The arrows rose high, glowing a solid white as they flew too far, much farther than a normal arrow should reach. At the highest point, the arrows exploded, and to her shock, the arrows fell, thousands of them, looking like shooting stars and the army below didn't move, transfixed by the show, the magic of their deaths.

The arrows landed, two circles of men fell, and there was silence.

Behind them, a loud booming had begun. Turning, she was stunned to see a mountain moving.

He was easily fifty feet tall and she stared in wonder at the enormous size of the King.

He wasn't wrong; his armour had grown with him, and he was magnificent.

She didn't think at all, throwing down the bow and sprinting away from the front line towards the King as his boots came down.

She realised immediately why there was such a large gap down the middle of the army's ranks. It was for their King.

She ran for him and his eyes found her, seeing her outrage and glee at the sight of him.

He stooped, his arm reaching; he was right, he was slow due to his size. She didn't need his help, however, except as a launching point.

Her foot landed on his cupped hand and she threw herself forward, leaping from his glove to his gauntlet, up to the lower edge of his shoulder guards, up to the spikes and over the wolf. All the way up until she stood gleefully on his shoulder guard and the air pressure as he straightened was enormous. All she could do was clutch at his hair as he looked at her, amused.

She felt like a God atop him, and her body swayed as he went forward.

Up over the crest, the sight must have been horrifying; the enormous, armoured King, taller than the castle, taller than anything had a right to be.

At the top of the crest, he glanced at her again. Etani drew her sword, holding it out, and screamed a battle cry.

His battle cry made her bones vibrate and then the army joined in on it. He reached behind him and drew the enormous sword, holding it out, and the armies moved as one.

They ran for each other, howling and raging like barbarians, their screams singing the deaths of the opposing army. Their army was smart enough to move around the King, because he moved forward with them, looming over all those below.

When he reached the enemy, his enormous foot rose backwards and then flew forward.

If they weren't hit by his foot directly, the force of the air sent men and creatures sent flying.

She had a huge grin on her face and laughed as soon as he moved forward with his soldiers and the dead flowing with him.

The armies came together in an enormous din, people screaming in rage, pain and death, or fear.

She revelled in it, wanting to see more and get involved.

"Up," she yelled in his ear.

She tucked her sword securely in its sheath, let go of his hair as his arm rose. Running down, she leapt off his fingers and twisted, her hand finding the loops of three of her throwing knives.

They loosed, flying to find flesh or bone or armour.

Rotating her body, she came down hard on the back of what she believed to be an ogre, her legs tight around his head. She turned first left, then right in a sudden movement, feeling his neck snap to the side.

She spun off him, landing on a helmeted head and using it to launch herself off. Reaching behind her, she drew her two long daggers as she landed on her knees atop the shoulders of a man she couldn't see for his armour.

Driving both knives down into the sides of his neck, severing his spine, she kicked off as he fell forward, coming to land neatly left foot first.

Turning, she slashed across the back of someone's legs, driving her knife into the back of another and still she hadn't paused, killing indiscriminately. It was still easy to tell which side was around her, they were all facing back the way she had come.

Using a corpse, she lunged up and landed on the back of a reptilian creature, his spines cutting her leg, but she ignored it. He hissed and she drove her knife into the top of his head, mostly to help pull herself up.

She rose as he stood rigid, then ripped the blade free and was on the next man in her next step.

Her hood was down, and her hair was coming loose of her braid, but she didn't care, she was high on blood and death.

A roar sounded and she spun, seeing an orc with a missing tusk coming for her. She changed course and ran directly for him, using a corpse to launch herself up and landing knees-first on his chest, driving him back as she drove both blades into his face. He fell and she was already moving on to her next target.

She had formed a pretty little circle of destruction in the middle of the field, Alaric lumbering in her direction and crushing whoever wasn't fast enough to get out from under his feet.

An arrow flew and she turned in time that it only grazed her cheek and she spun, throwing her knife at the archer.

It landed hard in his chest and he dropped to the ground, her blade deep enough to stick out of his back.

Those around her had realised the danger and they pressed back, but that only made them easier targets as she ripped the knife free and went after her next victim.

When her knife was lost, she switched to a sword and her heavy knife, glad to have options.

She grew bored of hacking when the first hour had passed and she laughed as she found the vial she was looking for.

Using the back of a centaur as a launching point, she twisted in mid-air and threw the vial; it exploded on the centaur's back and green bubbles exploded out all over the field.

'*Go, go, go!*' she thought as she used heads, backs, and shoulders to get away from the scene; over her shoulder, the bubbles exploded and spewed green corrosive goo everywhere.

Her first kiss came from a Naga, his muscular chest and writhing body made her turn in his direction, hoping it was the guard from Weorene, but it wasn't. He saw her as she stepped from his tail, his arms outstretched for her, wanting to sink his fangs into her.

But her lips found his before his mouth could open and he fell, his body writhing in death as her eyes flooded black.

She was lost to the death, ripping her way through human and creature, anyone that got in her way.

The buzz of mythicals never lasted long, and she was back to herself somewhat when she saw *him,* and he saw her.

He looked like a fighter so she lunged for him, gleefully cutting the hamstring of the humanoid she passed, left screaming in her wake.

She lunged for him and her first blow was deflected, along with the second and then the third before he managed to slam his fist into her chest and, finally, she had a significant hit on her.

She rolled, her knife lying on the grass between them, but she kept her sword.

She grinned and went for him again, her sword at the ready. They moved at a pace that was nearly impossible to see.

Her knee found his gut and he threw her back then came for her again and again.

Finally, his boot found her stomach and she was thrown back once more, growing angry, deciding she needed to figure this out. He was toying with her.

2

———

THE BEAUTIFUL DEMON

The male approached her slowly.

She lifted her sword out at her side she panted, her free arm protectively over her bruised and aching stomach where he had kicked her. He smiled slightly, his eyes an odd yellowish-gold shimmering colour she had never seen before. Short black hair and a chiselled face. There was a little metal ring in his lower lip just off to the side, another thing she had never seen before but that was not unheard of.

He wore a long black coat and black gloves that covered only his first three fingers, but he didn't have a bow as the gloves would suggest.

A large chain with a silver cross hung around his neck, loosely looping his slender throat twice with a third loop hanging down closer to his sternum that held the cross. The cross was inverted, and she watched it as he approached; she wanted that stupid necklace very badly.

Her eyes slid up from it, past his smiling face and to the top of his head, where two small horns stuck out from his wild hair. Sliding down again, she found the short, pointed shape of his ears. They carried a large number of rings in them, thick and thin.

He was a demon of some sort, attractive enough to stop most women, and when he smiled, her heart skipped a beat at the sight. He was a demon and she could guess which one.

Lust demons were the pretty ones.

She pushed herself to her feet, tightened her grip on the handle of her sword, ready for his next attack.

"Etani my love, I haven't seen you since you were but this tall." He stooped, holding his hand palm down around two feet off the ground.

That made her stop, her head cocking slightly to the side as she studied his face with renewed interest.

With his pace slow and relaxed, his hands shoved into the pockets of his trousers, he looked as though they were simply bumping into each other on the street, not in the middle of a warzone.

"Who are you?" she asked, her question making him scowl.

"Ah, yes I forgot. He died before he could tell you about me. The black sheep," his voice was honey and sex, all things promising, but she wasn't buying his act.

"I will ask again, who are you?" she demanded, her free hand going to the small of her back, fingers tracing names as she picked out the one she wanted.

He vanished between steps, and as her fingers closed around a vial, his fingers closed around her wrist from behind and jerked her arm upwards. She hated it when her adversaries could do that.

Forced forward with the pain, she gasped and lifted her foot, bringing her heel slamming down on the top of his.

He hissed in pain, but he refused to let go of her. "Stop being so difficult. I should never have added that damned siren, the lot of you have been uppity ever since," he growled in her ear.

She flicked the sword down to run along her forearm and drove it backwards and up, aiming for his chest or even his head if she could.

The sword deflected off his chest as though he wore armour, fabric tearing.

"Such a pain..." He sighed and tucked his foot around hers, jerking her foot out from under her.

Falling to her knee and bending forward, she realised she was running out of options. "Trust a demon to fight dirty," she snarled, tears in her eyes at the pain of her arm and shoulder.

"Now there's no need to be petty. You should be nice to your father,"

She went rigid as the words hit her and, in her distraction, she found herself face down on the grass.

"There we go. Now be a good girl and give me the sword." His hand clamped down on hers, squeezing until there was an ominous crack of one of her fingers and she reflexively released the sword.

Pulling that arm behind her back, he proceeded to sit on her backside, her hands in his lap as he pulled them up, presumably to see what they looked like.

"Who are you? You're not my father," she said in anger. She clenched her fingers into a fist to keep him from being able to do anything, but he simply pried her fingers back open and studied her nails.

"Mm, yes that one was a particular pain in my arse," he said as he flicked her nail, hearing the tap of metal. "Agnes, the iron witch," He pressed her hands onto her back and something clamped onto them, making it all but impossible for her to move them even half an inch apart. Standing up only long enough to roll her onto her back, he sat on her hips and leant down close to her face.

"Haven't you ever heard of personal space?" she asked, turning her face away from his.

He gripped her jaw and forced her face back to his and she smiled just a hint before she jerked her head up and her lips connected with his.

Bursting through his defences, she threw her consciousness downwards like an arrow, brushing his soul only to snap back to herself with a wrenching sensation as he forced her face down to the ground.

"You little bitch," he snarled, releasing her long enough to slap her across the face, his nails digging into her cheek. "Ought to muzzle you. There'll be no killing me." He gripped her bleeding face painfully hard, forcing her head back and to the side to examine her ears and the scars on her throat. "Vampires are always a problem for you lot," he murmured, irritable at her attempt to kill him.

"Get off me, demon!" She wriggled, but she wasn't moving even an inch.

"Daemon," he said, and she looked at him. "Shut up," he said, seeing the taunting sarcasm in her eyes.

"Those eyes though…" he breathed as he studied them. "Those were hard to get back." He pulled down on her lower lid and she jerked her head away from him.

"What do you want?"

He was driving her mad with the inspection and he noticed her teeth. Gripping her jaw with hard fingers, he forced her mouth open. "Damned vampires, I knew they would end up being a problem. Can you still procreate?"

The last question made her angrier and she bucked her hips in an attempt to throw him off, but he barely budged and settled again on top of her.

"Stop squirming. I haven't gotten this close to you in nine hundred years. I need to see my work," he sounded exasperated, and, giving a huff, she remained still while he picked at her hair and ears, her lips and then down the top of her vest. "You turned out a lot better than I expected," he said, turning around on her and tugging at her pants.

She kneed him in the face and he nearly fell.

"Fine, fine. But really about the procreation?" He turned around again to face her head.

"Yes, I can still procreate," she said angrily, glaring up at him.

"Then why haven't you? You've got two husbands, surely one of them could have done it by now."

The subject made her deeply uncomfortable and she wondered how he even knew about Epharis and Drizdan.

"That's none of your business. Who even are you?" she snapped, her arms straining to bring her hands closer to each other and away from her elbows. It felt as though he had glued her arms together, each forearm against the top of the other arm.

"I'm Daemon. I created you," he said simply as he leant down over her, examining her throat. "Can you sing?"

"Like a siren. What do you mean you made me?"

"I made you. Your father and his mother and so on. You are my pride and joy, my prodigy. You are the result of centuries of my very careful selective breeding."

His words struck her like a physical blow and her face paled as she took it all in. The family tree being a perfect straight line, the feeling that it had all been planned.

She had no words to describe just how horrified she was by the news, nor by his appearance now.

The battle raged around them, but through some magical anomaly, they were given a perfect circle of ten feet where no one entered, no blood splashed.

"Why?" she asked, trying to understand.

"The perfect weapon. The woman who will take over and rule all of the worlds. That is why," he said in a breathy tone while she shook her head.

"I won't let you continue to breed my family," she said, thinking of her children and grandchildren in the hands of a demon.

"No, my love. You are the weapon. You are the perfect being," he said, his nose a mere inch from hers. "A creature so beautiful it could blind, who can kill with a kiss, can sing children and men into endless sleep. Immortal and who can move between worlds with only a drop of blood, who can enchant any creature that comes into contact with her. You are the destroyer of worlds, the joiner and the creator. You are the one I have been working on for so long. It will be your womb that births an entirely new reality with no flaws like the humans suffer. It will be perfect, just as you are."

His speech made her feel ill and she looked for something to beat this crazy demon over the head with until he stopped talking.

"I know you're probably sick of hearing this by now, my love, but I'm going to marry you."

He wasn't wrong on that matter, and she looked up at him, eyes narrowed and jaw set.

"You're the fourth man to tell me that in a year. It's a tad old," she said sarcastically.

"Yes, but they aren't me. Together we will create infinite worlds, infinite beings," he breathed, and her flesh crawled at his tone.

"Well, thank you for the offer, but I'm afraid I will have to decline. I have no interest in being some universe broodmare, nor your wife, nor some perfect magical being." She squirmed again, managing to wiggle herself up an inch.

"I'm afraid your refusal isn't an option, Etania. I created you and I can always replace you with your sister."

She looked up at him and then laughed.

"Letari's been dead for a year, idiot. You need to keep better track of your toys."

He looked genuinely confused. "But I can sense her. She's near-by," he said, baffled.

"Yes, she's under you right now. We're both in here. She died and we touched in the spirit world." She was still laughing at the utter ridiculousness of the entire situation. "I'm all you've got Daemon the demon. Get off me." She jabbed her knee into his back, and while he was wrapping his head around what she said, she wriggled herself free of him.

"This is rich. After everything this world has put me through. After the men and the monsters, you come along and tell me I'm a dog you have bred. After everything I had to endure, after everything Letari and Avadari had to endure." She pushed herself to her knees and then to her feet, rage boiling up in her to a point where she was simply laughing. She was so completely beyond anger that she could do nothing else, standing before him with her arms bound behind her back, in the middle of an active war, laughing.

"Nine hundred years of running, nine hundred years of fighting to survive and there you are sitting all pretty in your ugly jacket." She advanced on him and he looked a little nervous. "Nine hundred years alone, Daemon, then I come here. One year of torture and men abusing me. One year of being lied to and manipulated and you decide to come walking up to me. In the middle of a war," her voice rose and her hair lifted off her shoulders and back, floating just off her skin.

Her eyes glowed white in her absolute and perfect fury. The demon backed away from her.

"One year, Daemon! One year of suffering and you come here to tell me you were watching? You just sat by and lamented your poor little pet experiment and wondered when she was going to become a killing machine for you?"

Her fury bottomed out and the entire field had gone silent, or perhaps she was just so incredibly enraged that she had gone deaf. "I'm going to kill you now," she said calmly and took one step, then drove her foot into his face.

The demon seemed to vanish, but then she followed a perfectly clean line of flattened soldiers and fighters where the demon's body had gone flying, landing finally to leave a gouge in the ground some two hundred metres away.

Those affected by the sudden projectile demon looked a little shocked, sprayed with blood from exploding creatures, and then turned to see what had caused it.

After a pause, they seemed to unanimously decide that their current location wasn't the best one to be in and scattered, shouting for others to run.

They didn't get very far as she turned, her eyes going towards the titan. He saw her at the same time, her long hair floating around her as the braid unwound, her eyes a bright white tinged with blue. Her arms peeled free of each other, her fingers in claws as she boiled inside, something building to erupt out of her.

Her mouth opened and the sound she made was not a scream; it was more than that. It was louder than that, deeper, and yet it was no sound at all. She screamed for those around her, for the dead who were already dead and for the dead who were dropping even as she sang their deaths for them.

Humans and mythicals dropped like cut flowers, mid-step and mid-rise to their feet. They simply dropped and the circle around her was perfect as though she had taken a scythe to wheat.

She was so beyond done with the lot of them, their taunting her, their abusing her, their using her for whatever goal, she wanted them dead and gone. She was going to destroy every last one of them and so she screamed, and ears bled, eyes rolled back and people died instantly, their brains exploding and their eardrums rupturing.

Glass all over the field seemed to evaporate at the sound, showering shards and killing even more with the projectile fragments.

Finally, the call faded and the sound returned to her ears, just in time to hear running footsteps.

She smiled, turning and throwing her arm up, punching the demon in the chest to send him flying just as far.

It was almost impossible to kill a demon, she knew that. But she wanted revenge and if he was going to make it easy for her, she was going to give him what he wanted.

She inhaled slowly, wisps of white lifted from the mouths of the dead and flowed to her in long, glittering streamers. Her body screamed with the energy that shot through her like a drug, hundreds dead in a second, hundreds consumed from a distance into the woman who had become death incarnate.

Stepping slowly over the corpses, her hair lengthened with each step, her attire changing into a long, flowing black gown that hugged every inch of her body before trailing back behind her, a long slit up the front revealing one slender leg.

Black metal encased her feet, delicate with vine-like creepers crawling up her shins with a modest heel. Her body was wrapped in a large black cloak that appeared at first to be made of feathers, until the feathers parted and enormous black wings spread out behind her, thick and full.

As they parted, a headdress leaked up from her now knee-length hair, two large horns pointing backwards behind her head, a glowing stone trailing from a single silver chain over the top of her head to hang between her brows.

Long black gloves snaked up her arms from her nails, stopping just below the hanging sleeve of her gown.

The demon was back on his feet, those odd yellow-gold eyes huge in terror and wonder as she stretched out one hand to her side and a massive scythe formed between her outstretched fingers.

He had wanted the perfect weapon, and she now stalked him in her demonic, God-like perfection.

The bodice of her gown was made of tight leather, cupping and supporting her breasts with a thin strip that traced down her front to join at the skirt, enclosing her in leather and cloth while leaving a healthy portion of her grey-blue skin visible, a large cross of leather running up her chest to curl around her throat like a lover. A crimson crystal hung between her breasts from a slender black chain, throbbing and glowing with her heartbeat which had kicked back into action as the transformation began.

She smiled at the demon and he flinched as she handled her new scythe with hypnotic precision. "Tell me, Daemon, can a demon greet death as a lover?" she whispered, her voice echoing a nanosecond behind her throaty purr.

He shook his head mutely, terrified and enthralled in equal measure.

"Shame, he's a nice creature," she whispered, her words echoing inside her head. "Tell him I said hi, when you see him." She swung the scythe and his body slowly, dramatically slid apart at the waist.

There was no blood, no gore or anything, the scythe moving so smoothly and perfectly that reality didn't have time to process what had happened before he slid apart.

He still had a shocked look on his face as she set the clawed foot of her scythe on the ground and contemplated what was left of him.

She didn't know if destroying his physical form would kill him, but she hadn't been able to resist.

Turning slowly to the booming steps of the titan, she smiled and headed in his direction, a gleeful excitement starting in her gut at the approach of the King.

She was going to kill him, too, just as soon as she got to him.

He stared down at her, seeing the destruction she had caused, seeing the change and yet he came for her, prepared to die in defence against this new, more lethal threat.

Most of the field had emptied before her and both sides huddled together out of the way, leaving her a clear path to the titan, though corpses still littered the ground.

His sword lifted and she swung the handle of her scythe up, holding the shaft behind her back. The six foot blade pointed up, curled over her head, and she grinned, a feral grin that had men cowering back in the trees.

The titan ran for her. She stopped, reaching up to caress the clean blade, down the shaft and as her fingers left it, the shaft seemed to stick to her. Black stretched to form a ribbon that curled lovingly around her wrist. Turning her head, she smiled and closed her eyes as she felt the weapon singing to her, loving her for her beauty and for her love of it.

Allowing the blade to fall, she jerked it and it flicked across her back and up, her fingers curling around the ribbon. Tilting herself just slightly, the scythe spun in a rapid circle by the ribbon.

Her eyes snapped open, bright white as she released the scythe and it flew for the King. The ribbon stretched, almost endless as it closed the huge distance to the titan.

Something struck the scythe before it could reach its mark and she lowered her eyes to the Lich, his eyes glowing a bright, flickering green. Pulling at the ribbon, the scythe shot back to her and she caught it as easily as a tossed apple.

Anduril was in his hand, smoking heavily with a new chip in the blade.

Alaric had stopped, not expecting her to be able to move so readily and he watched as his younger brother took on death given flesh.

Epharis paced forward, his right hand lifting to form a flickering green ball of fire, throwing it at her with a speed she hadn't expected.

Snapping her scythe around, the ball hit the blade and bounced off to her right, exploding a tree into evil green fire.

She smiled, watching her husband approach her with a second ball starting.

He was so cute when he was angry, furious that she had turned on them. But what had they expected? He was just as bad as his brother when it came to hurting her.

The second ball was deflected just as easily as the first and she paused, looking around at a soft rustle.

The scythe flashed and someone fell, blood splashing.

"Kai!" someone screamed, and a sudden shot of fear hit her chest as she vaguely recalled something important about the name.

She turned slightly to see what was going on, catching sight of Jaia over his brother. Kai was bleeding profusely from a large cut in his chest. She deflected a third ball of fire without looking and started for the two vampires.

Jaia moved to defend his brother and she used the butt end of her scythe to send him flying.

Kai was dying, looking up at her with huge, terrified eyes.

She smiled at him and tears welled up in his eyes. Oh how she loved that man, loved his fear and loved his beautiful death. She loved him more than he would ever be able to understand in that moment.

"Etani?" he pleaded as she knelt down, her scythe set aside.

She drew him up to her and even as Jaia screamed, her lips met the soft lips of Kai and she lifted him lovingly from himself, cradling him tenderly inside her even as his corpse fell to the ground.

3

DEATH

The entire battlefield was silent for a beat, and then Jaia was screaming, red running down his cheeks.

As she stood, she lifted her scythe back in her hands by the ribbon.

He ran for her and she spun, slamming the base of the handle into his chest to send him flying backwards, tumbling as he rolled to a stop only to run for her again, blind in his loss.

Her deal with him meant she was unable to raise her scythe to him; instead, she used the back and the butt on him, every attempt met with cold indifference and finally the handle connected with his temple and he no longer got up after he had finished rolling.

She felt part of herself reaching out for him and a loving caress told her he was still alive.

Turning, she saw Epharis was almost on her and she smiled at him, welcoming death to her. He was one of her creatures, dead and yet not dead, and she loved him for that.

Her hand reached for him, wanting his, and she saw his confusion, his burning need to join his mistress.

Something whipped past her and she blinked once, confused by the sudden movement that lacked even a trace of sound. She felt something missing, her fingers closing reflexively on the scythe but it was still there. Slowly, her hand that had reached for the Lich moved to her breasts and she found the crimson crystal to be missing.

Looking down, the light in her eyes sputtered and went out, her scythe exploded into mist and she looked at her hand as the ribbon slid back into her skin, digging a mark into her wrist as her gloves melted away.

Her eyes found him then, the vampire King holding the chain out to his side, the crystal dangling free in his fingers. Her wings exploded into a shower of feathers, her headdress dissolved back down into her hair and her dress seemed to melt into the ground, leaving her in her gear, the metal sinking back into her to be replaced by her tall boots.

She staggered forward at the loss of her wings, off balance as she dropped to her knees. Falling forward onto her hands, she felt the power leaving her, the strength and perfection, leaving her just a woman who could barely protect those she loved.

She screamed once the realisation of what she had done hit her, and remembered the little ball caressed against her breast that was Kai.

She had killed him because he had been injured; there was something there in the back of her head that urged her to move for him, to do something for him and yet she didn't understand the order.

Screaming her pain and loss, she felt a knife drive into her back and through her heart, her world going black as her body hit the ground.

She woke suddenly, sitting upright and looking around with frantic horror at the memories of the battle. But there was no battle, and she was in a cell, chained to a large bed.

Trying to figure out what was going on, she squinted in the dimness and Versalis seemed to materialise. She studied him, trying to understand what was different about him and then it clicked: his eyes were no longer crimson but had turned an odd pale lavender that matched him remarkably well.

"Versalis?" she whispered, trying to understand what was happening.

"Etani..." he said gently, holding the bars of her cell door. "You killed him."

Her breath stopped as the memory slammed into her and tears filled her eyes at the horrible, terrible realisation. Her heart seemed to break and there it was again, that need that itched at the back of her head.

"I need clay," she said, instead of begging for forgiveness as she had meant to do.

He blinked at her and then shook his head. "Why, Etani?" he sounded painfully tired.

She didn't know which 'why' he was asking and so she only looked at him.

Finally, he let out a breath and moved away from the door, his boots sounding loud on the stone.

Within a few hours, she was permitted to leave the room with gold linking her wrists, allowing her space to move.

They led her from the dungeons and up, though not to where she expected. They led her to the throne room where Alaric, Epharis, Uzo, Izziah, and Jaia stood.

Jaia looked broken, his face streaked with red and she couldn't look at him, even though she felt his eyes boring into her to leave her heart riddled with holes.

Versalis removed the chain to give her full range of motion, something the others didn't appear to appreciate.

"Etani, what is the meaning of this?" Alaric demanded, but she ignored him.

Instead she stripped out of her boots and tore the sleeves from her shirt, using one to bind back her hair. She didn't think, she only moved with a purpose she had never felt before.

The pile of clay that had been provided was too much by at least five times, but it was smooth and quality, squishing between her fingers as she tested it.

The King spoke again, but she still ignored him as she scooped up large balls into her lap.

Someone moved and Alaric stood, but Epharis stopped him with a hand across his chest.

She didn't look up, her eyes on her work as she began to mould and shape the clay.

A brain was her starting point, working the clay into a thick density and placing it gently on the ground. After, she constructed a skull and tenderly placed the brain inside.

Turning then to the spine, she pieced every bone together, that burning urge inside her turning to fire.

Each internal organ had to be crafted and then laid out inside the ribcage, connected and then checked.

Scooting around on her knees, she lovingly crafted every tiny bone of a set of hands and feet, placing them aside before she started on the ligaments, using them to connect each bone together.

An hour ticked by as she worked, then a second and third. The fifth hour had her finishing the ligaments and she moved on to veins, rolling the clay into tiny ropes that she laid out.

Hour ten had her finishing and she studied her work on his nervous system, turning then to the top layer.

Clay was flattened by her hands, smoothed with gentle touches and manipulations, and then laid out over the body, the seams joined and then she manipulated it, adding creases and lines. She didn't so much as flush when she crafted his genitals, as she had seen him naked any number of times with little interest aside from the fascination of seeing a naked vampire.

Each hand took another hour, his feet one each as well but it was his face that took the longest.

She worked his face back into existence, his full lips that tilted down just so, the smooth lines of his brow and jaw, the fullness of his cheekbones and the hollows of his cheeks. Round ears, a slender neck and then short, wavy hair.

The last thing she did was to apply hair over the rest of his face.

When she had finished, the night had disappeared and she stood back, pacing around him again and again, with her eyes sweeping and searching. She hunted for imperfections, wanting to find them and then smoothing them out as they were discovered.

Not a single sound came from the crowd, which had grown to include others, including Catherine, the elf, and others she didn't know.

Finally she looked up, her eyes finding Jaia, who was staring down at the perfect replica of his brother, a muddy brown. She hated herself for what she had done to him, despised herself for his loss, and she swallowed to keep the tears back.

Slowly she wiped away the excess clay from around him, ensuring that nothing would be touching him except what was supposed to be there.

She sat down beside the figure, his hands resting at his side, naked and alone in death.

Her fingers traced his brow gently as she had done a hundred times, touched his lips, his hand and found them to be exact. Her head bowed as her grief hit her again and she swallowed hard.

She turned inward and found the little ball, stroking its head and hearing it purr in contentment. The blackness wept out of her pupils to spill into the colour and then the white, spreading through the veins around her eyes and lips, turning them black.

After that, she leant down and she kissed him tenderly.

His chest expanded as she reached from herself to him, that little ball cupped in her hands as they stretched, finding that place in which it belonged inside his new form.

Clay cracked while the chest filled and lungs expanded, filling with air and exhaling dust. The little ball cooed at her as she released it, finding its home and settling in there, just so.

It found her as she retreated, a gentle kiss and she smiled, pulling away from it and back into herself.

Sitting up slowly, her lips parted as a black mist passed her lips, dissipating into the air as Kai's eyes opened and they were perfect.

He sat up, clay pattering to the floor and her eyes lifted to Versalis, meeting his, white-lavender.

She knew what they would think of her and she didn't care; she loved Kai and Jaia and wouldn't ever wish them apart.

As Jaia ran for his brother, her body fell sideways and she hit the marble floor.

She woke hours later in the arms of a man, but it was not the one she expected to find in bed with her. Versalis was wrapped around her, his warmth doing nothing to stop the violent shivering that racked her body.

Pulling away from him, she gasped for air and looked around. They were in her rooms beside Alaric's and she hadn't been bound this time, instead, there was only Versalis.

She dragged herself from the bed and into the bathroom with only one thought in mind: warmth. She filled the bath with entirely hot water and, still fully dressed, submerged herself in the heat. She continued shivering, even as she huddled beneath the water.

The bath had gone still with her stillness, her arms wrapped tightly around her legs and her face buried in her knees, a good three inches of water above her bowed head in the deep in-ground bath.

Something disturbed the surface and she looked up slowly to find Versalis had followed her, looking down at her. He wore a red crystal on a black chain around his neck.

She didn't recall his getting it, but it looked good on him.

He watched her with fascination, never having seen her when she was under water.

Unlike above water where she could be suffocated, when she was in the water she could go for hours without drowning and she bitterly thought it had something to do with her ancestry.

Lifting her head, her eyes peeked just above the water, sad and broken as they met him.

"Etani, come out of there. You can't hide forever," he spoke tenderly to her, but she only shook her head, not wanting to come out.

She was still cold, the heat of the water doing nothing to warm her.

"Jaia and Kai will want to see you," he said, frowning in concern as she flinched at the name.

She ducked her head back under the water; he stayed there with her until the water cooled enough and then he joined her, boots and all.

As he wrapped himself around her, she kept her eyes closed, burying her face in his chest and huddling against him as close as possible. He helped by pulling her tighter into his lap where they stayed, his need for air making him shift only slightly when the need arose.

It was some time before the cold water had her shivering and she reluctantly crawled out of the bath, her nightgown and hair sticking to her. Not bothering to get up, she slumped onto the marble floor and stayed there as Versalis got out and dropped down beside her, his face only a few inches from hers.

"Hey, it's going to be okay," he whispered, his hand moving to stroke her cheek as tears formed.

"I killed my friend. I hurt Jaia..." she whimpered.

"Yes, but you saved him," he whispered, his fingers light as he brushed her wet hair out of her face.

Someone had entered the bathroom and sat down, but she ignored them.

"I didn't mean to. I didn't want him to die in the field," she whispered. "I didn't want to hurt him, I just wanted him to be warm and safe in me."

Versalis was studying her face, confused. "Etani, you..." He stopped and changed tactics. "You got him safe again, he is safe and warm now because of you."

"He died because of me," she said, her voice breaking.

"And he lived because of you." He cupped her cheek and pressed a kiss to her forehead, even as she cried quietly.

It was only a short while later when two more people joined them, sitting down with the first person and she could see nothing but Versalis, clinging to him to keep herself from going mad.

They remained silent on the floor for so long that she had almost dried, her hair being gently combed by him, her eyes barely open as she tried to recall the events leading up to the death of her friend.

"Do you think they will ever forgive me?" she breathed sometime later, barely awake as the cold drove her towards sleep.

"They will; they both love you," Versalis said gently and his eyes moved past her as she fell asleep.

When she woke, she found herself amidst a pile of limbs and hair, most of it black, but it wasn't all hers. Against her back there was someone, his arms wrapped tight around her, a pair of legs lay over that person's waist and feet perched on her hip, an upper torso on her thighs using the legs as a pillow. She heard four sets of breathing, but only counted three bodies and the oddity had her eyes opening slowly to see Epharis sitting on the edge of the bed, one leg tucked up under him as he waited for them to wake.

When he felt her eyes on him, he turned to her and smiled slightly, extending his hand to trace his thumb down over her lips. She parted them slightly, placing a gentle kiss on the thumb before falling back asleep to his soft sigh.

A loud sound woke her later, coupled with three bodies jerking and she sat up sharply, head colliding with a shoulder and she squinted in the sudden brightness of morning.

Little had changed in the pile of bodies, except that the legs were now replaced by an entire body and the body belonged to Kai.

She jerked back so violently that he fell and slid between her and Versalis, Jaia falling down with Kai and head-butting him in the stomach. She shoved herself back from the pile of bodies and suddenly there was no longer a bed behind her and she fell, her back hitting the floor with a huff.

She blinked up at the ugly green pastel of the ceiling, her lower legs still up on the bed as she contemplated her life and what it was that she had done to deserve it.

The loud sound of armoured boots rounded the side of the bed and the form of Alaric loomed over her as she decided right there on the floor was the perfect place to stay. Versalis's face popped over the side of the bed and he looked down at her, seeing the stubborn set of her jaw, then he looked up at Alaric.

"Good luck," the vampire said before he went back and intentionally flopped down on top of the twins, who groaned and tried to shove him off.

Alaric didn't look very much amused by the lot of them. "Get up, we need to talk," he said to her, refusing to break their eye contact.

Given she didn't need to blink, she won the staring contest and she was allowed to look away.

Pulling her feet off the bed, she sat up and saw the twins watching her. Her face paled as she met Kai's eyes and her own dropped instantly, unable to look at him.

She didn't fight when Alaric grabbed her arm and pulled her to her feet, throwing clothes at her and glaring as she held them, refusing to get changed.

Finally he turned away and she quickly stripped off her stiff dress and pulled on pants and a vest.

She couldn't bring herself to look at the vampires; instead, she kept her eyes on the floor and followed after the King.

"Etani?" Jaia asked, sounding concerned. She didn't respond as the door slammed shut behind her.

Alaric led her out of her suite and then into his. Feeling eyes on her, she turned to see Epharis sitting calmly in a chair, Anduril resting across his lap.

She watched her husband for a moment before her eyes turned when Alaric cleared his throat.

"What was that on the field?" Alaric immediately started and she looked at him blankly. "Well?" the King demanded when she didn't answer.

Turning to Epharis, she found him watching her carefully. "What do you mean?" she asked when Epharis turned out to be no help.

King Alaric looked as though he would love to slap her, but Epharis cleared his throat.

"Your transformation," Alaric said.

"Transformation?" she asked, totally baffled. She didn't remember any such thing, though now that she thought back on it, she didn't recall seeing how Kai had been injured, only that she had to save him.

"You transformed, Etani. Into a great creature with black wings and a scythe," Epharis supplied and she spun to him, shocked by the news.

4

CHANGES

"*J* what?" she demanded and yelped as Alaric grabbed her, brushing her hair out of the way and ripping the back of her vest open.

There was nothing but pale, smooth skin and he growled, gripping a fistful of her hair as she bent forward, her arms raised to hold the remaining fabric to her chest.

"Alaric I don't know what you're talking about," she pleaded, using one hand to hold her vest over her chest and the other to grip his hand, trying to tug his fingers free of her hair.

He saw something and grabbed her wrist with his free hand, forcefully pulling it out straight between them.

On her wrist there was a mark, almost like a tattoo, in the shape of two arches with a single line running up between them. An additional line crossed the three as well as a small arch above the end of the middle line. A crescent moon crossed just under the top arch and she frowned, trying to understand it. It looked vaguely like an angel, the top little arch being the head and the two wider arches being the wings. But she didn't know what the crescent moon was.

They all stared down at the mark and she jerked her arm free, lifting it closer to her face. Switching arms against her chest, she checked her other arm as well, finding it clear along with both shoulders and what she could see of her back, stomach and sides.

"What is going on?" she demanded, finding that unless they were under her pants or hair, she had no more marks.

"Do it," Alaric said and Epharis stood slowly, looking tired as he set down Anduril.

Alaric moved behind her and grabbed her arms, shoving down hard and her back hit the floor.

She cried out, her wrists pinned to the carpet as Epharis swept across to her and grabbed her right calf. She immediately kicked him in the side with her left, screaming when her wrists were gripped together and Alaric struck her across the face.

Ears ringing, she thrashed when Epharis turned his back to her and held her leg under his arm as he placed something cold around her ankle that jingled obnoxiously.

Planting her foot against his lower back, she tried to pry him off her and then she screamed again as the clasp connected and she suddenly felt trapped in herself, bound to her immortal body.

A hand clamped down on her mouth and Epharis turned back to her, his grip on her calves to keep her from kicking him again.

The door burst open and the two men froze, looking up at three very angry vampires who took in the scene and immediately jumped to the worst conclusion.

Epharis's hands shot off her and he stepped back, making it very clear what it looked like was happening, wasn't happening.

Alaric, however, refused to let go of her, dragging her up off the ground and glaring at the trio.

She twisted her head and sank her teeth hard into his hand and he jerked, but not before she got a good taste of him. She shuddered at the deliciousness of his blood as he shoved her into the waiting arms of Versalis.

"Touch her again and I'll rip your head off," Versalis growled as he encased her in his coat.

Alaric said nothing, glaring back at the group before he nodded and she was allowed to leave.

Every other step jingled, but they ignored it until they reached her room and immediately turned on her, looking down at the tiny little gold chain around her ankle that held a small gold ball-shaped bell.

Not looking at the twins, she slipped free of Versalis and placed her foot up on the armrest of one of the chairs, trying to release the catch.

It wouldn't let go and she growled, tugging at it, but still it refused to release her.

Versalis had followed her and he gently moved her hands away before he tried to release it, both thinking it might work like the normal gold chains. It didn't release and he grew irritable when it refused to open.

Jaia was next to try and she stared at her foot, unable to look up and face his hatred.

His failure brought Kai sweeping over, an elegance in his movements that she had never seen before and his delicate fingers pressed and pulled at the clasp, eventually tugging it in frustration.

The mood soured as her foot landed back on the floor and jingled mockingly.

"What now?" Versalis said once he moved to her side, taking her hand and leading her to sit down and that bell jingled, alerting them to every movement she made.

"We talk," Jaia said and she flinched, knowing he was looking at her. She slid her hands into Versalis', she studied her hands in his, and jumped when a soft hand brushed her shoulder.

She looked up to see Kai looking down at her.

"Hey, don't do this to us, not when we need you." He pressed his warm palm against her cheek and brushed away a tear she hadn't noticed falling.

He wrapped his arms tightly around her, holding her hard against him.

"I'm so sorry... I never meant for any of this to happen." She was crying softly into Kai's chest as he stroked her hair. "I don't remember what happened. Daemon was there and then you were dying, and I couldn't let you die, not there. I couldn't just leave you." She clung to him as he held her, his jaw pressed against her cheek.

"It's okay, I'm okay now."

"Better than okay." Jaia sniffed, looking only a little jealous. "You make him into the perfect vampire and now I look like second rate trash. I used to be the pretty one."

Kai snorted, looking at his brother. "You were never the pretty one."

She shook her head, burying her face in his shoulder.

"Etani, I feel amazing," he whispered, and she finally looked up at him, tears streaking her face.

Jaia muttered something and they both looked at him while he pouted.

"Do you not remember what happened?" Versalis asked.

"No, just that."

"Who is Daemon?" Kai asked and she told them what the demon had told her. Around halfway through, the three vampires exchanged looks, and when she finished with pulling Kai to herself and then placing him in the host, she frowned at their looks.

"What?" she demanded.

"He was right. The reason everyone is so obsessed with you, it's because they can't help it. You are the most beautiful, enchanting, addictive creature to exist," Jaia said in a matter of fact tone.

Her cheeks burned and she glared at him. "Don't make jokes," she scolded him.

"Etani..." Versalis was gentle as he spoke. "Think of every man who has ever come to be in your presence. How do they react to you?"

She looked to him and frowned, going through the list of men she knew and slowly her scowl faded to be replaced by horror.

Every single one of them had in some way become obsessed with her, barring one.

"Aelen isn't obsessed with me," she said triumphantly.

"Aelen is absolutely obsessed. He watches you every second he can. He just both knows how to hide it, and can fight it. The rest of us can't. You are the sun for us, something so radiant and bright, but get close and you burn," Jaia said gently.

She looked between the three of them, not wanting to believe it but it was true. "I'm not a weapon," she said and another look was exchanged. "Stop doing that!" she cried, standing and beginning to pace, the bell jingling gently and making her even angrier. "I'm not. I'm just Etani, just a fae and everything else. I'm not a weapon."

"You didn't see the battlefield, Etani. He didn't create a weapon, he created death. You *are* death."

She turned and Versalis was holding out the red crystal. "When you transformed, this was around your neck. It matched your heartbeat so when I got my chance, I ripped it off you,"

She became transfixed by it, watching its dull silence and feeling a sudden, aching need to touch it. "That's what changed your eyes?" she asked.

"Yes, it happened as soon as I touched it, apparently."

Her eyes slid up to his face.

"I can feel you, like a presence in my mind. I can feel the power that is sitting inside you, coiled and ready. Etani, if you use this power, you can destroy our world, or even Faerie if you wanted to."

"No one can destroy Faerie," she retorted, fear flooding her.

"No, no one can. You can, you are the creator of worlds, and you are the destroyer."

Silence stretched between them as she tried to understand what was going on.

"Can you kill a demon?" Kai asked, looking thoughtful.

"No, they are eternal. They can only kill themselves," Versalis said immediately.

"But she cut him in half," Kai argued. She was baffled again.

"She killed whichever fool allowed him to take over their body, but I imagine he will be back. He orchestrated your entire family?" Versalis finally asked.

"He claims so," she replied and pulled her foot up onto the couch beside her, grabbing at the chain. "Do you suppose this will come off if we cut off my foot?" she asked and when the silence stretched on, she looked up at their horrified expressions. "It's not like it won't grow back," she said, frustrated.

"Knowing Epharis, it will be impossible to remove unless by him."

"What is the purpose of the stupid thing?" She ground her teeth as she again pulled hard on the delicate chain, trying to break it.

Jaia moved to her side and stopped her, meeting her eyes before she looked away and he frowned, palm on her cheek and forcing her to look at him.

"We'll figure it out, it's okay," he said gently, and she bit her lip, fear and pain filling her.

He leant up and his lips met hers in a tender, gentle kiss that made her whimper, her fingers finding his shoulders as she leant into the kiss.

A throat cleared and they looked up to a very irritable looking Versalis.

"Could you not?" he asked, Kai snorting laughter.

"Don't be jealous," Kai said.

Blushing, she leant back from Jaia and as he stood, she caught his hand and pulled him down beside her.

"Tell me what happened."

"Well, everyone was all riled up and there you were running for Alaric," Jaia said.

"The most amazing thing any of us have ever seen," Kai interrupted.

"And then you were up on his shoulder and you two were screaming. After that the fighting began," Jaia continued.

"And you were ripping a hole in that whole field," Kai interrupted again and Jaia frowned.

"It really was magnificent to watch," Versalis interjected.

"So you were off like an arrow ripping everyone apart and Alaric was going after you and everyone seemed to be having a great time but then Epharis said something was wrong – did you know he can see through all of those dead? Anyway, he said there was a stranger on the field and things weren't going well. So, we all decided to just go down and try to cover your back and then that Daemon guy had gone flying like a comet." Jaia paused, staring at her.

"We've never seen anything like it; you kicked him further than even Alaric can boot someone," Versalis said wonderingly.

"So we were trying to get to you and people were trying to get away from you and then you were screaming and we had to retreat. After that, you began to change and you cut Daemon in half and then turned on Alaric. I swear it looked like you were going to eviscerate him. We had to protect him and Versalis was shouting about the gem and Kai went for it. But you moved so, so fast and he was bleeding and you kissed him. Versalis had the gem and you were changing back." Jaia exchanged a look with his twin. "And then I stabbed you in the heart," he finished sheepishly.

She had been staring at him blankly, unable to process what they were saying. She didn't have a clue and she shook her head slowly.

"This is all insane," she breathed, but then looked down at the small mark on her wrist before turning her attention to the gem around Versalis' neck.

"We don't think it's a good idea if you touch that," Kai said gently and she frowned, disappointed.

"What did you do to Kai?" Jaia asked and squeezed her hands when she flinched.

"I don't know. I've never done that to another before."

"You can do that to yourself?" Versalis sounded fascinated.

"Yes, it's called a host and I was wearing one when I first came here. You create it out of clay, and I can sort of... put myself inside it. And then I *am* it." She bit her lip as she tried to understand how it worked. "You have to make a perfect replication of the anatomy of the creature you are wanting to be. Human is often the most difficult, and I don't specialise in male." Her cheeks flushed in embarrassment. "If an organ isn't attached properly the whole thing breaks apart. If a ligament isn't joined you can't walk or move. If you get it right, it's sort of like a kiss, I take myself and put it in the host. I took Kai's soul and put it into a host. I have never been able to do that before."

"You know, it sort of reminds me of the reanimation powers of a

Lich. Is it possible you're only being partially manifested into that rather than reanimating him in his body?"

"I suppose it could be possible. Taking my abilities and warping them," she replied, thinking.

Feeling a soft brush on her cheek, she turned to see Jaia watching her throat and she smiled slightly.

He had been on blood packets for some time and while they fed him, she knew he craved the real thing.

Turning to better sit, he lunged and bit down with ferocious need and she cringed at the pain while still pulling him closer.

"You have me wondering what else I am capable of doing now," she said in a strained voice as he chewed on her neck, growling between greedy gulps.

"It could be anything really," Versalis said, his eyes lingering on her throat, but he knew better than to try that now, especially with how things had gone between her and Jaia. Vampires didn't tend to like sharing much when they got attached.

Jaia drew back from her and licked the wounds gently, his face smeared and looking a little guilty at the ravaged flesh of her throat.

Biting the tip of his tongue, he licked up the side of her neck and she shivered at how sexual it felt when he did it. He responded with a low growl and her cheeks burned, trying not to look embarrassed at his flirting.

Versalis and Kai picked up on it and shifted uncomfortably, Versalis's eyes taking on a feralness that made Jaia glare and tug her closer to him.

"That's enough, you two," Kai snapped, immediately taking the side of his twin against Versalis by glaring at the King.

They had just settled into an uneasy truce when someone screamed from inside the castle.

5

WAR TWO POINT ZERO

The sounds of fighting sent them all running from the room and as the door opened, they saw a guard go flying and they turned to see what had done it. It was a centaur and his large, grey eyes found them. He heaved a spear and the four dove back inside as the spear hit the door and stuck there, quivering.

Shoving herself to her feet, she found his eyes on her and they were triumphant.

"Found you," he said as he came into the room and she backed away, leading him with the three vampires moving to circle him.

"And now what?" she demanded and he grinned.

"I'm not usually into your kind, but I'm sure we can enjoy some privacy before I take you back."

The thought repulsed her and she glared at him as he laughed, as though the taunting was a joke for him.

At least, it was a joke until his own spear burst out of his chest and sprayed her with blood. Tilting herself slightly, she saw Versalis standing at the door with a savage grin.

"My dear Etani, it seems your family has come to call."

She looked past him as the hall moved with creatures and she realised exactly what was happening.

The Winter Court had come to Ayathian in search of her.

"You'd think they would have gotten the hint by now," she said as she swept back to the door and watched as a huge boar with an additional tusk growing out of its forehead went barrelling down the hall. A handkerchief appeared beside her head and she accepted it, using the white fabric to brush away the spattering of blood from her face and neck.

They watched as the boar knocked over three guards before charging off again. They took advantage of the cleared hall to try and find others they knew.

Rushing through the halls they found all kinds of creatures, from a troll to a tiny winged fairy who hurled insults and then flew off to get backup.

"Worse mouth than you," Versalis quipped, but she ignored him.

They raced down into the throne room to find a very angry looking Alaric and Epharis, with Queen Tatialia sitting on Alaric's throne, a wide grin on her smooth, ancient face.

"Etania!" she cried when her eyes found her granddaughter.

Etani glared up at the woman before looking to Alaric. He had been stuffed into a cage that hung three feet off the ground. Epharis had been put in a full binding of silk and sat moodily on the top step of the dais.

Two young women were standing to the right and left of the Queen.

The right had long, blonde hair that seemed impossibly straight, a large headdress of pearls and sapphires. She was gorgeous, with dark purple lips and deep blue eyes, dark brows and pale creamy skin. Her dress covered her from neck to toes and was encrusted in more pearls and sapphires.

The woman on the left was almost impossibly pale with white hair and equally white skin. She was dressed in white as well, offset with dark red beading and embroidery in the pattern of runes. Her dress had large slits to show off hints of her breasts, arms and ribs, but she was otherwise dressed fully.

A string of black pearls hung around her neck, but otherwise she was undecorated with jewels.

"My daughters, Megara and Hercia," she said, pointing to the right and left respectively. That was unexpected. She hadn't known she had any other close relatives.

"What are you doing here, Tatialia?" she demanded, and the woman looked angry at the casual use of her name.

"Does it to me, too," Alaric said, and the Queen spun his cage.

"You will treat me with the respect I deserve, Etania. I am your grandmother!" the woman seemed exceptionally angry while she shrugged.

"I have yet to see you earn it. You trussed up a mortal King and a Lich," she spoke like that was no feat, knowing full well it would rile the old woman up.

"How dare you speak to me like that?" the Queen screamed, stepping down from the dais and when Versalis moved, her hand flicked in his direction and the man was thrown across the room. "Vampire scum," she snarled as she approached her granddaughter.

Jaia and Kai backed away quickly and she glanced up to see Uzo calmly walking into the room from behind the throne, tugging at his sleeves and looking around with interest.

Her eyes went back to the ancient woman before her and she smiled slightly.

"I'll not lie for you," she purred, the fact that she could lie angering the Queen even more.

Tatialia clenched her fist and pain ripped through her body, forcing her to her knees as she gasped to try and suck air into lungs that no longer seemed to work.

"You will respect me little girl."

"How can... I respect a woman who... sells her grandchildren to monsters?" she gasped, finally able to suck in air as the Queen released her fist.

"The Drow? I assumed you would have killed him by now," Tatialia said.

"You knew what he was," she wheezed. "You knew what he was

and what he did, and you still gave me to him." She looked up at the grandmother she didn't know she had and the woman stared down her nose at the granddaughter she had never wanted.

"You are weak, allowing a pathetic male to abuse you. You deserve to have that done to you if you cannot defend yourself."

The room had gone absolutely silent as everyone processed what she had said, the brutality of it and her lack of compassion for her fellow woman.

Her eyes lifted slowly from the floor to peer up at the Queen, fury filling her. She found her wrist itching, Versalis's chest beginning to glow with a rapid pace.

"I am your granddaughter, the child of your son, and you let him..." She couldn't even say what he had done to her, not to this woman. Her wrist burned and she sucked in a breath.

The vampires immediately moved to cover their ears but she wasn't going to scream.

Instead her hand flung out and the marking moved, liquid and flowing up to her hand and the scythe formed between her fingers.

The Queen backed away at the thing even as she stood and advanced, gripping it tightly.

"You knew he was going to do it. Did you enjoy knowing your blood was screaming in agony while she was defiled over and over? Did you *watch*?" The words were crude and the woman's cheeks had turned bright red in horror, but still she backed away. "Did you enjoy knowing he was going to do it again and again? Knowing he gained pleasure from the suffering of others?" She had lifted the scythe now, a threat that hovered over the woman. "Do it. Try and control me, try and hand me over to the next beast. *Do it!*" she screamed and the woman flinched, falling back onto the dais.

Neither of the two Princesses had moved, watching with calm poise.

"Perhaps it is you who is weak, Tatialia. You who have grown tired and frail with age and so you punish the young. You who are just as cruel and malicious."

Uzo came up behind her, but he didn't try and stop her. Instead he was grinning at Tatialia over her shoulder.

"Traitor..." the Queen breathed at him and then the scythe came down and the hall echoed with the sound of metal hitting flesh and then stone.

The scream of the Queen was loud, painful, and she smiled as she gripped the scythe tighter, feeling those tendrils reaching out through it for the woman.

Black seeped into her eyes and she sucked in a breath as the woman's soul was ripped from her body and up through the scythe into her fingers.

Her body blazed with the glowing white of the markings, her body blazed with the glowing white of the markings, radiant, and Megara moved, stepping down from the dais to kneel at her mother's side.

She knew nothing after that, her world lost to a blazing whiteness that was utter ecstasy of the kill.

When she came to, she had been bound very thoroughly to a chair, and she squinted as she tried to figure out what was happening.

"Why do I keep ending up unconscious?" she asked of no one in particular.

"Because you keep getting knocked unconscious," Alaric said and she jerked, looking around at him.

He watched her carefully with a grim smile on his face.

"I have a proposition for you, Princess," he said slowly as he leant forward in the chair.

"What would that be?" she asked warily.

"You have to understand my situation here. I have this being who is death given human form, and I have no way of controlling it, or keeping my people safe."

Her eyes narrowed at him. Yes, she understood but she didn't like where this was going.

"Now this creature could easily wipe out my entire city, could kill us all and is highly intelligent. This creature has rational thought and emotions. This creature just killed one of the most powerful beings to exist in either world. This creature is impossible to kill." He stood and paced, his hands behind his back. "Twice now this creature has saved my life, and then needed to be stopped from killing me. This creature is controlled to a lesser degree by a Lich whose loyalties are not entirely to this kingdom. This creature is free to do what it desires. Do you see how difficult this is?" he said grimly, and she nodded.

"Now, I could either let this creature go and do what it wants, or I could cage it and put it safely in a little box until it is needed, but then it would be resentful. So what else can I do about this creature?" He paused, watching to see if she would give him an answer.

She refused to speak.

"Well, the other option is to control it through some other means. The Lich is out of the question, but then there are friends who it would die for. Friends who it forced another to protect when things might be dangerous. It even gave up a priceless gift in the way of a fae owing it, in order to keep those people safe." He turned to her and she glared at him. "I think you know where this is going, Etani. Either you give me a way to control you, or I will have all three of the vampires executed and put you in a box for safekeeping."

The silence stretched between them and she watched him, her fingers tight on the chair.

"What form of control are we talking?" she asked warily, and he smiled.

"I want your name," he breathed.

"No," she said flatly and his eyes narrowed. "That is absolute control, Alaric, and I will not give it to you. You see, you are a megalomaniac and as you said, I am death. You having complete control over death would be disastrous."

He gritted his teeth and turned away from her.

"However, a deal might be struck," she said finally, angry at the situation.

He turned back to her, smiling.

"I will agree to do whatever it is you ask of me, without it conflicting with my current deals. You cannot attempt to stop us from seeing each other or my morals are wronged. Yes, Alaric, I have morals. I will also not be coerced," she growled at his snort. "In return you will never harm any of those I consider dear to me, nor will you order them, or even insinuate that they should be harmed, in writing, through speech or through any other means. Ever." She wondered if he caught the loophole and she kept her face irritable to hide the glee.

"Whatever I ask?" he insisted.

She narrowed her eyes and then nodded, wondering what he was planning. He thought over the deal and then he smiled.

"Very well, you have a deal, Princess," he said and extended his hand.

She took it and he sucked in his breath at the zing of energy as the deal was struck. She grinned and his eyes grew wary at her pleasure.

"What if I were to ask that you join me in my bed now?" he asked slyly, and she snorted.

"That would be coercion, Alaric. I am married."

He nodded and untied her. Immediately she stood and tugged her nightdress into place, but as she made to move, her world pitched and she fell forward. Alaric caught her and frowned.

"I need Versalis," she whispered and he scooped her up into his arms, stomping from the room and taking her outside.

The sun was high and she was shocked to see both Kai and Jaia sitting out in the sunlight.

They looked up at the approach and he set her down. Staggering forward, her world spun and Versalis was quickest to reach her.

His only warning was a low growl before she had grabbed a fistful of his hair and forced his head to the side, her bite ferocious and cruel.

He jerked back, but she refused to let go.

There was no sexual tension or need between them, only her desperate hunger that struck the instant she laid eyes on him.

His arms went around her and she clung to him, her eyes lifting to see the twins, their worry, and she gave a feral snarl, half-dragging the vampire back with her. Her vision had gone a deep crimson as she fed.

She drained him almost fully before she let him go and he dropped to the ground. Panting heavily, his blood dripped down her chin.

She backed away from him and gave the twins access to him, but he was already sitting up and looking confused.

Alaric hadn't left, watching the encounter and her as she sank down onto her knees, her thoughts racing.

She felt so much energy inside her, like she was going to explode.

Curling in on herself, she rested her forehead against the ground and tried to breathe through the sensation, her insides feeling heavy and strained.

She had never experienced the sensation before, but she had also never devoured a Queen of Faerie and then a vampire King.

She heaved but managed to keep it all down, not wanting to waste any of it.

Jaia moved to her and pulled her up into his lap, his eyes going wide at something on her face.

"Too much," she breathed and she drew him down to her, her fingers pulling at his shirt and pressing him down on her throat. Why had she fed on Versalis if she was already full? She didn't know and she whimpered as Jaia's teeth slid smoothly through her flesh.

Electricity shot through her from him and he groaned, drinking deeply of the energy that radiated from her.

His grip was painfully tight and yet she wanted him to squeeze her tighter, her pains seeming to ease slightly as he crushed her to him.

Her fingers slid inside his shirt and his breath sucked in as she found bare skin, touching first gently and then firmly as she slid her arms around his ribs, desperate to feel his skin against hers. She had never touched him in that way before and he trembled against her.

She smiled as he reacted to her touch, so cold against his warmth and he drank, needing to fill himself.

Her fingers found his back and traced slowly up his spine, each bump something to explore.

His teeth slid free of her throat and his head turned, his mouth finding hers in a hard kiss.

The taste of her own blood on his lips made her shiver and they had forgotten everything but their own feelings.

Her nails teased his skin, a threat and a flirt all in one and he clutched her jaw, stroking gently as one hand crept around the back of her neck.

Something moved and they broke apart, confused and not sure where they were.

Alaric stared at her with an enormous, malicious grin on his face and she knew instantly that they had made a mistake. She had let their secret out and he was going to use that against her.

6

TRUTHS ARE LIES

*A*laric dragged her back from Jaia, who was still high as the sky on her blood, and she struggled against him, knowing that neither Jaia nor Versalis could get to her and Kai was frantic.

"Look after them!" she cried and he nodded, knowing he was unable to help her anyway.

He didn't take her far, slamming her against the wall of the castle.

She gasped her pain and his face was near to hers.

"So, the little vampire, is it?" he growled, though she didn't think it was indignation about her betrayal of Epharis.

"Let go of me," she breathed, his fingers clenched in the front of her dress. "It's not like that, it's the blood." She was lying through her teeth and she did her best to sound convincing.

He narrowed his eyes at her and she glared up at him.

"You think there's nothing sexual about feeding from each other? Why do you think we're so close?"

"Just imagine how Epharis would react if he found out his wife was in love with a vampire," he breathed into her face and she glared up at him.

"We have a deal, Alaric." She was scared and she realised the flaw in their deal. She had worded it carefully, but she hadn't covered this entirely.

"Ah, but I am only concerned for my brother's wellbeing. How am I to know how he would respond to the news of his beloved wife with another man?" His words were toxic and she shook her head.

"I would never," she breathed, fear running through her system.

"But you already have, with Drizdan."

"That was not my choice."

His words stung her and she grasped at the anger to get past her fear.

"If you recall correctly, that was your doing when you handed me over to Winter." Angry now, she slammed her foot into his shin and he dropped her. She ducked out from under his arm and the merry tinkle of the bell made her eye twitch.

"What is the bell for Alaric?" she demanded and he turned to her, releasing his shin and smirking.

"An early warning system. Mythicals can hear it, humans cannot."

"That makes my job of killing harder, you have to realise that." She was above angry now, she was furious that he would dare put something on her.

"We have to be sure you're not going to try and sneak up on one of us with that kiss or scythe. Besides, it can be silenced when the need arises."

Her eyes narrowed in interest and Alaric frowned, knowing her thoughts had gone to her husband and what she could do to convince him to remove the damned thing.

"Epharis won't help you. He understands the situation, and understands the need to keep you contained," he said, and she shook her head in disgust.

"Versalis can control me," she breathed and Alaric made a soft sound of agreement.

"Yes, it seems that without that little crystal you cannot fully manifest, but you can still use that scythe and unless I can take that from you, there is nothing that can fully contain you."

The thought of his taking the scythe filled her with such terror that she immediately backed away from him though she didn't know why. It was just a weapon, but then, it was everything to her before she even knew it meant anything to her.

She would have to figure out why it mattered later, but for now she only thought to protect it from him.

"You will take it only if I am permanently dead, Alaric."

"Can you kill *death,* Etani?"

His question had her frowning in confusion. It wasn't like she was mortal before the events of Ayathian, but it raised an interesting thought in her. If she was death, then what happened to the death she had come to know? Surely if she had always been death, he would never have existed; or was there more than one death and he was just the one that came to her? Or were there many who had come to her and they all just looked the same?

She had become distracted and Alaric cleared his throat to bring her back to him.

She looked up at him, chewing on the inside of her cheek.

"What are you thinking?"

She hesitated, not to ignore his demand for information, but because she was trying to process her thoughts. "I have known death for a long time, since I was a young girl, in fact. If I am death, then what is he? Or is there more than one death? Is there a whole family of deaths?"

Her questions threw him off guard and he stared at her for a long time as he, too, tried to process what she was thinking.

"Death never carried a scythe when I saw him, so why do I have one? Am I death or something else?"

"I don't know what you are," he said finally, agitated.

"Well, that makes two of us," she sighed.

Alaric looked irritated but she could only shrug.

"I'm as blind to this as you are, Alaric."

"I have a task for you, now that I have you coherent and alone."

Eyebrows lifting, she smiled faintly at his calm. "And what task would you have for me, Alaric?" she asked curiously.

"You are going to assassinate the King of Weorene."

7

CONVERSATIONS WITH THE VOICE IN MY HEAD

"He has Aelen, why does he want me to be involved in this?" she demanded hours later when she had found the vampires in their basement, having burst in to exclaim her irritation at Alaric and the deal he had forced out of her. She conveniently forgot the reason for the deal and she knew they didn't believe her, but she wasn't about to tell them about Alaric threatening them if she didn't obey. They were smart men, they could probably figure it out but no one wanted to discuss it.

"He has been involved in an inquest into the deaths of a very large number of people under the city for the last several months," Kai said slyly, and she snorted her amusement.

"That makes sense I suppose, but it doesn't mean I have to like it."

"No, it doesn't, but it does give you the opportunity to get on his good side and maybe he will loosen the leash a little bit. If he thinks you are on his side, he will likely back off of you."

Pursing her lips, she considered that before she plopped down on the couch beside Versalis who had her family tree out and was studying the various species on the list.

Some were beings none of them had ever heard of, and it was

curious to try and learn what they all were. Versalis seemed to be a little obsessed with figuring her out.

"When will you be leaving?" Kai asked, and she made a face, his grin returning it.

"In a few days. Just enough time to get you enough blood and recover in case it takes a few months to get close to him. I imagine he's going to be quite paranoid. Why isn't Alaric waiting until after things settle down? Do you suppose there will be another attack?"

"Unlikely," Versalis said with a quill between his teeth as he flipped through the pages of the book and scowled. "They would be fairly demoralised after a loss like that. They didn't expect to come up against what we had to offer them."

Chewing on her lower lip, she recalled the titan King and the destruction he could cause, not to mention the army of the dead. "Yes, that makes sense. But does that mean they will be coming eventually, or do you think they have entirely given up?"

"Temporary seems a good assumption," Jaia said, and she let out a slow breath.

"What about Winter?" she asked and Versalis sighed.

"I tend to feel that we will get a break there while they transition, but it is impossible to tell with The Fae. Perhaps you could ask what Uzo thinks if he's still lurking around?"

Nodding her agreement, she made a mental note to hunt the man down when she got the chance.

"So, it seems like taking him out is the best option. So long as they don't suspect Alaric."

She considered her options as she picked up a book and flipped through it, pausing at the strange-looking creature with long, black fingers and an evil grin. It was human shaped and almost entirely black. She snapped the book shut, looked at the blank cover, and then put it down.

"Something to stop his heart. Injected between the toes," she was thinking out loud. "Quick death, looks like natural causes..." She picked over the books and frowned at another, lifting it up with index finger and thumb. The binding felt oily and it made her skin crawl.

"Kissing leaves a mark, bite would suggest vampire and there were no vampires there that I saw. Knife is obvious, that would never work. I could replicate a snake bite but with those covers a snake getting inside would be illogical. A sabotage?"

Letari perked up in the back of her mind, grinning widely.

'What about deadly nightshade?'

"No, it would take too long to concentrate and I don't have a supply."

'Cyanide?'

"I do have cyanide, but it can take time and we need this to go quickly."

'Do you remember that little yellow frog in the rainforest?'

"Oh yeah, we always meant to go back there and find it again. But again, we would need more time to find it and then get its poison. We should go there soon, having that would be handy."

'Aconite?'

"Aconite," Etani agreed finally, thinking hard. "Already in stock, easy to obtain and a small amount is all it takes. He'd be what? Ninety kilograms? Five milligrams should be plenty, but we can up the dose to make it quicker."

'Yes, that will work. If you want to really get back at him, go for the groin.'

"Tempting, the femoral would be ideal, but he's more likely to suspect that and it means getting closer. We can get to the dorsal venous easily enough from the foot of his bed, he will hopefully ignore it if we go under the toe."

Putting the book back down, she looked up and found all three vampires looking at her with various expressions of confusion, fascination and horror. "What?" she asked defensively.

"You were talking to yourself. Detailing how to kill the King," Kai said slowly, and she flushed.

"I didn't realise I was speaking aloud. Letari," she made a vague gesture to her head and they nodded slowly, but still looked wary.

"How do you know all of this?" Jaia asked.

"I have a lot of experience in this sort of thing."

The twins exchanged a look and she set her arms down in her lap, thinking.

"The other option is to aim for the external jugular. Inside the hair line. But it's sensitive skin and he might wake up. Any signs of a struggle would be bad."

She watched Kai for several minutes, thinking about her options, and he started to get nervous about her staring.

Versalis touched her arm and she looked at him, confused, and he smiled at her in amusement.

"Should we go with you?" he asked, and she laughed gently.

"No, darling Versalis. I can do this on my own."

"I wasn't implying that, it's just that you're valuable."

She silenced his concerns by kissing his cheek and stood, moving to collect the supplies they would need to draw her blood.

The jingling of her bell seemed louder than normal, a reminder that no matter how relaxed she seemed, she was very much a prisoner.

After setting up the supplies, she got herself comfortable on the couch and squeezed the pump, feeling the gentle pull that was her blood being sucked from her body by the tube in her vein.

Humming softly, she rested her head against the corner of the backrest and armrest, staring up at the ceiling while the vampires calmly went about their business.

A gentle hand lifted her feet and rested them in a lap, his fingers warm and soft as he gave her a tug and she slid into a more comfortable position.

Rolling her head she saw Versalis smiling slightly, though his eyes were still on his studies. Sitting up to replace the bag with a fresh one, she listened in silence to the work going on around her. It was a moment of peace they rarely got to enjoy.

The door opened some time later and Epharis swept into the room, looking around and finding her lounging on the couch, her face pale and eyes hooded as she squeezed the pump, a small pile of packets on the table and Kai moving around her, his fingers touching her throat and wrists to feel the size of her veins.

She mumbled at the warmth of him and he gently took the pump from her limp fingers.

"That's enough, sweetheart," he said gently, carefully removing the needle from her arm and pressing down on the spot to help her blood clot.

Epharis moved into her field of vision and she looked at him sleepily.

"Are you planning to go somewhere?" he growled and she let out a slow sigh, knowing he had come to pick a fight.

Gentle arms slipped around her and she found herself pulled into Kai's lap as he settled down in her seat.

He was so incredibly warm that she was unable to resist snuggling into his chest, her eyes heavy.

"Kill Varsas for Alaric," she murmured quietly, pressing her cheek against Kai's collarbone and neck for the warmth of him.

"Since when did you start killing for him?"

Turning her head just enough to look at her furious husband, she gave him her best sleepy, irritable glare.

"Your brother is manipulative, Epharis, he was bound to find something to threaten me with eventually."

"What could he possibly have threatened you with? You're death!"

Kai made a hushing sound and she growled gently, not wanting to fight with him. She just wanted to sleep there in Kai's arms.

"You're a smart man, you'll figure it out," she breathed and her next inhale brought the spicy scent of angry vampire to her senses, lulling her closer to sleep.

There was a pause and then Epharis seemed to explode. "You would give up your freedom for vampires?" he yelled. "They're vampires, Etani!"

He seemed to have forgotten there were three of them in the room and the silence was enough to hear a pin drop.

"I will ask you to leave only once, Epharis," Versalis said in a low, warning voice.

"Give her to me, you are clearly incapable of taking care of her," Epharis snarled in response and Kai's warmth was stripped from her as Epharis' hard chest met her side and she whimpered at the cold.

"You can't even stop her from draining herself to keep you all sane, you ungrateful little boys. You have one task, to keep her safe, and you fail at even that."

"That's hardly fair; she's an assassin and vanishes like smoke when she wants to. How are we expected to keep her safe all the time? Do what *you* do and just leash her?" Jaia had stood, his face dark with anger.

"At least putting a leash on her has kept her alive."

"And how is that working out for you? You failed at turning her into a Lich, you failed at keeping her from Drizdan, you failed at keeping her out of the hands of Winter. You failed at keeping your brother off her, you failed at keeping Versalis from her, or Daemon, or Harla."

"Who is Daemon?" Epharis demanded and the three vampires exchanged a wary look as they realised they had revealed information she might not have wanted to share.

"A demon, the one from the field," Jaia said resentfully.

"What has he got to do with anything? He's back where he belongs," Epharis snapped.

"He is after Etani."

"Isn't everyone after her? Why does he matter?"

"You'll have to ask her," Kai piped in, throwing his brother a warning look.

"Keeping secrets, too? You lot and she keep more secrets than you have combined hairs."

He shifted his weight to get a better grip on her barely-conscious form in his arms.

"Be nice..." she mumbled, but no one was listening to her.

"I cannot be held responsible for the latest creature in this world who wants to get his hands on her."

"She's your wife! It's your job to protect her!" Jaia yelled, his cheeks flushed in his anger.

Epharis stiffened, but he had no defence. It wasn't wrong and they all knew it. He had failed at keeping her safe.

"Now look at her, bleeding herself out because your brother is obsessed with using her as a weapon," Versalis said gently.

"Why do you need so much?" Epharis demanded, eyeing the packs.

"We don't know, she just kept going and we stopped her just as you came in. She was talking to Letari before she started drawing," Kai said gently, trying to diffuse the situation.

"Talking about what?" Epharis asked.

"A yellow frog in a rainforest, aconite and cyanide, injection sites. She didn't realise she was speaking aloud."

"Odd, she's never done that before. Letari has been dormant for quite some time." Epharis looked down at her, her eyes almost closed but she was still clinging to consciousness.

"Letari apparently doesn't like any of us very much so she likes to stay back and watch the fun," Jaia said and Epharis turned to him.

"She told you that?" he demanded and the three nodded. "Why would she tell you that and not me?"

"It might be because we're her friends and you're the man who forced her into marriage and turned her into a Lich. Did you not see her reaction to you on the field?" Versalis said dryly, curious about their reaction.

"No, what happened?"

"She was desperate to get to you when you started calling, and her eyes began to glow green like all the other dead."

Epharis looked to the twins for confirmation and they nodded their agreement. "I have control over her?" he said warily, earning a worried look from the vampires. No one wanted Epharis to have more control over her.

"It seems so, at least in the moment when you were so close," Versalis finally said.

Epharis let out a low sigh and ducked his head to see her face, her eyes barely slitted.

"Hi," she breathed and he growled softly at her incapacitated state.

"You could have stopped her earlier; what if there is an emergency? You are never to allow her to take so much again." Epharis was getting angry again, his tone icy.

"I can give her some blood to help replenish," Jaia said, but Epharis stepped back, his arms tightening around her.

"I think you three have done enough. I'll take it from here. As you said, she's my wife and my responsibility," he threw their words back in their faces and turned, stalking towards the door.

"Let us at least help," Kai cried and her eyes opened wider at his distress, turning slightly and pressing at Epharis to get him to stop.

"Kai..." she breathed, a dull ache starting behind her eyes as she strained to see him. She could feel his distress at a distance, a part of her immediately wanting to go to him and comfort him.

"Everything will be fine, Etani," Epharis said, but she squirmed weakly, her hand outstretched for him.

Warm fingers found her hand and he kissed her palm gently, her eyes finding his over Epharis's shoulder.

"You're okay?" she whispered, her nails digging into the Lich's collarbone as she strained to lift herself up enough to see the vampire. Her panic at his sorrow faded slightly at his nearness.

"I will be," he said gently and she frowned, her fingers tracing his cheek in a bare hint of a brush.

"Don't be sad, I'm here." She rested her cheek against the shoulder under her and smiled sleepily at the sight of him.

He seemed concerned for her and she saw Jaia and Versalis looking at each other in confusion.

"I'm going to go to sleep now, but I'll just be upstairs. Come see me if you need."

His slow nod made her tension melt and the adrenaline made her fingers tremble in his hand.

"I love you, Kai," she breathed. *"Puer Meus."*

Sliding back down into Epharis's arms, she had exhausted herself entirely and shivered as the chill of blood loss set in.

"Don't come see her, little vampire. Use your blood and stay away until she is back," Epharis ordered and while she felt Kai's pain, she had no energy left to reach him.

Epharis fumed and her head bumped gently against his chest as he started towards the door. Then it slumped back as she passed out in his arms.

8

CHILDREN

She was groggy when she woke up later and crawled from the bed and onto the floor to reach the jug and sat down on her heels, gulping water directly out of it. The water tasted off from sitting for so long in the ceramic, but she didn't care.

A soft moan escaped her as she drank and a low chuckle made her look around.

Epharis was still in the bed and he had watched her going for the water, enjoying the view of her in the abnormally short nightdress he had ordered for her.

Flushing at what he had likely seen, she shifted around so that her back was to him and finished off the jug, her belly uncomfortably full and sloshy with the liquid.

Epharis sat up with the sound of shifting fabric and she peeked at him over her shoulder, making sure he was still on the bed.

She felt relatively okay, all things considered, and she had to wonder if he had given her something to speed up the blood production, or perhaps she had slept longer than she intended.

"Come back to bed," he crooned and she narrowed her eyes at him, half teasing and half wary of him.

"And what if I don't want to?" she countered.

His eyes narrowed in return, his grim smile making her unsure if he was teasing her or not. "Don't make me come over there," he said in a playful tone and her body relaxed slightly.

Setting down the jug, she crawled back to the bed and peeked at him over the mattress before finally climbing up and settling on the edge.

Her legs felt a little weaker than she would have liked, but that was to be expected after severe blood loss.

His arm snapped around her waist and she yelped as she was yanked from the edge of the bed and into his side, his grin wide and feral.

Slapping at his hands, she wriggled around until she was comfortable against his chest.

"I miss being this close to you," he purred as he breathed in the scent of her hair and closed his eyes in bliss.

"Do you now?" she said playfully and pressed a gentle kiss to his cheek. "I miss it, too."

Did she though? She wasn't entirely sure now, something inside her had changed when it came to him and she suspected it was the chain around her ankle.

He growled a soft sound of pleasure and his lips were hard on hers, pressing her back into the pillows. She kissed him back, but she hesitated at the hunger in the kiss, a nervousness settling into the pit of her stomach as she thought of having to reject him again. She wasn't ready for that, not yet.

He felt her hesitation and frowned against her mouth, his hands insistent as they found the hem of her night dress and pressed it upwards over her thighs.

Turning away from him, she caught his wrist before he could reach up between her legs and forced it back down again. "Epharis please, I can't," she said gently, trying to find words to explain to him. "Not yet."

His anger was so thick she could almost taste it and he shifted, sitting up to glare down at her. "When, Etani?" he demanded, his eyes trailing down her beside him as she shifted to put more space between them, sitting up to hug her knees to her chest.

"I don't know, I just need time—" her voice cut off as his hand struck her face and she gasped in shock, her hands flying up to cup her raging cheek.

When she looked up at him, his eyes were cold and his fingers curled around her ankle. He jerked her hard and her back hit the bed.

Planting her foot on his chest to pry him off her, she cried out as he grabbed her ankle and twisted, the audible pop of breaking bone sounding loud in the room.

His fingers closed around her throat as he reached between them and forced her nightdress up over her hips and he struck her again as she tried to pull the fabric back down again.

Her whimpers of pain and struggles were ignored as he clamped one hand down on her mouth and used his body to keep her pinned to the bed.

Her cries as he took her were muffled, and he made barely a sound at all, angry at her refusal to submit.

When he had finished with her, she rolled from the bed and left without a word, heading for the bathroom and locking the door securely behind her.

She stripped off the nightdress, threw it in a heap in the corner and ran the bath as hot as she could, her teeth clenched as she struggled not to make a sound, crying silently.

She hated him in that moment, knowing she had no grounds for accusations. As her husband he had a right to her body and he had been patient up until that point, but she hadn't moved on fast enough for him, hadn't gotten over the abuse and the loss at a pace that suited his desires.

Her body ached, and she grimly recalled that she would have to endure that pain every time she died as she had not been intimate before her first death.

She sank into the bath, scrubbed herself hard enough to leave her skin red and aching, but it didn't matter to her. She only wanted to be alone and away from him and his ravenous desires.

For an hour she remained in the bath, her arms wrapped tightly around her legs as she allowed the scalding water to seep away her muscle aches and sooth her as much as it could, but in that moment she just wanted to run to the basement and hide there. She wanted to be with the vampires who would protect her. But then she realised that if Epharis really wanted to, he might just kill them all out of spite.

Fear racked her and she felt suddenly frozen, her heart aching. Realising what was happening, she immediately got out of the bath as her breaths grew ragged, her limbs trembling and her vision blurred as tears filled her eyes.

Her body felt tight, her mind flicking from terrifying event to horrific vision and back again, tormenting her with the past and possible future.

She dug through the cupboard until she found something she hadn't seen before and huddled in the corner of the bathroom, staring down at the little jar of pink salts. She forced herself to focus on it, the way the salt moved as she turned it in her fingers, the gentle click of her metallic nails on the glass and the texture of the little cork stopper.

Giving it a little shake, she listened to the sound of salt on glass and her thoughts began to slow, her breathing easing though the tightness in her chest lingered spitefully.

When she had finally calmed down, she pulled on her pants and vest, the little jar going into her pocket, and she made her way back out of her room.

Upon glancing towards the bedroom, Epharis lay naked on his back, sunlight beaming down on him with the sheet lazily flung over his hips to guard his modesty. His left arm over his eyes blocked out the sun while he slept.

She moved slowly and closed the door before she headed into her small laboratory and prepared for her orders from the King, wanting to keep her mind occupied from the night before.

She carefully set out the empty bottles and drew down supplies from the shelves and cupboards, her hand in her pocket and the jar twisting between her fingers as she tried to keep her mind occupied.

By the time he had gotten up, she had a healthy supply of minor chemicals that would make things easier if the situation turned sour on her, though her pride and joy was a tiny vial of yellow liquid, big enough to hold around ten millilitres, with a foil cap for easy extraction.

Stuck to the side with a dab of glue was a small syringe with a tiny needle that she had first thought impossibly small to have been made.

Content with her work, she was still toying with the jar in her pocket when Epharis walked into the room, a towel around his waist and his hair wet from the bath.

He didn't say anything, merely watching her as she worked with narrowed, suspicious eyes.

She had of course thought about sticking the needle of aconite in him, but decided that it wasn't worth the retaliation if it did nothing to him. Instead, she kept her eyes down and pretended he wasn't in the room while she worked and fidgeted with the jar of salt.

He watched her for a good twenty minutes before he left to get dressed and her tension eased, muscles aching as they released.

Piling the vials into a small pouch and arranging them so that she could easily feel the raised lettering, she picked out a couple of strips of leather from the pile, a bottle and vial, and a sewing kit, almost bumping into him as she walked back out of the room.

Backpedalling fast, she looked up at his stern face and his eyes narrowed at her moment of panic.

"I wouldn't have to hurt you if you just did what I asked," he said coldly.

She didn't respond, slipping out of the door and placing her kit on the table before sitting down and setting out the strips: a longer, thin strip on top of a much thicker one.

Picking out a thick needle, a metallic, leather padded thimble, and a length of heavy string, she set to work sewing the ends together.

He approached her slowly, his hands coming down on her shoulders and she went still, her eyes wide as she wondered what he was going to do. "Do not ever refuse me again," he murmured in her ear. She nodded once, her stomach a tight knot of fear before he kissed the top of her head and swept from the room to leave her alone and trembling.

She felt she had no recourse with him, since he was a powerful Lich and immortal. Her instinct told her to run or kill, not submit. It left her confused and feeling helpless, which she hated.

Setting the bottle underneath the thin strip, she pressed the leather down and sewed it into place, her hands shaking hard enough that she was forced to stop and she stared down as drops of black splashed down onto her thighs.

She wasn't weak; far from it, she knew that. But in that moment she felt as weak as a human, unable to defend herself against her own husband. Unable to even tell him no without risking his violence.

He had not been as violent as he could be, easing up on her when she stopped fighting him, but she knew he would do whatever it took to get what he wanted out of her and that was the worst part of it all.

Forcing herself to calm down again, she got back to work and once she had sewn in five pockets for the bottles and five for the vials, she stood and tested the length of the leather strap around her thigh, moving to the lab for a knife and buckle.

She cut off the end, attached the buckle with more careful sewing and then dug a hole into the leather, forcing the buckle pin through repeatedly until it slid freely and she was happy.

The sewing reminded her of Sasha, and she bit hard on her lip at the remembered pain. Cain had caused so much destruction in her life and yet she found her mind going to Nayishma, the one victim who hadn't been his.

Cocking her head to the side, she allowed herself to sink into herself and she poked around in search of that little pretty box she had created in order to house the woman. Finding it, she gave it an experimental nudge and it quivered.

Sudden joy filled her as she swam upwards. Leaving everything behind, she sprinted from her room and down through the layers of the castle to the cold room, where her backup host had been waiting for her all that time, stuffed in the back somewhere.

The shape would be wrong, she knew that, but it was still a body for the woman and she would create a better one later.

Rushing past startled servants and guards, she threw open the doors of the cold room and prowled inside, her nose catching the scent of clay, and she grinned wildly at the sight of it. It had a few marks, but they were easy to smooth out.

"Oh, my dear friend, forgive me for the shape I am giving you, but this is on short notice," she whispered to herself and reached down once more, opening that tiny box.

Inside she found the sleepy soul, warm and content in its little box and not particularly happy about being disturbed. When she thought about it, she felt that it looked like a tiny kitten, all warm and fuzzy, sleepy and content just to be what it was, mewling happily when its mother came to it and gave it love.

Kai had been the same, and now Nayishma opened her sleepy little eyes and purred at the warmth she shone down on her.

She moved automatically, leaning forward over the clay form and pressing a tender kiss to the host.

Nayishma was confused, not understanding and not liking the cold, but she went willingly enough.

She gave a huff, pawing at the gentle fingers that reached through herself and into the new shape that had been given life.

The sound of cold clay splitting was loud in the silent room and she leant back even as golden eyes opened and she inhaled hard.

Etani smiled as she felt herself falling; the woman was so incredibly beautiful, even without a head of snakes.

9

NAYISHMA REBORN

*S*he woke to sharp slapping on her face and gasped, her body stiff and aching from the cold and she sat upright so fast she almost banged her head against the golden angel sitting at her side.

"Etani?" the familiar voice asked and she turned, her mind reeling as she tried to recall everything without overloading her brain.

Studying the woman, she was pleased to see that the red-bronze skin had returned, her crimson hair falling in thick waves around her head. Her golden-brown eyes were large and luminous. She was small, full figured, but still somehow seemed delicate.

Etani had made that form for herself, but she was very aware that it suited Nayishma perfectly. "Yish?" she asked, and the bronze beauty nodded, grinning widely with sharp little canines that didn't belong to her.

Before she knew what she was doing, she hugged the woman hard and Nayishma was hugging her back just as hard.

"What happened? I was bleeding and then I was warm and in the dark, then I was here and half frozen." Her voice was the same; gentle and warm with a faint hint of a hiss that Etani found endearing.

"You died, I took your soul and then I..." She paused, trying to think of the right word. "I gave you a new body. You were reborn? Resurrected?" She didn't know what the word was there, but it didn't matter.

Nayishma looked indignant and shook her head, suddenly looking down at the crimson curls that weren't snakes. "What?!" She sounded horrified, but Etani placed a finger against those full lips to silence her.

"It's not your old body, I had this one just sitting here and when I realised, I came straight here to bring you back. I will make you a new host but I will need your help designing it. I can't do it without you."

Nayishma calmed slightly and nodded, her jaw moving as she felt around the inside of her mouth.

"I have your little kitten teeth," she laughed, looking down at herself and admiring the shape she had.

"What happened to you, you look so different?" Nayishma asked, clicking her deep brown nails together experimentally. They had been shaped like Etani's, but hadn't been formed of metal.

"Where do I start?" She laughed, but then she had to actually think about it. "Well, I am married to Epharis here and Drizdan in Winter. I killed Tatialia, the Winter Queen, I am apparently death given human form, I have three vampires as my best friends, a demon created my entire family line, there is a lord of Faerie who was my father's friend, we just went to war with your father, and Nidhogg the dragon is living in the north with his husband, who I am fairly sure isn't human. My sisters were murdered, Megara has replaced Tatialia, but we haven't seen the results of that just yet, the man who killed my sisters is dead. Oh, and I gave you and Kai life after you both died."

She spoke quickly and Nayishma laughed around her mention of Nid, and then quickly stopped when she realised Etani was entirely serious.

Nayishma swore, and Etani smirked at such a well-bred lady cursing. "What is wrong with this kingdom? Is everyone insane? Why is my father at war with Alaric?"

"Everything is wrong with this kingdom. Yes, they are all insane, and your father is at war because he wants Ayathian, but we knocked them down and are just waiting for him to get back on his feet. And we're waiting for Winter to attack again."

"Why is Winter attacking?" She was sounding a little tired.

"I'm the Princess; they know about me and they want me back."

Nayishma stared at her, lips slightly parted, and then laughed again. This time Etani joined in and they hugged again tightly.

In order to keep Nayishma from freezing, she pulled the woman from the cold room and up into the warm sun, stunning Etani with the way her skin seemed to almost glitter and small flecks of gold in her hair reflected the light. She had never seen such a beautiful, pure creature.

"Oh, I missed the sun," she said as she held out her hands to it, warming herself like the snake she was.

A delicate cough sounded and they both looked around at no less than three guards who were staring at them, eyes wide and mouths slightly open.

"Are you a Goddess?" the middle guard asked and then flushed bright red, right along with Nayishma.

"No, I'm not," she said, laughing.

Etani nudged the woman towards the group and stood back, her eyes watchful of the men and their intentions but it seemed to be just harmless flirting.

It wasn't long before they had to leave, their duties not allowing much in the realm of fraternisation while on duty and they were sad to go, but duty to the King came first.

"I've never had someone flirt with me before," Nayishma said giddily, her cheeks a rosy pink.

"Is that right? Must have been you hiding under the veil all that time." Etani found Nayishma attractive in any form and found it hard to believe that her having snakes for hair would have dissuaded anyone in their land of reptiles.

"Sometimes I had to wonder if father was forcing them to stay away, but it might have been a combination of the veil and fear of trying to get close to the King's daughter," she said, smiling warmly.

She was not entirely accustomed to the new form and she wasn't happy with the dress she had been stored in, but they stopped by Etani's rooms in the royal quarters to both give her time to examine herself and pick out something she preferred to wear.

"How long was I out?" Etani asked as she moved behind her friend, carefully combing through the crimson curls and arranging them around to better show off that slender neck and feminine profile.

"Only an hour or so, I think. I was getting worried but you were still breathing so I knew you weren't dead." Nayishma turned her head to better examine the fall of her hair. "How do you create these bodies?" she asked, touching the smooth lines of her throat.

"Clay. It takes around a day to create them, but you can make whatever you want so long as you understand the anatomy,"

Nayishma blushed and met her eyes in the mirror. "My anatomy at the moment is like yours?"

"Very similar, I made that host to be somewhat smaller and more agile. It was going to be my escape host but you need it more."

"What happens to this one if you make me a new one?"

"It will crack and fall apart. They don't usually survive a withdrawal, though I have had some success with submerging them in water. Cold wasn't working, and I didn't often have access to hot water. I may be able to mess around with the composition to make it stronger, but that means there is a higher risk of it failing while wearing it, and you really don't want to experience that."

"What is it like?" Nayishma asked with a horrified fascination.

"Imagine vomiting so hard you turn yourself inside out, but instead of everything coming out of your mouth it comes out of your chest and every cell in your being hurts for a week."

Nayishma looked slightly scared. "What happens if I no longer have a host?"

Etani looked at her and friend, studying that beautiful face before wrapping her arms tightly around those small shoulders and resting her cheek against her crimson hair. "I don't know, but I'm going to make sure you don't have to worry about it."

Nayishma nodded slightly and a knock at her door made her jump.

Leaving Nayishma in the bedroom, she moved to open the door and lifted a brow at the giant form of the King. He took her in with one sweep and then searched the room at the sound of movement. His eyes found Nayishma and they almost popped out of his head.

"What is going on, Etani?" he demanded and pushed past her.

"No, please. Come on in," she said sarcastically, closing the door as the King swept across the room and into the doorway of her bedroom. Nayishma studied him in the mirror, her expression carefully neutral. "Your majesty. I hear you've been having troubles with my father."

Alaric choked slightly, turning back to Etani with a look of terror and wonder that she was sure was going to get her in trouble later.

It didn't take long for her to fill the man in, her being covered in dry clay plus the previously dead Princess sitting at her side, looking radiant.

"You can't just bring people back on a whim," Alaric said after they had finished talking and he had taken a good five minutes to process the information they had given him.

"You don't control that aspect of my life, Alaric. Besides, I can only bring back those whose souls I currently hold," she said.

"You should have asked first. Think of the implications of that man learning you have the ability to resurrect his dead child."

"I was thinking of giving a woman a second chance at life, not about your political struggles." Not entirely true; it had mostly been a selfish need to have her friend back, but that was irrelevant at that moment. "I will not ask your permission, not ever."

He looked like he very much wanted to throttle her, but he restrained himself in light of Nayishma, and she knew he had begun to think. She didn't like it when Alaric was thinking. "Would you like your father to be made aware of your... situation?" Alaric asked.

Nayishma frowned, trying to think. "There is no way of knowing how he will react. He might see it as a means of stopping any further threat, or he might see it as an excuse to invade to come and get me. He could really go either way depending on his mood, time of day or season," Nayishma said dryly, her tone suggesting she wasn't particularly fond of her father.

"There is option two," Etani said, mind racing as she thought over the implications of their situation.

"What's that?" Alaric asked.

"We continue on with the current plan and Nayishma takes the throne," she spoke in a matter-of-fact tone, her eyes on Alaric's.

He studied her for a long moment before turning his eyes on Nayishma. He was thinking hard.

"You were planning to assassinate my father?" she didn't sound particularly upset about that, only mildly curious.

"We were; I was planning to leave tomorrow, in fact," Etani replied and their eyes met for a long moment, both women trying to think dispassionately.

"If I were to become Queen, I would not continue on with this war," she said. "Perhaps we could come to some form of agreement?"

Alaric looked like he wanted to kiss her, and she smiled, enjoying his lack of repulsion.

"Very well, the plan goes ahead. Nayishma will go with me and we will allow Varsas to announce her being alive. That night his joy will result in his having a heart attack and how very lucky it is that they have their Princess back with them," Etani said and stood, their eyes following her.

"I'm sure you two can sort it out without me. I need a to take bath." With that, she swept from the room and did exactly that.

10

ALL THINGS COME TO AN END

*S*he could hear them talking, though not enough so that she could hear the topic, and she found herself interrupted from the warmth and luxury by a gentle knock on the door to her suite.

She decided she had been basking long enough, got out and wrapped a towel around herself, heading for her clothes when a voice rang out.

"Who the fuck are you?"

Looking to the door, she frowned in confusion before heading for it, clothes forgotten.

"Nayishma," the response came, cold and resentful. "Who are you?"

"Kai," Kai responded and his eyes found Etani as she opened the door.

He moved towards her and she saw his tension easing slightly as he reached for her, taking her hand in both of his.

"Kai, is everything okay?" she asked gently, her fingers tracing his jaw.

Nayishma stood, glaring at him. "Yes, everything is fine," he said, his hand releasing her and instead going around her waist, his eyes on Nayishma over her head as he hugged her against him gently.

The two seemed determined to stab each other through the face with their eyes and she frowned, the room tense and heavy.

"Didn't Epharis tell you not to visit?" she asked, her fingers finding his and interlocking with them. Nayishma looked like she was about to burst into flames at the intimate gesture.

For one fleeting moment, she thought Nayishma was jealous of her closeness to the vampire, but she dismissed it as ridiculous.

"Since when do we listen to him?" Kai asked, and she laughed gently.

Kai was still staring at Nayishma, his cheek atop her head with spiteful glee.

Alaric cleared his throat gently and all eyes turned to him.

"Why did Epharis ask you not to visit?" he asked suspiciously.

"He is under the false impression that we are responsible for harm that comes to Etani," Kai said, speaking to the King but not taking his eyes off Nayishma.

Alaric grunted softly and crossed his arms, eyeing their closeness. "Do you not have a mission to prepare for? Or clothes to put on?" Alaric demanded and she nodded, turning in Kai's arms and planting a gentle kiss on his cheek.

"Nayishma will be coming with me, I'll explain when I get back," she said to Kai, who finally forced his eyes from Nayishma to look down at her. He didn't look very happy.

"I'll come too, keep you safe," he said and she arched a brow.

"You need to stay here in case something goes wrong. I'm not here to keep *him* alive. Need someone to keep his arse above the grass." She motioned over her shoulder at Alaric, who she felt glaring at her back.

Hugging Kai, she gently untangled herself from his grip and headed for the bedroom, turning to see both he and Nayishma had followed her like ducklings. Nayishma jabbed her elbow into his arm when he tried to squeeze past her.

"What has gotten into you two? Stay out here with Alaric," she backed away and they followed, looking unhappy at her demand. "Stay."

Holding up her index finger, she opened the door with the other hand and slipped inside, closing it quickly behind her and locking them out.

"Everything was fine until you got here," Nayishma snapped.

"Everything was fine until you were reborn," Kai hissed back.

Turning her back on the door, she rubbed her temples and dressed herself in black pants and a relaxed tunic. She would change into her gear later.

Walking back out, she froze as she found the two standing on either side of her door, glaring. Jaia had come in and was staring at them in wonder, Alaric looking like he was holding back laughter.

"I didn't mean literally stay *right* there," she said and frowned when each of them took one of her hands tightly.

It was disturbing and she had no idea of how to deal with them, nor even what the problem was to start with.

They weren't looking at her, they were staring at each other, their grips tight on her hands.

"Okay, Kai, let's go," Jaia said, but Kai wasn't listening.

"Yeah, Kai, you should go. We have plans to make," Nayishma said and all eyes turned to her, trying to piece together what the issue was.

Kai looked deeply upset but Jaia had moved to him, pulling him away.

"Don't worry, Kai, I'll only be gone a few days," she said gently, but he was staring resentfully at her hand still clenched tightly in Nayishma's.

When she forced her hand free, Nayishma looked upset but it seemed Kai relaxed and then finally allowed himself to be pulled away from her.

"Don't tell Epharis, we were just worried," Jaia said gently as he shoved his brother towards the door. Smiling slightly at Jaia, she shook her head and they left. There was a brief scuffle and then the sound of someone being dragged off, whimpering sadly.

Turning on Nayishma, she glared at the woman who looked a little sheepish, but they both remained silent.

The remainder of the day and night passed without issue and the plan was set out. Nayishma would be provided a guard and a carriage, then she would be returned to Weorene. Etani would follow behind to act as a second guard and backup. Versalis was to join her up to the city, though Alaric didn't tell her why. She suspected it was because of the gem, but she didn't ask.

Instead, she collected her items and checked everything to ensure it was clean, prepared, and in good condition.

Versalis arrived shortly before dawn, wary at the sight of them all sitting calmly together, his eyes lingering on Nayishma.

"Nayishma, Versalis the vampire King. Versalis, Nayishma the Princess of Weorene," she said, her eyes flicking up to him only briefly as she worked on polishing one of her knives.

They murmured a greeting as Versalis joined them, taking up a cloth and one of her knives.

They filled him in on the plan quickly and he nodded, glancing towards the sky out of the window to gauge the time.

"I'll get dressed," she said finally, heading into her room to gear up.

It took a good twenty minutes and once she was dressed, she padded back from her room with her boots under her arm, her hands working through her hair into a long braid, the leather tie between her teeth.

She grunted a thanks to Versalis as she noticed he had finished her weapons and was lounging back against the chair, and he smiled at the sight of her. Nayishma looked around and gave a little squeak of shock. She had never seen the skin-tight black ensemble before and her eyes widened.

Dropping her boots onto the chair, she frowned at her hair and unwound it again, realising she had twisted the braid and the second time she had a pull. Sighing in frustration, she eyed off one of her knives, Versalis catching the intention.

He slapped her hand away from the knife, moved behind her, and bundled up her hair.

"You are not allowed to cut it off. Well, unless it stays the length it is when you go all death on us, but not like this," His fingers made quick work on the length and she sat, pouting, knowing better than to argue.

He bound the end tight with the thong, then dropped the long rope of hair down the back of her shirt, adjusting it, and let go.

She tilted her head forward to loosen the braid for freedom of movement. As he moved away, she caught his hand and kissed the palm gently.

He made a happy sound in the back of his throat before starting to bundle up the weapons.

She tugged on one boot and started sliding weapons into place, followed by the second boot and then the new straps around her thighs. Crouching down to feel the flex of the leather, she adjusted them and Versalis dug a new hole in the second strap.

Content with the tightness, she slipped her belt around her waist and buckled it in place.

Looking up, she found Nayishma and Alaric both staring at her and Versalis' quick work of her weaponry and the movements of her body in the tight outfit.

"Don't you have to get ready?" she asked Nayishma. The woman jumped, hurrying into the bedroom to get dressed.

Alaric was still watching her. But she chose to ignore him and tucked the lockpick up under the corset, then the last two knives.

She left her hood and mask down, not needing them for the time being and she stretched, feeling everything settle against her frame.

Versalis stared hard at her, searching for anything out of place, and reached out to hitch the corset up and then pulled the strings to tighten it.

"Ow..." she complained and he looked over her shoulder. Without a word he reached down the front of her shirt to adjust her pinched breast and then nodded.

"Better?" he asked and she flung out her arms, twisting her torso and nodding.

Alaric seemed to be struggling and she lifted a brow at him. "You just let them touch you like that?" he demanded, and she shrugged.

"It's not like he hasn't seen me naked before. We've all seen each other naked. It's just a body."

Alaric stared at her chest and she snorted.

"Don't even think about it."

Versalis was smirking when she turned to him, Alaric's jealous glare alerting her to his doing something he shouldn't be.

"Do you want to stay behind?" she threatened.

"No, Ma'am," he said, but he was unrepentant in the face of her glare.

Lifting her hand, she gave his nose a gentle flick and his head jerked back, shocked at the tap.

She laughed gently and moved away from him, the gentle jingle making her look down. "That is going to be a problem," she murmured, lifting her foot and even through the boot it tinkled.

"Have Epharis look into it," Alaric said, his brows furrowing as she flinched and dropped her eyes.

Versalis growled softly in response, his eyes dangerous, but she calmed him with a touch on his arm before she swept from the room to check on Nayishma.

"Come on, Yish, we have to be moving," she said and stopped at the sight of the woman struggling in an attempt to reach back for the strings of her corset. She was still only half dressed, her dress hanging around her waist limply.

Laughing, Etani moved forward and together they got her dressed in the soft black gown, her hair piled up on top of her head with long tendrils falling down around her face and shoulders.

She looked lovely, elegant, and sophisticated.

"Perfect," she murmured as she selected a small emerald necklace and placed it around her neck.

Slipping her arms around her friend's shoulders, she hugged her tightly. She was going to sorely miss the woman, but at least she was alive.

A gentle knock came at the door and the two turned as Versalis came in, his eyes straying to the bed for a moment before finding them at the vanity.

"It's time to go," he said, and Nayishma stood, her gown rustling as she swept from the room to a murmur of surprise from Alaric.

Before she could leave, Versalis caught her arm, his lips near her ear. "I will kill him if he abuses you again."

"Versalis, don't get involved. You don't want to have to deal with him."

"You deserve better," he growled and she smiled, cupping his face between her hands and pulling his head down. Placing a gentle kiss on his forehead, she felt his sigh of resignation.

They both knew there was nothing that could be done and worrying about it would only make it worse.

"Don't worry about me," she said as she released him and smiled, heading out of the room.

Nayishma had waited, her face curious, but when Etani shook her head, she smiled and they turned to leave. Nayishma curtsied to Alaric and Etani gave him a flippant two-fingered half-salute as she left, feeling his eyes lingering on her. Versalis gave him one finger in farewell and that earnt a soft chuckle.

Heading down the main stairs, she gave Nayishma a tight hug and watched as she was helped into the carriage by a guard, his eyes lingering on her.

A voice called her name and she turned to see Uzo of all people.

Waving to Nayishma, she waited for the Fae to join her and he grinned, gazing after the Princess.

"Who was that lovely creature?" he asked, intent on the carriage.

"Nayishma, Weorene's Princess. We are taking her home."

"Didn't the Princess die?" he asked, frowning after the carriage now.

"Yes, and so did Kai, but that's no longer an issue."

She looked to Uzo, whose eyes had snapped to her. Meeting his intense gaze, she offered a quirk of her lips and watched as Versalis fidgeted, wanting to go.

"We have time, don't worry," she said to him and turned back to Uzo. "Will you keep an eye on the twins and Alaric, I don't want to come back to a burning city."

Uzo nodded, looking down over her form and scowling, but she wasn't about to tell him what she was up to.

"Hurry back, Etania, we haven't had a chance to talk yet. We need to discuss things."

"I might be gone a while," she said and smiled at his narrowed eyes.

Touching the side of her nose, she winked at him and then turned, sprinting suddenly at Versalis, who yelped and jumped backwards to avoid her swipe.

He was on her tail in an instant as they followed the carriage from a safe distance, having more fun trying to catch each other than anything and with an uneventful trip, they were just glad for the chance to burn off some energy.

Etani especially felt the need to move, still overly full and energetic from Tatialia.

They never strayed far from the carriage and guards in case anything happened and they slept in trees, huddled together for warmth and comfort while on the road.

They eventually reached Weorene and the city seemed to be rather subdued, the pair watching the procession as it passed through the forests and along newly built bridges to get to the castle.

The King was quickly informed and he came out to see what was going on, not expecting any visitors.

When he saw his daughter, he took a moment to try and process just who she was and then he bellowed and tackled her in his joy.

He almost dragged her into the castle and the two remaining

outside breathed a sigh of relief and settled themselves in to wait. They would wait outside until the time came.

The King threw an enormous celebration in the light of his daughter's appearance, the palace filling up with people and creatures of all kinds.

It was exceptionally interesting to watch as they sat in their trees and kept an eye on things.

They were only a few minutes away and remained alert all through the night and then the next day, where drunk and hungover revellers finally piled back into their carriages and headed home.

The guards from Ayathian had left, taking the carriage with them and everything settled into quiet once more.

It was that night that the pair moved, slinking closer to the palace and setting themselves up.

Etani checked her weapons again, ready in case things went wrong, but there was no reason why anything should happen that they didn't expect. The bell was wrapped several times over, forming an uncomfortable wad of fabric against her ankle, but it silenced the thing, at least mostly.

11

KING VARSAS

As the moon rose, the two began their descent from the trees and picked their way across the streams and gullies that broke up the city into smaller slivers, making it more difficult for them to get closer. It was better than trying to get across during the day.

Using ropes to get across the streams without having to go swimming, it was closer to midnight before they reached the palace and she gave Versalis one last kiss on the cheek before she pulled up her mask and hood, leaving him to act as her backup.

Being near him felt wonderful, and she hated to be away from him, feeling that constant pull towards him and the crystal he held.

She felt his eyes on her as she slunk across the palace grounds and located the room Varsas slept in, one story up.

Scaling the decorative wall was easier than she thought and when she was up there, she carefully worked away the edge of the screen to pull it free, the sticky substance that held the screen in place likely to leave prints if she wasn't careful.

Using the palm of her hand to flatten out any prints and smear them, she slid inside the tiny gap she had wiggled loose and pulled it down behind her.

Excess bugs in the room would lead them to suspect tampering and she didn't want that.

The room was very dark, the only light coming in from behind her, and she breathed in the odd scent of fur and male who didn't bathe often, coupled with the humidity and the general smell of the swamps.

Pausing just inside the room, she listened but found only one set of breathing. Waiting to give her eyes time to adjust, she kept her eyes off him. Some humans had a weird ability to sense when they were being watched and she wasn't keen to learn whether he was one of them.

Her eyes adjusted to the dimness and she crept silently across the room, her feet placed slowly to ensure she didn't make a sound as she approached the bed. Kneeling down, she felt along the covers and cursed silently when she found them tucked carefully under the mattress.

Looking up at the sleeping form, she placed her arm against the bedspread and began to slowly pry the sheets out from under the mattress. It was a slow process and she mentally berated the servant who was responsible for that inconvenience.

It took a good five minutes for her to get the blanket and sheets out, every second making her anxious.

Reaching down, she picked out the syringe and vial and slowly eased the sheets up just enough to see his feet. She was very glad he wasn't one of those people who slept with their toes scrunched up.

At a snail's pace, she slid one knee onto the mattress and slid the syringe into the foil, drawing out enough to fill the syringe around halfway and then she leant forward, her lips pursed to keep her breath from brushing his feet.

Once she was settled, she searched the skin of his foot and then slowly pressed the needle into the firm skin between his first and second toe. The needle was incredibly fine, almost as thin as a strand of her hair, and she smiled as it slid cleanly into the skin.

He grunted and she froze, her eyes wide as she tried not to breathe, but he didn't move.

Letting out her breath in a quivering exhale, she pushed the needle slowly deeper until she felt the resistance and then the pop of the needle finding the vein.

Smiling, she pressed down on the plunger, and emptied the syringe into his system. She waited, not wanting to remove the needle just yet, and counted the time passing.

He jerked and she pulled the needle out quickly to avoid tearing the skin, backing away as the man wheezed. She checked the spot of skin she had injected and found it to not be bleeding.

Tucking the blanket back under the mattress, she smoothed it out and looked up to find him looking back at her, his eyes massive and bulging as he clutched at his chest, gasping and straining.

The veins in his neck popped into stark relief and he clawed at himself.

She could only smile, watching as the man's body betrayed him, natural functions seizing wide open and refusing to close again, blood rushing and then blocked when no more blood was pumped.

She stood silently and watched as his body jerked and then he was still. It took all of about six minutes and she remained to be sure he was indeed dead.

Placing her fingers against the side of his neck, she found his pulse had gone quiet and she moved efficiently, arranging him in a more comfortable position.

When she was satisfied with how he looked, the bed sheets tucked around him as he had been in sleep, she crept from the room and carefully pulled the screen down, pressing at the goo until it resembled the rest of the window.

Throwing one last glance into the room, she descended the side of the palace and found Versalis waiting, calm and patient, for her.

She took his hand and they hurried away, leaving the grounds and retreating to the trees as though nothing at all had happened.

When the morning came, they heard the scream as someone found the corpse and the two assassins smiled at each other, the job done.

They lingered for several more hours to watch the goings-on around the palace, Nayishma seen to be wandering around in mourning clothes, crying and lamenting the loss of her beloved father.

Those who had left only hours before were rushing to return, dressed in black and looking horrified at the ill luck of the man. He had just gotten his daughter back and then he died, how awful for them both.

Once she was sure they hadn't been noticed, she released the needle from the syringe and threw it into the stream, the canister and the jar washed out and buried in separate locations. If they were ever found, it would be unlikely that anyone would make the connection.

Content with their efforts, they started back towards Ayathian and set up for the night in a tree together, her leaning back into his chest with his legs dangling off the sides of the branch.

"Do we go straight back or do we run off and conquer the world?" he asked after several hours of watching the night sky, tracking the moon and enjoying the peace of the outside world.

"I am not going back right away," she said, feeling him tense behind her.

"What do you mean? Where are you going?" he demanded and she sat up, turning to face him on the branch.

"Away, for a few more days at least." She didn't want to tell him.

"Etani, where are you going?" he didn't sound happy and his hands curled around hers, clutching them firmly as though it would stop her from leaving him.

"I need to be away from them. Away from the city, and I have something I want to get."

"What do you want to get? I can come with you."

She frowned, looking into his handsome face, those white-lavender eyes making her want nothing more than to curl up in his arms. "Versalis, I can't go back to Epharis," she breathed and his face went stony.

"We can kill him," he stated, but she shook her head, smiling sadly.

"No, we can't kill him. At least not yet."

He frowned, not understanding, and she pulled one hand free to brush his hair back from his face.

"You need to go back, tell them I ran and you couldn't catch me," she said gently and he shook his head stubbornly.

"They would never believe me."

"I can run places where you can't follow me, Versalis," she reminded him, lifting up her index finger.

"That's not the point. Etani, he will be furious when you get back. He will hurt you worse."

Dropping her eyes, she shivered at the idea of what he would do to her.

"I cannot refuse him again. He and Alaric will kill you and the twins and I can't allow that."

Versalis sucked in a breath and he grabbed her arms, shaking her slightly. "Why didn't you tell us?" he demanded.

"Because it makes no difference, I am trapped there no matter what. I can't escape them and if one lets go the other will grip tighter. Then they just swap, passing me between them over and over again. Alaric owns the twins, Epharis knows I care about them. It is only a matter of time before he kills them and then goes after you."

Her voice was anguished, wanting him to understand and yet she desperately wanted him to convince her to stay. "There are things I need to do. Alone," she added when his mouth opened to complain.

His eyes narrowed and he shook his head, refusing to accept that. "You're not leaving, he won't harm any of us ever again," he sounded certain but she knew he wasn't. There was nothing that could stop the Lich.

"Just go back and give me a few days. I left plenty of blood for them and you."

Understanding dawned on his face and he clenched his jaw. "You were planning this the whole time," he accused and she gave a slight shrug. His grip tightened on her arms.

She flinched and he immediately let go as though she had shocked him.

"Etani, please... don't leave us. We need you." His words struck her and her eyes immediately filled with tears.

"Versalis, I have to, I'll die if I go back." She saw his pain and fear, his need to cling to her, but she drew him closer, her forehead pressed against his. "Please, my love, you have to do this for me," she breathed and his body clenched, his need to keep her close and safe being forced down.

Her eyes lowered to the crystal that glowed a warm red under his shirt and she shivered, wanting badly to take it from him.

"All right, but you have to come back as soon as you can," he whispered, and she nodded. His fingers touched the underside of her chin and lifted her lips to his in a tender kiss. "Don't abandon us," he breathed and she shivered, his lips warm and soft, his breath cooling them sharply.

"I would never abandon you," she replied in barely a whisper and her lips found his again, firm and loving.

He clutched her to him, her smaller frame fitting perfectly into his hard chest, and they remained like that until morning, simply existing together.

When morning came, she bid him farewell for the time being, feeling his eyes on her as she thought of where she wanted to go in Ceress and opened the door with a single drop of blood.

Stepping through, she found herself in that place and shook her head in wonder.

Something had changed inside her.

Turning, she saw one last glimpse of his handsome, worried and angry face as the door closed and they were split apart between worlds.

She felt a terrible urge to go back and throw herself into his arms but she knew he would have left already, facing the wrath of the Lich and the titan all on his own and she was sorry for his having to face that, but she had her own needs to attend to right then.

Breathing out a soft sigh, she focused on where she wanted to go and opened the door once more, stepping out into a dense rainforest.

She spent the remainder of her day trying to catch the elusive pain-in-the-neck frog who was determined to stay away, just as she was determined to have it with her.

Eventually she caught it and unceremoniously stuffed it into a bag before it could spit on her or whatever it was the thing did. She soon found out that the frog secreted the poison and she was very glad for her leather pants when that happened.

She prepared a small fire, slipped through into a new little town and stole a pot and some other supplies. Taking them back, she used the pot upside down to cook the frog and the secretions collected, leaving her with a healthy supply of the poison she needed.

It was mostly for backup, but she had other plans.

She had just finished dousing the flames when a cough came from behind her and she whirled, staring into the yellow-gold eyes of the demon she had met on the field.

"Hello, Etania," he purred, and she recoiled slightly from the wash of sexual tension that filled her at the sound of her name. She wasn't wrong when she thought he was a lust demon.

"Hello—" she cut off, wracking her brain for the name he had given her.

He looked a little put out, his face falling as she struggled to recall that one simple detail. "Daemon," he offered, and she snorted.

"Oh right, Daemon the demon." She snickered, his eyes narrowing in response to her amusement. "What do you want?" She picked up the pot and walked away from him without waiting for a response, leaving him to run in order to keep up with her as she fetched more water.

"I want to talk with you," he demanded, but she ignored him.

Filling the pot with water, she turned and he was right behind her, her sudden jolt sloshing water over his nice white shirt.

"Excuse me," she snapped, but he refused to move.

"You have to be the most stubborn one of the lot," he growled and then he was staggering, the loud bong of the pot bouncing off his head loud in the quiet forest.

"Firstly..." She stopped again and squinted, his name escaping her yet again. "Firstly, demon, you are the one who is interrupting my day." Was it David? Samuel? Eli? Why couldn't she remember it? "Secondly, I have no interest in talking to you, ever." She turned back to the stream and refilled the pot, even as he was still sitting on the stones and holding his head.

Stalking past him, she yelped when he grabbed her foot and she spun, the pot glancing off his skull as he ducked.

Trading up her foot for her wrists, he squeezed the soft insides until she let it go and it hit the ground between them.

Instead, she lifted her foot and drove it into his shin and he yelped in pain, letting go of her wrist. Using the freedom, she smashed her palm up into his nose and dropped him. "Why is it so hard for men to understand what 'no' means?" she demanded as she tried for a third time to collect water, this time dumping it on the fire while he recovered from his injuries.

"Why is it so hard for you to just be nice?" he growled as he followed her, jerking back when she turned and held the pot out in a blatant threat of violence

"You have five seconds to tell me what you want, and then you are going to leave."

"I want you," he said and she rolled her eyes.

"I'm married, enslaved to a King, and currently not in the mood for yet another suitor," she retorted and when he reached for her, she clocked him on the side of the head again.

He lost his temper and ripped the pot from her hand, throwing it hard enough that it made a very neat little circle in a nearby tree before lodging in the second one. "You are wearing on my patience!" he yelled, gripping her wrist and jerking her arm down roughly. Forced to her knees, she pulled at her arm but it wasn't moving.

"I will force you to obey me if you do not cooperate," he growled, teeth bared.

"Oh, like you're the first man to tell me that," she snapped and punched him in the stomach.

He grunted and doubled over but refused to let go of her arm, even as she stood.

Heaving against his grip, she swore and drove her knee up into his face.

He flipped backwards onto the ground, and finally she was free. She didn't wait to see if he got back up.

The instant he was down, she had bolted and she heard him screaming her name as he raced after her.

Cursing at the difficulty of men, she forced herself to move as fast as she was able within the trees and foliage, the sounds of the pursuing demon growing closer as he simply breezed through the trees instead of going around like she did.

Biting down on her fingertip, she flung out her arm and laughed as the door opened, streaking through it and into Ceress.

Sprinting at top speed along the border between Ceress and Summer, she headed in the direction of Winter, her mind racing.

Glancing back, she saw him rip his way through realities to leave the door in shattered shreds, his eyes finding her and immediately coming after her.

She pushed herself harder, but knew she wouldn't be able to keep it up for long.

A second fling of her hand and she blew back into the human world atop a small hill that was entirely green, huge and majestic mountains capped in white to her front and a large lake to her right. Turning for the valley to her left, she heard him ripping his way through and she knew he was catching up to her.

She couldn't maintain the speed and he was drawing on strength from Faerie, something she had never tried to do before.

His arm slid around her and the sudden loss of momentum had knocked them both to the ground, rolling and leaving a long gouge in the green hill.

She panted and threw herself to her feet and ran to him, driving her foot into his side and sending him flying up the hill but he was on his feet again within a breath of her foot finding his side.

Growling, he ran for her and she ducked, lifting up enough to drive her elbow into his back, and he staggered.

When she reached behind her, she drew out the large two knives that crossed against her lower back and she went after him, her mind set on destroying this new mortal host of his.

Seeing her coming, he was able to block her first thrust for his chest, the second grazing his cheek as he tilted his head back in an attempt to dodge it.

His eyes glowed a rich gold as he retaliated, throwing a hard underarm punch for her stomach and her body twisted, his fist grazing her but missing a damaging shot.

He deflected another slash that barely missed his throat, and caught her attempt to drive the second knife into the side of his neck. Fingers closing around hers, he spun her and used her own knife at her throat to hold her still.

His fingers were painfully hard on hers, keeping her from being able to release the blade as he pulled her firmly against his chest to prevent her from busting his nose open with the back of her head.

He panted heavily in her ear, his free hand curling around her waist to trap her other arm at her side and they stood still, trying to recover from the sprint and fight. "Now be a good girl and don't struggle," he breathed as he pressed forward and she was forced to bend with him until he drove his knee into the back of hers and she buckled, landing hard on her knees with his body leaning over hers.

"Let go of the knife," he said slowly and she released the blade at her side, the one at her throat unable to be released. "Good girl. If you try and stab me, I will hurt you," he said slowly as his fingers loosened on hers and the second blade fell to the ground with the first. "That's my girl."

He kept his fingers on hers, pulling her arm down until it was wrapped around herself and he was able to hold her by the wrist. Using his body weight, he finally pressed her to the ground and sighed in relief, releasing her wrist and placing his hand against the centre of her back to keep her pinned.

Sitting on her backside, he looked down at her and smiled, her head turning just enough to see him seated on top of her. "That wasn't so hard, was it?" he asked and she glared at him. "Don't be a spoilsport, I won fair and square. Now I get my prize."

His fingers pulled the length of her hair out of the back of her shirt and he began to unwind the tight braid, his fingers smooth and fast. Once it was free, he took one of the throwing blades from her thigh and used it to cut a lock of her hair, holding it up to examine in the light. He smiled happily, tied it into a smooth knot, and then tucked it away in his pocket.

"What do you want?" she demanded, shivering as he leant down and the tip of his nose traced a line on her throat as he breathed in her scent.

"You, Etani, only you," he said gently as he reached under her and began to unbuckle her belt.

"Is anyone in this world capable of taking 'no' as an answer?" she snarled and he laughed, removing the belt and throwing it away.

"Oh don't worry, I'll be gentle," he paused and then laughed again. "No, I won't."

She waited, his hands tracing down over her backside and then up between her legs as he released the straps and they too were thrown away, far out of her reach.

The laces of her corset were next and he pulled them free, grinning as he used the strings to bind her hands and then the second going around her throat, suddenly pulled tight and cutting off her air as he leant down.

"You have no idea how long I have waited for this moment." He relished her gasping for air, his eyes cold on her as she choked. "Since you were but a little girl, crying for your daddy when that Cain fellow killed him. Then screaming for your mother to wake up, but she never did."

His words cut her, the string pulled tighter as he forced open the back of her corset and pulled it out from under her, throwing it away.

"I tried to get to you when you left Ceress, but that damned cat was there. He wouldn't let me near." She could see blackness creeping in on her vision, fear washing through her as he undid her boots and shoved them off, leaving her with nothing but her base clothes.

"Then you ran, and you ran." The string pulled tight until no more air could slip past and she felt herself fading. "And I followed, and followed. But you always managed to get away from me," he whispered in her ear, watching her face as her eyelids fluttered.

She was suddenly able to breathe and she gasped in air, her head spinning as she heaved.

"No, my darling girl, I want you conscious," he said maliciously, enjoying her struggles. "You were so beautiful, prowling your way through the human world and killing without mercy. Anyone who crossed you ended up dead, anyone who looked in your direction ended up dead."

His free hand gripped the back of her shirt and pulled it up, his body shivering as his hand pressed against her bare skin, feeling the softness of it. "Such a perfect creature, so hungry and never satisfied." He leant over her and dragged his tongue hard up the side of her face, grinning when she shuddered. "I knew I had created the one, especially with what happened with Faerie. Such a waste of perfectly good Fae."

He forced his hand up under her and found her breast, squeezing and fondling her painfully.

She felt her boot and her attention immediately snapped to it, the soft pad of one of her custom knives giving her hope.

"And then the Lich caught you and I was certain you were lost to me. They're not the sharing type," he said, and in a whip, he flipped her over and pinned her back down.

She didn't try and struggle, not wanting him to restrain her further, instead she worked on trying to inch her boot up towards her hands, her attention turning to cutting the string. The string broke in a matter of seconds and she was free. Not that it meant much in that instant.

"Then I found out about the war and I was so excited to join in. I knew you would be involved, that idiot King has no idea just how powerful you are."

At her not fighting, his hands went to the hem of her shirt and he pulled it up to expose her, his eyes bright as he leant down and bit her breast.

She cried out as he drew blood, using her unconscious squirm to wiggle the boot up, but it wouldn't go any further. Cursing, she thought over her position and then she did either something very stupid, or very clever.

She shifted herself, pulling her legs out from under him and parting them, one of hers on either side of his hips.

He went still, staring down at her, and then growled. He assumed she wanted him, but the position allowed her to move the boot up and her fingers grazed the leather. He licked the trickle of blood from her breast and moaned at the taste of her before he gave her a warning look and kissed her hard.

She wanted to kill him, she really did, but she resisted the urge to try. Instead she shifted the boot up a little higher and edged it around to find the knives.

Her lips moved against his, meeting the ferocity of his kiss with hers. Her fingers found his hair and she gripped it hard, controlling his head as she bit his lower lip.

He sucked in a breath and growled his pleasure at her cooperation. Fingers closing on the knife, he rolled and she suddenly found herself on top of him, his arousal obvious under her as she straddled his hips.

Leaning down, she kissed him with as much passion as she could give a man she hated and couldn't remember the name of.

While she was down, her hand extended and she fished one of the knives out of the boot and her thumb pressed off the woollen ball cap. She ground herself down on him to keep him occupied, his hands finding her hips and pushing her down harder.

His eyes were closed and so he missed her lifting the knife, but they opened in some primal warning system, even as the blade plunged into his eye.

The side of her hand was covered in blood and ichor as she let go of the knife that had plunged in up to her fist and she wiggled it, scrambling his brains just to be sure.

His body jerked and she felt the malicious intent of the demon leaving the human as the human died.

She knew he would be back and he wouldn't fall for her game again. But until then, she had time to escape. She jumped off him, scrambled to pull her boots on, and gripped the handle of the knife in his eye, jerking it sideways to snap off the thin blade.

She had made them so that the blade would easily break and remain lodged in the wound, making it harder to heal. In this case it only meant he was still dead, but that was irrelevant.

She dressed quickly and bit her finger to open the door, throwing one last glance at the beauty of the land she had just left before stepping through into Summer.

12

___

THE SUMMER COURT

She had never had reason to wander around Summer and she didn't intend to stay there then, instead trying to place herself in an unexpected ancient ruin.

Why were there ruins in Faerie?

Giving the question a pass for the time being, she looked upwards to try and find where the skies met and she cringed at the distance she would have to go.

She didn't hear anyone behind her until a large hand closed around most of her face and she was yanked back into a hairy body.

Screaming out of shock, thinking it was the demon, she jerked free of the hand and spun, a knife seeming to materialise in her hand at the speed of the draw.

Her eyes met the chest and then lifted to see the face of Barron, the centaur she had met once before.

"We have to stop meeting like this," he said in an amused boom.

"You shouldn't sneak up on people; you'll get stabbed," she warned, glaring at him before sheathing the blade again.

"I'm not overly concerned," he said and beat a fist on his chest. "Hard as nails, we centaur."

She snorted, recalling the centaur Versalis had killed in

Ayathian but she shook her head. A thought occurred to her then and she tilted her head slightly. "What are the odds of us running into each other twice?" she asked and his grin made her considerably nervous.

"Not high, unless we've been waiting for you."

She had only just processed his words when a dart thudded into the small of her back. "Seriously?" she demanded, plucking it out and throwing it at the centaur. "What is wrong with you people? I'm a perfectly nice person if you just leave me alone."

She turned, trying to see who or what had darted her, but she only saw ruins and yellow-leaved trees.

"Nice or not, Princess, you are in Summer," Barron said and as she turned, the world suddenly tilted sideways and she staggered, gripping a broken wall to keep from falling.

"How did you know who I am?" she asked, her voice seeming to be coming out as a wobble from far away.

"Your father killed many of us; we recognised your name," he said and smiled as she plopped down onto her backside, her hands seeming to stretch and warp as she lifted them.

"I should have killed you when I had the chance." Her vision was going fuzzy and she stared up at the large blur of brown and tan.

"Yes, you should have. Sleep well, Princess."

She did sleep then, dropping back onto the stone and unconscious before she felt the collision.

When she woke, she found herself bound tightly at her arms and legs, sitting in a chair. Everything else was still a blur around her and she blinked hard to try and figure out what she was seeing.

The marble under her bare feet was white streaked with gold and she was sitting in a chair that was also gold, the straps were at least not the gold ones she knew to be owned by her husband, but they were tight and she was unable to move enough to cut them.

She was able to feel that she had been carefully disarmed, a tilt of her head telling her they had even gotten the vials from her hair and she sighed, frustrated at the foresight of the inhabitants of Faerie.

She was in a small room with nothing but her chair and a tapestry of a blonde woman with blue-green eyes and bronze coloured lips in a black dress. Squinting at the tapestry, she leant forward to try and focus on it, then jerked back violently when the eyes moved. She might even have squeaked a little in shock.

The eyes focused on her and then narrowed before turning to gaze into the distance again, and a door behind her opened.

A massively tall figure stalked into the room, clad from head to toe in black amour, followed by a little wisp of a girl with a million freckles on her honey skin and a mass of wild red hair down to her backside.

The two looked at her and then the girl smiled.

"Behave and we won't have to hurt you, we are going to unstrap you and bind you. Do you understand?" She sounded disgustingly chipper and Etani nodded, staring at her.

The male made quick work of her bindings and then tied a simple yellow ribbon around her wrists in front of her. The sight was so incredibly odd that she tested it and then hit the ground as all of her strength vanished, only to begin to return in a slow seep that made her feel ill.

"You'll only ever do it once," the girl said happily.

"Yes, thank you," Etani said sarcastically as the enormous, faceless man helped her up.

They led her from the room and she found all sorts of creatures staring at her with the same amount of fascination that she levelled on them.

Aside from the obvious differences between Winter and Summer was the blatant colour differences between the two. Winter was all cold blues, blacks, silvers, and whites. Here everything was yellows, reds, oranges, and oddly, blacks.

She saw a sphinx with haughty gold eyes watching her, her long tail swaying in agitation. Beautiful women and equally beautiful men, dryads with their earth tones and leafy clothing, pixies and fairies, even a unicorn watching her with a creepy level of consciousness.

She seemed to be the centre of attention, a sharp contrast from the warm tones with her coldly dark colouring and the ribbon binding her hands.

She found herself turning to try and see the sphynx again, fascinated with the creature. Her affinity for felines had her wanting to go back and yet the sphynx seemed uninterested in her. It was a little disappointing, but she let it go.

The pair pulled her through that hallway and into another, then finally into an enormous hall so packed with creatures she was surprised there was room to move at all.

At the far end of the hall a tall dais held three thrones, two small and casual with the large middle one being made entirely of gold and looking weirdly leaf-shaped with the tip curling up to provide the Queen a place to sit.

The woman sitting on the throne was the woman from the tapestry, her long, blonde hair bound in a braid coiled with gold atop her head. She had large gold earrings with aquamarine stones set into them, the design that of a flower. A matching necklace hung around her throat, a series of flowers and stones covering her chest.

Her dress was rather ordinary compared to that of the girls at her side, only a simple black flowing thing with long streamers of black fabric that fluttered around her, hanging from her shoulders and up over her head.

She wore no shoes and Etani found the sight of her pretty feet weird though she wasn't sure why. The woman looked older than any Fae she had ever seen, looking to be perhaps in her forties with laugh lines and small creases at the corners of her eyes.

"Queen Cecelia, may we present the Princess Etania of Winter. Captured while trying to travel between worlds," the faceless male at her side boomed out in a huge, echoing voice from inside his helmet.

The crowd went silent as all eyes turned in their direction and she looked up at the Queen, her chin lifted and effecting her best 'yes, and?' expression.

"Welcome to Summer, Princess," the Queen said gently, her copper coloured lips pulling into a wide smile and revealing perfectly straight white teeth.

"Pleasure. Can I go now?" she asked, making a vague gesture towards the door.

A snort came from somewhere but no one seemed willing to own up to the sound.

The Queen had looked in the direction but then her eyes returned to Etani with that same kind smile that made her skin crawl. No one was that nice, or maybe she was jaded.

The Queen didn't seem to be overly bothered by the rudeness and she gave a slight shake of her head. "I'm afraid we can't let you leave, we haven't been able to gain control of a Winter Princess for a very long time," she said happily.

"You're wasting your time. If you want a real Princess go after Megara or Hercia. Though I suppose Megara is the Queen now. Who's the second Princess now?"

"Xena," the Queen supplied and Etani nodded.

"Xena then, go ask for one of them. I'm sure they'll be glad for something to do. I however have things to do, people to see and all that."

The Queen didn't look overly impressed by her argument on why she couldn't stay in Summer and Etani sighed.

"Don't make me kill you, too..." she said finally, tired of the games of the Fae.

"Too? Ah, so it *was* you who killed Tatialia?"

"Didn't you already know that?" She tilted her head, curious at how the woman hadn't already been informed.

"No, our spies haven't been able to get through with the added security. They seem to be under the impression that a Fae killer was on the loose. Or maybe you're just a Queen killer?"

"No, I'm not all that picky on who I kill," she said flippantly.

The Queen frowned at her, trying to figure out if she was serious or not.

"Really though, I think you're great, love the colouring of this place, but I have to get back before my husband blows a vein and starts setting things on fire."

"Sit down," the Queen said and suddenly her legs no longer held her up.

Finding herself on her backside, she squinted up at the woman.

"I really don't appreciate your holding me, Cecelia," she said coldly.

She expected a reaction but again the Queen seemed unbothered by her rudeness. That in itself gave her pause and set off all sorts of warning bells. No one was that calm, unless they were unable to get angry.

Her eyes swept the room, searching smug and curious faces; some displayed pity and others looked like they would have enjoyed beating her themselves.

She had assumed that Summer would be the nice side of the coin but the more she looked, the more she doubted that. Something was wrong here and she couldn't quite place her finger on it.

Finally her eyes returned to the Queen and she still had that same calm smile; the sight of it making her skin crawl.

"Given you are quite a hostile creature, we feel you should remain contained for the time being," the Queen said, and Etani looked down at the obnoxious yellow ribbon.

"Of course you do..." she said sourly, irritation filling her.

What was she going to do? She needed to get back, but this Court was refusing to let her go and she had no means of contacting anyone for a retrieval. She realised with cold certainty that her desire to keep secrets from her friends was what got her into that situation.

"I believe this calls for a celebration!" the Queen declared.

Etani turned her attention from the Queen to the other two on the dais with a note of curiosity. Unlike Winter, these two were watching her just as curiously.

The heir was a slender woman with hair the colour of blood. Her lips were a rosy red and her eyes were a deep blue. She was lovely in a copper, orange and red dress.

The second heir was an almost ordinary looking woman in a

cream coloured billowing dress. A simple silver tiara atop her brow. She had long, wavy blonde hair and soft green eyes. Her face was a smooth, round shape and she looked as though she was likely the nicest person there.

Looking between the two as they studied her, she lifted a brow and the youngest smiled, dimples appearing in her cheeks.

She turned back to the Queen, who had been speaking to the crowd; she realised it might have been a good idea to pay attention to the speech, but she hadn't.

"On the eve," she was calling out and the crowd cheered, faces excited.

Frowning, she was certain she had missed something important and large hands caught her upper arms and gently lifted her to her feet.

Turning to see the little redhead and the giant in black armour, she gave them a sheepish smile.

"I missed the speech, what's going on?"

"Another ball. Third one this month," the female said with a roll of her eyes and Etani pursed her lips in frustration. She wanted to go back, but that didn't seem to be happening.

Sighing, she followed between the two without argument and they led her through more corridors until they reached a large wooden door. Two guards stood outside the door in armour that matched the giant at her side.

She was horrified to see the inside. Pastels. Pastels everywhere.

"Oh mother, what happened to the room?" she gasped, finally digging in her heels when they tried to lead her in. "No, this is cruel and unusual torture! How am I supposed to sleep in there? It looks like a unicorn vomited!"

They didn't give her a choice, pushing her inside, and the door closed with a loud snap.

Turning to the room, she stared around in horror.

It was so incredibly bright that it made her eyes water, the walls a soft peach and the ceiling a warm yellow. The bedspread was green, the carpet was beige, and the furniture was a soft white gold colour.

"No wonder everyone here is homicidal. This place would make anyone a murderer," she said and a laugh came from behind her.

Turning, she saw an ancient woman sitting in a little alcove. Her skin was a pure black she had never seen before, white hair and no less than six arms.

"Who are you?" Etani asked cautiously, her mind immediately going to how effective having that many arms would be in battle.

"Arachne," the old woman said, her eyes on her work as she weaved thread. It was the most bizarre thing she had seen, and that was saying something.

Frowning, she tried to place the name. "You lost a bet, didn't you?"

The woman looked delighted, glancing up with milky white eyes.

"Indeed, I did. Turned into a spider as punishment."

Now that she thought about it, she did look rather spider-like.

"Tried to have it reversed and now I'm this," the woman said as she stood and hobbled over.

"You need a dress for tonight. Another ball; these Fae are obsessed."

Etani sighed gently, looking down at the tiny woman. "Strip?" she asked

"Strip," the old woman responded, and Etani obeyed.

The measuring of her body didn't take long, the old woman was incredibly efficient and before she knew it, she was allowed to dress.

"Who created those undergarments?" the woman asked as Etani pulled on her pants and top.

"They were modelled after Sthiss. A maid for the Princess Nayishma."

The woman didn't know them but she seemed impressed enough. "Sit, you're making me anxious when you loom like that," the woman said.

Etani had moved to watch the work and blushed.

Sitting down, she watched the skilled fingers flying. When the basic shape material was made, the woman pinned it into place and then muttered something.

The dress suddenly pulled tight around her, hugging every inch of her skin from halfway down her neck to her toes. It flowed like silk and left her arms and back entirely bare. The fabric curled up around her throat and then down over her chest before spilling out around her hips and flowing behind her in a short train. It made her look incredibly elegant and the colour was so deeply black it seemed to pull in the light and consume it.

The woman whispered to herself and she watched herself in the mirror as long strips of black fabric fluttered around her, pulling up her hair into a messy knot that left long tendrils to brush her shoulders and back, the yellow ribbon changing to expand and turn black, floating up and then behind her to form a constraining shawl.

Turning slightly, she examined herself with fascination. She looked like a drop of ink given feminine form. Her pale skin contrasted and the blackness of her dress enhanced both the white grey-blue of her skin and the vivid blue of her eyes.

She smiled slowly at herself, cautious at first but then slightly more sure as she came to see herself as at least exotic, if not attractive.

A last remaining ribbon fluttered up and twisted itself into a coil before coming to rest atop her head, hardening until it formed an elaborate tiara that reminded her of Winter's frozen trees, all spikes and sharp angles.

Arachne grinned at her and lifted her chin, Etani mimicking the gesture.

Yes, she was the Princess of Winter and she wasn't going to let Summer control her, even if that meant destroying a quarter of Faerie. She would bring them all crashing down if that was what it took.

The woman looked gleeful as she watched Etani sweep from the room, a soft cackle of pleasure following her out.

13

THE SUMMER BALL

*M*usic led her through the halls and she followed it curiously, finding the corridors oddly empty though the sound of voices came from ahead. She went still, peeking over a low balcony to see the mass of movement below.

They were talking, dancing and laughing with excitement and there were so, so many of them.

They all wore bright colours, all unusual and rare creatures she had never imagined to actually belong to a side before. Now that she thought about it, she had never really thought about the sides of Faerie as actual sides. The only sides she had thought of before then were Faerie and her, but now there was Winter, Summer, Ceress, and then her in her own corner trying to escape them all.

She was still watching them when a soft cough came from behind her and she ignored it at first, simply watching and finally, she felt she had ignored her companion long enough and turned.

The man before her was easily the most attractive man she had laid eyes on. He was muscular without being repulsive, with a smooth face and honey-coloured skin. His eyes were so pale a blue that they were almost white and his hair was short and the rich brown of tree bark. He had long nails on one hand, oddly long for a male, but they suited him well. Atop his head there was a large headdress made of some unknown metal with wings pointing up and out, elaborately carved and engraved with swirls. Several long chains trailed down from the sides to brush his chest. Tucked behind his back were two sets of deep violet wings and he wore nothing but a black belted skirt.

She stared at him, her mind utterly blank as she realised she was looking into the face of one of the Fallen.

The Protectors had been the guardians of Faerie, keeping the Courts from killing each other when things got messy and the Courts were still fighting, but when Faerie failed to bring down the human world, the Protectors had fallen from the sky and been unable to get back up. They had been called the Fallen ever since and they all looked like that, all impossibly beautiful and perfect.

Neither of them spoke, simply watching each other for a long moment before he finally bowed to her, his jaw set.

She had no idea how to respond, but she was getting the distinct impression her presence bothered him in some way.

"I'll not give in to your charm, succubus," he said in a deep voice.

"I beg your pardon?" she said after a pause, trying to process all the information at once.

"I can feel you pulling me, trying to draw me in." He straightened and his eyes were stern on her.

She had no idea what to say to that, namely because the Fallen were born without reproductive abilities, or even the tools to use them. They were all men, all gorgeous and all totally lacked genitals. The fact that she had any effect on him at all was baffling. "It is not intentional," she said, forcing her eyes from him to see as trumpets blared and the Queen swept into the room with her two daughters.

"You are not trying to seduce me?" he asked, seeming amused.

Looking back to him, she arched a brow. "Not hardly, you're pretty but I'm not stupid. The Fallen aren't capable of bodily pleasures."

His lips parted in shock and she returned her attention back to the crowd as they swarmed to make room for the royals. "How did you know what I am?" he said and she jerked, realising he was now mere inches away from her.

"Four wings, the mask, the beauty. It's not that hard to figure out," she said dismissively, and her frown matched his.

"I could have been any number of beings. But you knew what I was immediately."

"It's a talent for remembering species."

"Except that our existence has never been put to paper," he said slowly, searching her face for a hint of the truth.

"Then someone likely told me."

"It's impossible for those who know to share the information. Only one of the Fallen can mention the Fallen."

"Well, I do believe your rules are incorrect, because I just did," she quipped and moved away from him, hearing him follow her, his bare feet a soft whisper on the marble.

Rounding the balcony, she allowed herself a better angle to observe the crowd.

"You cannot be a Fallen, you are female." He sounded utterly baffled and she sighed, turning to him once more.

"I'm also a crossbred freak, stop following me." She was growing frustrated with him, but he ignored her and followed again as she moved away. She didn't think he was out to harm her in any way, only fascinated by her. Whatever the reason, it was irritating.

"What manner of creature are you?" he asked as she stopped again and finally she gave up trying to get away from him.

"A little of this, a little of that," she said evasively, not wanting to get into it with him.

"Vague," he complained, and she turned her attention to the crowd as a young man swept the heir onto the dance floor and they moved beautifully, looking like flame with her blood coloured hair and his soft yellow.

"As far as we can tell, I am descended from at least fifty different species of Faerie," she said, still watching the couple. "All leading down to Winter and Ceress."

The man jerked slightly, surprised to hear what she was.

"I did not know the Celestrials permitted cross breeding."

"They don't," she replied darkly and his head tilted.

"You are an odd creature, I think I rather like you." He smiled, only the barest hint of the lips, and yet she felt warmed by the smile as though he had wrapped a heated blanket around her.

"Stop that." She glared at him, but it was hard to be angry at such a likable man.

"It's not intentional," he said, repeating her words back at her.

She glared at him before she finally shook her head. It was impossible to be angry at him, there was simply too much innocence to him.

The protectors had been entirely neutral, and they had a charm that outshone any creature. They had always been like that, born to calm the angry masses and keep the Courts from destroying themselves.

"What is your name?" she finally asked and he smiled again, washing her in warmth.

"Galad," he said, and after a pause, he offered his hand to her. "You are the Princess Etania?"

"Etani," she corrected as she accepted his hand and he drew her towards the grand staircase that would lead them down into the ballroom. The crowd parted for them, eyes wide at the sight of the dark Winter Princess and the fallen Protector Galad entering the dance together.

She felt like a blot of ink on a perfectly pressed white shirt, moving amongst the colourful crowd, and it caught the attention of everyone in the room.

The music slowed as the band watched and then swelled into a song she didn't recognise. The pace was steady and without a word, Galad took her by the waist and pulled her into the steps.

When it came to dancing, the Fae did it best. They were born with a natural grace and beauty, able to pick up almost any dance in record time and remember it for centuries. They loved the formality of dance and Etani was no exception.

One hand resting in his, the other on his shoulder, she moved with him in perfect time. It wasn't long before the dancers joined them and she couldn't help but smile at the perfection. It was as though it had been choreographed, each step and twirl perfectly timed in the ancient art.

After the dance had finished, he kissed the top of her hand and moved to his left as was custom, leaving him with another woman and her with a new male.

Looking up, she found the warm brown eyes and bare chest of a satyr. "You keep your hands where they belong, my good fellow," she warned, and he grinned sheepishly before he pulled her closer than was custom and swept her into the next dance.

Satyr were a playful bunch, lovers not fighters. For them, random orgies were commonplace, and they never wore clothing. Thankfully, the thick fur around his legs made that a non-issue. His hooves made a pleasant tap on the ground, adding complexity to the beat of the music and when the song ended, he was sad to be drawn away.

The creature that appeared next gave her pause, not because he was abhorrent in any way, but because he seemed to be utterly human.

Unable to help herself, she leant closer and inhaled the warm scent of him and the rush of blood to his cheeks had her mouth suddenly watering. "What could a human possibly be doing in Faerie?" she asked curiously, his fingers trembling a little on hers.

"I'm a changeling," he said, and her brows shot up.

"I didn't know that custom still existed." She had thought the custom of stealing human children only to replace them with identical Fae children had died out, but here he was and he was less than thirty years old.

"There are those who cling to tradition," he said wryly as his arm extended and he spun her, drawing her back in with a gentle tug.

"I see. What do you think of Faerie?" she asked. His eyes narrowed in suspicion and she grinned, though she thought that might have been a bad idea when his eyes locked onto her sharp double set of canines. "Do not fret, I have lived in the human world for a very long time, I tend to prefer it."

"Faerie is all I have known, but I am not fond if it."

"We should escape together," she said in a matter-of-fact tone and his eyes nearly popped out of his skull.

"Why would you want to leave?" he asked, and she realised he had no idea who she was.

"I'm the Winter Princess, my dear friend. And like you, I am very eager to get out of Summer."

He looked like she had slapped him, his face pale and eyes huge.

"Well, what do you say? If one of us figures out how to escape, we tell the other?"

He nodded and she smiled at him.

"I promise to not leave you behind if it is within my power. You're a cute little human. I won't eat you, at least not this time."

She laughed as he was swept away and she turned, her laugh dying as she found herself face to face with the demon. "Not you again..." she said as his hands caught her and he pulled her smoothly into the next dance.

"Yes, me again," he said in a nastily happy tone. "You and I have some things to discuss, namely you *killing* my human hosts." His fingers clenched hers painfully as he said 'killing.'

She kept her face neutral and her mind was again racing to try and remember his name.

"This time you're not getting away from me. You appear to be a prisoner." He grinned at the shawl and she bit the inside of her cheek as fear ripped through her. A prisoner at the mercy of a man. The memories sent her mind into a panic and she forced them down, tasting blood as she chewed on her cheek.

"I know you're all for the whole rape and torture thing, but could you not?" she asked and he laughed, drawing her closer.

"No, my love. I can't not. You have no idea the effect you have on me just by existing."

She pulled herself back from him, but something in the back of her mind spoke up and Letari laughed at the thought. "How about we make a deal?" she said, grinning.

14

A DATE WITH THE DEMON

His eyes narrowed on her as they moved, pulling her as tightly as he could without being obscene. "What deal?" he demanded, suspicious of her and any deal they could possibly make.

"I will do whatever it is you desire for one night, if you help me escape," she said calmly.

His eyes lit up, exhilarated by the idea and yet he was still suspicious of her. "Anything I want? If I help you escape?" he said, his eyes going from her to the room, sweeping it for guards.

"Oh, and you have to bring my human along with me," she added, tilting her head in the direction of the unfortunate human man who was struggling with which of Arachne's arms to hold.

"Lunch?" he asked, glancing at the human.

"A pet," she said dismissively. She had no such intentions, but didn't want... Richard? To know what she was thinking. "What was your name again?"

"Daemon," he snapped and glared at her.

"Oh, right, so do we have a deal, Damion?"

It had already slipped.

"You will surrender yourself to me for one night if I help you and the pet escape?" he confirmed and she nodded, smiling sweetly at him. "No tricks?" he demanded.

"No tricks," she lied.

"Deal," he said quickly, and as her grin grew wider, his smile faded.

"Excellent," she purred, and leant forward to place a single tender kiss on his lips.

Electricity shot between them and he was gone, swept away to the next woman and replaced by a cyclops who looked a little drunk. He moved well enough and after him, she bowed out and was replaced by the young Clea.

Sweeping across the room to get herself a drink, she was sniffing the crystal goblet suspiciously when the scent of roses permeated her, and the small, blonde Princess swept up at her side.

She wore a deep cream dress with white lace at the bodice, neckline and arms. It hung off her shoulders and looked lovely, flowing around her like a cloud, her lips a stark contrast in a deep mauve. Her necklace was white lace and more of the stuff decorated her wavy blonde hair. A simple tiara against her forehead, silver and undecorated.

"Hello, Etania," the Princess said and picked up her own crystal goblet.

"Princess," Etani replied politely, taking a sip of the drink and frowning at the contents. It was weirdly spiced but she thought it might be some form of wine.

"Nyrellia," the Princess said, and offered a small, undecorated hand.

Taking it, they shook once and let go quickly, both wary of the other.

"It is unfortunate that we had to meet under these circumstances." Nyrellia had a sweet, gentle voice and Etani found she rather liked the softness of the young woman.

"It is at that. I don't suppose you have an idea of how long your mother plans to keep me here?" she asked, and Nyrellia shook her head.

"I'm afraid not. It is a delicate situation with your being the natural born heir of Tatialia and not taking the throne with the death of your grandmother."

Etani had lifted the goblet to her lips but then froze, her eyes lifting to the young woman.

"Oh, you don't know?" she sounded surprised and Etani set the goblet down hard.

"Know what?" she demanded.

"Being that you are the natural heir and not the chosen heir, you should be sitting on the throne of Winter, not Megara. Tatialia only had one child, and he had two. One of those is deceased and that leaves you. You're the Queen of Winter."

Etani was stunned into utter silence as she stared at the woman, terror filling her. "What if I have no desire to be the Queen?"

"Then you will remain a Princess in the line of succession. I believe you are currently fifth. But as Megara is not the rightful Queen, she will struggle wielding the power. It will resent her, but she can do it."

"I'm not a Queen. I'm barely a Princess," Etani said, almost pleading with the woman, and Nyrellia smiled gently.

"You of all people should know what it is like to not want to be what you are," Nyrellia said gently.

"How do you know that?"

The Princess blushed a deep pink that made her look lovely. "I have become obsessed with studying you after we found out of your existence. It was quite funny really, we never would have learnt about you if you hadn't mentioned your name to Barron. You would have been ignored as a minor Princess of Winter. Dangerous and exceptionally powerful, but not a threat to the crown. But then you said your name and it was realised that the Queen's only son had given birth to a daughter. A daughter who could take the throne when her father could not. You became an interest to us all because of who you are and I'm afraid a very large number of us became obsessed with this unknown heir to the throne. We learnt everything we could, right from the moment of your birth up until you left

Ceress and then again when you surfaced in Ayathian. You're quite the skilled little kitten, aren't you?" She was grinning, but Etani wasn't amused.

"So I have stalkers?" she demanded

"More like... admirers," Nyrellia said happily

"Wonderful. Don't suppose any of my *fans* would like to help me get back to the human world?"

Nyrellia shook her head and Etani sighed, frustrated by it all.

"How did you kill Tatialia?"

Etani looked at the small woman, those bright eyes glittering in her amusement. "I drove a scythe through her chest and consumed her soul."

Nyrellia's smile faded at the bluntness of the response.

"Don't forget, Princess, I'm a murderer and a monster, no matter what a pretty dress tries to claim."

"I know that," Nyrellia said gently. "I just didn't expect you to use a weapon like a scythe. It seems too... cumbersome."

"I would have thought so, too, before it started manifesting," she said dryly and picked up a new goblet, examining the contents carefully.

"Manifesting?" Nyrellia asked, sounding fascinated.

Before she could respond, she heard someone screaming her name and she turned, expecting to find a red-faced Alaric glaring down at her. But he wasn't there. Instead, a fair few creatures were looking at her with interest.

"Did you hear that?" she asked Nyrellia, a slow ache beginning to form in the pit of her stomach.

"Hear what?" Nyrellia asked.

"I could have sworn someone just called out my name," she said, frowning as she heard it again and turned in a slow circle, staring up into the balcony but there was still nothing.

"I can hear a bell. Where is that coming from?"

Etani glanced down and gave her bare foot a tap on the marble, the bell jingling.

"Why do you have a bell on your ankle?" The Princess looked

intrigued and she had a horrifying thought that a new fashion trend would be starting by morning.

"It's a long story. You can't hear someone yelling my name?" she asked.

"No, nothing. Are you feeling all right?"

There it was again, and she clenched her jaw as her stomach started to burn.

Clutching at it, she held the table with her free hand and the goblet spilled.

"Etania? What happened?" Nyrellia sounded panicked, but she couldn't speak, her brain aching as she realised what it was.

She was reneging on a deal and Faerie was punishing her.

"Alaric... we have a deal," she breathed, her fingers clenching the tablecloth.

Someone seemed to materialise at her side, a second someone being dragged along behind, and a hard arm wrapped around her middle.

"Nice meeting you, Princess, but I will be going now and I'm taking these with me. Have a pleasant evening," the demon said in one breath and then threw himself backwards, ripping a hole through reality that made her scream as it felt like he was ripping her in half with it.

They landed in snow and Etani landed hard on her knees, panting as the feeling of being ripped sealed over and she was whole once more.

She felt herself to see where it was she had been ripped apart but found herself whole.

"What is going on?" the human was saying, backing away from the two. Etani blinked as drops of blood splattered onto the snow under her and she touched her nose, feeling it wet.

"Stay still, human, or you'll fall off the mountain," the demon said, and then the human was screaming in terror.

The burning in her stomach had eased somewhat and she looked up, watching the demon holding onto the human man by the arm, allowing him to dangle out over a cleanly cut cliff face.

Pushing herself up, she swayed, but moved forward and grabbed the poor human, dragging him back from the edge.

"You... your eyes are bleeding," he said and she frowned, wiping at her cheeks and finding they too were bloody.

"Why are your eyes bleeding?" the demon demanded, grabbing her face and forcing her to look at him.

"And her ears..." the human said, staring at her in horror.

"This can't be because of that King of yours," the demon said, worry written all over his face as he turned her head to look at her ears.

"What did you do? I thought you were ripping me in half," she asked, confused, and the burning in her stomach had started up again.

"You felt reality tear?" he demanded and scowled when she nodded. "I see."

Pushing the demon off her, she staggered and the human caught her arm, keeping her from falling. "Where are we?" she said finally, clutching at his soft, warm hands.

"A mountain in a place the humans haven't named yet. There are no humans or mythicals in this part of the world," the demon said as he scowled, clearly wanting to inspect her for injuries.

The human handed her a scrap of cloth and she used it to wipe her face and neck, the scarlet bright against the white fabric.

"We need to get back to Ayathian," she said and glanced at the human. "We can discuss your life later, but right now I have to go back. What is your name?"

"Thomas," the human said, sounding like he was about to cry.

"Well, Thomas, I'm afraid you're going to have to stay with me for a while."

He seemed scared, but didn't protest.

"Can you take us?" the demon asked and she frowned, trying to focus, but nothing was coming to mind. Her hesitation made him sigh and he wrapped his arm around her, his hand on Thomas' shoulder, and it happened again.

They ripped through reality and she was screaming, making

others scream around them as they forced themselves into Ayathian. She fell forward onto her knees, seeing the familiar marble floor of the throne room. It felt worse the second time, feeling blood dripping from her chin and onto the floor as she huddled there, simply trying to breathe through the pain of being ripped open and stitched back up again.

"Hi, honey, we're home!" the demon called happily, tossing the human away from him as he threw his arms out wide.

There was silence, the room taking in the scene and then the smell of Versalis hit her like a brick to the senses.

He didn't have time to reach for her before she threw herself into his arms and he caught her, his hold tight around her as he smelt blood and her fear triggered his instincts.

"Etani?" Kai called, and his chair toppled in his rush to get up, hurrying to them and kneeling at her side, his arms encasing both her and Versalis.

"Jaia!" Kai yelled and footsteps could be heard pounding back.

All three of them nearly fell as Jaia tackled them, his lips on her hair.

"What happened? Where have you been?" Alaric demanded and she looked up, the sight of her bloody face making him stop dead.

"Hi, Alaric, sorry I'm late..." she breathed, and collapsed into someone's chest.

15

HUMAN

When she woke, she found herself the centre of a dogpile of vampires, a Fae, and a demon, the men all piled haphazardly on top of her. Someone was snoring.

She understood the vampires, but not the other two, and she planted her foot against the demon's side, shoving him off the bed.

His yell woke everyone else in confusion.

"Why are you all in my room?" she demanded, but then realised they weren't in her room. "In the basement?" she asked finally.

"Epharis set your room on fire when you didn't come back," Jaia said sleepily, wriggling himself around until his head was in her lap rather than on her arm.

"We got your supplies out, just in case the fire blew the city up, but everything else was lost. Sorry, Etani."

Cursing the Lich, she wriggled herself out from under the pile of bodies and staggered, looking down to find the ankle with the chain was tied to the bed.

The vampires took one look at her and immediately dove for cover as she screamed.

She was so angry at being tied up, so sick of them all controlling her, and she lost it.

The jug and mugs exploded, the loud shatter downstairs indicating that the cells had just failed again and the glass in the cabinets in the sitting room were reduced to a fine powder.

They heard yelling and splintering glass from upstairs, too.

Uzo had just enough time to clamp his hands over his ears as she sucked in her breath, but the demon wasn't so lucky. His eyes went huge and then they simply ruptured, his ears leaking blood and he slumped, dead.

The scream ended slowly and she panted, her body heaving at the energy it took to simply stop the sound. She wanted to scream and scream again, but she forced it down and covered her own mouth.

Slowly the vampires surfaced, looking scared with blood running down their necks from their ears.

She turned on them, trembling, and they exchanged a look.

Without a word they were on her, hugging and squeezing her tightly while Uzo sat, his brain scrambled and looking like he would have died had he not been prepared.

She didn't cry, but instead she stood there with the three men she loved the most all around her.

They hadn't been able to remove the shawl and it still curled tightly around her wrists, the fabric seeming to be made that way rather than sewn shut to contain her.

The door to the basement burst open and she growled softly, irritated though she kept her eyes on Versalis'. His forehead pressed against hers, trying to calm her, and it worked rather well.

She didn't know if it was simply his power as a vampire King or the crystal, but whatever it was, it was effective.

The door to the bedroom opened and Epharis stalked into the room, stopping at the sight of the four of them standing close, her eyes locked on Versalis and his on her. Uzo was slowly starting to move.

"What is going on?" Epharis demanded, but no one spoke; they were doing their best to keep her from panicking. "Etani?"

Slowly her eyes turned to him, her hand going automatically to slip into the tight grip of the vampire King.

Kai and Jaia released her enough to allow her to move and they all looked at him, a single unit of resentment and hatred towards the Lich.

"Where have you been?" he asked coldly.

"Summer," she said and everyone looked at her in surprise.

"What? Why were you in Summer?" Epharis demanded.

"The demon was trying to catch me. I stuck a knife in his eye, and when I tried to get to Faerie I was distracted and ended up in Summer. They had some sort of way to ensure I ended up where they wanted and they darted me. When I came to I was taken to see Cecelia and there was a ball and..." She broke off. "Where's my human?" she demanded.

"Your human?" Kai asked, sounding shocked.

"My human, Thomas. Where is he?"

"The human boy? I think Uzo took him somewhere."

She turned on Uzo, but he wasn't functioning while his brain regrew from its exploded state.

"Take this chain off me right now!" she snapped at Epharis and his eyebrows rose at her tone.

"Excuse me?" he asked in an icy tone.

Turning to him, she glared. "I have been beaten, kidnapped, abused, kidnapped again and then held captive in Summer. You let me out of this chain right now before I kill you!"

The room was tense, but she glared at Epharis and he glared right back at her.

When he didn't move, she felt her fury begin to build and Versalis groaned, clutching at his chest.

Flinging out her hand, she felt the hard handle of the scythe drawing down from the mark on her wrist, swirling into existence.

It hadn't fully formed when Kai grabbed her arm and forced it up behind her back, pitching her sharply forward under the strain of her arm being bent into an unnatural angle.

He moved and covered her mouth with his hand. "Now, now. No

need to fight, you two," he said cheerfully, trying to defuse the situation.

Tilting her head, she glared up at Epharis who looked livid that she had been more than willing to cut him in half.

She wasn't about to back down, but with her arm up she was unable to get away and they all knew it.

Uzo groaned and shook his head, taking in the scene with confused eyes before he leapt to his feet.

Biting Kai's hand, she stamped on his foot and he released her. Though it wasn't enough to actually hurt him, it did make him let go.

Turning on Uzo, she was jerked to a stop by her ankle caught around the foot of the bed and she stumbled.

"Uzo, where's the human?" she demanded, and he blinked at her in confusion.

"The human?" he asked, sounding lost.

"The human! The redhead! Where is he?" she demanded, and Uzo blinked again.

"Oh, I took him up to my rooms to keep him safe," he said and she relaxed, rocking back onto her foot and taking in a deep breath to calm her nerves.

"Good, keep him safe," she said finally, not knowing why she suddenly cared for him; he was just a human. But she did care.

Stepping back to try and unhook herself from the end of the bed, she backed into a hard chest and looked up to see Epharis, his teeth bared, and she gave a low, warning growl.

"You and I need to talk," he growled.

Turning to face him, she glared up at him and the three vampires sidled out of the room, looking worried but not willing to argue.

Uzo, on the other hand, had his hands on his hips, watching the Lich.

"If you try and hurt her, I will be back in here for your arse," Uzo warned and then slunk from the room to leave them alone with the human corpse that had been the demon.

As she stepped away from him, she trod on the corpse's hand and grunted, looking down to see it.

Taking advantage of her distraction, his fingers curled around her throat and she found herself suddenly pinned to the wall, her feet a good few inches off the ground.

Gasping, she clutched at his wrist to try and ease the pressure on her neck.

"You ran, didn't you...?" he breathed, his face only an inch from hers.

She shook her head, but he could see the lie for what it was.

"Don't lie to me, Etani. Do you remember what I told you? If you tried to leave I would ensure you never can."

He had reached that level of anger that left him entirely calm and she shook her head again as fear flooded her body.

"Epharis please..." she wheezed, her nails digging into his wrist.

"You are mine!" he screamed and she flinched, her eyes wide in fear of what he was going to do to her.

He threw her; her back hit the wall and the headboard, then she slumped down onto the mattress, groaning as she tried to push herself up.

He moved to her and gripped her hair, forcing her head down onto the mattress. "If you struggle I will make sure you never move again," he said and flipped her onto her back. He sat down on her stomach, gripping her jaw and smirking down at her.

"You, my precious wife, will be unable to use magic again unless I deem it worthy. You will never be able to attack me, never be worth anything more than a human until I deem otherwise," he said slowly, his long fingers hovering above her face.

She shook her head furiously, straining to get free from under him.

His fingers glowed green as he lowered them toward her face and she whimpered, struggling more violently to free herself of him. He was tormenting her, terrifying her, and when his index finger touched her forehead, she screamed.

It was a terrible sound as his power reached into her and turned off the switches in her mind, turning off her abilities, and she could hear Letari screaming as well.

The door heaved but it refused to budge.

Her scream did nothing; it was just the anguished scream of a terrified woman and it strangled off into a sob as he lifted his hand from her.

He smiled as he reached down and took up one of her hands, using it to cut her arm. He watched with savage glee as the cut bled, and then continued to bleed. He laughed as he saw crimson dripping onto the sheets, and she was forced to resettle in a brain that was so incredibly human it hurt.

She screamed again, a sound of pure anguish, and as he left, the three vampires piled in.

The smell of her hit them first and they froze, unable to move towards her as she curled on the bed, her hand over her bleeding arm. She no longer smelt of magic, the draw towards her was gone and she was left huddled and alone, the voice in her mind snuffed out.

Crying, the tears came forth clear, staining the sheets under her.

Hesitantly, Versalis slipped his arms around her and found her to be warm and soft. His eyes were huge as they met hers, still a shocking vivid blue, still an unearthly beauty, and yet the magic had gone, leaving her as less.

The gem against his chest had gone silent and dark.

She stared up at him for an instant before she buried her face in his chest and he looked up at the twins, horrified.

"She's human..."

She had remained in his arms all night, the vampires suddenly on high alert for any threat now that she was so easy to kill and her death could possibly be permanent.

Even when she found herself with an uncomfortable pressure in her stomach and learnt that she suddenly had a working bladder, Kai followed her to ensure she was safe.

When her stomach growled, Jaia found her food. She tasted human food, finding it bland and revolting, but she still ate it.

Everything felt strange, the air less sweet, and her heart beat at a terrifying seventy-three beats per minute.

After she had eaten, she sat back on the couch and pulled her legs up to her chest, staring down at the plate that had held a variety of meats and vegetables between slices of bread.

A pile of red berries had been delivered, but she ignored them for the time being.

A hand stroked her hair and she found it to be oddly cool compared to the warmth she normally felt from him. He hesitated at the warmth of her, as well.

Versalis hadn't so much as left her side except when she rose to use the bathroom. She knew how it all worked theoretically, but actually experiencing it had been eye opening.

Then she felt dirty and so she took a bath, quickly finding out that water, when hot, was actually hot. Her hand was bright red as she looked at it and Kai sighed, taking her by the arm and running her hand under the tap.

"Kai I don't know if I can do this," she whispered, watching the water running over her burnt hand.

"You can," he breathed, and she looked up at him.

They had all suddenly seemed larger than life, unbelievably beautiful and hypnotic. She could understand how the humans must suffer when around their kinds, all that unreachable beauty.

Kai was gentle with her, having her remain at the sink while he pulled the plug out of the bath and topped it up with cold, his movements too fast for her to see.

"If I die I might stay dead," she breathed, flexing her stinging fingers.

He was back at her side and she jumped, looking up at his anger and fear.

"You aren't going to die, we will fix this," he said and she nodded, not believing him.

They had managed to hide out in the basement for three days

before Alaric came looking for her, wanting his report, and he blinked at her.

The sight of him, so incredibly huge and strong, ruggedly handsome and feral, had her eyes going wide and she shrank back into the couch.

He stared at her, this small creature suddenly smaller and frailer.

"What happened?" he demanded and she shivered at the sound of his voice in the air.

"Your brother," Jaia snapped.

"What did he do now?" Alaric asked and moved forward. His fingers were on her jaw and she cried out as he gripped her, the normally unremarkable touch leaving her jaw aching terribly and she jerked back from him, his fingers leaving red marks on her skin.

"Don't touch her!" Kai yelled and his arms went around her protectively.

Alaric took a step back, horrified, staring from the marks to his fingers and back. "I'm not wearing iron," he said, feeling the tension and the fear.

"Your brother! That bastard made her human!" Jaia screamed, his anger and fear bursting out of him.

Alaric looked at him and then down at her, small and fragile as glass in the arms of the protective vampire. "How is that possible?" Alaric demanded, taking another step back from her as though she were going to bite him.

"I can only assume he tapped into the Lich aspects of her and used it. She's entirely human."

There was a long, terrified silence

"I will get him to reverse it. She's no good to any of us like this," Alaric said.

She knew he didn't mean to sound like that, but his words cut her and she whimpered as tears filled her eyes.

She hated being weak and she had no control over her emotions anymore. Kai glared as Alaric stalked from the room, and they fell into an uneasy silence.

No one knew what to do with her; they were as lost as she was.

They did their best to keep her safe and comfortable, but she could feel her body dying around her, feel it aging and growing frail. She hated it and couldn't understand at all how the humans managed to survive like that.

Looking up into the devastatingly handsome face of Versalis, her heart skipped a beat as he smiled at her, and they all heard it.

Flushing, she dropped her eyes to his chest and extended her hand to touch the gem.

Without a word, he pulled it free of his shirt and she felt the cool, dead stone. It had no power without hers and her power had gone. It was just a pretty stone now.

Letting it go, she sighed as her stomach growled and she picked up the bowl of berries. She glared down at their weird shapes, the seeds on the outside to make it look like it was rotting.

Making a face, she popped one into her mouth and then froze, her eyes huge as she chewed it and the divine taste of it flooded her mouth and throat.

Making a happy sound, she picked out another and popped it into her mouth, looking up at the three vampires. They were talking so quietly that her human hearing couldn't pick it up and she frowned at them, popping a third berry into her mouth.

She didn't like that they were talking about her in a way that meant she couldn't hear and she took aim, throwing a berry at the trio.

It bounced off Kai's head and he caught it, looking around at her.

"Stop talking about me," she snapped, glaring at them all. "I'm human, not stupid."

They all looked rather guilty and she found her breath hitching. Vampires had a very particular charm about them, an ability to enchant humans into being willing to surrender their blood and bodies. It was working spectacularly on her.

Shaking her head, she demanded the berry back as they returned and she chewed it, glaring at the three like they were naughty children.

Feeling the bowl, she found only two left and looked down, horrified.

"Where?" she asked, looking at the floor and then touching her lips, realising she had eaten them all.

"I'll get more," Kai said and kissed the top of her head as he left.

Watching him go, she bit into the second-last berry and then turned her attention to the two remaining vampires.

"What are you thinking?" she demanded.

"We are trying to come up with a plan, but nothing is surfacing yet. We don't want to worry you," Jaia said gently and she held the berry out in a threat.

"Worry me, just keep me informed. I need to know."

He nodded and they exchanged a look as she chewed silently and moodily on the last berry.

16

STORIES

They had several hours of peace before the next intruder arrived, and she had devoured an entire garden of berries of the straw, blue, and black variety. She found she had a very particular fondness for the mulberry variety, even if it stained her fingers and lips.

They had even found a treat for her, a dark slab of hard something that she eyed suspiciously.

Daemon burst in the room, golden eyes bright with fury as he found the three vampires. "Where is she?! I know you've dropped her off on some random corner of this stupid ball you call a world and I can't sense her! You have exactly three sec—" His gaze found her; her eyes were on him and she had gone as still as a human could manage.

The demon absolutely and utterly enchanted her with his rage and the pheromones that kicked into the air and then her lungs.

His fury seemed to go out like a candle and they all heard her heart skip when his lips quirked up into a slightly sheepish smile.

"Etania," he purred, and she swallowed. "What's wrong with her?" he finally asked, all three vampires looking at her even as she stared mesmerised at the demon.

"Hello, Daemon," she breathed and the fact that she remembered his name twisted his face with fear.

He crossed the room in a blur and six other blurs moved around her; finding herself entrapped in their arms, Daemon's fist closed on the front of her shirt and he pulled her closer, suddenly restrained by the protection of the vampires.

He ignored them and leant closer to her, his nose an inch from her throat and hair as he inhaled.

She shivered and made a soft sound that was very nearly a moan and he let her go.

"Who did this?" he breathed, eyes glowing yellow in his fury.

"Epharis," Kai said, guilt in his voice as he saw what would develop into bruises from their attempts to protect her.

"The Lich husband? Why?"

"He feels it is the best way to control her," Kai said, worried.

"Or get her killed. We need to reverse this."

The pheromones being kicked off by all four of them made her dizzy and she picked up the bowl of mulberries and slid from the couch, padding away from the lot of them to try and get some fresh air. They all watched her carefully.

"This is sick..." Daemon breathed "How could any mythical do this to another?"

The three shook their heads and sighed.

"We need to keep her safe. If the Lich won't reverse this, I'll find a way to fix it. You three need to protect her."

Sliding down onto her backside against the wall, she watched the four of them and chewed, her lips stained a deep red from the berry.

"How do we protect her? She's so... soft," Jaia said, looking worried.

"Feed her, idiot," Daemon snapped.

"We have been feeding her!" Kai snapped back.

"Your blood! Give her enough blood to make her stronger without turning her!"

The three vampires looked first shocked, then embarrassed. None of them had thought to feed her blood to give her strength.

"Versalis, you're the strongest," Kai said, and Versalis nodded, looking worried.

"Yes but there is always the risk of bonding."

"Do it anyway, we can deal with that later," Daemon said angrily, unable to take his eyes off her. He approached her finally and with two fingers, he lifted her chin as he crouched. "Etania my love, we're going to fix this," he breathed.

Nodding, she felt the world leaving her as she stared into his golden-yellow eyes, captivated and entranced.

Daemon looked away and she blinked hard, unable to understand what happened.

"I'm not going to seduce her, idiot. The humans don't survive if I take them to my bed. I need her alive more than you do."

Looking up, she tried to process everything and then Versalis was at her side and none of it mattered.

He slid down the wall beside her and slipped his arm around her back, pulling her gently into his lap and curling his arms around her. "Sweetheart, you need to take my blood to get stronger, do you understand?" he purred in her ear and she shivered as delicious desire flooded through her system.

They could all smell her reaction to him but she ignored it, her head turning to his.

"I understand, Versalis," she whispered and he smiled, tilting his head away.

He used his nail to dig a smooth cut into his neck and she bit her lip, watching the blood before she licked up the side of his throat. His body went rigid at the feeling of her wet tongue and hot breath on his skin as she sealed her lips around the cut and began to drink.

Energy flooded her and he clutched her tighter to him, bruising her and leaving her trembling with need.

He growled his desire, his fingers finding her hips but Kai and Jaia were there to restrain his arms and keep him from trying anything.

She drank as much as her stomach could handle and then Daemon had her in a gentle embrace, pulling her back from the vampire. His blood stained her lips, dripping down onto her chin.

She felt both weak and strong at the same time, her mind racing to trying to process faster, but unable to.

She whimpered as she reached for Versalis and he strained to reach for her but they were both held back until the high came down and finally she was able to think.

The moment she was let go, she spun on Daemon and made to slap him, but he easily caught her wrist and grinned.

"Nice try, but you're not fast enough." His grin and firm tug of her towards him had her heart speeding up but she ignored it, instead focusing on her anger at him. His mouth came down on hers and she very nearly melted in his arms, finally jerking back and glaring at him.

"See, that's how you're supposed to react to me," he said happily as she pulled her arm free and backed away.

Her cheeks glowed and she felt an uncomfortable tightness between her legs that made her feel awkward, especially when all three vampires seemed to be responding to her every reaction to them.

"Don't ever touch me again," she growled, the threat no longer very effective.

"Oh, but we had a deal, Etani," he purred, pushing off the couch and approaching her.

She retreated from him and she saw the twins' stress. They needed to keep Versalis contained and that left her mostly on her own.

"You had a deal with a Fae," she countered, and his grin grew wider.

Her back hit the wall and he closed the distance, his arm against the wall at her side and he ducked his head, meeting her eyes.

"And as soon as you are one again, we can complete the deal."

His finger traced her jaw, her hitched breathing making him press closer to her and she gasped as he bit her earlobe.

He was suddenly gone, and she found herself trembling at the promise of pleasure beyond her imagination and oh did she want it, so badly. Her entire body was screaming for him and he knew it. He was using her humanity to get her riled up, and she was not strong enough to kill him now.

Versalis had broken free of the vampires and gone for the demon, who had leapt away with a laugh and bowed to the lot of them before sweeping from the room. She was left trembling, both aroused and horrified by the whole incident.

She had never been sexually aroused before and she was confused by it all. With Epharis it had been drugged, the sensation was overshadowed entirely but now she was human and her body was responding in ways she couldn't understand.

"Make it stop," she pleaded, and Kai moved to her, glancing at the two remaining vampires.

To her shock and horror, his hand slipped easily down the front of her pants and she froze, her eyes wide as he cupped her between her legs and then she buckled, his fingers soft against her.

He dropped with her, kneeling at her side and his free hand found her jaw, lifting her head.

He kissed her hard, greedy and demanding even as she whimpered and moaned against his lips, her fingers tight on his forearm, nails drawing blood.

It didn't take long for her to reach climax and she was left gasping as sparkles lit up inside her and she struggled to breathe. Smiling gently, he curled his arms around her and hugged her to him as she tried to process what had happened and what he had done.

"What was that?" she whimpered and Versalis tilted his head. Jaia looked stunned and glanced at the vampire King.

"Was... was Epharis your first lover?" Kai asked, sounding utterly confused.

Her cheeks flamed red and she looked up at Kai.

"Oh dear..." he breathed and laughed gently, kissing her forehead.

They were very matter-of-fact about what a normal woman should come to expect from her partners and she blushed the entire way through it.

She had extensively studied the anatomy of humans, but had never bothered to learn about sexual pleasure outside of the realm of procreation and that had left her entirely unprepared for masturbation and then an orgasm.

But if she didn't lie to herself, she found she had enjoyed it immensely.

The demon had returned a few hours later, sensing the change in the room and he looked around in confusion at her and Kai still on the floor, and she dozing in his arms.

"Epharis told me to jump in a volcano and that he would do what he liked with his things," Daemon said angrily and dropped into the chair.

"So now we have to look into alternatives."

"What alternatives do we have?" Versalis asked, still standing as far away from her as was physically possible in the confined space.

"Well, we can either have Etani kiss some serious arse and try to get him to do it, or we try and force the abilities to return. The former is only dangerous to her pride, the second could get her killed."

The idea of begging Epharis made her feel ill, but that was the better alternative.

"They're both a risk. What if he hurts her? If it would amuse him to break her bones?" Kai demanded.

"Talking to him is the safest option at this stage. We might not be able to trigger the return, we don't know where it is."

Something about his tone made her think he was lying, and she frowned at him.

"What do you know?" she asked and his eyes found her.

She shivered at the clench in her stomach, and he narrowed his eyes at her.

"Not all your talent comes from magic, hm?" he asked snidely.

"Shove it, Damion. What aren't you telling us?" she said, her intentional use of the wrong name making his eye twitch.

"Your magic would have returned to Faerie, and back into the ones it originally came from," he said slowly.

Everyone was still confused as they tried to understand.

"What does that mean?" she demanded, and it was his turn to look confused.

"What *do you* mean? Surely you know where your magic came from?"

They all looked perplexed, none of them having any idea at all.

"You can't be serious. It's obvious if you stop and think about it," he was indignant. He pushed himself out of the chair and paced. "Think about it. What happened on the day you were born?" he demanded, and still everyone looked confused. "Do you not know the date of your birth?" That seemed to confuse him even more.

"Not at all. Why would I know that?"

They all looked at her, baffled.

"Everyone knows the date of their birth," Kai said gently.

"It wasn't important. It was just a day, my parents never kept track."

"Your father did, I suppose you were too young. He always ensured he was there on the day."

Etani frowned at him, trying to recall.

"Well that makes sense with you, but you two? You're scholars, the Lich is a scholar. How did none of you make the connection?" Daemon demanded

Kai and Versalis exchanged a glance and then shook their heads.

"What happened on the day?" Kai asked.

"It was the day the creators tried to bring down the human world!" Daemon shouted.

"So? Lots of people were born that day," Etani said, frowning.

"I'm not sure if you are messing with me..." When they all just looked confused, he sighed. "The attempt failed, because there was a great vacuum of power in Faerie. Something sucked it all up, right at the point where things were looking good for Faerie. Something stole all that magic and, specifically, stole all the magic from the Creators and the Protectors. Very few others were affected in any meaningful way. But those two groups were hit the worst. Why would that be? Why those two in particular?" he paused, hopeful.

But no one had anything to say. "Because you took it all!" he exclaimed.

"I stole magic?" She felt sick, thinking of her doing to others what Epharis had done to her.

"Not like what Epharis did. You took their ability to create and to protect. It is generally believed that the Protectors were born to protect Faerie from itself, but it was actually to protect Faerie from the inhabitants. These Creators could bring down the human world, but they also had the power to change Faerie and the Protectors existed to change that. To stop them from upsetting the balance. So when all the powers of the Creators was sucked away, they no longer had a purpose and so they fell. You're the Creator now; you're the one who can destroy this world and change Faerie. I already told you that you were capable of creating worlds, infinite worlds. You are the Creator, and the destroyer, of worlds."

The silence was palpable and she chewed on her lip.

"So what now?" she asked, thinking she might already know.

"Now, the powers have gone back to Faerie and the Creators will be reborn. They will have the power to bring down the worlds and because so many were killed, more will be changed. The Protectors will be able to fly again."

She looked at Versalis for confirmation, and found him staring at her in terror.

"You have to get your magic back. Right now," he said.

There was a sudden whirl of movement around her as the vampires moved and she found herself on her feet, having no idea of how she got there.

"I don't know if he should be told," she said slowly.

"Only if he refuses. A last resort," Daemon breathed and she turned to find him behind her.

He cupped her cheek and kissed her, her entire body flooding with a sudden need. "Be careful. Don't take any risks until you are back to yourself," he said gently, and then stepped back before Jaia could grab him.

She was deeply confused, accepting Jaia's hand quickly and he pulled her to him.

"We will come with you, but we will stay outside so you can have privacy," he said gently and she nodded, her eyes wide with fear.

"I'm scared, Jaia," she whispered and his smile was devastating. How had she never appreciated just how incredibly attractive he was? Even more so than Versalis and Daemon, more so than the fallen Galad.

She swallowed and he gave her a wicked grin, unable to help but enjoy her reaction to him.

"You be a good girl and keep us all from dying," he said.

"I'm not a hero," she said gently, not wanting them to think that of her.

"No, but you're not a villain either. You are both and neither. Just save the world this one time and you can get back to killing things like any other day," he replied

"Don't make jokes," she complained, and he kissed her hard but briefly.

"It wasn't one, my love."

And then he was gone, leaving her alone.

She stared after him, eternally grateful that there were no mind readers in the area. Sex had never been something that interested her, but now all she could imagine was him and what it would feel like to be with him.

Forcing her mind away from the subject, she shook her head and followed the others out of the room. She could feel her body working as she made her way up the stairs and while she didn't feel out of breath, she felt warm from the muscle use.

Turning, she glanced around and squeaked, finding Daemon right behind her.

"We are going to stay close in case something decides you look particularly tasty," he said, smirking at her surprise.

It seemed that her guard was what drew the attention, not her.

Guards she had seen a hundred times looked bigger and more intimidating, their eyes curious. They noticed the differences in her and she felt them watching with interest.

She felt horribly fragile and exposed, sliding her hand into Kai's as he prowled at her side. His movements were impossibly smooth and graceful, more like a cat than a human. No wasted movements, nothing spared. His fingers squeezed hers gently as they swept past the throne room and Alaric's voice reached them.

Cursing, Kai pulled her to a stop and they turned back to see what the King wanted.

"Where are you lot off to?" he boomed, all eyes turning to the small group.

"To see Epharis," Jaia said, and Alaric found her behind the vampire. She offered a weak smile, but a whisper went out as people saw and noticed her.

Inching closer to Kai, she glanced around nervously and found there to be far too much attention on her. It made her nervous and she didn't like it at all.

"He will be in his rooms," Alaric said and grinned.

Etani realised he had pulled them back for that exact reason: to have people notice her and what had happened. She clenched Kai's hand and he glanced at her, curious, as she gave a gentle tug back towards the door.

He wanted people to see her, wanted them to know she was weak and defenceless.

Jaia and Versalis glanced back at something she didn't hear and Jaia forced on a smile, bowing to the King.

"Please excuse us, we have a meeting to attend," Jaia growled.

A man caught her attention, his wide face split into a malicious grin as he watched her go and she immediately knew she needed to arm herself.

They moved quickly through the halls and as they reached the rooms the Lich owned, the man in question stepped out with his head lowered over a book, scowling.

Jaia cleared his throat and the Lich looked up.

She had gone still, watching the man she had never seen before. It was hard to tell if he was beautiful or not, gaunt and terrifying as he was. Those eyes burned into her soul as his attention dropped to her.

She wanted to run very fast and very far away from him and never come back.

"You two need to talk," Versalis said slowly, doubt in his voice as he heard the frantic pounding of her heart.

If she ran he would catch her; if she stayed there his eyes would set her alight. She was frozen, fear radiating off her in waves.

Giving a grunt of irritation, he jerked his head towards the door and Kai gently pushed her forward.

She moved slowly, her eyes locked on him, and sidled under his arm, never once turning her side or back to him.

"Hurt her and Alaric will spend the next year trying to piece you back together," Versalis warned.

Snorting his amusement, Epharis turned to follow her into the room and closed the door on them.

She had backed away until she was as far from him as she could be without having her back against the wall, wary and afraid of the man.

Setting the book down, his eyes found her and he smiled slowly. The smile sent shivers down her spine and she inched another step backwards from him.

"What do you need?" he said with a malicious tone.

"You know what I need, Epharis," she said and his brows lifted.

"My, don't you look different as a human."

He was across the room and on her before she managed to take two steps back, his fingers curling in the front of her shirt and pulling her closer to him.

Her body moved on instinct, driving her palm up into his nose.

He growled in pain, blood beginning to drip, and she retreated.

"Little bitch..." he growled and turned on her.

He lunged; she suddenly found herself lifted off the ground by the throat and she choked, her nails digging into his wrist as she struggled to breathe.

"You would think that after everything you would finally have learnt to be nicer to me. But you're too stubborn. Don't forget I can kill you easily now, if I choose to," he whispered, sneering at her as her face turned red.

"Let... go!" she gasped and then she was falling, landing hard on the ground at his feet.

Looking down at her, he cupped her jaw and tilted her head back up to look up at him. "What will it be like to have you now?" he asked with a leer, and she jerked back, pushing herself to her feet once more.

"You know full well you would kill me if you tried," she said and yelped as he caught her again, pinning her to the wall.

With a growl, his hands found the hem of her dress and he lifted it to grip her thighs, his fingers painfully hard and bruising.

"Stop!" she cried and he only laughed, removing one hand to grip her jaw.

"Or what, Etani?"

She didn't have a response, looking up into his cruel, terrifying face so close to hers. "Reverse what you did," she whimpered. His nails cut into her skin and she flinched.

"Why should I? You're so much more agreeable now," he grinned, nudging her cheek with his jaw. Sliding one leg forward to wedge between her legs, he hoisted her dress up higher and she squirmed, trying to wiggle herself free of him.

"Please!" she gasped, his hands cold on her and his nails cruel on the soft skin of her stomach.

"I've never had a human before; it'll be quite interesting," he replied and grinned as she tried to shove him back. His grin vanished when she slapped him though, the blow hard but hardly enough to do more than sting.

His eyes seemed to glow in his anger and his fingers curled in her hair, dragging her from the wall and throwing her against the back-rest of the couch.

He followed, his hand on her back as he forced her forward against the backrest. His nails cut her skin as he forced the fabric up over her rear and she shoved herself back, stamping down on his foot and turning, driving her elbow into his sternum.

He staggered back and growled, eyes furious. Reaching for her so fast he was nothing but a blur, he gripped the back of her head and slammed her head down on the end table.

She screamed in pain, blood flowing, and she found herself upright again as he turned her to face him.

A boot slammed against the door, flinging it off its hinges to land hard on the floor, Versalis stalking into the room.

They both froze, her hands on his wrist to try and free her hair from his grip, his using her hair to try and force her back onto the table.

His teeth were bared, but his eyes had turned to the door and while he was distracted, she kneed him in the groin.

Clutching himself, he snarled and she saw his hand moving, aimed for her face, and then everything went black.

17

RECOVERY

When she came to, she found herself wrapped tightly in hard arms, her head feeling like it was going to explode and she squirmed, reaching up to find heavy bandages wrapped around her head.

Making a small sound in the back of her throat, she looked around to see the vampires all asleep and sprawled out on the chairs and couches in the room, plus one Uzo across from her; he was apparently the one who snored.

Glancing behind her, she found that Daemon held her and she scrambled to get off his lap, intentionally standing on his foot as she did so.

He jerked awake and looked around, confused at the rude awakening. "Oh good..." he said sleepily and stood, reaching for her while she made to dodge him but he was faster and he caught her gently, pulling her closer and frowning when she struggled.

Without a word he pulled her into the bathroom and lifted her up onto the bench beside the sink.

Giving her a warning look, he closed the door quietly and then returned to her side. She watched his movements, that same tingling starting in her belly and spreading as he gave her his attention. His hands were quick and sure as he removed the bandage and examined the small cut and large bruise, then down to the second bruise on her cheek and eye.

"He got you good..." Daemon said, and she frowned but said nothing. Picking up a small bottle, he popped the cap and applied the liquid to the end of the bandage, using it to dab onto her cut. It was blood and she knew whose blood it would be.

Flinching at the gentle touch, he sighed and lifted her jaw to better examine her. "At least you're still beautiful," he said and smirked at her when she jerked her head away from him.

"Why are you looking after me?" she demanded, wanting Kai or Jaia, but left with Daemon instead.

"Because your beloved vampires are trying to preserve energy. They don't know when there will be more blood and they don't want to risk feeding from you directly unless there is no other choice," he said, and she bit her lip, frowning at the oddity of the sensation without her sharp canines.

"Well, thank you then," she said grudgingly.

He grinned and pushed aside her hair to see how far back the bruise went.

"What happened?" she asked, resentfully remaining still while he worked.

"When your husband tried to knock your head off, King vampire almost ripped the Lich apart, but Jaia managed to stop him. Kai was checking on you and there was an argument. Versalis was screaming about you being killed and the risks but Epharis wasn't buying it and he was really mad at the cheap shot. Nice job though, you got him right in the goods. I'm quite proud of you for that." His grin was proud and he picked out a new bandage from under the bench, wrapping it around her head.

"After that, Epharis said he would kill you if that was what he felt like and then Jaia was letting go of Versalis and they went for him, but he was ready and there was lots of fire. Kai got you out and the other two were trying to get to him but then they had to retreat or catch fire. They're both pretty keen on killing him and I'm *so* for it. I'm not keen on you having a half Lich child. Demon would be best, but I'd take one of the vampires as a close second since the Drow is gone. I haven't managed to get one of them yet. They're worse than your lot when it comes to breeding with others." Finished with the bandage, he took her by the waist and lifted her off the bench to set her down on her feet.

"What were you doing during all this?" she asked, and he laughed.

"Watching. It was highly entertaining, the measures these men will take to keep you at their side."

She scowled and turned away from him, starting towards the door, but his hand caught her wrist.

"Etani, you know we have to get your magic back. There's more at risk than just you," his voice was low and she turned to him, seeing his concern.

"How do we get them back if Epharis refuses?" she asked curiously, and he let out a gentle sigh.

"Well, it's not going to be easy. But I think we can get them to reactivate if we go back along the line and ask each species to gift you some of their magic."

"You would have an easier time turning off the sun," she snapped, giving her hand a tug and he jerked her against him.

"It will be difficult, but I think it can be done and really what other option do we have?"

Looking up at him, she frowned and shook her head, pushing herself back from him.

She stalked from the room, he man following close her and intentionally slammed the door behind him.

Everyone jerked awake, alert and ready as she turned and glared at him angrily.

"Really? What are you, a child?" No longer needing to be quiet, her voice was cold and sarcastic.

"You need to get over this and find a way to deal before we all get disappeared," he snapped "Do you think the Creators won't be preparing to finish what they started at your birth? The human world is using Faerie magic and they think they can do a better job the second time around. They will wipe this world away, along with everyone in it!" He was angry now and her face had lost all colour. "They will vanish this entire world and it will be because of you!"

"That's uncalled for..." Jaia growled, rising to his feet.

"You shut up, boy!" Daemon turned on him, fuming, as he pointed at her. "That is the only thing standing between you and either death or a life in Faerie, then death when they wipe your sorry species out of existence. Vampires do not live in Faerie!"

She turned on the three, her fear reflected in their eyes as they stared at Daemon.

"They wouldn't do that," Kai said, his voice small in his uncertainty.

"Vampires are part of the reason this world was made! To dump you off somewhere safe and away when it was realised that this world wasn't suitable for Faerie!"

"How do you know that?" Jaia demanded.

"I was there! I was in Faerie when the decision was made to expand Faerie and then when it was decided to bring this world down again!"

"How old are you?" Kai asked.

"I was one of the first demons born after Faerie came to be."

That stunned the room and they stared.

"Why not let them bring down this world?" Uzo asked slowly, his eyes on Etani as she stood frozen, panicking.

"What?" Kai and Jaia demanded, turning on the Fae.

"Think about it. Everyone goes to Faerie and then they expand Faerie, and everyone lives there, happily ever after."

"Except that mythicals don't want to share Faerie," Versalis snapped.

"Because they haven't had to. Do you really think the mythicals would kill all the humans?"

"Yes!" Jaia yelled.

"Etani can't stay a human in this world or the next one!" Daemon said angrily.

"We could turn her into one of us," Versalis said, glaring at the demon. "Just because it would foil your stupid plan to make some Goddess doesn't mean she would want to be your creature."

"You know we can't make that choice for her," Kai said, turning to Versalis.

She hadn't moved and still Uzo watched her, frowning.

"If you think about it, there are only two choices," Uzo said quietly and they all stopped bickering to look at him, but he was talking to her. "Either we find a way to return your magic and you become his creature, a slave to destiny and what he intended for you, or we all abandon this world and let the Creators bring it down."

She met his eyes, her body trembling slightly as she shook her head. They were all looking at her and she took a slow step back from them. "How can you ask me to make that choice?" she whispered, looking between each of them. "How could any of you make that choice?"

Kai dropped his eyes and Jaia frowned, Versalis closing his eyes and Uzo still staring at her intently.

Daemon, however, shook his head. "That is not a choice. It's death or being what she was born to be!" he snapped, and all eyes turned to him. "The vampires would not be an option. If nothing else she would be better off as a demon."

They fought again and her eyes turned back to Uzo, searching his face for a decision she couldn't make.

"How long do we have?" she whispered, and he gave a slight shrug.

"No way of knowing, but less than a year I'd guess," he mouthed, and she closed her eyes, turning and walking from the room.

They called for her, but she ignored them, heading upstairs and out into the hallway. She didn't stop for anyone, instead breaking into a run and heading straight for the tower.

She didn't pause to think about what she was doing, nor the danger she had put herself in as she climbed. She only thought to climb as high as she could go and escape them all and the burden they had placed on her.

She was not responsible for humanity or the human world; she was just a creature who lived in it and yet they were demanding she take that responsibility and choose. There was no way all of the human world would fit into Faerie; that meant she would be responsible for the deaths of millions in a heartbeat. Not because she chose to devour them, but because she simply couldn't save them all.

The Creators wanted power and that meant bringing down the human world; if they brought it down the humans would end, at least most of them.

They were asking her to either become the one who gave up on humans and ran to Faerie to hide, a coward and weakling, or to be a hero and save them all. She was neither weak, nor a hero.

As she climbed up onto the roof of the tower, she sat down and stared out at the land around her, searching it for some hint of what she had to do.

She knew it already, she knew she really had no actual choice. But then she thought of the option.

She could become a vampire and then run to Faerie. It would mean she would be hated by those who came from the human world, but what if the creators were successful this time? What if they could expand Faerie and gave them all enough room? But then, how would she be able to decide who went to Faerie and who stayed behind to die?

Or was there a third option? Could the human world be entirely parted from Faerie and left to exist without magic of any kind? Would the humans not be happy without magic?

She bit her lip and tried to think through her fear and worry. Would that last option not be best for the humans? Let them live their lives without any magic while the mythicals expanded Faerie? Or was the human world needed in order to rebuild the magic? Could the human world survive without magic or was its existence reliant on the magic of Faerie?

Surely the Creators would have thought about that and simply tried to dump the human world off, it would have been easier than trying to dismantle it. Simply cut the string rather than pulling apart the anchor on a sinking ship. One might make you float a little longer, but was it rope or was it steel you were trying to cut with a butter knife?

She climbed down after several hours, shivering and hungry from sitting up there in the wind so close to sunset and she had not come to any conclusion on her situation.

Heading back into the castle, she ignored the staring and headed in the direction of her rooms in the royal quarters, not wanting to see her friends and their fear. She didn't want them to be afraid of her, or what she was capable of.

A small sound caught her attention and she turned to see that same man who had appeared so excited to see her helpless and protected.

Blinking, she had no idea who he was and so she paused to see what he might want.

"Hello, Princess," he said and she tilted her head, curious.

"Hello, do I know you?" she asked.

"No, but you knew my brother, Jacob," when she looked confused, he smiled wider. "Jacob Carriger."

It took her a moment to place the name and then her eyes widened as the name clicked in her mind. He was the first man she had killed for Epharis.

"Never heard of him," she lied, sliding her left foot back in preparation to run.

"Oh don't bother, Princess, we already have you trapped."

She glanced behind her and three men were standing there, grinning only five paces away and they weren't human like the man before her. Tilting herself slightly to the right to see around him, she found another two standing some eight paces away.

"Six against one? That seems fair," she said slowly, trying hard to remain calm.

"We had to be sure we could get you down and keep you down," the man before her said and she offered him a weak smile.

"Can't we just blame the Lich and call it even?" She didn't sound very hopeful.

"No," he said bluntly, and she sighed.

"All right..." She exhaled and then stepped forward, driving her foot up between his very unprotected legs.

He dropped like a stone and she went for the two, knowing they would be easier to beat than three, but they were all so much heftier than she was.

As she moved, the three behind her had started forward and she knew she needed to move fast. They thought that she was weak because she was human? She was about to teach them a lesson.

Reaching the two grinning men, she had a flash of worry that the right seemed to be an elf of some sort and so she aimed for the left, her fist driving hard into his gut and he doubled. As his companion turned, she spun, her hair flying, and drove her elbow into his cheek.

He staggered but didn't go down and he spun to try and catch her but she was out of his reach.

Cursing her lack of speed, she sprinted for the end of the hall and then ran straight into a massive chest and bounced off, landing hard on the ground.

Looking up, she found the broadest man she had ever seen looking down at her. Damn, they had known where she would run, and they had backup.

Crawling backwards, her eyes went to the space between his wide set legs as a means of escape and rolled forward onto her knees and the balls of her feet when a boot landed on her calf and she was jerked back down.

Yelping in pain, a fist found her hair and a cloth was smashed down on her mouth and nose.

It smelt sickly sweet and chemical and she immediately tried to hold her breath, but it was too late. She looked up to see Carriger approaching, his face furious but turning gleeful and she collapsed against her captors.

18

REUNION WITH A FAMILY FRIEND

She woke to a sharp slap across her face and she jerked, trying to push herself up but she had been bound by what felt like rope. The thought of being successfully bound by rope was disgusting and she squirmed, jerking back as Carriger tried to slap her again.

In retaliation, she kicked him hard on the shin and he danced back. The idiots hadn't bound her feet, only her arms to the backrest of the chair.

Cursing, the man waved and she found hands pressing down on her shoulders and she tilted her head back to see the elf holding her down.

A touch on her foot had her reacting and one of the three, a small man with a long nose and greasy black hair, earnt a knee to the face as he knelt to restrain her legs.

They were amateurs, and while she was scared, she wasn't about to go down quietly.

The tallest of the bunch, a willowy male with deep brown skin and long pointed ears stepped up and struck her with the back of his hand.

Her ears rang and her head hit the backrest of the chair. Recovering quickly, she glared up at him and rolled her jaw to ensure it wasn't broken, though she could taste blood on her lip.

"Real classy, beating on a bound woman," she said and he glared right back at her while the man she had decided to call Grease bound her feet to the legs of the chair.

"You're not just a bound woman though, are you?" he said, and turned as Carriger approached.

Prepared for his retaliation, she turned her head in time with his fist as it struck her cheek and while it still hurt, it wasn't as bad as it could have been. Still, it made her head ache and she swore softly and slowly.

"I'm going to kill you, too, Carriger," she hissed, and he laughed.

"Not if we kill you first," he said snidely, and she jerked, a slender knife pressing against her throat.

The elf had a knife and he seemed wonderfully eager to use it on her.

"What now?" she asked Carriger, fuming but mostly helpless at the moment.

"We are going to enjoy your company, then the boys can do whatever they like, and then we kill you," he said and she narrowed her eyes.

"Not even a ransom? You're boring," she quipped and the knife pressed hard, a drop of blood oozing down her throat.

"You think we could get a ransom for her? Then send her back in parts?" Grease said and Carriger frowned, thinking hard.

"Don't strain yourself; thinking looks like a foreign concept to you."

She deserved the next slap he gave her, but it was the knife that made her flinch, held still so that her body moved against it.

"You've got such a smart mouth, maybe we should send your tongue back to your husband in a gift box."

"I'm sure he'd be thrilled. He's wanted to have it removed ever since he met me." She shifted, trying to inch herself away from the knife, but the elf seemed to be aware of her every movement and inched it closer. "Could you not?" she asked and in response, the knife pressed firmly against her throat without cutting. "No then…"

"You wouldn't believe how happy we were when we saw you in the throne room. We've been waiting for a year to get a chance to capture you and then there you were, all soft and human. It made my week," Carriger said, and she sighed, giving him her best 'get on with it' face.

He looked at her and smiled. She wasn't prepared for it this time and his fist drove hard into her sternum, the knife cutting deep as she doubled over, gasping in pain and lack of air.

He grinned as she lifted her streaming eyes and closed them just in time for his fist to meet her jaw.

For ten solid minutes he hit her, finally needing the elf to hold her head up when she went limp, laughing his pleasure at her suffering.

She had always half expected to go out in a way similar to this, finally captured and a soul stealing knife slid into her chest, but she had never expected to be human when it happened, her body on fire, certain he had broken something.

Finally satisfied, they had unbound her and shoved her to the ground, leaving her there while Carriger moved away to wash her blood from his knuckles.

"Who's first?" he asked and there was a soft murmur before her hands were unbound and then bound once more above her head.

Opening her barely functioning eyes, she looked up to see Carriger holding down her wrists, grinning as someone moved at her feet.

The elf kicked her feet apart and knelt between her knees, his eyes intent and face neutral. Feeling a sudden thrill of terror, she looked up to find that knife in his grip, his eyes on her chest.

"What do you think?" he asked, Carriger only laughing.

"She's the Prince's whore, isn't she?" Grease asked, his attention focused on her breasts.

The elf nodded once, contemplating where to start cutting. Lifting her leg, she slammed her foot into his stomach. Grunting in pain, the elf doubled over to protect it from another attack but he was disturbingly fast to recover. Motioning for something, she hissed as hands gripped her ankles.

Squirming violently, the elf gripped her dress and ripped it from hem to neckline, the men around her laughing as they took in her body, her modesty thankfully preserved by her underwear.

The elf dropped down onto his one free hand above her and she growled in warning, the sound hardly as threatening as it used to be. He only smiled at her, using the knife to cut the left band of her undergarments. As she strained to wriggle herself away from him, she bit her tongue to keep from whimpering as he used the blade to flick away the fabric, leaving several cuts on the soft skin of her hips.

As he lifted the knife, she clenched her eyes shut, expecting the blade to be driven down into her chest, but instead she felt the blade glide over her chest, just above her right breast.

She hissed in pain, her eyes snapped open, and she glanced down to see that he had carefully carved a large 'w' into her skin, his face intent as he moved on to the next letter that would leave her body scarred with the crude word.

He never got the chance.

There was an enormous sound of wood screaming in protest, metal being warped, and then the elf no longer had a head atop his shoulders.

Blood sprayed and the two who had been holding her legs were gone.

Scrambling back, she yelped as an arm went around her and the knife was pressed against her throat.

Dragged to her feet, she struggled to pull the scraps of her dress together as Jaia seemed to materialise, covered in blood and looking like he was going to set fire to the entire world in his fury.

His eyes were a vivid crimson, taking in the knife and then Carriger before he simply vanished and the man behind her jerked, suddenly falling. She turned slowly, Jaia holding the man's severed head by the hair.

He threw the head and it made an unpleasant thud against the wall and he was on her, his hands rough as he yanked her to him, leaving bruises on her arms.

He didn't speak, only stared at her bloodied face and bleeding body. His lips pulled back and he bared his fangs at her, a thrill of terror going through her. She didn't have time to scream before his teeth found her throat and she shuddered, pain closely followed by sweet pleasure as his saliva hit her system and triggered every sexual urge she had.

His hands moved from her arms to her hips and he lifted her, her backside hitting the table in the next second. Those fantasies flooded her again, the thought of crying out his name as she moved atop him, his hands roaming her body and her blood coating his lips. But that was a fantasy and she knew now she was in danger. She couldn't fight a vampire, she knew that and as he drank deeply, she felt her world spinning.

Clutching her tight enough to break her fragile bones, he ripped his teeth free of her and smiled, lips glistening as he lifted his wrist to his mouth and bit.

Pressing the wound to her lips, she resisted at first but then she got a taste and the world vanished around her.

Grasping his wrist, she sealed her lips onto the wound and drank greedily, a soft moan escaping her that had his breath sucking in. She could feel that he desired her with him pressed so close between her legs, but he forced himself to remain still, watching as she fed from him and energy began to flood her system.

He pulled away reluctantly and those glowing crimson orbs searched her face, hungry.

Giving in to her own need, she hooked her bound arms up over his head and pulled him harder against her, her lips meeting his and mingling their blood against each other's mouths.

He went still at first, reacting to her in shock as his fury came down, but then he leant into her and his lips were demanding on hers.

Her moan made him shudder and he gripped her hips, jerking her into him and his hiss at the warmth of her made her giddy.

She wanted him and she could feel how badly he wanted her, her fingers tangling in his hair and clutching him to her as she deepened the kiss, passion and raw need spilling from her into him.

"Jaia?" Kai asked and the vampire seemed to vanish from her arms, ducking out and turning on the intruder to protect her from the new threat.

But it was only Kai standing there, looking confused and nervous.

Jaia gave a deep warning growl, his arms up and ready to attack his brother if he made any move to come closer.

"Jaia, it's me, Kai. Calm down," Kai said slowly and she realised that Jaia had lost control. He was guarding her as any vampire would protect his mate and solitary food source.

She hadn't been able to help herself, and then she had made things worse by kissing him. Regardless of who was at fault, she felt guilty for making it harder on him.

"Kai?" she asked weakly and Kai's eyes flicked up to her, widening at the sight of her sitting there, then to the elf who had slumped down on his front. It didn't take a genius to know what had been happening and he clenched his jaw, the realisation of Jaia's state clicking in him.

"Jaia, Etani is safe now. You can relax."

Jaia's eyes snapped to her, then around the room before going back to Kai, unsure and wary.

"Etani, I need you to calmly step down and come to me," Kai said and the feral, animalistic sound Jaia made had her shivering.

She did as she was told though, slowly sliding down from the table and his eyes locked onto her, hungry and furious in equal measure.

He reached for her when she tried to step away and she didn't try and resist, his fingers closing painfully around her arm and drawing her to him. He straightened and clutched her to his chest with one arm, protective and possessive.

"Jaia I'm okay," she breathed into his ear and the feeling of her breath made him shudder though his eyes remained on Kai in the doorway. "I'm fine love, you can relax," she was speaking softly, but she knew Kai would hear her without issue.

Jaia finally looked at her and he sniffed gently at her hair and face, testing for a lie, but he found none.

The vivid redness seemed to fade and he slowly eased his grip on her until she was able to breathe properly.

He wrapped both arms around her and crushed her to him in a fierce embrace, his nose nudging her jaw as he nuzzled into the hollow of her throat.

She wanted to wrap her arms around him, but her hands remained bound, but he didn't seem to care.

It took another ten minutes for him to fully recover, and yet he was still incredibly defensive of her, high on adrenaline and his need to protect her.

He refused to let her go to Kai, instead keeping her pressed against his side and inhaling the scent of her hair.

When Kai was allowed closer, his eyes searched her face and then her body, but Jaia's blood had done a wonderful job reducing the damage and she was feeling somewhat better.

"Kai, how did you find me?" she asked, extending her hands, and he cut the bindings without getting any closer to him.

"I don't really know. Jaia said he could smell you and when he smelt your fear and blood, he panicked. We thought you were dead. He ripped the castle doors off their hinges and came streaking out here," Kai said gently and her arms went around Jaia, her fingers gentle on his hair and face.

The touch soothed him and he blinked at her, frowning his confusion as he tried to see through the blood lust and terror rage.

"Your face..." he said in anguish, touching her swollen lip tenderly.

She had completely forgotten about it in her passion and when he touched it then, it made her flinch.

"Oh, Etani, what did they do to you?" he breathed, and she shook her head, not wanting him to know.

"Don't think on it." She kissed his temple gently, leaving a smear of blood on a mostly clean patch of his skin.

Glancing at Kai, his eyes were again on the elf and a crease had formed between his brows as he saw what was wrong with the picture. His eyes snapped back to her dress and the scrap of what had been her undergarments, but she turned herself, settling firmly against Jaia's chest.

His arms were around her in an instant, cradling her there tenderly.

"I was so scared you had been killed," Jaia whispered and she made a soft hushing sound, not wanting him to worry.

"I'm fine now thanks to you," she said gently and he nodded, resting his cheek against the top of her head.

"Versalis will be ripping the basement apart if we don't get back soon," Kai said and Jaia looked at him, nodding his agreement before scooping her up into his arms.

"Jaia?" she asked, barely daring to raise her voice as Kai led the way. "If I can't get my magic back... will you turn me?"

His shoulders tensed and he looked at her, frowning. He nodded after a pause and she smiled, resting her head on his chest as he carried her back to the castle and into the basement where she felt safest.

Daemon was beside himself at the state of her, fretting like an overbearing mother as she was set down on the chair in Jaia's lap, her fingers tight on her dress to hold it shut. "Give her your blood!" Daemon demanded and Jaia stared up at him in anger.

"If I give her any more we run the risk of turning her," Jaia snarled, his arms tightening around her.

Daemon stared, seeing the posture and her willingness to stay in his arms, her body turned to him and legs curled up. His eyes narrowed suspiciously but he said nothing, turning and stalking away.

"What happened?" Versalis asked, coming to examine her face and the bruises on her arms as well as the cuts on her throat and chest.

"The brother of the first man I ever assassinated in Ayathian. He had been trying to get to me all this time," she breathed, her mostly untouched cheek nuzzling against Jaia's chest.

Jaia let out a slow breath as he finally let go of his tension and his turned to rest his jaw against the top of her head, eyes lowered in his knowledge that she was safe in his arms.

"They beat the living hell out of her and it looks like a knife wound," Versalis said quietly and Kai murmured a soft agreement.

"They were all men. Her dress was ripped open. I think they were only a matter of minutes from slitting her throat," he said, anger in his voice at the implication.

"We need to fix this," Versalis growled, understanding.

"I think I know how," Daemon murmured and the group dispersed, leaving her alone with Jaia.

Tilting her head, she looked up at him and she motioned for the bedroom.

Without a word he lifted her up and took her into the privacy of the room, setting her down on her feet and slipping the ruined dress from her shoulders. He reached behind her and removed the clasps of her brassiere and the shreds of undergarments.

Sitting her down on the bed, he got a cloth and filled a bowl with water from the jug. Coming to kneel before her, he wiped blood from her face and neck.

She watched him, unmoving as he tended to her so gently that she barely felt it.

He worked slowly, careful not to hurt her and she smiled, her eyes lowering as she caught his hand and pressed it against her cheek. His breath hitched, and in response, she leant down and placed a tender kiss against his lips.

Dropping the cloth, his hands found her jaw and he kissed her back firmly.

Her hands found the buttons of his shirt and she slid them free quickly, her fingers finding his bare chest and she smiled when she felt him sucking in a breath at the gentle touch of her against him.

She traced her fingers slowly down over his muscled chest and abs, feeling him tensing as she trailed lower, but then she stopped and he felt her grin.

He gave a warning growl, though it was more playful than threatening as he gripped the back of her thighs and jerked, her back hitting the bed.

In the next instant he was over her, his knee between her legs and his elbows on either side of her shoulders. He kissed her fiercely, passionately, and she kissed him back just as passionately, need and fear warring inside her as she used his shirt to tug him down, easing his weight onto her.

"Jaia?" Kai called out and he froze, eyes snapping open in realisation of their position.

He pushed away, his fingers moving down his shirt to correct the buttons and she frowned at the ceiling, frustrated and hungry.

Kai hadn't seen them and Jaia licked the blood from his lip, giving her a wolfish smile as she sat up.

He was gone in an instant and she flopped back down, left wanting.

19
____

ANSWERS

She started a bath after Jaia left to discuss tactics with the menfolk of her life, ignoring them as she moodily paced across the living room naked and ignoring Uzo, who covered his eyes, and Daemon, who turned to stare.

They had a weird dynamic, with Uzo feeling more like family and Daemon being the obsessed ex-husband who wouldn't go away.

But she felt other eyes on her and it was like his lips brushed the back of her neck, leaving her flushing as she slipped into the bathroom and closed the door quickly behind her.

She could hear the soft murmurs of voices that sounded angry, but she ignored them as she prepared for bed and when Jaia came in, she smiled.

He looked tense but she moved to him regardless, meaning to pull him towards the bath with her but he resisted, looking down at her with an odd expression. "No, Etani I can't," he said stiffly, and she went still, confusion written across her face.

"What's wrong?" she asked, a note of fear in her voice.

"We can't do this," he breathed, and cold shot through her. She didn't understand, and his words stung.

"What? Why not?" she asked, doing her best not to start crying.

"You're human. I would kill you."

"You wouldn't kill me," she whispered, unsure and yet not caring.

"Yes, I would." His voice was cold and she searched his face, but his eyes told her nothing at all.

"I don't understand," she breathed and his lip curled.

"Yes, you do, you know what I'm talking about. You know you're too weak."

His words cut her like a knife and she took a step back from him. "Why would you say that?" she whispered, barely able to speak.

"I need someone stronger. Someone who can keep pace with me." And then he said the words that destroyed her. "You will never be enough for me."

Her head swam as he stared down his nose at her and she couldn't even bring herself to cry.

"I see," she said finally, unable to focus on him anymore, only the way the room swam around her. "Thank you for telling me." She meant to sound sarcastic, but her voice was empty and he nodded, stalking from the room and closing the door sharply behind him.

She looked at the bath and then the rest of the room, everything seeming to sparkle around her and she touched her eyes to find them wet with clear tears. Human tears.

Reaching into the water, she splashed her face to remove the last of the blood and removed the plug from the drain, forcing herself to calm down. She needed to deal with this, she could fall apart later.

She looked at her face in the mirror, then turned away from the woman who was not her, the human that had given her heart to a man who didn't love her.

That thought broke her; the first time she had given herself a chance to love and it had ended before it even started. Sinking to the floor, she cried silently but didn't give herself time to focus; instead she picked herself up by the scruff and packed up her grief, forcing it down in the back of her mind. She would not think about him again.

Something bright caught her attention as she got dressed and she looked down, a moment of pristine terror filling her as she saw that gold chain and little bell at her ankle. It was only then that she realised she hadn't been tuning it out.

She tapped the ball of her foot on the ground and listened. Nothing.

There was no sound coming from it, it was silent.

For one blissful instant, she felt relief that maybe, just maybe the thing had broken and then her bliss popped like a soap bubble. No, it hadn't broken. It was working just fine, it was she who was broken. She couldn't hear it because she was not a mythical.

The realisation hit her like a physical blow, the full knowledge that Epharis had stripped her of everything until she was raw and naked.

She gave the bell a flick, and a sob escaped her when nothing came from the stupid gold.

It might have been a symbol of her enslavement, but it had also been a friendly reminder that she was something more, something powerful and something that could make a difference and she felt a sudden, desperate need to hear that bell again. She wanted it like her human body wanted food.

She didn't want to be human, she wanted to be a mythical.

It took her several long minutes to be able to move on from the horror and fear of her realisation that she was very much a human now before she had the mental capacity to leave the room.

Slipping from the room after she had dressed, she found Jaia missing and no one seemed to notice that anything was amiss. She went immediately for Versalis, sitting close at his side and his arm went around her tightly.

"What are we planning?" she asked, and Versalis frowned in irritation.

"Well, at this stage we have three choices. You have three choices.

Two of them involve us running to Faerie and hiding out until it can be expanded. The last involves you getting your magic back."

Looking up at Versalis, she frowned as well. "How do you think we might get my magic back?"

"Daemon has a plan."

"We go through the line and have each species share their gift with you. We go along in order, just in case."

She tilted her head and frowned, turning to the shelf that held her family tree. Standing, she fetched it and all the paperwork, setting it out on the table between them. "Do you remember the order?" she asked and he snorted, looking at her.

"I wrote that tree and left it for you to find. Of course I remember," he snapped and she looked up. Her face made him pale slightly and he made an effort to moderate his tone.

"I wanted you to know what you were. So I made sure it was there when you went looking."

Lowering her eyes to the tree, she tapped her index finger on the first two, only having the name of the woman and the species of the male.

"Ah yes, Villaria. My beloved wife."

The silence that followed was absolute and they all looked up at him in horror.

"Excuse me?" she finally asked and he blinked, looking confused.

"Villaria was my wife. I started this all off."

"That... that is so gross..." Uzo said though Etani had been thinking it.

"You have been trying to sleep with me all this time, and you're related to me?" She couldn't hide the disgust from her tone and her face showed her horror.

"You are the fifty-first child born to this line, Etani. I hardly consider that a close family connection."

Kai was choking on his laughter while making a half-attempt to hide it and failing.

"She's still your direct descendant. That's revolting!" Uzo exclaimed, but she had stopped listening.

His words had triggered a memory and her head tilted as she tried to pick up the tantalising hint of information.

"I'm the Winter Queen," she said finally, the memory bursting back into crystal clarity.

"What?" Versalis demanded, looking at her.

"I'm the Queen of Winter," she repeated, her eyes turning to Uzo who was smiling slightly.

"No, Megara is," Versalis said and he frowned when Uzo laughed.

"Megara is the chosen heir. Etani is the direct bloodline. The only remaining female born to Tatialia. It makes her the actual heir and Megara the heir apparent. Who told you?"

"Nyrellia, the second heir to Summer."

Uzo nodded and she shook her head at the thought.

"Why is it I can't tap into Faerie if I am the Winter Queen?"

"I suspect it is because you never accepted your role. Now you are no longer a Fae, you cannot. Faerie will not recognise you."

She looked at Versalis; he nodded slowly and she let out a slow breath.

"So it is safe to assume that because I am not a Fae, Megara is now the Winter Queen in full?"

Uzo nodded and she looked around the room.

"So what happens if I take back my magic?"

The room was silent for a long moment.

"Then you have to deal with an angry ex-Queen who wants to be Queen again. But while you're alive, you're a threat."

"And dead, she becomes the Queen," Etani finished.

"Unless she kills you, you will always be a threat," Uzo said slowly, looking at Daemon who seemed like he was going to explode.

"We will worry about that later. Either way, you will be a target." He seemed to perk up slightly. "And if you're a human in Faerie you are at a greater risk. Even a vampire in Faerie will be at risk.

"Those are your choices, Etani. You can be hunted as a human, a vampire or a Fae. Regardless, you will be hunted," Uzo said, his words sounding harsh although he said them gently.

"Well, I guess there really is no choice is there..." She sighed, wanting desperately to just live a normal life.

"Yes, there is," Versalis said. "The choice is between Faerie or the human world. The choice is for you to be human, a vampire or a Fae. You are the only woman in history who can choose what she is," he turned her face to his and he smiled. "You get to pick what you will spend the rest of your life as."

She wanted so badly to say that she would be a vampire and have Jaia turn her right then and there, to give herself to him body and soul and be enough for him. But she knew she couldn't do that and even if she was a vampire, he would not have her. No matter how badly she wanted to say that, she would never be able to live with herself.

She wanted so badly to try and be normal, but there was no 'normal' for her; she was meant to be Fae and she felt a sinking resolve at her loss and the knowledge that she had to do the right thing.

"We get my magic back," she said gently.

Daemon cheered and Uzo looked massively relieved, though he had been working hard to keep it hidden.

"Good choice," Versalis said, and kissed her cheek.

"Prepare to fight tooth and nail for it, my darling girl," Daemon said as he approached her and, without warning, his lips came down on hers and his fist slammed through her chest.

The room was suddenly moving, voices shouting, but she had become lost to the pain and deliciousness of his lips.

She couldn't move as his index finger was an inch from her racing heart, his nail becoming long and black inside her. She felt it when the razor tip touched her and suddenly there was silence around her.

Inside herself, she found she was standing in the cavern she came to know as her soul home. Her soul was looking at her curiously, making little squeaking and humming sounds.

Turning at its alarm, she found Daemon approaching. He looked even more beautiful in that state, his horns long and curling back over his head, his eyes wicked. He was sex given flesh and he was looking right at her, making her quiver.

"There's my precious love," he purred, golden eyes going from her to her soul and back again. "You have to want it Etani."

She shook her head, fear washing through her, and her soul inched back.

"It's this or nothing, you know that. Give in and you can fight at top strength, you can protect those around you, you can create the world that we were always meant to live in."

Tears fell against her cheeks as she tore her eyes from him to her soul and it looked back at her with those large round eyes. "Will Letari come back to me?" she whispered, and the soul gave a single bob of its head.

Daemon grinned, an inch from her face as she turned back to him and she nodded. He kissed her gently and then moved past her, going to the glowing form that was her soul.

Arms lifting, her soul took him into itself and a violent slash of red streaked through.

Daemon's mouth was bloody when he stepped back and her soul looked down, touching the streak.

Their eyes met and her soul's smile was bloody. It lunged at her and she was suddenly thrown back upwards, slamming back into herself with a scream of agony that ripped through the dungeon before she collapsed.

She felt it inside her, the little tendrils of black that sped through her system from her brain downwards, poisoning her and tainting her like a drug.

It burned like acid and she writhed in herself, the pain peaking with a sudden crystal clarity. Her mind opened and she felt herself expanding.

On the inside she burned and writhed, but on the outside her body changed.

20

DEMONS AND VAMPIRES

*S*he was left slumped against the couch, limp and lifeless as the hole in her chest healed and then closed entirely, her face mending before their eyes and those minor changes that had marked her as human seeming to evaporate.

Inside she could feel herself growing stronger, her body alight, and she screamed at the pain, she screamed at the heat, and she screamed as she saw herself changing. She didn't like it. It was as though someone was breaking her bones and then setting them back again all wrong and yet nothing had actually changed.

Someone was pulling out every strand of hair one at a time and then digging them back in individually.

Every pore was raging and yet nothing seemed overly different; they were subtle changes, but exponentially more, the pain of their happening that she could feel.

Her eyes snapped open and she inhaled sharply, the world coming into focus, and it was off somehow though she couldn't quite place it. Her gaze immediately went to Daemon and a sly smile pulled at her lips; his golden eyes went wide as he found her attention on him.

"Sweet mother..." Versalis whispered as she lifted herself from the couch and stretched.

She felt different, her muscles loose, and yet she knew she was stronger. She felt graceful, sexual. Turning her eyes on Versalis, a sudden need to go to him struck her in the chest and her sly smile turned into a seductive one. "Versalis," she purred, and he swallowed.

She didn't have wings, horns, or a tail like those depictions of succubi that the humans always drew. No, there were no outward signs of her, but the men were all paying her very close attention and every tiny movement she made was tracked like a hunter tracking a deer.

Her hips swayed in a way they never had before as she closed the distance to the vampire King and she knew they were being watched. Before she had been more like a vampire, not wasting movements or energy. Now? She wanted their attention and so her body moved in ways that would captivate men of all species.

Her hands came up onto his chest and she found them to still be pink and white, the sight irritating her somewhat.

Versalis's hands found her hips and a growl came from behind her as she pressed into him.

She could feel him trembling and when she leant forward to whisper all the terrible and deliciously depraved things she wanted to do to him, her lips brushed his ear and his breathing stopped.

A hand came down on her shoulder and she turned, spinning to drive her elbow into the jaw of whoever had dared to touch her without her permission.

Daemon was sent flying and he rolled to his feet, teeth bared as she turned on him.

"What's the matter, Daemon?" she whispered and even she could hear the sexual promises in her voice that all the men around her responded to. It was the voice a lover used in bed, fingers inching lower in a promise of pleasure and satisfaction. "Jealous?"

His eyes flashed as he started forward and she grinned, feeling those sharp little teeth against her lower lip.

"Come on then, old man, I'll rip to you shreds." The threat was there and yet her tone suggested it was going to be pleasurable for him in some disturbing way.

"What do we do?" Kai asked in a strangled tone. Turning her head slightly, her voice rang out in a throaty laugh that had all men tensing.

"I'm sure we can arrange something to keep us all happy." Was she suggesting an orgy? Yes, she was.

Kai flushed and dropped his eyes, all very aware of each other and how much sexual energy there was in the room.

Daemon nodded to Versalis and the touch on her arm was tentative.

Turning to Versalis, she smiled as she saw his need, feeling it radiating off him in waves that her body instinctively responded to.

His arms went around her as she moved against him, a soft sound of delight escaping her as she felt the warmth of him.

Leaning into him, her head tilted and her lips found his. It was slow and gentle, but then building and he shuddered when her tongue traced his lower lip.

His arms became painfully tight on her, gripping her so hard that he could easily have broken her. Drawing his lips back from hers, he traced them along her jaw and she sighed, her head tilting away from him, thinking only of the pleasure his lips left on her skin.

His teeth found her flesh and she gasped at the sudden pain of her skin breaking under the force of his fangs. His hold went around her in a vice, trapping her arms between them as he fed in a way that hurt every inch of her body.

He was pulling too fast, taking too much, and by the time she realised that it wasn't a sexual need of his, her head was already beginning to spin.

Someone moved behind her and she whimpered softly as her arm was pried free and a second bite found her wrist.

She felt the loss of the third bite more than she was willing to admit, and she couldn't fight them, part of her hoping they would drain her dry.

Teeth slid free of her throat and a burning tongue dragged up the side of her throat, making her quiver in pain and delight.

Her eyes found his, hooded and confused. She saw his battle, his fight to drain her or to throw her down on the ground and make her his. His logical brain won out and he lifted his hand to his throat, leaving a long cut.

Her eyes focused on it, watching the blood well and trail down the length of his throat. She had never seen anything so beautiful in her life, the contrast of white and crimson, the way his skin seemed to glitter in the low light of the basement.

There was no ignoring it and even as she felt woozy, she dragged the flat of her tongue up his throat. She heard his moaned expletive at the action and the sound of it made her laugh gently in his ear.

"I'll fuck you later, drink," he demanded, seemingly desperate to feel her tongue on him again.

She didn't need to think about it, his blood would only enhance their pleasure and endurance. She only thought to fill herself with his blood. Sealing her lips against the wound, the taste of his blood on her tongue sent a shock through her system and her arm was ripped free of Kai.

Wrapping them both around Versalis, she crushed him against her and her sharp little canines dug into his flesh, tearing at the skin and increasing the flow. She wanted more; it wasn't enough and she bit again, opening a third wound.

She heard people yelling, hands on her, but she ignored them, she refused to stop. There was something inside him that she could reach for and she had never wanted anything more in her life.

He struggled weakly, trying to push her off him, and the weaker he got, the stronger she became.

A hand found her face and someone jerked her head back, more hands coming down on her, trying to rip her away from him and trying to rip him away from her.

She strained to keep her grip on him, but there were too many hands on her, too much strength pulling them apart. She snarled as she was pulled back and her fingers left him.

Uzo had her by the face, bending her backwards against his chest in a way that made it impossible for her to bite him or anyone else.

Versalis collapsed into Kai and his throat was a bloody mess of torn flesh and muscle.

She strained to get back to him, but they were holding her back.

She became aware of a burning inside her mouth and she whimpered, her tongue finding the loose teeth that wiggled freely.

"Let go," she pleaded, and Uzo let her go. Throwing herself away from him, Daemon and Jaia, she staggered and fell to her knees, her hands over her mouth to find it wet with blood.

Something fell against her lips and she spat out the tooth, whining softly at the ache of the second row of fangs growing in. The second tooth came free and she dropped them, clutching at her face as it burned, her teeth growing in at a pace that felt like her gums were being shredded.

She could smell Uzo at her side, his hand on her back in comfort, but she shook him off.

Her heart pounded and she screamed, the sound terrible and unearthly as the two halves of her screamed and raged against each other. Demon and vampire clawed at each other, wrestling for control, and she didn't know who she wanted to win.

Clutching at her head, she could feel that expansion that made her head spin.

Her nails dug into her scalp, her blood screamed, and then her body jerked as her heart gave one last violent throb and her breathing stopped.

The silence in her chest was loud, final.

She collapsed onto the ground, certain they had finally killed her and glad for it. She wanted to be free of them, she wanted to die and finally she felt herself shutting down. She would be free in death. She welcomed death and called for him, pleading for her to die.

She didn't. Death was a bastard and wouldn't come to her.

Sucking in a breath, she whimpered and curled in on herself. Why were they torturing her? Why were they ripping her apart just to piece her together again? Why wouldn't they just kill her and be done with it? Because they loved her? No, because they wanted to live.

A hot hand touched her cheek and her eyes snapped open, taking a moment to focus.

Uzo was at her side and he smiled gently, his fingers burning on her cold cheek.

"Hello, love," he said gently and she shook her head, turning from him.

She hurt so badly, every pore screaming in agony, and her throat stung.

"She'll have to feed," a gentle voice said. She knew who it was, but she ignored him. What if she refused?

In a matter of hours she had suffered more than she had from an entire lifetime of fighting and attempts to kill her. She had experienced too much pain, too much loss.

She couldn't do it. She wasn't strong enough to get her magic back. She was a coward.

Uzo ignored her attempts to claw her way away from him, and instead he scooped her up into his arms and stood, ignoring her whines and feeble attempts to escape.

He clutched her to him and glared at the others. "You're all idiots. You're going to destroy her. Two in one go? Do neither of you remember what it was like to be turned? You will break her mind under that pain!" he was furious, and she felt their eyes on her.

"The quicker the better," Daemon said defensively, but Uzo turned a furious glare on him.

"You shut your mouth, demon. You need to stay away from her." He stalked from the room with her bundled tightly against his chest and kicked the door shut behind him.

As he dropped onto Kai's bed with her cradled in his lap, she frowned at the scent of his anger and she tilted her head up, sniffing at the air curiously. It was a wonderful smell and his eyes met hers.

"You don't want to do that, little vampire," he said gently. "But then again…" Giving a hint of a smile at something in his mind, he cupped his hand against the back of her head and drew her to his throat. The smell was utter bliss and she found her mouth watering in anticipation of what he might taste like.

Her tongue darted out and touched his skin and he shivered. His throat was pristine, no bites at all.

Unable to resist, her lips parted and her teeth slid through his skin like butter.

The sensation was oddly satisfying, the pressure against her double canines triggering something in her brain and she wanted to do it again. It felt good to bite.

His blood hit her tongue and her entire body tensed at the first taste of him. Without thinking, she latched onto him and pulled, his blood filling her mouth, and her brain, and every sense her body possessed.

She knew instantly what it was the twins had felt in her when they tasted her; she could taste it then. Uzo was made of magic and light, he was the sun and the moon. He was everything that meant anything to her and then he was so much more.

She knew she was hooked as soon as the blood touched her tongue and she fed greedily.

His arms were both tight and gentle on her, keeping her close to him but he was ready when he felt the effects of her taking too much.

He pushed her back gently and she looked up at him, her eyes wide and her brain buzzing with the energy that filled her. She wanted to move, to run and dance and sing.

Grinning at her, he used his thumb to wipe away blood from her lower lip.

"Now they can't try and steal you away from me," he said, and she frowned in confusion. It clicked and she jerked herself back from him.

He had manipulated her so that she would feed from him and she would be left craving his blood like the twins had been with her. He was a Fae after all, and she pushed herself from his lap, her head spinning as her body sang.

Stumbling, she held the wall and just tried to breathe through the high that his blood gave her. "Why?" she breathed, trying to understand why they were so cruel.

"Because you are precious to me and I will not let them take you," he said calmly, and she shook her head, her body screaming for her to go back to him and get more. To force him into submission and rip open his throat.

She resented him for what he did to her, and yet a part of her entirely understood why he had done it. He had no real hold on her before, but now he had his claws in her and she was stuck with him. He had ensured she could be monitored and in a weird way, it had ensured she would forever be safe.

She looked at him over her shoulder and his eyes were wide, but she didn't feel that same sexual need from him that others had. He really didn't see her as anything but his family and that protected him completely from her.

"You make for an exquisite vampire," he breathed, and she made a face, turning away from him.

"You're such a bastard," she said, and her voice surprised even her.

It was that same throaty purr that she had known to be her own.

He stood and approached her, taking her by the arms and turning her to face him. His eyes studied her and then he drew her in, pulling her towards the mirror.

The woman standing there couldn't be her. That creature was exquisite with large, vivid eyes and milky white skin, a radiance about her drew all eyes and she found even she wanted to go to that woman. The woman reflected her movements exactly and it took several long seconds for her to process that it was in fact her. She had become that creature.

Her cheeks flushed red and Uzo laughed, hugging her tightly from behind.

A gentle knock came at the door and they ignored it, both captivated by the creature before them.

When the door opened, she could smell Kai and then the others, though the strength of his scent told her he alone had come in.

"Versalis will be okay," he said gently and Uzo made a soft sound of satisfaction.

"Good, I wasn't sure I got her off him in time."

Kai shifted, trying to see her, but she stayed where she was, her eyes on Uzo's in the mirror.

She wasn't ready to see Kai but he shifted sideways to force the issue and she found his face in the mirror.

"Sweet mother..." he breathed and she had to agree with his thoughts as she studied his face. He had been beautiful to her when she was human, but now he was also powerful, her eyes picking up on every detail she had never noticed before. A possessive feeling rose in her stomach; the need to be close to her own kind.

Forcing her eyes from him, she looked around the room. She could see it all as she had the first time they had turned her.

"Is that what a vampire Queen looks like?" Kai asked, and Uzo nodded.

She wanted to be away from them. She was faster than them both and the handle of the door crushed in her grip, the door ripping free of the wall and she blinked, looking at it in her hand. She dropped it and it crashed to the ground and all eyes turned.

Looking down at the door, she crouched and splayed her fingers against the wood, slowly digging in and closing her fist. Wood splintered into crumbled nothing and she smiled at the sight.

Peering up, she found an unusual number of men looking at her, her eyes going from Daemon to Epharis and then to Alaric, skipping over Jaia without stopping and settling on Versalis who was staring at her with an open mouth.

They all looked shocked, many of them seeming to have stopped working entirely at her appearance.

Dropping the splintered wood, she blew off her hand and stood, the air seeming to want to refuse her under the speed of her movements.

Her eyes found Epharis and her smile was slow and malicious. He barely had time to process before she tackled him, driving him to the ground.

He rolled and she rolled him to keep him from getting a good hold on her.

Sitting up, she straddled his chest and punched his face once and then again and again. The sight of him being beaten and her fists doing it was glorious.

He screamed, clawing at her and then her fingers were around his throat. Strangling him, she grinned in triumph as she saw him suffocating.

Arms went around her and she screamed, dragging the Lich up with her.

Someone was gripping her around the middle and still she refused to let him go.

"I'll kill you!" she screamed, her nails digging into his throat to keep her grip on him.

His teeth were bared at her, eyes wild as he struggled to get her off him and tried to rip her apart in the same move.

A hand found hers and she screamed as she felt her wrist break under the force of the blow. Letting go, she knew she had lost her chance to kill him; instead she drove her foot into his side and sent him crashing through the wall and into Kai's room.

Thrashing, she looked up to see Jaia before her and her eyes narrowed, fury bubbling over at what he had said and that he would dare touch her after he had ripped her heart out and crushed it in his fist.

"Get away from me," she hissed, and his face went cold. She didn't care, she was hurting and she wanted him to hurt, too.

Whoever was behind her clamped her arms against her sides, and she looked down. Blonde hair meant Alaric.

She didn't fight him, knowing her chance had passed and the

Lich was getting back to his feet, eyes a burning green. He stalked forward but Kai stopped him and there was finally stillness.

"Are you calm?" Alaric asked at her ear and she nodded.

Slowly he released her, and she flung his arms away from her, turning on him and stepping away. "Why wouldn't you let me kill him?" she demanded, her attention flicking to Epharis to find him glaring at her furiously.

"He's my brother," Alaric said, a point of calm in the chaos.

She bared her teeth at him and his lip curled in response, but she didn't attack him. She knew better than to attack him.

"What did you little beasts do?" Epharis snarled, not taking his eyes off her in case she went for him again.

"You refused to return her magic. We're trying to get them back," Kai said.

Epharis turned on him and sent the vampire flying.

She took advantage of their anger at the Lich to go for him again but he was prepared, his fingers around her throat and her foot landing in his side.

He grunted and she snarled but his arms were longer than hers and she couldn't get her nails into him. "I made you this, I can do it again," he snarled, drawing her closer.

"I'll kill you before you get the chance," she whispered and she shoved her arm through his chest.

He threw her before she got the chance to reach his heart and her body hit the wall.

Dropping to her knees, she looked up to find Kai and Jaia between her and the Lich. "Move," she hissed and Kai shook his head, his hands out to calm her.

She glared at him, refusing to look to Jaia at all.

"Etani please, you can't kill him," he breathed and she shook her head.

"Of course I can; he's my husband," she said snidely.

Epharis sneered when she threw his words back in his face.

Versalis had finally gained his feet, a bag of blood clutched in his hand. "She's high on the energy. I freaked out when I was turned as well. Just try not to get in her way," he said. Her eyes turned to him and her stomach clenched at the sight of him.

She had been mostly ignoring him as a half corpse, but now that she paid attention to him her body ached for him. There was a sudden, burning connection between them and she could only think of him; he was her creator and she loved him with a sudden fire she had never known.

"Versalis..." she said in a tiny, little girl's voice and his eyes snapped to her. His face darkened at her fear and hurt, protective of what was his.

He was at her side in an instant and she stood to meet him, his hands on her cheek and in her hair.

She murmured softly at his touch that left tingles on her skin and she leant into him.

His eyes took her in and she filled herself with him, revelling in his closeness.

The others in the room ceased to be; he was all that mattered and she drank in his attention and affection.

Turning her head into his hand, she kissed his palm gently.

He gave a low growl of happiness, his free arm going around her and drawing her closer at a scuff that pulled their attention away from each other.

Epharis looked like he was going to rip Versalis into pieces and Jaia looked like he would have happily joined in and added a few kicks for good measure.

She leaned into his chest, his arm tight, and the pressure made her feel better in ways she couldn't understand.

Glancing to Kai and Daemon, the demon looked worried, but wasn't homicidal. Kai looked at his brother in concern, not understanding his anger.

"You're okay, my little Etani," Versalis whispered and her attention turned back to him.

She smiled, nodding her agreement. If he was sure that she was going to be fine, then she would be. He would keep her safe.

Uzo watched the events from the door to Jaia's room, bemused and enjoying the chaos. "Well, those were the easy ones," he said and everyone was suddenly anxious.

"What do you mean?" Kai asked, inching closer to her and his fingers were gentle on her hand.

She jerked away on impulse but then she realised who it was and she slid her hand into his, his fingers feeling pleasantly soft against hers.

He smiled at her tentatively and she offered him a wary smile in return but they were both tense and the room felt like it had narrowly escaped an explosion.

"Well, we already had a demon and a vampire in the area. The rest won't be so easy. If you think about it, we now have to find all the rest and that will mean leaving Ayathian and hunting them down," Uzo said, his eyes lingering on Epharis with a crease between his brows.

"You're not leaving Ayathian," Epharis snarled.

She turned on him, but Versalis touched her cheek and she calmed, looking back up at him.

"We are, Epharis, and you can't force us to remain," Versalis said gently, speaking to the Lich though he was still looking into her eyes.

"She's my wife!" Epharis screamed, and Kai moved to grip her hand with both of his.

"You do not get to control me anymore, Epharis," she murmured, unable to tear her eyes off Versalis.

"Vampire, demon, or human, it makes no difference. I own you," he snarled, and Alaric moved to restrain him with a hand on his shoulder.

She tore her eyes from Versalis and looked to the Lich, her eyes narrowed at him in irritation. "You are the one responsible for the destruction of the human world if we can't get my magic back."

He looked taken aback and then he laughed, but their seriousness made him pause. "You can't be serious? Because I stole one Fae's magic?"

"Because you returned her magic to the Creators and they are going to be coming to tear down the human world. They want Faerie to be whole and this world is dragging it down," Uzo said, still watching Epharis.

"You're lying," Epharis snapped, but then he frowned, realising that Uzo was a Fae and he was incapable of lying. "This is insane, you're not a Creator."

"No, she is The Creator," Daemon said gently, a small smile on his lips. "I created the mother of all future worlds. Etani will be able to repair Faerie and create as many worlds as she desires."

Epharis turned on the demon, fuming. "Rubbish. It's impossible!"

"It's true. Etani will birth a universe of worlds on a whim. There is nothing she cannot do," Uzo said, while Epharis started to look distinctly nervous.

"And what if she doesn't get her magic back?" he asked.

"Then the creators bring down the human world and we all die," Uzo said simply. "We will all vanish."

Epharis looked like he was going to be sick and he searched her face but she simply looked back at him blankly. "I can't return her magic," he said, and the room tensed, everyone hopeful that he would have made it easier for them all.

"Why not?" Daemon demanded, and Epharis looked only a little guilty.

"I banished it. I shredded her connection to Faerie."

Daemon sighed and shook his head at the pettiness of them all.

"Idiot. I don't know how long we will have before the Creators come and wipe us all out. We have to get through fifty more species, and we can't do it fast or it might break her mind."

She watched the group, her face empty, but she thought she might be perfectly content right where she was, a vampire and demon. It would be easy and she could already think of a few choice people she would gladly leave behind. She knew it was spiteful, but she couldn't really help it.

"Alaric, we need your permission to go," she said simply, and Alaric jerked at being addressed.

Epharis turned on his brother, fuming that she had gone over him. "Don't let them. We can find something else," he hissed, but Alaric was looking at her with calm eyes.

"You have my permission to take anyone you need with you. You need to do this and save our world."

His words made her flinch and she bit her lip, hating the idea that they were relying on her like that. She didn't want to be the one who would fix it, she just wanted to be alone. No, that was wrong now; she wanted to be with Versalis.

Looking up at the vampire King, she found him watching her and he bowed his head to brush his lips against hers.

A soft hiss sounded from someone in the room, but she ignored them and enjoyed the sensation of his love and adoration.

Melting into him, she made a sound of contentment and closed her eyes.

"If we do this, we will have to move fast. Very fast," Daemon said, looking around the room at the various men. "We will need to be a small group to go unnoticed."

"I'm coming," Epharis said immediately, and her eyes snapped to him.

"You are staying right here," she said. She would not permit him to come with them. She would kill him herself before she let that happen.

"You are too recognisable. It will be daemon, myself, and Uzo," Versalis said, but Kai looked distressed.

"I'm going!" he cried, hating the idea of being left behind.

"If Kai is going then so am I," Jaia said, but she shook her head in refusal.

"You're not going," she said simply.

His eyes found her and he glared, but she simply turned her eyes away from him and back to Versalis. Versalis never broke her heart and left her soul bleeding. He would never hurt her like that. But she would never give her heart to another; she was not a foolish woman.

"Don't leave me," Kai whispered and she looked to him, seeing the fear in his eyes.

She shook her head and turned, cupping the back of his neck and resting her forehead against his. "Never..." she breathed, and he seemed to relax into her.

"You're not going without me," Jaia snapped, and Kai looked to his brother and then back at her.

She frowned at the pleading in his eyes and shook her head, but then sighed at his little whimper. "Fine," she said moodily, and Kai tilted his head, not understanding her reluctance.

"You're not going!" Epharis yelled, but she ignored him.

"So Kai, Jaia, Daemon, Uzo, Versalis, and me?" she asked, a little concerned at the size of their party. But what choice did they have, really?

"Six isn't bad," Uzo said, knowing her fear.

Alaric nodded, looking between them all, and then he sighed at the loss of so much power in one go. But they all knew it had to be done. There was nothing else they could do. "Very well, go save the stupid world," he said, and stomped from the room.

21

MOVEMENTS

Over the course of the following days, they packed and repacked their supplies, mostly blood and weapons in case they needed them.

Kai was unwilling to feed from her yet and she wouldn't let Jaia near enough to bite her, something they all pretended not to notice in the hopes that the issue between them would go away on its own. It wouldn't, but they were hopeful.

The next step was to find the Dragonkin and they were going to be harder, given they were so reclusive. She had never met one and was eager to find them, but they only had a rough idea on where they might dwell. It was going to be a month's travel and that was even if they ran the whole way, night and day.

The question of Etani's being able to walk in the day was very quickly answered when they had been weighing the pros and cons of testing it and she simply walked out of the dungeon and then had to be dragged back by Versalis, even though nothing happened to her. He was still angry along with the rest of them that she simply risked her life like that.

Her interest had been more inside her family tree and she was fascinated to see just how many of the men in her family were creatures that had never been reported to have a male population. She was amused that even inside Faerie, each species kept their men a very closely guarded secret indeed.

The Dragonkin were not actually dragons, but they had a very close affinity with the beasts, and were even rumoured to mate with them, though she doubted it. They were largely an elf species that had existed long ago, changing their name when it was discovered that they were so closely linked to the dragons and now no one remembered what they had been called before.

It had only been fairly recently that Dragonkin of other species had come forward, expanding their variety. Daemon told her that his daughter had married an elf and that it was unlikely for her to be a dragonkin given how far back this was in her family line. But the idea of being able to communicate and grow close to a dragon was something she hoped for.

When they were finally prepared, it was decided that rather than running the whole way, they would take a ship and she had been very, very opposed to the idea.

When she had been Fae, she struggled to contain her hunger when crammed into such a small space with that many human men, their attraction to her kicking off her hunting instincts. It had once resulted in her being left alone on a ship, watching sharks swimming around and not keen to become dinner.

It had taken seven months for the ship to drift close enough to a landmass for her to risk swimming to shore. She hadn't known what sharks were then, but they looked mean and she had later learnt that they were man eaters.

When the option of taking a ship had come up, she simply refused and crossed her arms. They had beaten her down and she had been forcefully dragged onto the stupid floating death trap and confined to her room to stop her from eating anyone.

She was the first to leave the ship once they came to port in a small fishing village and she glared at her companions sourly, their amusement irking her.

It had taken them another day of travel to reach the forests in question, and they settled in to make camp.

The task of finding wood was decided and Etani stalked away with an amused Versalis following after her to keep her safe. She was still sore about having to be on a ship and them laughing at her.

His eyes met hers as they moved, collecting wood and kindling for the fire. He kept close by in case she needed him, but she was calm and had little need to worry with so many within shouting distance.

"Do you think it will take long to find them?" she asked, and his grunt made her sigh.

"They will always hide, especially if they think they are being stalked. We should have been more careful, but it's too late now,"

"Isn't everything too late now?" she asked, and he chuckled.

"Don't pout. We'll get this figured out. It's only a matter of time." He moved to her side, tenderly brushing his fingers over her cheek.

"Yes, but is it going to be too late?" she said, turning her cheek into his palm and kissing his wrist.

He made a soft sound of pleasure and she smirked at his reaction. She couldn't help it, his pleasure satisfied her in ways she would never be able to understand. "That's cheating," he growled, eyes hooded as he looked down at her.

"All's fair in love and war, my darling," she purred.

He growled and moved away from her, needing space from the vortex of pleasure and fantasies that she was. Her grin was wicked and he glared at her, but she knew he was only teasing her.

Moving away, picking up another branch, she moved to his side, her eyes sweeping the trees. It was a natural instinct for her to keep watch and she jerked when something touched her.

Spinning, she found a laughing Versalis with a branch that he had brushed her arm with.

"So tense, little vampire," he teased, and she growled, throwing her whole bundle at him.

He ducked and she grinned, but then her grin vanished as he went for her. She yelping as he caught her around the waist and slammed her to the ground. On top of her, he grinned and pinned her arms down above her head.

"You're getting slower," he purred and she stuck out her lower lip in a pout. "We'll have to bleed that Fae a little more." His face was an inch from hers and she smirked.

"Why don't you join me next time? He's delicious." It sounded innocent enough, but her tone had him pausing, his eyes narrowed.

"You'd like that, would you?" he was teasing her again, but she lifted an eyebrow.

"What's wrong? Don't want to share your things?" she challenged.

His lips pulled back from his teeth and she pushed him. "Maybe Jaia will." He snarled, one hand going from her wrists to her throat and she lifted her chin, defiant.

He exhaled slowly, and then his mouth came down on hers in a fierce, possessive kiss. Her lips met his in turn, her head lifting off the ground in her effort to reach him.

He growled in response to her groan of satisfaction at the taste of him. It was the most amazing thing she had ever tasted. His hand moved down from her throat lingered around her breast, tracing around and never quite touching her.

She whimpered as he drew back, eyes wary, and he seemed to have a rational thought that wasn't driven by her being a vampire or his being her creator.

"Versalis..." she breathed as he moved off her, standing with his hands trembling.

He turned away as she stood, not understanding him.

"Etani, stop," he growled, holding out his hand to stop her approach.

She caught his hand and lifted it to her lips, a gentle kiss making him shudder.

Smiling, she tilted her head and bit his wrist. She didn't bite enough to break the skin, but it made him tremble and he looked back at her, trying to contain himself.

He watched with horrified fascination as she opened her mouth and bit hard on his wrist.

His blood filled her senses and her saliva triggered his need.

Spinning on her, he thrust her up against a tree and his mouth was on hers ferociously. She met his need with her own and groaned into his lips as her fingers dropped, tugging the buttons of his shirt free and shoving the fabric of his shirt off his shoulders.

Her fingers found his chest and her nails dragged down over his flesh.

The force of his kisses pinned her head against the tree and he reached between them to grip the hem of her shirt. Hitching it up.

He forced himself back from her with a feral growl, his entire body trembling as he worked to fight against his senses. She was panting gently, need radiating off her in waves that his body responded to unconsciously.

"Versalis," she moaned softly, her entire body aching for him. "I need you."

It was those words that broke him and his body was against hers, his fingers in her hair as he bruised her lips and she clutched at him.

Impatient, she broke apart from him only long enough to pull her shirt off over her hair and throw it.

His mouth found the upper curve of her breasts and she gasped as he bit her, licking away the blood. But before he could move again, a loud snap froze them both in place.

Looking around in confusion, she couldn't see anything but that didn't mean they were alone.

"Let's get back," he said nervously, posture protective as he studied the area in case there was something there seeking to hurt her.

Dressing quickly, they headed back in the direction of the camp, sweeping the area for signs of threats, but they found nothing.

The wood had been forgotten and they returned to camp, all eyes turning on them as a possible threat but no one said a thing, at least not until Jaia appeared and made a note of blood smeared over his chin.

Grunting, Versalis wiped at his face and found that indeed there was blood on his face from her breast.

Her cheeks flamed and she turned away to pack up her things, footsteps following after her.

Moving further into the trees, she stopped at a small stream and crouched to cup water in her hands, drinking, and the growl made her look around.

Jaia had followed her, his dark eyes furious.

"What do you want?" she asked, straightening, and when she turned to him, he was on her.

His forearm pressed across her throat as her back met a tree and she grunted in pain, her hands immediately going to his wrist. "Why him?" he demanded, fury and hurt in his eyes as he glared down at her.

"Get off me!" she hissed, struggling to shove him off her even though he had the weight to keep her pinned.

"You could have chosen anyone, why Versalis?"

She met his eyes for an instant, frowning in confusion. "Why do you care?"

His face darkened and she felt a thrill of fear go through her at the remembered sight of him when he lost his grip on sanity.

"You lost your chance to have an opinion on my life when you decided to rip out my heart and stomp on it."

He jerked back at her words and she shoved him away, glaring at him.

"You are the one who decided I wasn't good enough. You are the one who left." She advanced on him now and he backed away. "You are the one who told me I would never be good enough and now you're acting all hurt and lost because I found someone who believes I am good enough?"

His eyes narrowed and he bared his teeth at her.

"You don't know what you're talking about," he snapped, and she fumed. She flung out a hand to slap him, but he caught her wrist and yanked her forward into him, his lips near her ear. "If I ever see you two together again, I'll kill him," he breathed and she went cold.

He had seen them? How had he seen them?

"You were following us?" she whispered, indignant.

"I was following you. You're mine."

"I stopped being yours a week ago. You decided that." With her attempt to get away from him, he only tightened his grip on her until it hurt. "Let go, Jaia!"

He growled, clutching her until she was sure her bones would break. "Never again, Etani." He released her and she staggered back from him, frustrated and hurt that he could come to her like that.

"If I want to be with him, I will be."

It was the wrong thing to say. He gave a deep growl and slammed her against the tree again, his fingers tight around her throat and cutting off her air. "The Lich has nothing on what I will do to keep you," he breathed, ignoring her trembling fingers as they scratched at his hand. His free hand stroked through her hair though it was tender at first.

"You can't tell me that and then be angry when I find someone else," she whimpered, barely able to suck in a breath.

"You know why I said it." His voice was a whisper, his body so close to hers that not a breath of air could pass between them.

"No, Jaia." Tears filled her eyes and she tried her best to force them down. "I never loved anyone before you, and you..."

His face went blank as he processed that and she took advantage of his confusion, slamming her foot into his shin. He yelped, his grip so tight that he pulled her with him as he jerked back.

Spinning her, he crushed her against his chest with his free arm wrapping tight around her middle.

"Stop! Let me go, Jaia!" She squirmed in his arms and still he clutched her tight and hard against him.

"Stop fighting me," he snarled and the tone of his voice made her go still. He was breathing hard in her ear and she knew he was close to losing control, so she remained still and gave him the chance to calm down.

"I have loved you since the day I saw you in that dining hall," he whispered, his words cutting through her.

"You told me..." she whimpered, not knowing what to believe any more.

"So you would be safe," he breathed. "So you would make the right choice. So you wouldn't choose to be one of us and run because you wanted to be with me."

Her knees gave out and she buckled, his body lowering with hers as she gave in to her pain.

He pressed against her, shielding her from the world while she cried and her body trembled under him.

"Let me go..." she pleaded, wanting to run from him and hide, wanting to be there as the world vanished into nothing and to feel her pain end with it.

He murmured softly in her ear, drawing her into his arms and she struggled, hitting his chest. He took every blow without flinching, his eyes focused on the distance.

"How could you do this to me?" she pleaded, needing to know and not understanding.

"Because I had to. You had to make the choice on your own. You had to make the choice we all knew you needed to make."

Shoving him off her, she shuffled back from him and sat on the muddy ground, her head in her hands and her mind reeling with the news that he had manipulated her into making a choice she thought she had made on her own. How far back did the manipulation go? She didn't know that, but she hated him and all of them for it.

"You used me..." she whispered, her mind beginning to clear as anger covered her grief. "You're like Daemon, just doing whatever it takes to make sure I move to your dance."

His face was devastated and when he reached for her, she shuffled back from him, not wanting him to touch her again.

"You just wanted me to save your stupid world, that's it. Did you ever even want me?"

"I always wanted you, I will always want you," he breathed, but she shook her head, glaring at him.

"You're all the same. Epharis, Alaric, Daemon, and now you! I'm just a piece in the game, just your pawn you move into place and wait to see if it's taken out or does the taking out."

Her mind reeled and his head shook, reaching for her and pleading for her to listen to him. But she couldn't listen anymore, she couldn't hear what he was saying.

The whole thing had been his plan, making sure she was in position.

She scrambled back and shoved herself to her feet, retreating from him and the voices they could hear calling for them from the camp. "I should have left you all here..." she breathed, knowing it was cruel and harsh but though she thought he had broken her heart before, it was nothing compared to what she felt then.

"Etani, please, it's not like that at all," he pleaded, pushing himself to his feet and following after her. "I have always loved you, I have always wanted to make you mine." He sounded panicked and she shook her head, stepping back into the stream but not caring.

"Stay away from me, all of you," she whispered and he saw her body shifting before she could take more than a step. He knew she was going to run.

He crashed into her and they landed hard in the stream, water rushing over them as he wrapped his body around her in a bear hug, refusing to let go of her.

She screamed her rage, thrashing against him and then forcing them both down into the water, holding her breath as he wrapped his legs around her thighs and she was unable to run. Hands grabbed them and dragged them from the water, people cursing as they tried to understand what was going on.

Jaia was dragged from her and he swore at top volume as she took her chance, scrambling up and sprinting into the trees. "Etani!" Jaia screamed and she heard someone coming after her.

He was a lot faster than her but still she tried to push herself as hard as she could, resenting that she was no longer a Fae because of the men in her life.

Arms encased her and she was dragged to a stop, the grip on her like a vice.

"Stop, Etani stop," Kai gasped in her ear, the sound of more pursuers coming towards them.

"Let me go!" she screamed, struggling against him but the others were on them and she was tired. She hadn't fed in days and she regretted it then.

Struggling violently, he held her tight and then they were all there, looking nervous and afraid.

Jaia skidded to a stop before her and she snarled, planting her foot on his chest and using him to launch herself over Kai, his body forced backwards, and she was able to break free, but Daemon had seen her use the technique before and when he hit her, it was like a boulder.

She landed hard on the ground, his arms around her and she struggled to get her breath back. He rolled into a sitting position with her clamped between his legs, her arms pinned to her sides; she was trapped.

"Let me go," she whimpered, struggling against him, but she knew it was pointless to try and fight him. They had her and they weren't going to let her go.

"What happened?" Daemon snarled, his grip leaving bruises on her skin even as a vampire would.

"She thinks we are manipulating her," Jaia said, his hair plastered to his head and clothes soaked just as hers were.

"Why would she think that?"

"I..." Jaia broke off and all eyes went to him, his face showing his distress.

"Idiot. Stupid little vampire scum," Daemon raged, his golden eyes beginning to glow. "All you had to do was keep your mouth shut and feelings to yourself for a few months. That's it!"

"Why tell her now?" Kai asked, and Versalis shifted, looking nervous.

"Because they were together," Jaia snarled, pointing at Versalis. "They were almost on the ground instead of collecting wood."

Her cheeks flamed but she wasn't able to deny it, her eyes dropping to the scuffed ground beneath their feet.

Kai swore gently under his breath.

Uzo looked like he was going to throttle the vampire King. "You took advantage of your sired?"

"I didn't take advantage of her!" Versalis snapped, and her eyes went to him, feeling his distress and wanting to be at his side.

"You know there is no consent possible in that situation. She would do anything for you."

Their eyes turned to her, but she was squirming in Daemon's arms even as he refused to budge an inch.

"Let go, Daemon!" she pleaded

"Etani, stop, you need to stop."

She refused to listen, wanting to be free of him to get to Versalis, her fear at his anguish burning in her.

"Etani, listen to me, this feeling you have for Versalis, it will fade with time," Uzo said gently as he came to her side, his fingers gentle on her cheek, and then he jerked away when she snapped at him.

"Stop that right now, young lady," he snarled, and she went still, looking up at him with wide eyes at his demanding tone. No one had ever spoken to her like that. "He might love you with all his heart and soul, but you two can never be together like that. It's not healthy."

She looked from him to Versalis and back again, shaking her head. "I want to be with him," she whispered, and Uzo smiled gently, both of them ignoring the strangled sound Jaia made.

"I know, love, but it would destroy you both. A vampire and his sired can only share so much blood before it begins to destroy them. Their blood eventually becomes toxic and they die."

He spoke gently, and she had been about to say that they wouldn't feed off each other, but then she recalled his bite and she went still, her eyes locked on Versalis who was staring back at her.

"Etani, you two will be together forever, but you cannot be lovers if you want forever with him. You know what it was like before you were made human."

She shook her head, not wanting to believe it, but Versalis had dropped his eyes and she whimpered.

Why did the world constantly want to break her?

"Etani, I'm sorry," Jaia murmured, and she turned on him, jerking Daemon as she tried to kick Jaia in the shin. He danced back and bared his teeth at her.

"You are a liar! Stay away from me!"

"Etani, he's not a liar," Kai said, but she wasn't listening, resentment flowing through her at all of them.

"Etani, listen!" Kai cried and she looked up at him, hatred burning inside her. He remained silent, face pale under the force of her fury.

22

LIES

Daemon pulled Etani to her feet without letting go and he hoisted her up over his shoulder, his arm tight around her legs to head back in the direction of the camp and the last of their supplies.

Kai followed close behind; as the fastest he would be able to catch her easily and hold her long enough to give the others time to catch up and contain her.

She glared at him the entire time, his eyes wide and hurt at the murderous intent in her face.

Jaia moved ahead in the hopes that she wouldn't try and escape if she couldn't see him, and Versalis took up the rear with Uzo talking to him quietly.

She wanted to go to Versalis, but she was starting to wonder at his intentions as well. Was it possible they had all turned on her?

The thought had her death-glaring Kai and he shrank back a little, the unfortunate victim of her fury.

When they returned to the camp, Daemon dumped her down on the ground and she growled. He ignored her, instead grabbing her arms and twisting them behind her back. His fingers clamped down, that same weird glue magic keeping her arms trapped.

She swore at him, straining to free herself, but there was no escape.

She saw Jaia stalk away from them and dropped onto the ground, his head in his hands, but she had no pity for him; instead she found Uzo crouching in front of her, his fingers on her jaw as he forced her to look up at him.

"You should have taken us on a much merrier chase," he said, and she narrowed her eyes, snapping at his fingers.

He slapped her, not hard but enough to shock her, and she jerked back, staring up incredulously. "Stop that, you're a grown woman," he snapped, sighing at her resentment.

He lifted his wrist to her mouth and she resisted at first, but the call of his blood was too strong and she bit down hard, chewing out of spite, but he didn't make a sound while she fed and his energy washed into her.

He pulled away after only a few minutes and she followed him until he was out of her reach, licking her lips. She had to admit she was starting to feel better. Had her absolute irrationality been hunger? She didn't know, but she felt somewhat foolish.

He smiled at her and kissed her forehead, standing and moving over to Jaia.

She was still angry at him, but when her eyes met Kai, he looked hopeful at her improved mood.

He approached her slowly, coming to sit at her side, and nudged her gently, finally resting his head on her shoulder when she didn't reject him. "I love you, even if you do go crazy when you're hungry," he said gently, and she snorted.

"That was hunger?" She was indignant when he nodded.

"Sure was, all of your moods get sour and everything makes you angry. We didn't manipulate you," he said, and she looked at him, her expression wary.

"Jaia did." She saw Jaia look her way at the sound of his name, knowing he was listening even if she had been talking quietly.

"No, it wasn't like that. Daemon said it would be impossible to be with you. He couldn't touch you and couldn't love you. He had to stop what had started, he couldn't risk hurting you and he couldn't risk your choice being a result of your feelings for him."

"So instead of choosing to be a vampire and going to Faerie, he made me hate him and want to be a Fae just so I can be away from him," she said sourly, and Kai jerked, looking up at her.

"Why would you hate him?" he demanded.

"Monsters don't love, Kai. Not like that," she said, and turned away from him, dropping onto her side with her back to him to end the conversation and try to get some sleep while the group packed up their things.

She got around an hour of rest before Uzo shook her awake and helped her up. She was allowed to be free so long as she didn't try and run off again, or they would find a branch, tie her to it, and carry her the rest of the way. Or so Daemon threatened.

Setting off at a quick pace through the trees, they scoured a good fifth of the forest by the time the sun set and they were forced to make camp for the night.

She refused to sleep with the group and instead climbed a tree and settled into it, exhausted from her lack of sleep.

When she woke, she found she wasn't alone and it wasn't one of the men in her group.

An elf sat on the end of her branch, a long spear touching her throat, and she offered him a wry smile.

"Morning," she said conversationally, and his eyes narrowed.

He had blue skin, as blue as the sky at midday. His eyes were black as night. He had white hair the colour of clouds and was naked except for a fur loincloth, fur boots, and a necklace of long teeth.

"What are you doing here, vampire?" he demanded, and she was surprised to see he had two rows of sharp teeth.

"Looking for you, I suppose," she said and he looked confused.

"Why me?"

The spear pressed closer to her throat.

"I came looking for someone to grant me a favour."

His white brows shot up and the spear lowered slightly, resting against her collarbone. "What kind of favour?" he asked and she smiled slightly, moving on instinct.

She swatted the spear out of the air and grabbed him by the necklace, pulling him closer. "Never drop your weapon, little boy," she purred as he looked terrified. "I need you to take me to your elders, they and I need to talk."

He nodded slowly and she smiled, watching the young man as she climbed down. She stayed close to him as he started off into a section they wouldn't have entered until day three.

She kept a firm grip on his arm as they walked and he was nervous, but she was perfectly calm and all the more amused because she had managed to ditch her guard again.

The terrain became rockier as they walked and she wondered how long he had been following her when a weird, squeaky growl made her look around and up.

The tree behind her was absolutely filled with tiny dragons of all shapes and colours. It was mesmerising to see them all, the poor tree straining to stay upright with the weight of them.

"Wow..." she breathed, and the boy stopped, appreciating her wonder.

"Dragons," he said, and she nodded, fascinated. He tugged her on and she reluctantly followed him into what she had thought was just a depression in the landscape but turned out to be a massive hole in the ground.

He led her down the steep incline and they came out into a cavern so large she couldn't wrap her brain around it; it was entirely covered in tents and hanging domes.

The sight of the place was baffling and she stopped again to stare around.

People and dragons stared back when they saw her and she jerked at a huff behind her; a huge feline dragon glared at her.

Utterly in love with its white scales and fur combination, she had to be dragged off by the boy and she whined, reaching for the dragon and its big, purple cat eyes.

"I want him..." she whimpered, the dragon cat's ears flicking forward and he prowled after her for a moment but then he was drawn back to his owner.

As he led the way through the milling people, she marvelled at the sheer number of people and dragons.

They reached a large tent towards the far end of the cavern. The boy pulled her inside and she blinked, looking around at a small table of four people, three men and a woman.

They all had purple hair, something she had never seen before. All had purple eyes and grey skin. It was bizarre to see when they turned to look at her with interest.

"Shon?" the woman asked and the boy left her behind to run to the woman.

She doubted that was his mother, but he seemed happy to see her.

Turning slightly, she looked around the tent with curiosity. There were four perches, all empty, and four beds hidden by a divider in a corner.

They all lived there, it seemed.

"Isn't she one of the vampires wandering around the forest?" the oldest of the men asked, his long purple beard streaked heavily with grey.

Shon nodded.

"I went out to capture her and bring her back! But then she captured me and told me to bring her here anyway," he said, seeming proud and then rather sheepish.

Etani snorted, crossing the tent to peer behind a divider and a large washtub.

"What do you want, vampire?" the smallest man demanded. He had a long scar running down his face.

"Do you want the easy version or the full version?" she asked, picking up a book and examining it. She could read this one and she found it to be a book on keeping a dragon clean.

With a sound of delight, she flipped through the pages to see them wonderfully illustrated.

"Who are you?" the woman asked, and she turned to look at them, the book still in her hands.

"Well, I was Etani, the royal assassin of Ayathian." They seemed to tense at that. "Then I was Etania, the Winter Princess of Faerie. Then I was Etani the human and now I'm Etani the vampire."

They blinked at her and she smiled, snapping the book shut, and they all jumped.

"So, short or long?"

"Might as well go long," the eldest man said and she grinned, her teeth giving them pause.

"All right. I'm not here to kill you, I have little interest in your people aside from a fascination with your species and dragons. Especially the white cat out there." She pointed over her shoulder with her thumb. "But that's not the point. As I'm sure you all know, nine hundred years ago, or thereabouts, the Creators came to this world and decided they were going to pull it down." She paced around the room, the book still in her arms.

"As you won't know, because apparently none of us figured it out, that whole attempt failed because of a single little Fae girl was born and sucked up all the magic of those Creators, and the Protectors, and pulled it into herself. That girl was me, if you weren't getting the reference. When I stole all that magic, the Creators couldn't bring down the human world and many of them were killed. A few weeks ago, my husband decided that the best way to get obedience was to make me into a human. In doing so, he released all that magic back into Faerie and the Creators, who will be ecstatic to have it back with all new Creators coming into their powers.

"Now you see, that's where we start having issues. Because if you think about it, what are they going to do when they realise they again have the power to destroy the weighted anchor that is the human world?" The woman gasped and she smiled. "The lady gets it. We all get vanished into oblivion. And I don't know about you lot, but I like living." Coming to the table, she rested her hands atop it, the book seeming to have vanished in the time it took her to get to them and the back of her pants felt oddly heavy.

"So as you can imagine, I'm real keen to get my magic back. Both so I can kill my husband, and so I can keep the Creators from making us all disappear. That's where you all come in. You see, there is this demon who thought it would be real fun to start messing with the lineage of my family and he intentionally bred each girl with a new species. Demon, vampire, Dragonkin, Harpy, you get the idea. Now we've already hit up one and two, you are three." She grinned widely, enjoying their fear. "I need your magic, and you're going to give it to me, or I'll kill you all and take it that way. Your choice."

There was absolute silence at the end of her speech, and she had to wonder how many times she would have to give it. She would have to cut down the words next time.

"You're insane!" the oldest man said, and she laughed, moving to stand behind him, and her hands came down on his shoulders

"Perhaps, but do you really want to risk it? I only need a little bit. Just enough to trigger that part of my brain that was Dragonkin. Now if you could do it enough that I could have a dragon, I'd be extra happy. But beggars can't be choosers."

She crossed her arms atop his head and dropped her chin onto them, smiling at them all.

"And if we refuse?" the woman asked.

"I kill every last person in this cave while you watch, then kill you, too. I'm quite good at it."

The man under her arms was shaking, though she didn't know if it was rage or fear.

"Do it," the woman demanded, and they all turned on her, but she wasn't going to argue with them. "What is a small bit of magic to you? We don't use it once we have our dragons."

"There's a good girl," Etani said happily, everyone ignoring that the woman seemed to be almost twice her age.

"Just give her enough to get this to work and we can all live. How many do you have?"

"After you? Forty-nine." She shrugged at her look of horror. "Got to start somewhere."

"Do you know how long we have if you fail?" she whispered, and Etani bit her lip.

"We can only guess."

The room was tense and the woman stood sharply, coming around to her.

Turning to the shorter woman, she tensed at the touch on her hair and face, the woman fixing her hair in a motherly way, and then pulling her down so their lips met in a gentle kiss.

Inside her, her mind warped and she could feel a part of her streaking out as though it had wings, touching on a million lights and then retreating back to her and settling as she felt the warm glow of a million lives she had never known before.

They were everywhere, all around her on the walls of the cavern and sprinkled about on the ground. Over a thousand dragons, all of them alert to her and her to them.

"You see this all the time?" she whispered and turned to the woman who nodded.

Turning in a slow circle, she could feel them all around her and she smiled.

"It will be a shame not to have one," she breathed.

"Perhaps you will one day," the woman said, but she doubted it.

Finally she decided it was time to leave and she thanked the woman, making a quiet promise to do her best in the journey to get her magic back. It wasn't like she wanted to die any more than they did.

The woman kissed her cheek and she smiled, leaving the place, but she had not found the cat dragon again on her way out.

She stopped outside to see if she could coax down any of the dragons in the tree, but they only looked at her like she was an idiot. She felt like one.

Heading back in the direction of the camp, she knew the others would have discovered her missing long ago and so she wasn't in any particular hurry to get back to the moody bunch.

As she approached, though, she could hear her name being yelled and she ignored it, tired of having to be a good girl.

She was only a few minutes from the camp when someone hit her from the side and she was sent sprawling, Kai atop her and pinning her to the ground with his teeth bared.

"Don't you ever leave like that again! Do you hear me?!" he screamed in her face and she looked up at him in shock. She had never seen him lose control before and it was scarier than when Jaia had done it. Kai was so gentle and sweet, but this was a furious monster. "Never! I will make sure you can never walk again if you do that again!"

She could only nod, her eyes huge as she looked up at his gleaming fangs and wild eyes.

Seeing her fear, he seemed to calm down somewhat but he was still angry and his shouting had brought others.

"Kai it's all right, she's back," Uzo called as he reached them and tried to pry the vampire off her, but he had latched on.

"Never..." he snarled in her face, and she whimpered.

"Yes, Kai, never," she whispered, and finally he let her go, allowing her to push herself up and crawl backwards from him into another pair of legs.

Looking up, she found Daemon grinning. No, not grinning. He was baring his teeth at her and she made a soft squeak in fear.

Before she could get away, he had her by the hair and dragged her to her feet.

Shoving her up against the tree, he glared at her.

"Hands," he said simply, and she swallowed, holding her hands out in front of her.

He wrapped his long fingers around them and then she was bound, trapped with no chance of getting her wrists apart.

Daemon refused to let go of her again after that, instead keeping a firm grip on her, and she frowned, but didn't argue. It was easier not to argue with him and he was exceptionally angry, which was odd because she had never seen him quite so angry before.

When they dragged her back to the camp, he sat her down by the fire and she remained quiet, letting them talk before they finally had to stop pretending like she didn't exist.

"Did you get it?" Kai asked, and she nodded, smiling at his look of wonder.

"They are logical beings, once I explained the situation it was relatively easy. I also found that I needed very little magic shared to be able to trigger the dormant links in my brain. This may not be the most difficult task in the world after all. Some of them will be harder than others."

Kai and Etani looked at Daemon, who grimaced at their glares.

"I tend to think the general creatures will be easy enough, but I recognised some of those names and it will require us to go to Faerie, and even the underworld. Why did you breed my family with the Gods?" she demanded.

"Because they were powerful," he said snippily.

"How many Gods are we talking about?" Uzo said warily.

"I counted six," Kai said, and Etani nodded.

Daemon ignored their moodiness and looked away.

"Not only that, but we have a shapeshifter and a damned thunderbird... How do you even procreate with a thunderbird and why would you go with one?" the vampire wondered.

"Eyes," Daemon said simply, and they all looked at him, then turned to her and those eyes that had no way of being described fully.

"That's why I was trying so hard to get them back, look at them," Daemon said, and she snapped at him when he went to grab her face.

"What about the Strigoi?" Kai asked, and they all shivered.

"That one will be just as tricky. There aren't many left. They all gave into infighting and trying to gain territory," Versalis said, staring at the fire.

"Wouldn't Versalis be enough?" Etani asked, glancing at the man.

"I am a vampire King, but they are King of Kings. Think of it like my being a prince and their being the King. I am King only because I stole that from a Queen and a vampire Queen controls a coven. The Strigoi control us all."

Biting her lip, she sighed and motioned for the pack. Kai handed it to her and she unfolded it.

"So we have covered the first three. Demon, vampire, and Dragonkin. Next we have a Harpy and... who is Mara?" She frowned at it, not knowing the name.

"Sort of like Hades but from a different background. Big, lecherous, evil," Uzo supplied.

Rubbing her eyes, she let out a slow breath. "This is going to be impossible. How are we going to hunt down this being? Are they in this realm or Faerie?"

"Mara never leaves Faerie unless the humans need him," Versalis said.

"Unless there's some great battle to keep him entertained."

"What is he a God of?" she asked.

Daemon hesitated and she looked at him suspiciously. "Destruction and desire," he said finally, and the group let out a collective sigh.

"If I ever get back to myself, I'm going to kill you," she said, her head in her hands.

Daemon snorted, looking at her bound and held captive. "You did that already, three times."

"At least you won't have to worry about this again." She sighed, skimming over the enormous list again before turning to the map.

"What does that mean?" Daemon asked.

"This line will end with me," she said, tilting the map upside-down and frowning at it, not sure of where they were in relation to anything else, plus she wasn't able to hold it very well with her hands bound.

The silence of the group made her look up and she noticed everyone was watching Daemon. Looking at the demon, she found him staring at her intently.

"What?" she demanded, shifting herself a little away from him.

"I think you need to repeat what you just said, I feel like I misheard," Daemon said in a weirdly formal, dangerously calm voice.

"You heard me. There will be no more after me. Letari is dead, I will eventually be killed and that will be the end of it. You can start with some other messed up game."

His teeth flashed in a manic grin and she met his grin with her own neutral expression.

"You think you will end my line? I will put a child in you by force and keep you down if that is what it takes."

Her face flushed and she glared at him.

Kai was on his feet, Jaia baring his teeth, but Uzo looked relatively calm.

Versalis had vanished, a movement of him catching the corner of her eye, but she pretended not to see it.

"You will not. You will accept that you have gone as far as you can with this game. It is time to stop."

He was on her before anyone saw him moving, her body slamming back so hard she cracked her head. "You listen to me, you little bitch. I will not allow you to ruin my work just because you have had a hard time. You will do what fifty others of your family have done and give me the next generation. Or I will make the next generation from your body." His nose touched hers in a light brush, his fingers curled around her throat only tight enough to keep her down.

"Then I suppose that's what you'll have to do. I will not procreate, I will find a way to destroy it every time like with Drizdan."

Uzo twitched but she ignored him, instead staring up into those feral gold eyes.

Daemon bared his teeth at her and she responded in turn, knowing he would make good on his threats just as she would. "What's to stop me from keeping you immobilised?" he whispered.

"Them," she said simply.

Daemon glanced up to see every other member of their group inching in on him, murderous intent on their faces.

Looking back down at her, his sudden switch to calm had her immediately suspicious of him.

"No, you're right. It is your choice, of course." He let go of her and pushed himself away. Kai appeared above her and took her hand, pulling her up to her feet and immediately put his arm around her protectively.

After that there was no further discussion and they decided it was a good time to start packing while they figured out what to do next.

23

HARPIES

"The Harpies aren't hard to find, but finding one who will help might be more difficult," Uzo said quietly, his mood pensive since the argument and near incident with the demon.

"I had a thought on that," Etani said gently, only able to help with the basic tasks as Daemon adamantly refused to release the magic that bound her wrists.

"Oh, here we go..." Daemon said sourly and she glared at him.

"We capture one and threaten her, magic or death."

Glancing around at the men, she found mostly thoughtful looks. Uzo didn't seem to be listening.

"That would actually be the best idea. The Harpies aren't exactly the nicest creatures in the world, threats might be the only thing that will work," the Fae said finally.

"Do you think they would take surrender over death?" Kai asked, his efforts to help clear up limited to what he could do around her without moving further than a few steps from her side.

"From what I remember, they will take just about anything over death, pride be damned," Jaia said, throwing a glance in her direction but she ignored his attempts to start a conversation.

"Well, the only other question is, how do you catch a Harpy?" Daemon asked.

"How did you do it last time?" Kai asked.

"Pretty much just threw Rosa at him. She was a sweet girl and Digne took a keen interest," Daemon said.

"How do you remember their names?" Etani asked, fascinated.

"I remember them all. When you have to live with them for a thousand or more years, you remember their names easily."

"So how do we catch one?" Kai asked.

"Well, there is an easy attempt we can try. We only need to find a Harpy, not a male. So we throw a pretty boy at it and wait," Daemon said and then studied the faces of the men around him.

The moment was rather awkward, but she found it rather amusing. She thought of Kai for his sweetness, but the name chosen made her stomach clench in an emotion she didn't fully understand.

"Jaia, you're going to be our test subject. If that doesn't work, we'll send out Kai," Daemon announced.

Uzo had been watching her and she did her best to cover the flash of... what was that emotion? She wanted to dig her nails into him and scream at anyone who dared try and come near him, especially if that someone was another female.

Blinking at the sudden surge of emotion, she glanced at Uzo and immediately wiped her face clear, but he was watching her with a sly smile on his face.

"Why not Uzo?" Versalis asked.

"They can sense the Fae, but I don't think the vampires have enough magic to sense," Daemon said.

"So where is our best bet?" she asked, putting down the map.

"We aren't going to be able to get there on foot," Daemon said and all eyes turned to him.

"Why not?" Etani asked immediately, dreading another sea voyage.

"It would take months. We'll have to go my way."

Fear ripped through her and he had been watching her to see her reaction. That feeling of being ripped apart, every cell screaming in agonised protest.

"No, Uzo can take us," she said, her voice wavering slightly.

"No, darling, I don't know where to go and it could take months to get the right location." Uzo had come to her side, taking her hands and smiling into her pale face. "You're not what you were, it should be okay."

She didn't believe him, but what other choice did they have? They outvoted her and she sat sourly, dreading the coming trip. Her dread was unwarranted and much to her surprise, the rip in reality that they passed through felt like nothing at all. Stepping out into an unfamiliar world. It was humid and hot, with a sky so perfectly blue she was certain she had never seen the likes before. The sound of crashing waves came from behind her and she spun, eyes wide as the colour and size of the ocean.

Ignoring the men who called out to her, she ran for the water and shed her shoes as she went. The water was deliciously warm on her feet and she gasped, staring down at the perfectly clear liquid.

The others had come down to join her and she turned, grinning widely.

"Like the ocean, do you?" Daemon asked sourly.

"I've only seen it once, go look for the Harpies with Jaia, I won't be long."

Dismissing them, she returned her attention to the ocean and crouched down to dig her pale fingers into the sand.

Scooping it up, she watched the wet clumps splash back down and she ran her fingers through the water to clean them. Turning, she searched for a shell and went for it, scooping it up and examining the pretty pink and purple fan shape of it.

Turning, she found them all watching her and she grinned. Uzo saw it coming first and jumped away, just being missed by the spray of water she kicked at them, and then she ran as a soaked Kai glared and bolted after her.

He caught her easily and she shrieked as they both went down into the water, his arms tight around her waist. Meeting his eyes, she smiled at him and kissed his cheek before shoving him away and kicking off the soft bottom to the surface.

He popped up beside her and they waded back to the shore, dripping but happy, and she was still clutching her shell.

Giving them all time to get used to their new surroundings, they devised a plan that would involve Versalis and Jaia going into the surrounding mountains and hills, then Jaia would go on alone. He had been given two days to find himself a Harpy and then ask her to come with him.

If successful, they would ambush her and threaten her with her life. Etani would then get the magic and she would be released without harm.

Versalis seemed doubtful that it would go that well, but that was their best bet for the time being. Etani had her doubts as well, but she kept them to herself and instead focused on rinsing out her and Kai's clothes in a clean stream before setting them out to dry under the hot sun.

She had been given the generous liberty of having her hands parted, but at most she could move them six inches from each other. It was enough to work, but would limit her escaping in that terrain.

When darkness fell the two vampires set off, Versalis after giving her a tight hug and kiss on the cheek, Jaia only getting a glare as he slunk off into the night.

Turning back, she saw Kai's expression and decided to go check on their clothes, a gentle crunching behind her leading her to think the vampire had followed to scold her.

Pulling the dried clothes from the rock and checking them for dampness, she felt his presence before he started speaking.

"You're in love with him," Uzo said gently and she turned just enough to see him over her shoulder.

"What makes you think that?" she asked defensively, handing him

Kai's clothes and flicking out her own to get any residual sand and stiffness out of them.

"You were jealous when it was recommended that Jaia go out to seduce the Harpies."

"You're mistaken. I don't love anyone," she snapped, pulling on her pants and tying them into place.

"There's nothing wrong with being in love, Etani," he said gently and moved forward to catch her hands, holding her still to look up at him.

"Monsters don't love, Uzo, and love gets you killed. It will always get you killed. I died for my sisters, my sisters died for me, my father died for us both and my mother died for us all. Being in love is a dangerous curse granted only to those who are stupid enough to fall for it," his brows had risen and he frowned at her anger but she wasn't done. "Don't try and say he loves me either, because he doesn't. It's all a lie the stories tell you so you remain content in your life. Love is for the humans and their fleeting existence. It is not for the immortals."

Pulling her hands free of his, she sighed at the sight of her shirt and how difficult it was going to be to get on.

Without a word, Uzo picked it up and held it out, helping her into it and as he tugged it down over her arms, he kept a tight grip on her. "He loves you. And you love him. Accept it and embrace it. It will make someone like you stronger."

"What is that supposed to mean?" she hissed, trying to wriggle herself free of him but he only tightened his grip.

"You are a dangerously powerful creature who has little compassion for humans or many of the beings of this world. You need someone who has those things you lack and Jaia is that someone."

She didn't want to listen, but when she tried to drop her legs, he only heaved her up against him in a bear hug, her feet unable to reach the ground. "Put me down!" she cried, his hand coming up over her mouth and she was furious to see just how strong he actually was.

"Listen to me. You need someone who will love you like that, or we will all be doomed. Don't let your fear and resentment cloud you to the fact that you need love. Our entire existence needs you to love or we'll all be destroyed."

She shook her head furiously, refusing to accept that he might be right. She wasn't that cold, was she?

"If it is a choice between you destroying us all or you being trapped in this state and us all in Faerie, I will drag your stubborn arse there right now and let this world be damned. All of those creatures you need to become yourself will be lost and you will never be that Etani you enjoyed for the last nine hundred years. No Letari, no magic, just a sad little vampire demon brat who couldn't handle it."

He let her go and she landed hard on her knees, falling forward onto her hands.

"Shut up..." she whimpered, hating that his words had left a hole in her stomach that caused her eyes to well with tears.

"I will take you there right now and I will leave all of those you find precious behind. Then you can watch as they are all vanished from this world," he said cruelly, leaning over her to speak into her ear.

"Shut up!" she screamed, turning on him and slapping him across the face. "I won't let you kill them!"

He only smiled at her, grim and satisfied. "No, Etani, it will be you killing them," he breathed and walked away from her, taking Kai's clothes with him.

Looking down, she picked up a shoe that had fallen from the rock and found the other, sitting against the rock and hugging them to her chest.

She knew he was right; she had survived by putting only two things before her own survival and that had been her two sisters. Without them, she had nothing left and had considered letting that world be destroyed because it was easier. She was cold and indifferent to the humans unless it was something she could eat.

Bowing her head over the shoes, she rested her chin against the soles, watching a tear rolling off her arm. Her hair formed a perfect curtain around her head, shielding her and her traitor tears from the world.

When had she become so cold, or had she always been like that? She had loved her sisters or else she wouldn't have bothered keeping Cain distracted. But that was the love of family and that was entirely different from the kind of love Uzo was talking about.

Did she love Jaia? She didn't know; she had never experienced that kind of love before. But when she thought of Kai being vanished, she felt a terrible pang in her heart, and she gritted her teeth to keep from sobbing.

She loved Kai, but what kind of love was that? It was like the love she had for her sisters, but still different. She had essentially adopted him as her sibling, but no, that still wasn't it. She loved Kai like she had loved that little ball of light that had grown inside her. He was more like her child than her brother; it was the same with Nayishma.

She considered that and frowned, clinging to something that wasn't her fear and confusion over Jaia.

Kai and Nayishma were both a result of her bringing them back to life, she had to suppose that meant she had created them in a weird way. They were her children.

Chewing on the inside of her cheek, she contemplated the two and then snorted, realising why they had so disliked each other. They were siblings trying to fight over the attention of their mother.

The thought amused her greatly, and she looked up in the direction of the camp. Daemon was watching her from a distance, but he left her be. She didn't doubt he knew the topic of their conversation, if he hadn't been listening in and didn't know every word that had been spoken.

Dropping her eyes back to the sand, she tried to turn her attention to the problem that was Jaia, and immediately shied away from the subject.

No, she wouldn't go there, not yet anyway.

Pushing herself to her feet, she made her way back to the camp and dropped the shoes down beside Kai. Wrapping her arms tightly around his shoulders, she rested her cheek atop his head. He looked up at her with a wide smile. Kissing his hair gently, she sighed and let go of him, pausing when he took a gentle hold of her arms and held her there.

Leaning his head back against her stomach, he closed his eyes and simply enjoyed being close to her again.

They remained like that and she found herself absently combing her fingers through his hair, something he seemed to enjoy immensely, and she found him and Daemon exchanging glares. Kai was smug and Daemon was irritable, but she decided it was good that the demon should remember his place in her life.

Turning her attention to the passage, they were left waiting.

The night passed and finally she had to move, folding herself down onto a patch of grass beside Kai. Unable to help a smile when the sleepy vampire rested his head against her shoulder, she fell asleep in less than a minute. Versalis had returned and been sprawled out for hours, Daemon moodily staring out at the ocean and Uzo had wandered off to explore the beach. Shifting Kai from her shoulder, she stretched her legs out in front of her and rested his head in her lap.

He nuzzled her thigh in his sleep and she smiled, watching him but remaining alert to any sounds around them.

By the time Uzo had returned it was almost dawn and he sat down at her side, her head immediately finding his shoulder and her eyes sliding shut.

She was exhausted but hadn't wanted to risk disturbing Kai by moving him again and Uzo wrapped his arm tightly around her.

It was almost noon by the time she woke, finding herself wrapped up in Uzo's arms and resting in his lap. Kai had vanished but she knew he would be around somewhere.

Yawning, she stretched and Uzo grunted softly as her change in position allowed blood to return to his legs.

Squinting up at him, she frowned groggily.

"No news?" she asked, and he shook his head.

The smell of him so close made her mouth water and she found herself staring at his neck.

He laughed gently at her and had only just managed to tilt his head away when she wrapped her arms around him, her lips on his throat.

The sensation of her teeth slicing through his flesh was as beautiful then as it had been the first time, a delicious pressure she never wanted to lose. His blood was another story altogether and she shuddered as it hit her tongue.

Pulling greedily, she clung to him and he held her just as tightly, his attention on something else behind her.

It was he who terminated the feeding, pressing her back from him and she growled softly, wanting more. His blood was like nothing she had ever tasted, but he would start to suffer if she took too much. That didn't stop her from trying to pull herself closer to him again.

A pair of arms slid around her ribs and pulled her off the Fae, while she snarled and reached for him.

Slowly she came down from the high, her desperate attempts to get back to him easing until finally she stared at him sullenly.

"Thank you," Uzo said as he used a scrap of cloth to wipe away saliva and blood from his throat, the bites already healed over. "The more we collect, the stronger she gets."

"I think the blood lust will fade as we move down the line," Daemon said, easing his grip on her, and a low growl came from him.

Looking around, she smiled at the sight of Kai as he approached. Wriggling herself free of the demon, she immediately went to his side and he used his thumb to brush away a smear of blood from her cheek.

Licking her lips, she went into his one-armed embrace, his hug tight but fleeting.

"Still no sign of him," he said, and the mood on the beach dulled.

"He has time, he can do it," Uzo said gently.

Everyone agreed, but no one was particularly happy.

"I didn't see anything, but you got the general sense that the trees had eyes," Versalis said, and all eyes went to the trees in the distance.

The day wore on and it was night again, then day, and everyone grew anxious. Pacing the beach, Kai looked irritable; she had taken to drawing symbols in the sand, focusing on the perfection of them before wiping them away and starting over.

The others had wandered off somewhere and had all returned by nightfall.

"I don't like this," she said as the sun set with no sign of the vampire or the Harpies.

"Do we wait or go in for an extraction?" Kai demanded.

"Jaia is a fully capable soldier, we will give him until noon," Uzo said calmly, his eyes lingering on the passage.

She was impatient and found herself pacing, interjected with anxious glances in the direction of the passage.

It was close to dawn when they heard the loud laugh, and everyone froze for an instant.

Uzo seemed to melt into the sand, he moved so fast. He had sprinted far enough away that the Harpy wouldn't be able to sense him, and the rest of them moved into position around the entrance of the passage, alert and ready. Daemon, however, had gone the other way, knowing she would feel him if he was near.

A low, raspy, female voice joined in with the laugh and Etani felt that same clenching in her stomach. She resented it, knowing she had no claim over the vampire, and she resented that just as much.

Shaking her head, she tucked herself under the ledge of a rock, her knees nearly touching her chin as they waited. Kai had lowered himself down onto his stomach under a bush and Versalis had hidden behind a tree that hugged the wall of the cliff.

As the two came through the passage and out onto the beach, she got her first look at the Harpy.

The Harpy stood around five foot five, making her a good foot shorter than Jaia, though wild reddish-brown hair made up another several inches on her head. She was naked, legs changing slowly into taloned claws from just below her knees. Her arms were strewn with feathers, the limbs seeming to form the basis of her wings though she had hands at the pinnacle.

There was no denying she was a beautiful creature, her skin melting into feathers and scaly claws seamlessly. But seeing her with Jaia had Etani wanting to rip out the Harpy's throat.

Versalis moved, holding up one finger; the three readied themselves as the pair headed, leisurely, towards the water.

A second finger rose and they tensed, seeing Kai shifting his weight, ready.

The third finger went up and then Versalis dropped his hand and they lunged forward.

A sound must have alerted the Harpy; she turned and screeched a terrible sound and Jaia threw himself out of the way.

Kai, being the fastest, reached her first and he caught her by the wings, spinning her and throwing her into Versalis, who caught her.

Etani immediately went for the Harpy's feet and as she spun to try and gouge the vampire, Etani caught her ankle and yanked it out from under her. The Harpy fell and they went down with her, pinning her down to the ground. Kai sat on her writhing legs.

The sounds she made were terrible and Versalis clamped a hand over her mouth, only to get bitten by sharp teeth.

Deciding on an alternate course, she waited a beat and then slapped the Harpy across the face. "Shut it! If you listen, we will let you go!"

The Harpy did so, looking sullen and scared with a bright red handprint on her golden cheek.

"What do you want, vampire?" the Harpy hissed, her eyes large and golden, searching for Jaia and then realising he had been in on it when he hung back, looking guilty. She bared her sharp teeth at him and Etani smiled. Versalis held tightly to the Harpy's shoulders and glared down at her.

"Good job!" Uzo called as he approached and the Harpy hissed at him, sniffing at the air.

"There's a good girl. Just listen and we'll let you go. What we want from you is a tiny bit of your magic, then you're free to leave. However, if you refuse we kill you, and I take it all."

The Harpy didn't look particularly happy about that, glaring up at her with full lips pursed. "What do you want it for?" the Harpy asked, and Etani paused, considering the creature.

"Why does it matter?"

"We Harpies like our secrets. You give me that secret and I'll give you magic," she countered.

"It's no longer a secret if I tell you. Nothing stops you from sharing it."

The Harpy smiled slyly and Etani narrowed her eyes. "It harms you none if I know. Your secret is safe with me."

Etani looked up to Daemon who shrugged, frowning down at the Harpy.

"Very well. I want your magic because if you don't, this world gets vanished by the creators. If you don't give it to me I will kill you very slowly, removing your wings and then your talons. If you don't give it to me, I will destroy every Harpy in this area and then take all their magic."

Even Daemon was looking at her, but she ignored him.

"If you don't give me your magic I will obliterate your entire species and ensure that not a single creature in this world ever recalls the name 'Harpy.' You will be nothing but an impossibly bizarre memory of the ancient Faerie species and no one will lament your demise."

"Etani," Kai whispered but she ignored him, too.

"Do you really want to know what it feels like to have your veins screaming as every last drop of moisture is drawn from them? The agony of being drained by a vampire and the pounding pain as your brain is starved of oxygen right before you die? Because I'll do that to you."

Her face was close to the Harpy's and she looked utterly terrified. "You can have it! Take it all," she squeaked and Etani smiled, her fingers clasping the Harpy's face and pressing that tender kiss onto soft, plump lips.

The magic flooded into her and she shuddered, drawing it into her with greedy abandon.

The warping in her mind was the oddest sensation, her head seeming to stretch outwards and she threw herself back from the Harpy, clutching her head and screaming as her mind swelled and then recoiled, spinning and stretching in ways she had never experienced before.

Her body changed, her shoulder blades cracking with a sound like cannon fire, the bones stretching out, growing, and as they did, black feathers sprouted.

Falling forward onto the sand she whimpered pitifully; arms found her and pulled her against a warm body.

She was blind, her screams terrible in the quiet of the beach until finally they died down. She staggered to her feet, her eyes opening as she felt oddly off balance and she shrieked as she fell backwards and landed hard on her backside.

Looking up at the fear and shock on the faces around her, she first looked down at her feet but they were normal. Slowly, with terrible trepidation, she looked behind her and screamed again at the sight of the wings, spanning eight feet and weighing far more than she ever expected them to.

They were a glossy black and thick, the light reflecting off them in blues and purples.

"What did that bitch do to me?!" she screamed, struggling to reach for one of the wings that seemed to move with a mind of its own.

Finally grabbing one by the feathers, she pulled it around her and stared at it, then up at the stunned men.

Kai was the first to move when she tugged at the wings, attempting to rip them out of her back, and he stopped her, his grip tight on her hands.

"Stop, Etani they will go away. We just have to finish the process. Stop trying to rip them off," he was firm, and she latched onto his calm, staring up at him.

"I feel like my brain is... everywhere," she whimpered, not liking it, yet it felt more normal than her mind before.

"I know, sweetheart. Just try to focus and calm your nerves. It's going to be okay."

Nodding slowly, she let go of the wing and it flicked out as though needing to rid itself of her touch and she whimpered. She could feel the muscles working, an odd sense of awareness of their movements, yet she had no idea how to control them.

"Can you stand?" he asked gently, and she threw her arms around his neck. He pulled her slowly to her feet while she clung to him like a child, reluctantly letting go of him and immediately latching on again when she began to topple.

"Lean forward slightly," Daemon suggested, and she turned on him, nearly falling again.

"You shut up, Demon!" she snapped, and to her surprise, her right wing batted him clean off his feet.

Uzo laughed and Kai grinned, but she was still mildly concerned by the things.

"Don't even try and make me fly..." she warned and the things folded behind her back, almost sullen. "Where's the Harpy?" she asked, looking around as she planted her feet and tried to focus on simply staying upright.

"We let her go when you stopped screaming and seemed to be okay," Jaia said, lingering near the back of the group.

She only nodded, taking Kai's hand as he offered it to her.

Sitting down slowly, she looked at the others and frowned. "Mara is next, right?" she finally asked when no one else seemed willing to speak for fear of annoying her.

"Yes, and that will require us going to Faerie," Uzo said, packing away his possessions and handing Kai his shoes and socks to put on.

"Where does Mara live?" she asked.

"Winter, but he doesn't like the Courts," Daemon said. "At least not when I saw him last."

"No, he is still very much in dislike of the Courts, much like all of the Gods," Uzo said softly.

"Why do they call themselves Gods?" she asked, watching Kai putting on his shoes after flicking the sand out of them and his socks.

"The humans started that, and they liked it. It's easier and more flattering than 'Ancients,' isn't it? So those who took a fancy to it started demanding everyone call them that, and so the rest just ended up being that too. Most of them don't particularly care," Uzo supplied, handing her a skin of water and she drank eagerly, handing it back once she was done.

"They are an odd bunch," Daemon said, and they all nodded their agreement.

"So when do we go to Faerie?" she asked.

"As soon as you are ready to move. We are all prepared," Daemon said gently.

Etani frowned, looking from him to Uzo. "Why aren't you taking us?"

"I can't take anyone but myself, love," Uzo said. Etani narrowed her eyes at him. "I didn't tell you before because I didn't want you to worry. Most of us can only move ourselves, it's only those special cases who can open a door. Gatekeepers they're known as, but it's not a particular species. Much like the Celestrials, only a handful can do it in each generation."

"Why can I do it, then?" she asked and he smiled.

"You're special, like them."

She shook her head but then shrugged it off as a future worry. She hadn't ever really thought about it, she had simply done it. But now that she thought on it, she didn't recall any other Fae being able to open a door like she could.

"Might as well go deal with it now," she said slowly.

"At least after Mara we have several mostly easy goes," Daemon said as he stood.

"What is there? Werewolf was after Mara," Jaia said as he pushed himself up.

"Werewolf, dragon, faun, Naga, and a shapeshifter," Kai listed off automatically and offered his hands to her. She accepted and pulled herself up.

"Let's not get ahead of ourselves. We have Mara to deal with first," she said, and they nodded.

Taking Kai's hand, she watched as Daemon gripped the other, and pulled the line of them through the rip and into the crippling cold of Winter.

24

MARA

Immediately she wrapped her arms around herself and shuddered, squeaking at the cold and snow falling around them.

Kai stripped off his coat, but her wings had already moved to wrap around her and he laughed at the sight of her, nothing but a ball of feathers with a head and feet.

Glaring at him, her wings twitched, but he was already dancing out of range.

"Imagine if we pushed her down a hill like that..." Uzo said with a wicked grin and she turned her glare on him, silently daring him to try.

He didn't dare; instead, he grinned at her and set off. Accepting the jacket and wriggling it on backwards under her wings, she muttered about their immunity to the cold, even if it would affect them eventually, and Daemon's sheer body heat melting the snow around him.

They set off in the direction away from the four points and they could see the palace a good day's walk to their left.

Turning, she stared in the direction of Ceress and chewed on her lip, knowing she was incredibly vulnerable to attack, but also difficult to track.

Turning to see the men heading off, she hurried to catch up and smiled as Kai lingered to wait for her. He ruffled her hair and then set off again, smiling at the tips of her fingers only barely peeking out of the sleeves of his jacket.

Daemon led the way with a set jaw, remembering the path to the home of the ancient Mara.

It took them several hours to reach it, but while they walked he explained everything they needed to know, starting with the reason for their distant approach being because Mara didn't like strangers barging into his land.

"Mara is a dangerous man," Daemon said as he melted a path through the snow. "He is very intelligent, very attractive to both men and women, he is a God of lust and worldly desires. He will try and seduce you and keep us trapped, think of him like a siren but much worse."

Etani chewed on her inner cheek and contemplated what the man must look like.

The place they were looking for came upon them rather suddenly, though they were the ones moving toward it. It simply seemed to loom out of the snow.

It was a large dome shape, white and sparse, and the group paused, curious about it.

Set into the front of the dome sat a pair of doors that were open, inviting them in, yet the building only grew bigger as they drew nearer, seeming to grow before their eyes.

When they reached it, the dome seemed to be the size of Ayathian, smooth and without imperfection.

Daemon didn't stop; he simply walked inside, and the others paused to exchange looks.

Shrugging, they followed him in and the sight had them staring around in wonder.

The inside was a deep blue with gold and silver patterns painted everywhere from bottom to top of the dome.

The ground was strewn with pillows and little day beds, pillars carved into giant spouts of water. Fire kept the dome up and allowed for long strips of gauzy fabric to hang and break up the space.

In the centre of the room a man sat in a pile of cushions, two young women at his sides.

They were succubi, judging by their sumptuous bodies and little horns.

Mara looked up and Etani froze at the sight of him.

He was glorious to behold, a rich honey colour with black hair that seemed to suck in the light.

Luscious, glistening lips and full cheeks.

He was naked from the waist up, revealing his toned, gorgeous body painted in gold and six arms moving, stroking hair and teasing flesh all while lifting small green fruit to his lips or holding a goblet. He wore a bright green, blue and gold skirt and little gold clogs on his feet.

As he took in the group, his eyes seemed to bore into her like a physical touch and her breath sucked in. He was a God indeed.

Atop his head he wore a large, elaborate gold crown and his eyes were an unusual, heavy lidded almond shape she had never seen before, only enhancing the exotic beauty of him and captivating every cell in her body.

He smiled at her and she felt herself filling with light, his eyes moving from her to Daemon. "Daemon!" Mara boomed, brushing away the succubi to rise to his feet. He moved like a snake, smooth and graceful. His arms outstretched for the demon who went to him immediately.

A sudden thought struck her at how close the two seemed to be and a flush crept up her cheeks as the idea of those two together made her blush.

"Mara, my dearest friend!" Daemon said and the two kissed, deep and slow in confirmation of her tantalising thoughts.

Her mind lingered on the thought of having both the demon and the God giving her that kind of attention and she bit hard on her lip to keep from making a sound.

"What entertainment have you brought me?" Mara boomed, his words seeming to echo inside her mind and low in her stomach.

"Not so much entertainment, my friend. These are my companions and a special guest just for you," Daemon said. "This is Versalis, the vampire King; Uzo you likely already know," he pointed to Versalis and Uzo nodded once, wary. But Versalis hadn't moved, his lips slightly parted as he stared at the God.

"Next we have Jaia and Kai, vampire twins."

"Twins?" Mara asked, a suggestive tone to his voice as he eyed them.

Jaia and Kai seemed both terrified and enthralled by the God.

"Yes, twins. And then we have Etani."

Mara's eyes found her and she felt herself warming up inside, her breath coming in a slight hitch as Mara moved towards her. He took her hands in two of his, a third stroking her cheek and fourth trailing through her hair. He drew her closer and she quivered at the scent of sandalwood and lavender that tickled her senses.

"I'm sure you recall Ivette and Jeanette," Daemon said, and Mara nodded absently, his gentle touches stroking her skin and hair and she found herself unconsciously moving forward to him and his remaining hands found her hips.

His head bowed and his lips were an inch from hers when Daemon spoke, laughter in his voice.

"Etani is Jeanette's descendent."

The God froze, his breath brushing her lips and she desperately wanted to feel his lips on hers, her entire body battling against itself to reach for him.

"Jeanette had children?" Mara asked her, his eyes a warm honey brown as he studied her face.

"Just the one. Her name was Gennevote."

"How far back was this?" Mara asked.

"There are around forty-five generations," Daemon said, and the God gave in to her need and his lips found hers.

Her entire body melted into the kiss and he pulled her to him, hands finding their way between her protective wings and touching on bare skin at the small of her back.

She whimpered softly against his lips and he smiled against hers, a hand finding its way up to the back of her neck and her hands reached for him.

Without knowing how she had gotten there, she found herself on her back in a pile of cushions, his tall frame laid out beside her with his hands trailing over her, his lips moving against hers.

Daemon coughed and Mara broke the kiss to look at the demon, frowning.

"What? It's not like we're closely related," he said, irritated at the interruption. "I don't imagine you've managed to resist. You're further back than I am." He placed a gentle finger against her lips at her quiet protest and his lips quirked when she licked the finger playfully.

"I have, actually. She won't let me touch her and they're all very protective,"

"I can imagine," Mara said, and his eyes turned back to her as she gave his finger a nip, demanding his attention. "Quite the vixen," Mara crooned, and she tingled all over.

His fingers had found her stomach and he was tugging at her pants, his mouth heavy on hers as the ties came free.

"Mara, we're not here for that," Daemon sounded angry now, but Mara ignored him as his hand delved down the front of her pants and she gasped as he found her, teasing her.

"Come and join us, Daemon, bring a vampire or two with you," Mara muttered against her mouth and she moaned softly against his lips.

"Mara, we're here for your blessing so Etani can get her magic back. She's the one I was trying to create."

Mara paused, though his fingers still moved against her and she grasped his wrist, gasping as he teased and toyed with her, keeping her in pleasure without giving her anything real. "What are you talking about? That fantasy of yours? Daemon, can't this wait? I'm busy."

Daemon seemed to materialise at her side and she whimpered as Mara's hand was yanked free of her pants. Mara looked annoyed as he sat up and her eyes found Kai and Jaia.

Jaia looked livid, Kai only confused and scared. Versalis seemed to have fallen in love, but at Mara's annoyance, her own being grew annoyed at the demon's interruption.

"Think about it, Mara: she's nine hundred, what happened nine hundred years ago?"

Trying to distract Mara, she licked slowly up the side of his throat and he gave a low growl, two hands gripping her hips and jerking her against him to feel his need.

"I don't know, Daemon. Come back later, we're busy."

She had slid her hand slowly up under the pleated, colourful skirt and her nails teased his legs.

"Nine hundred years ago, magic left Faerie and no one knew where it went. That's where it went."

Glancing at him, she found him pointing at her and she grinned, grabbing his wrist and yanking him down into the cushions beside her.

Her lips found his and Mara laughed gently, watching Daemon struggle to keep himself composed as both Mara and her own demonic lust triggered his own. "Now you want me..." he growled, pushing her back, but his eyes burned with need.

A loud slapping sound came from somewhere, but they ignored it, Mara reaching for Daemon's pants while another hand went to her hair and pulled her hair back roughly to make her moan.

"You've got yourself a masochist, that's what you have, Daemon. Why haven't you taken advantage yet? You know how much fun they are."

Mara bowed his head over her and he kissed her hard, catching her lower lip between his teeth and biting firmly.

She whimpered, relishing the pain while a hand found her pants once more. It didn't get any further, Daemon snapping both hands away and shoving himself off the pillows.

"Damnit, Mara listen to me!" Daemon snarled, glaring down at his friend.

"Stop being difficult. She wants it, you can smell it on her. She practically screams sex with every beat of her heart," Mara purred, and she shivered.

Something grabbed her foot and suddenly she was yanked out from under Mara's hands, her back hitting the hard marble floor and her wings jarred.

Looking up, she found Versalis glaring down at her, a large red welt on his face.

"Hi, Versalis," she purred, and his pupils dilated suddenly as her need hit him. Swallowing hard, he grabbed her arm and dragged her to her feet, a second pair of hands gripping her other arm and she glanced at Jaia, his nails digging into her arm painfully.

"Stop this now," Versalis snapped, glaring up at the God.

"Fine, fine. But I get to keep her for a while after I've listened to your story."

"Over my dead body..." Jaia snarled, his hands shaking.

Mara only sighed and crossed his arms with the other two sets on his hips, looking at Daemon. "Fine, if I can't even pleasure the poor creature, talk."

"I managed to create a Creator like no other. When she was born she sucked up all the magic from the Creators when they were in the middle of trying to bring down the human world. She is the reason they failed and now they have that magic back. They are going to try again," Daemon said, and Mara glanced at her; this time she felt no wave of desire and she was coming down fast, wilting in the grip of her friends.

"You did that?" Mara asked.

"No, she did that. But now we need to get her magic back before the Creators can destroy the human world."

"Why not just come here to Faerie and stay? It would be easier," Mara said and threw her a sly smile. The thought of spending years with him had her shivering and she smiled in response, only to have Kai step in front of her and her sexual desire seemed to sputter out like a candle.

"Kai?" she asked, confused that he would be there. He was her child, not a lover.

"Hey, honey, it's okay, just focus on me," Kai said, and she swallowed, staring into his face.

The need faded and she could hear Mara and Daemon talking, but she focused intently on what was before her, searching every inch of his face until finally she felt back to normal, at least mostly.

Mara laughed and her attention flicked over Kai's shoulder, her cheeks flushing as she found Mara approaching, all six arms stretched out for her.

"It's okay, Kai," Daemon said as the vampire turned on the God.

Kai was reluctant to move but as Mara closed the distance to her, she shook off the two restraining arms and met the God, her chin lifting as his head bowed and their lips met.

There was no expanding of her mind; rather, it entirely shut down and everything went black.

Waking slowly, she frowned at the sight of the dome above her covered in lengths of colourful cloth.

Sitting up suddenly, she looked around the room and found the small group of people sitting at a low table she hadn't noticed before. They were all sitting on the cushions, the table only high enough to allow their knees under it comfortably.

Looking to her side at a soft grunt, she found Jaia and she went still, staring at him suspiciously.

He had been asleep, sprawled out beside her with his arms protectively around her middle but he was stirring and looking around groggily.

"What happened?" she demanded, and he squinted at her, grunting something unintelligible. Pushing herself up, she went still and looked down at herself. She had been changed and she wasn't much impressed by the change.

Her breasts had been hitched up far closer to her ears than she had ever wanted them to be, cupped in a silvery metal brassiere that barely covered them at all, patterned with vines and sharp thorns. It crossed up over her chest, enhancing the appearance of her rather spectacular cleavage.

Her skirt seemed to consist of nothing but a single strip of fabric that ran up between her legs and over her pelvic region and backside, held around her hips by a matching silver belt.

Fabric hung from the underside of the brassiere by small loops and trailed down to the ground behind her, leaving her front and sides, including much of her backside, open to the view of others when she walked.

A band was tight around her upper arm, and she found her hands to finally be free, just in time for her to strangle whomever had dressed her.

Her long hair had been combed back, smooth and silky with a band holding it in place, though feeling it she found it to be a delicate silver crown.

Growling, she stalked towards the group and Kai gave a little squeak at the sight of her.

Turning, the men stared at her, her eyes flicking from one stunned face to the next before landing on Mara and his amusement.

"I'm going to rip your ears off!" she snarled, making him laugh.

"Well, I see the temper didn't get bred out of her," Mara said as Versalis stood to stop her and her eyes went to him.

"Touch me and you're next."

He took a step back, but he was clearly, obviously admiring her figure.

Turning on him, she slapped him so hard he was suddenly on the floor and she jerked back, staring at him and then her hand.

Versalis had left a rather large indentation in the ground and he was very clearly, at least temporarily, dead.

"Versalis?" she asked, whimpering softly as she knelt at his side, seeing the side of his skull crushed in where it hit the ground.

"Well, that's unfortunate," Mara said and she glared at him.

"Vampires heal, he'll have a migraine, but he'll be all right," Daemon said, picking out one of the green berry shaped things Mara had been eating.

Cradling Versalis in her arms, she stroked his hair and tried to ignore the disturbing cracks and pops his skull made as his brain swelled and the fluid replenished, pushing the bone out and back into place.

"What are you doing? Who put me in this, and why did I just kill Versalis?" she demanded, looking at the fruit on the table and the little pots of a pale red-brown liquid.

Mara offered her a little bowl of the berries and she took it, looking at them suspiciously.

They were smooth, oval shaped, and hard, but had a soft, fibrous flesh inside when she broke them open.

Sniffing it, she found it pleasantly sweet and refreshing. Slowly she popped it into her mouth, and it crunched as she bit down, a sweet deliciousness filling her mouth.

"Etani recently discovered the joys of fruit," Uzo said happily, drinking the liquid from the little pots.

"What were you before all this?" Mara asked and she looked down as Versalis gasped, his eyes snapping open then slamming shut again as the light scalded its way into his brain.

"My mother was a Celestrial, my father was Lutheral Daewen," she replied, placing her hand gently over Versalis's eyes to help shield them from the dim light in the room.

"Lutheral? Tatialia's boy?"

She nodded, giving Versalis a tight hug in apology, to which he groaned softly.

"You're the Princess they have been hunting?" Mara asked, bemused.

"The runaway? That's me," she sighed.

"Explains why you have so many little friends to try and help you.

You killed him so easily because you have my strength. I assume it would be similar to what you had before?"

"She only retained the abilities of the last twenty or so, from what I can tell," Daemon said.

Taking up one of the little berries, she placed it against Versalis's lips and he bit it, still pouting. "Oh I'm sorry, Versalis, I just lost my temper and didn't realise," she said gently and he lowered her hand enough to glare up at her, then smiled and hid his eyes behind her hand once more.

"You're just lucky she only used one hand. My mother had six, and being slapped like that by three isn't fun," Mara lamented.

Stroking his hair gently, she accepted a cloth and bowl of water from Kai, using it to wash the blood and tissue from his hair.

"We didn't dress you, that is what your clothes became," Uzo said gently and gave her a wicked grin. "If I wasn't almost related to you I might be after you myself,"

She wrinkled up her nose and he laughed, throwing one of the berries at her. She caught it and popped it into her mouth.

"What are these?" she asked, offering Versalis another one.

"Grapes. A human treat we get brought in on occasion," Mara explained. "There is another one I am particularly fond of, a big green ball with red flesh inside, makes your mouth water."

Versalis sat up finally and he held his head in his hands, groaning at the change in position.

Mara offered him a small pile of a strange brown and cream root. "Eat these, it'll help with your pain," he said and Versalis accepted the roots, popping them into his mouth and chewing with a revolted expression.

"What is that?" Etani asked curiously.

"Piper Methysticum. A plant known to relieve pain," Mara said.

"Isn't that a human plant?" she asked, taking a small piece and examining it closely.

"Yes, but it works when we get it brought in." Mara was dismissive, and she contemplated why a God of pleasure would need pain treatment.

The realisation hit her and she flushed, his grin telling her he had followed her line of thought and his wicked stare had her stomach clenching. "Stop that," she said, throwing the plant root at him. He caught it and tossed it back to Versalis, who stuffed it into his mouth and flopped back onto her lap.

"What are you after next?" Mara asked and she glanced at Daemon, who shrugged.

He must have filled the God in while she was out.

"Werewolf. Jeanette married a man named Fenrir, she didn't know he was a werewolf until a few years later and they had a daughter. Gennevote married a dragon named Loco, they had a daughter named Miriela and it goes on for ages," Daemon said, and sipped the drink.

"Who else have you involved in this game of yours?" Mara asked slyly, and Daemon flushed.

"I don't know what you mean," Daemon lied.

"Which of us ancients did you seduce with one of your girls?" Mara elaborated, leaving the demon no room to lie.

"Well, there's Hades, Loki... not *that* Loki, the other one. Related to the Thor boy. Theseus, Spophis, Sobek... Stacius, and then Dominick."

Mara whistled low under his breath, staring at the demon. "What's that? Six Gods, a Nephilim, and a Strigoi? I don't envy you. I doubt you'll make it past Hades. He's been in a right mood ever since Minthe," he stopped and looked at her. "Minthe? I thought it would be the other one."

Daemon snorted. "No way I would have gotten someone like her, she's got a temper worse than all of my girls."

"I didn't know Minthe had a child," Mara said slowly, frowning.

"No, she kept it a secret. I knew things were going bad with Hades so I took Sibbe and we went to the human world."

Etani had lost track of the conversation, frowning at the two. "Wouldn't you be considered a God, Daemon?" she asked suddenly, and Daemon choked.

"I am, but at the time I was going by another name."

"Why?" she asked, curious.

"It was a running joke I had going with Hera, she hates me. You probably know me as Eros."

The room was silent as all eyes turned to Daemon and the news that he was the God of lust.

"Is it really all that surprising?" she asked, and slowly the vampires shook their heads. Even Uzo looked surprised.

Shaking her head, she picked up one of the pots of liquid and took a sip, frowning down at it.

"It's tea," Mara said. "My children make it; it's quite good."

Looking up at him, she swallowed the bitter liquid but the more she thought about it, the more she liked it.

"Your children?" she asked.

"We all have our children. Hecate has the witches, I have mine, though they don't have a name yet. We all have those who worship us."

Etani nodded slowly, trying to imagine humans like him, but it was impossible. She could imagine all forms of mythical creature, but a human who looked like him? Not even remotely, but that made her wonder about the different types of humans and she was left wondering if it was possible.

"Do you?" she asked Daemon and he grinned.

"Of course, I'm much loved."

Snorting, she shook her head and drank the last of her tea before setting the pot down and looking down at Versalis who had been watching her for who knew how long.

"You're so pretty..." he breathed, and she shook her head, Daemon and Mara laughing.

They packed up, preparing to head off to the human world once more, but Mara stopped her before she could leave, four hands catching her around the waist and he drew her back into his chest with warm lips brushing her ear.

"If you fail in your task, little Etani, I'll welcome you back into my home and into my bed just as soon as you come to me. I'll give you pleasures you can never know with any normal man," he breathed, and smiled as she shivered.

His fingers were tantalising against her navel, but then he kissed the side of her head and let go of her, leaving her tingling and aching for him.

Turning, she found he had vanished and she frowned, wondering where he could have gone.

A hand took hers and she found Jaia tentatively pulling her along, and she allowed him to, the others waiting.

Stepping out of the dome, Daemon pulled them through into the human world and they stepped out into pelting rain.

25

WEREWOLVES AND DRAGONS

Stepping out into rain was unexpected and her wings moved automatically to shield her from it, leaving her to smirk at Daemon. Kai huddled in beside her at one side with Uzo at the other. Jaia didn't seem to care, but Daemon glared at them all resentfully that he was being left out.

At least there wasn't a lot of fabric to her outfit to get wet. She took Kai's hand and they followed after the sullen demon and continued deeper into the dripping forest.

"Where are we?" Kai called out, sticking close to her side.

"Most of these places don't have names. But we are in the birth-place of the werewolves. The humans here don't speak Common, so there's no point in trying to communicate with them. But they're an interesting looking bunch."

He wasn't wrong, and she found herself distracted by the universal beauty of the humans. They had deep fawn coloured skin and dark eyes, dark hair, and most of the men had facial hair. They wore bright colours, the women in long flowing skirts that Etani immediately wanted.

"Are they aware of mythicals?" she asked as she watched a small village from the ridge above.

"Yes, mostly. I don't think they are that aware of the spectrum of species, but they do know we exist."

"Can I go down there?" she breathed, desperately wanting to see some of them up close.

"No, we're looking for a werewolf," Daemon said, but she ignored him.

Flicking water off one wing at the demon, she leapt off the ridge and while she didn't fly, her wings stretched out and slowed her fall.

The people in the village saw her and their language was musical, animated.

She heard the growling and knew she was going to be in trouble, but she wanted to see. She mustn't have seen all that much of the human world; she had never seen anything except the soft whites and creams of the humans near and around Ayathian's continent.

But these humans looked entirely different, huddling under rooves or holding up little canes with a circular sheets on top to protect them from the easing rain.

Landing gently in the soft mud, she started towards the people and they for her, both sides equally fascinated by the other.

When they touched her arm, she found them to be warm with rough hands and wide, white smiles.

Up close she was astonished to find such perfectly smooth skin with barely an imperfection amongst them. They spoke almost constantly in that musical language and Etani shook her head, not understanding.

Taking one young woman by the face, she studied the young beauty whose cheeks had turned red at the pleasure.

Slowly, she leant forward and pressed a kiss against the woman's forehead, and she giggled. At least that was a universal sound she could understand.

She lingered there with the humans for only thirty minutes or so, finally pointing to the skirt and then at herself and a small group of women left and returned with a pile of clothing. Etani was delighted and pulled the clothes on, twirling to feel her skirt fluttering up around her thighs.

Reaching up under her new skirt, she wriggled out of the metal skirt and offered the silver to them in exchange and they took it along with the fabric, chatting away happily at the precious metal.

Smiling, she waved goodbye to the humans and headed back out of the village and back up to the waiting vampires.

She rather liked the way her skirt moved around her calves, made of a large number of colourful strips of fabric stitched together and then attached to a wide belt that tied at her side. It moved beautifully around her, and when twirled, it formed a vivid circle around her. The colours were perfect, browns and deep greens interjected with a soft cream and dark red.

Her top only just reached below her ribcage, leaving her midriff bare, but it was a rich brown colour and hung off her shoulders.

Only Kai and Uzo remained when she reached them and she tilted her head, curious.

"They went on," Kai said gently, staring at her new outfit with a slight smile. "It suits you," he said as he took her hand and they set off into the forest.

The rain picked up again as they travelled north, their fast pace allowing them to catch up with the others within an hour. Much to her surprise, a stranger sat with them and he beamed at their appearance.

"Is this her?" he asked cheerfully, and Versalis nodded.

"Etani, this is Benjamin. He's graciously offered to share his magic with you."

Immediately she was suspicious and she glanced at Kai who was staring at the man with narrowed eyes. "Why?" Etani asked after a pause.

"In exchange for a future favour should I ever need one," Benjamin said.

She tilted her head and studied the man. He was a native, the same rich skin tone and warm smile, the same colourful clothing, and yet he seemed hairier than the rest. "You know I am not a Fae, you can't hold me to a deal," she said warily as she approached him.

"I know that. But you seem honourable."

Daemon snorted and she shot him a glance, her eyes turning to Benjamin.

"That's all? A future favour if you ever need one?"

Benjamin nodded and she finally shrugged.

He smiled brightly and pushed himself to his feet, approaching her with arms outstretched.

Silently, she closed the distance to him, and his lips were warm on hers, soft and rough all at once.

She felt the gentle brush of fur on her soul and something settled deep inside her, warm and safe.

Nothing about her had changed, her mind didn't warp, and she felt oddly disappointed by that.

"What is that?" she asked after he had stepped back and she turned inwards to the shadowed thing.

Benjamin frowned, looking at her.

"You feel it? You feel the wolf?"

"Oh, that could be bad..." Uzo said nervously. "When is the next full moon?"

"Two weeks," Benjamin said, his eyes both cautious and fascinated. "I've never met a female werewolf. I wonder what you would look like..."

She shivered as the beast gave an odd rumble at her touch, fur thick and soft, muscles tight and yet relaxed. "I will turn into a wolf?" she asked, snapping back into the present as one large, vivid blue eye opened and she felt her mouth begin to water at the smell of the man in front of her. Watching him, his pupils dilated at something she couldn't understand, and he grinned at her.

"Careful, you'll wake her up. Vampires don't taste good," he laughed.

Shaking her head, she kept herself as far from the wolf as was possible within her own mind.

"What's up next for you?" he asked, and she inhaled sharply at a hypnotic scent that hit her body like a blow, the wolf lifting her head to sniff at the air.

Benjamin had a lascivious grin on his face, and she realised he had tapped into his wolf to release pheromones that her body reacted to, the sensations very similar to what she had felt with Mara.

Moving upwind of him, she glared and he laughed.

Kai looked confused, but she only shook her head at his questioning glance.

"Dragon. I can only hope it will be as easy as this."

"Take jewels. A large ruby or something," Benjamin offered, shifting until he was upwind of her and grinning widely.

It hit her again and she found herself suddenly struggling with the wolf, trying to force her back down again as she snapped at the shoving.

She panted softly, Daemon frowned and stepped between them, grabbing her arm and pressing a cloth against her mouth.

It didn't help and she threw him off her, her joints aching as though she had strained them all at the same time.

Someone swore and Benjamin grunted in pain, the scent washing away in an instant to leave her able to breathe.

"Etani? Listen to my voice and focus. You are not a wolf."

Looking up, she found Uzo in front of her, tapping her cheek to get her attention and the wolf snarled, her own lip curling in response.

"Come on, you know you're not. Just thinking about what is happening, you're not an animal."

Someone was laughing painfully, but she focused on Uzo and what he was saying, the wolf reluctantly pressing down into a crouch.

"I'm okay..." she breathed and Uzo smiled at her, pulling her into a tight hug.

"I'm sorry, okay? I wanted to see her change, I promise I won't do it again."

Etani turned at the voice, clutching a fistful of Uzo's shirt and pressing it to her nose.

Daemon had Benjamin in a headlock, his face red and clutching at his stomach where he had been hit. He was grinning at her with clear desire in his eyes.

"You can't deny she'd make a pretty wolf," he said.

Eventually the werewolf was let go and ordered to stay downwind of her at all times, and the tension eased.

They didn't linger long after that, everyone eager to get away from the area.

"What are we going to do?" Etani asked after they had passed through another rip and the rain was suddenly gone.

Stepping away from the group, her wings flicked to rid themselves of the water and she turned to her friends, smiling at their being soaked while she had remained relatively dry.

"The mongrel was right about one thing, a gift will do the job," Uzo said as he took off his jacket and wrung it out onto the grass.

"Where do we get a gem that would tempt a dragon?" Kai asked, waving his own jacket before him to try and dry it. Jaia had spun his, water flying out in an arc.

Daemon looked like a drowned puppy and was moody, but he did at least seem to be thinking. Then, he smiled, and without a word, vanished through a tear in reality, and left them alone.

She looked to Kai in concern, the vampire staring at the spot the demon had vanished through, a small crease between his eyebrows before he turned his attention to her.

"What do we do if he doesn't come back?" Kai asked slowly, and she frowned, realising that unless Uzo was able to get help from another demon or a gatekeeper, they were trapped in an unknown place. They might be a year's walk from Ayathian if they were even on the same part of the world.

"I don't think he will abandon us," Uzo said gently.

He was right; the demon returned in only a few minutes and he was laughing, a shout coming from inside the portal, and they got a glimpse of a long hallway before it zipped shut and the voice was gone.

All eyes turned to Daemon and from under his coat he drew out an enormous ruby.

"Where did you get that from?" Etani asked, wondering, her breath sucking in as she stared greedily at the ruby. She wanted it so badly it hurt, and she didn't understand her sudden urge to jump on the demon and take it from him.

"Ayathian vault," Daemon said with a wide grin.

She laughed, imagining the fury and indignation of Alaric when he found out they had stolen one of his rubies.

"I don't even know what to say," Uzo said, staring at the pretty thing.

The twins were smiling, Versalis was frowning but seemed happy enough.

"Alaric is going to skin you alive," she laughed, taking it and looking it over curiously. It was a very pretty red colour, polished and cut to perfection. It was lovely, really.

Offering it back to Daemon, she met his grin with her own and they set off in the direction of a mountain to the west.

The cave was weirdly easy to find and she could only assume it was because most people weren't stupid enough to try and annoy a dragon like they were.

Inside the cave, they followed along a large passage that led downwards. Around midway down they came across skeletons and scorched armour, some of them having marks of enormous teeth.

They grew nervous around that point and Daemon toyed with the ruby, ready to throw it at the dragon if they needed to.

The passage was fairly well-lit from behind at the opening, and from a warm red glow below, allowing them to see when the passage ended and a large cavern was filled with a mass of jewels.

The rumour about dragons being hoarders wasn't wrong and she stared around at the sheer mass of gold, jewels, and precious stones the dragon had collected.

To their left, a post stood and hanging from a cuff was a single arm from elbow to fingers. It looked fairly old and the small hand suggested it had once belonged to a woman.

Kai squeaked when he followed her attention and she turned back to the cavern, searching for the dragon, her mind reaching out but she found nothing.

"Is he not here?" she asked finally, stepping away from the group to peer around a large pile of coins. The others had spread out, searching, but she felt nothing.

"He is here," a voice whispered in her ear and she spun, coming face to sternum with an enormously tall man.

Looking up slowly, she found a pair of ruby red, slitted eyes, and a wide, fanged grin staring back at her. His fingers caught her around the throat and hoisted her up off the ground, his grin growing wider as the vampires moved to help.

A single wave of his hand was all it took to stop them, a line of fire bursting up between them and his eyes returned to her, watching as her cheeks flushed and she tugged at his fingers.

When they didn't budge, she pulled herself up and planted her foot against his chest, using her legs to help push herself back from him. It only aided in tearing the skin of her throat and she whimpered, stopping that line of escape.

He was wearing long black pants and black boots, his chest bare though massive spikey shoulder guards stuck out up around his head and trailed down the tops of his arms to protect his hands. She hadn't realised his fingers were so sharp with the guards.

There was no denying the man was incredibly attractive, his chest muscled without being bulky, with glittering silver hair that reached to the middle of his back. Grey faun skin and a strong jaw added to his rugged attraction. She might even have fancied him if he hadn't been choking her.

"What are you doing here, little winged vampire?" he asked, and smiled as she gave him a hard kick to the stomach. He didn't so much as twitch and her foot burned.

"Let go!" she snarled, using his belt as leverage to keep herself from choking.

He seemed to be enjoying her struggle more than wanting to hurt her in any real way.

Tilting his head slightly to allow his silver-white hair to fall away from the left half of his face, he studied her with both eyes. "Pretty thing, aren't you..." he said thoughtfully, his eyes turning from her to her friends who had moved to circle the dragon though they were unable to get any closer. "And you have a collection of pretty friends."

He let her go and she landed hard on her feet, staggering only to have him grasp the front of her shirt, and he bent down to her level. "Why would so many pretty things come wandering into my home?"

"We've come to make a deal," she said, wiping at the blood on her neck though the wounds had already healed.

His brows lifted in a note of surprise. "What kind of deal?" he asked curiously.

"We have a jewel to exchange for magic," she said and motioned to Daemon.

The demon lifted the gem out from under his coat and the dragon's slitted pupils thinned even further as he saw it. "Is that right? What use have I for such a little bauble?"

Frowning slightly, she studied him and then smiled, prying his fingers off her shirt and taking a step back from him. "Don't try and fool us, dragon. You seem to be lacking in the department of rubies."

His eyes snapped to her, narrowing at her attitude. When he reached for her, she danced back and out of his reach, though that only seemed to amuse him more than anything.

"Who are you?" he asked curiously, taking a step forward to try and catch her again, but again she evaded him.

"Etani Daewen," she said, and the dragon paused, squinting at the name.

"Daewen? That Fae's spawn?" he frowned down at her, taking her in and coming to some conclusion. "I don't like liars."

"I'm not lying. Lutheral was my father, but a Lich stole my magic and now I need to get it back."

He looked doubtful and he tried to catch her for a third time, barely missing her as she skirted him and the flames while trying to avoid slipping on coins. "A Lich stole Fae magic? How is that even possible?" he looked irritated that he couldn't catch her, studying the way she moved.

"A Lich who also happens to have a hold on me."

The dragon growled in understanding and his hand seemed to vanish, then appeared again, and everything went dark as his fingers curled around her face.

She yelped as he tugged her closer and his armour grazed her jaw as he leant down to sniff her shoulder and hair.

"You smell like a newling vampire, and a number of other things. Is that werewolf?" He lifted her just enough that she was on the very tips of her feet, gripping hard onto his wrist in case he pulled her any higher.

"Let me go!" she yelled, her voice muffled by his palm against her face. Growling, she pulled herself up using her arms and swung forward, wrapping her legs around his arm.

He grunted and straightened, lifting his arm up to study her clinging to it. "Strange creature you are. Why are you here if you need your magic back?"

"I need your magic!" she yelled, unsure how well he could hear her.

"My magic?"

"Yes, your magic. Dragon magic."

Finally he let go of her head but his free hand caught her by the shin and pulled her from his arm.

Immediately she reached for her skirt and held it up front and back, though thankfully the metal brassiere held her breasts in place when her shirt fell up around her chin.

She blushed when she found him looking at her legs, but she was out of ideas. The dragon was going to do whatever he felt like doing.

"Tell me why I should give you dragon magic," he said, his eyes trailing down over her exposed torso and lingering at her chest with a slight quirk to his lips.

"Well, I assume you like pretty things, your gold and gems. If you don't help, all of that will vanish."

His smile faded and his eyes found hers, her face turning red as blood rushed from the rest of her body.

Letting go of the back of her skirt, she heaved herself up and curled her hand around his forearm, allowing her to tuck her skirt between her legs for modesty.

"Little monkey," he purred and she lifted two fingers. The rude gesture made him laugh, but he didn't let go.

Tilting her head back to look at him upside down, she glared at him. "If you don't give me your magic, all of this world will be torn down by the Creators and you will lose everything, *if* you manage to flee to Faerie in time."

He studied her face carefully, considering her. "The Creators lost their magic a long time ago," he countered, and she nodded.

"Yes, but they have it back now and are gearing up to come here. Everything will be gone and most of us with it. You know we all can't fit in Faerie."

Letting go of her leg without warning, he wrapped his free arm around her waist and as she fell against him, he trapped her there, looking down at her.

"You assume I care which world I live in," he said quietly, smiling at her discomfort.

"You care about your hoard. There is no gold or jewels in Faerie. They all came from the humans, so what will you collect then?" she countered.

"Pretty creatures like you and your friends," he said, and his grin grew wide as her triumph faded.

"Creatures die, but gold is forever so long as you look after it. You would give up your gold to run to Faerie like a coward?"

His grin vanished and he glared at her. "I'm no coward, little girl," he snarled, squeezing her against him until she cried out and an ominous crack sounded. He released her as she screamed, feeling the rib shattering inside her.

Gasping, she hung limp in his arms and his eyes went to Daemon.

"You're an ancient, aren't you? How are you involved in all this?"

the dragon asked as he cupped the back of her head, keeping it from falling back.

"She's telling the truth; she needs your magic," Daemon sounded tense, the ruby gripped in his clenched fist.

"Tell me why, and I will consider what you say. Why does she need her magic back?"

"Because she is the reason the Creators lost their magic. She took it all and when the Lich banished it, it returned to its owners. We are trying to create what she was before. She was a creator and she was death."

The dragon looked down at her as she lifted her head, the bone knitting back together and whatever organs he had punctured repairing. "Is that right?" he breathed, and she looked up at him, frowning at his tone.

"You can have the ruby for a trace hint of your magic. That's all I need," she offered, but he had begun to smile.

"No, I will exchange you *temporarily* for the ruby, but for my magic I will insist you return to me once you have your powers back in full."

The room went silent as they considered what he could possibly mean.

"What does that entail?" she asked warily, and his grin seemed to stretch from ear to ear, but he didn't answer her question.

"Do you agree? Your freedom now for the ruby, and your return for my magic. We'll say you will return to me for three months every year for the rest of eternity," he bargained, and she narrowed her eyes.

"Three days," she countered.

"Two months."

"One week."

"Two months," he repeated, and she gritted her teeth.

"One month," she said, and he laughed.

"One month a year for eternity, you will come to me here," he said finally, and she nodded, knowing she would regret it.

He bowed his head to hers and his lips were burning hot as they met hers.

The wolf screamed inside her as something enormous grew out of the shadows in her soul, a furry and feathered body and massive wings, a large form and trailing tail.

She didn't know when she had kissed him back, the beast inside her calling for him, but finally she forced herself away and he laughed, setting her on her feet.

"You are a fascinating creature. Very well, you may go. You will return to me within a month of your magic being returned," he said, and the encircling fire faded, his hand reaching for the ruby.

Daemon stepped forward and placed it in the outstretched hand, his eyes on hers as she backed away and into the arms of Kai, who poked at her bruised ribs to ensure the bones had set.

"Goodbye for now, little Creator Princess," the dragon said, and flames burst up around him, his tall frame vanishing into nothing. Immediately she turned to Kai and threw herself into his arms, his grip on her painfully tight but welcome and they left the cave quickly in case he decided to come back and mess with them again.

Outside of the cave, she sank to the ground and simply tried to breathe through the fear and stress of the encounter, her head spinning as she tried to settle herself down with so many changes going on inside her.

"It's like with the werewolf, there is a dragon," she breathed, relieved somewhat by the gentle stroking of her hair.

"It's almost like when she was a Fae," Jaia said, irritation in his tone.

"Not exactly. Then it was an addiction, now it's just the desire to collect her. She's powerful," Uzo said, his hand coming down on her shoulder.

She didn't feel powerful; she felt weak and yet she revelled in the magic that was burning inside her, scorching new pathways in her brain and leaving her tingling.

It felt good to be powerful once more.

"How is it he was so much stronger when I have Mara's strength?" she asked.

"Dragons can neutralise magic when they are in physical contact. That's why he kept trying to catch you. As soon as he touched you, it made you only barely stronger than a vampire, which was the last physiological change," Daemon explained

Shaking her head in confusion, she looked up at Kai and he kissed her forehead.

"Seven down," Kai said gently, and she sighed.

"Forty-three left," she said miserably.

They gave her time to recover, but they knew it was time to move on. Any wasted time was a risk and they were already on borrowed time.

"Why do you think they haven't already pulled this world down?" Etani asked as she fixed her clothing, shaking her head at the offered jacket.

"They will take time to get ready. Bringing down this world isn't as easy as strolling along and ripping down a curtain. It takes preparation, organisation and a massing of power," the demon explained.

"Do you suppose we could delay it somehow? Kill some of them on our way through?" she asked, and Daemon frowned, thinking.

"If they weren't so protected then yes, but I think everyone will be watching them and getting to them might be difficult. We can certainly look into it when we go there for a faun."

"Are the faun aligned?" Jaia asked.

"Generally they are Summer, so it will be dangerous and we will need to be careful."

"Summer? Great..." she said with a scowl and Daemon laughed, catching her hand and pulling her closer to him.

"They won't care much about you right now. You're not interesting enough."

She growled, but he only smirked and they joined hands, allowing him to pull them back into Faerie.

26

FAUNS, NAGA, SHIFTERS, AND REPTILES

Summer was beautiful no matter what time of year it was in the human world, all bright greens and colourful flowers. Little fairies and butterflies fluttered around in the grass, but Etani knew better than to fall for the prettiness of the place. The Summer Court was just as ruthless as Winter.

Looking around, she moved away from the group to try and get her bearings, her eyes finally turning upwards to the sky and following the clean cut line that marked the divide between Summer and the Heathen lands.

They were very close to the Heathen quarter and the memory of the spider attempting to trap her made her shiver.

"What about the hunt?" Uzo asked nervously; his presence there made him a spy in the eyes of Summer.

"If they come I suggest you skip out. We are unwelcome, but you will be captured," Daemon explained, his tone somewhat anxious.

"Aren't you Winter?" she asked and he shook his head.

"The ancients are neutral in most cases. Most of us come and go as we please and would dare either Court to try and stop us. You shouldn't be bothered if you stay near me."

Making their way through the Court, they found it rather

disturbing how quickly they came across a small group of faun sitting around and playing music in a little circle.

They were all too happy to help when asked simply if someone would kindly share their magic with her, and she was suspicious of them all, not understanding why they would agree without explanation. Was it just lucky or were they being guided?

She didn't know, but she accepted the offer and the tall faun moved towards her, naked with thick fur starting just below his navel.

His kiss was gentle and again she felt no physical or mental changes, though the two inside her had calmed significantly and her own pleasure at gaining more power began to grow.

He gave her more than she needed and she took it in greedily, wanting it.

After he had broken the kiss, he smiled at her and traced a finger along her jaw. She smiled slyly and shook her head at the invitation.

She knew exactly what they were inviting her to do and she wasn't having any of it.

The fauns laughed and the group turned away, still worried by the sheer ease of their path.

"Did no one find that too easy?" she asked finally, glancing back at the fauns who had begun to dance.

"It was too easy. I think we need to leave," Uzo said cautiously, peering around, but there was no sign of anyone watching them.

Regardless of their fears being true or not, the group fled through to the human world and the rip closed behind them, leaving them in the darkness of night.

The smell hit her first and she turned on Daemon, her eyes wide in realisation.

He grinned at her and she gave a cry before she sprinted for the trees, the group following along behind her. Daemon, however, was enjoying her surprise.

Bursting through the underbrush, Weorene stood before her and she shrieked, a woman's voice shrieking in return and the flame beauty of Nayishma spun around, her eyes alarmed before going wide.

Etani ran at her and tackled the Queen to the ground, hugging her as tightly as she dared.

"Yish!" she cried and pulled the woman up into a sitting position, hugging her again tightly.

The group slowed as they realised what had happened and Nayishma laughed in surprise, hugging her friend back tightly.

"What are you all doing here?" the beauty asked, frowning as she got a better look at Etani. "What happened to you?"

"Epharis." She waved it off and grinned, taking the woman's hands and squeezing them. "We came looking for Naga magic, I didn't know we were coming here!"

She turned on Daemon and he was grinning, watching the two with amusement.

She wasn't about to complain as she clung to her friend and then noticed another woman. She was as soft as Nayishma was warm and her eyes were wide in surprise.

Her eyes were a warm, golden brown and her hair was a rich pink-purple. She was absolutely stunning, her lips pulled up into a confused half smile and as she turned, Etani saw that she had six webbed points to her ears.

"Mermaid?" Etani asked immediately and the woman smiled warmly, though she looked a little defensive.

"This is Adella, she's my partner," Nayishma said and Etani's eyes immediately narrowed on the mermaid.

She dragged her eyes down the woman's slender, graceful form and then back up again. "I suppose she'll have to do," Etani said finally and Nayishma snorted her amusement.

"Glad we have your approval," Nayishma said and Etani smiled.

"What are the odds of you having a shapeshifter here?" Daemon asked, watching the mermaid with curiosity.

"Relatively high, why do you ask?" Nayishma asked, her lips turned down in a frown at his attention on her love.

"That could deal with three in a row. Naga, shapeshifter and reptilian," Daemon said, his eyes on Adella's feet.

"Stop staring, Daemon, it's creepy," Etani snapped and he blinked, looking away.

"I haven't seen a mermaid on land since Ferrand," he said as explanation, and Adella smiled, her cheeks a soft pink.

"What do you need these creatures for?" the mermaid asked in a softly sweet voice.

"It's a fairly long story, but the gist is... I need magic or this world is going to be vanished. So far we have obtained eight of the fifty we need. Hey, we're almost a fifth of the way through," she said to the men behind her and they didn't seem as happy with the news as she did.

"This is Daemon, the demon responsible for the mess that is my life, my father's—" She paused, glancing at the man in question. He was more than that to her, more than just a family friend. "My uncle, Uzo," she said, the man's cheeks flushing with pleasure. "You know Kai. Yish, that's his brother, Jaia." She pointed to each man in question and aside from Kai, they all waved awkwardly. Kai glared at Nayishma.

"How long have you two been seeing each other?" she asked, and Adella blushed.

"A few months," Nayishma said, her chin lifting.

Etani narrowed her eyes at her friend.

"She nice?"

"Very."

"If you hurt my Nayishma I will scale and eat you," she said to the mermaid, who looked more than a little horrified.

"Etani!" Nayishma cried, though she was amused. "Etani is the one who brought me back to life."

Understanding filled the mermaid's eyes and she swallowed.

"I would never dream of hurting her. She is precious to me."

"Are you intending to marry her?" Etani demanded.

Nayishma choked but Adella nodded and Etani nodded in return.

"Good girl," she said and then smiled at Nayishma. "Oh calm down, I'm allowed to be protective of my Yish,"

"Yish?" Adella giggled and Nayishma turned on her, the mermaid slinking back with a fluid grace.

"So you need three? I'm sure we can collect them. Why don't you stay for dinner while we hunt them all down?"

Etani nodded eagerly and the group headed inside, the palace having changed very little in the time since she had been there.

The three that had been collected were an odd bunch, the Naga being the guard who had assisted her on her visit with Izziah, the shapeshifter being a very confused looking young woman with a mass of curly brown hair and green eyes, the reptilian being Yhiss, Nayishma's lady in waiting.

Etani went to Yhiss and hugged her tightly, the woman happy to see her again.

"You smell different," Yhiss said gently.

"After all this is over, I'll explain better," she said, and stepped back to address the trio. "You have all been called here to provide a favour for me. I am the Princess of Winter and when I am back to myself you will be entitled to one favour in return should you ever wish to accept it. Should you choose to refuse, I'll find someone else." She looked at the shapeshifter, who looked ready to bolt. "Except for you, it's not easy to find your kind. My favour is simple, I require you to impart me with a sliver of your magic. That's all. Your returned favour may be anything you ask, within reason."

The Naga and the shapeshifter exchanged a look, but Yhiss simply nodded her agreement without question.

"This favour, it could be anything?" the young woman asked.

"Within reason. I will not perform sexual favours, but generally outside of that, yes."

"What if I asked you to kill someone?" the woman countered.

A low, dark chuckle sounded from the various people around her who knew her.

"I would accept that. However your favour will have to wait until after I am back to my powers."

The shapeshifter shrugged and all eyes turned to the Naga.

"Did you have anything to do with the Queen being placed on the throne?" he asked.

She studied him for several long moments before she smiled. "I thought it would be beneficial to my eventful escape if Nayishma was on the throne," she lied, leaving out the involvement of Alaric.

The Naga nodded once and glanced at his fellows, the young girl looking horrified by the news that Etani had been involved in the death of the King.

"We must do this in a particular order, just to be safe," she said, nodding to the Naga. He smiled stiffly as he stepped forward.

He had a human torso, yet up close she realised his skin was made up of tiny scales and that made his lips oddly smooth and cool when they met hers.

The wash of magic left her skin tingling and she gasped. The physical change was minor, her skin seeming to ripple as long stretches changed to form smooth scales. It made her skin feel hard on those areas, but it was difficult to notice the difference if one didn't look closely.

Drawing back from him, she panted gently though she calmed down in only a minute, her eyes going to the young woman.

She looked scared.

"What do I have to do?" the woman asked.

"It's simple," Yhiss said quietly. "All you have to do is touch lips and will some of your ability into her. That part of yourself that you tap into to change, just feed a little of that into the Princess."

The girl looked even more scared, but she stepped forward and her lips were warm, but she broke away quickly, her eyes huge.

"I can't, I don't know how."

Etani frowned, not having considered the possibility of their coming across someone who had never shared their magic before.

It was common among lovers and siblings, but this girl seemed to have neither.

"Do you not have siblings or a partner?" Etani asked curiously and the girl shook her head.

"That could be problematic," Uzo said slowly, watching the show with a professional interest though he had remained close at her side since she introduced him to Yish.

"You simply have to want it," Kai said as he stepped forward and she met Jaia's eyes over Kai's head. He glared at her though she wasn't sure what his issue was.

She turned her attention to the girl and Kai, who was talking to her quietly, and she moved away to join Nayishma and Adella.

"What if you can't get her to do it?" Adella asked softly.

"We'll have to find someone who can," Etani replied and frowned, looking over to the clustered group trying to get the girl to share.

"I never really considered that someone might not know how. I just assumed everyone could."

Nayishma shrugged, chewing on her lower lip.

"What will happen to me if you don't get your magic back?" Nayishma asked, and Etani looked at her.

"You will remain as is until you die and your soul will go to the spirit world to await your next life."

"Can she die of old age?" Adella asked, and Etani shook her head.

"No, Nayishma will never age past the point of death. Mermaids are ageless, aren't they?"

"Unless we choose to age," the mermaid replied, and she looked between the pair.

"Well, don't do that and you two will have an eternity together."

The couple exchanged a happy glance and Etani turned away, hiding her flash of jealousy.

She didn't desire Nayishma like that, but there was a part of her that wanted to keep the Gorgon Queen to herself. It was a stupid feeling and she crushed it down, refusing to give in when her friend was so clearly happy.

"Etani?" Kai called out and she left the two to join the little group around the young woman.

"I want to try again," she said gently, and Etani nodded.

The second kiss left no result, nor the third, and Etani grew irritable.

"What if I bite her?" Etani finally asked, unsure of her sudden anger at the young woman.

"That would work, but you don't want to start forcing magic. It works better if it's consensual," Daemon said, frowning at the anxious young woman.

"Do you consent to my taking your magic through a bite?" she asked, and the girl nodded slowly.

Shrugging at the demon, she took the girl's arm and her teeth slid through the soft skin like butter.

Closing her eyes at the rancid taste of blood that was not Uzo's, she drank and her body sang.

The girl, however, screamed, and Etani jerked back, lips crimson.

"What's going on?" Uzo demanded, the girl clutching at her arm.

"It burns!" The girl screamed, but Etani tuned her out, focusing instead on what it felt like to be a shapeshifter. It was like a secret she held within herself and it was both similar and entirely different to the others inside her. It was odd to think about how many forms she could take.

Blinking, she found Yhiss before her and the reptilian woman smiled at her, rough mouth without lips and a flash of warmth through her. The air suddenly felt pleasantly warm but she wasn't sure why.

"You keep us all alive," Yhiss demanded in a whisper, and Etani nodded.

She could hear the girl's screaming, but she ignored it as she thought about what she could do.

With a smile, she willed herself to change and so her form changed, her mind going to that of her twin and the little black cat she had always become.

Nayishma shrieked at the slow, graceful change and then Etani found herself looking up at the friends who were suddenly giants. She could hear everything, from the rapid heartbeat of the girl, to a soft squeaking that turned her head, ears moving of their own accord in the direction the sound was coming from.

Her tail flicked and then she curled it around her little black paws and she watched. The room was in uproar; the girl had fainted and Uzo scolded her, demanding she regain her own form again.

She understood completely why Letari had chosen that form; people adored her.

Uzo reached for her and she leapt back, hissing her anger that he would dare touch her.

He swore as she bolted and three sets of boots came after her.

She was small, she could hide.

She darted under a dresser and then crouched there, watching the men peering under and trying to coax her out. She didn't want to come out, she didn't like the noise.

She growled and swiped at a hand and Daemon swore, his hand bleeding as he withdrew it and he peeked under the dresser.

"Lift it up, I'll grab her," Daemon growled, and she narrowed her eyes at him in return.

"She'll just bolt, won't she? Kai come here," Uzo called.

A new set of feet joined the three she could see and Kai's face appeared, his eyes wide as he saw her.

"Come on, sweetheart, come out here and I'll keep you safe."

She stared at him for a long moment, trying to decide if he was lying or not. He seemed to be telling the truth and she watched as he reached a hand towards her but didn't try and grab her like the others.

He smelt wonderful and she nearly collapsed as his gentle fingers found her head. She understood why cats liked to be petted and slowly she inched forward.

He scooped her up and she settled into his arms as he stood, the ground seeming to be a thousand miles away.

A hand grabbed her, and she yowled as she was hoisted up by the scruff of her neck.

Curling herself into a little ball, she found herself face to face with the demon, her tail flicking in irritation before she tucked it up under her belly protectively.

"Change back, right now," he demanded, and her ears flattened back against her head as she hissed at him, baring her sharp little teeth.

"Don't you take that tone with me, young lady! Change back right this instant!"

He seemed to be very angry and she wilted a little, putting on her best pleading look.

She gave a tiny, hopeful mew, more question than anything else. She was trying to get his pity so he would let her go. He grunted, glaring

"You can try all you want to be the cute little kitten, but it's not going to work on me."

Kai appeared at his side, his hands cupping up under her rump to take the pressure off her scruff. "Put her down, Daemon, you'll hurt her," he sounded genuinely distressed at the sight of her and she took full advantage, turning big blue eyes on him and mewling pitifully.

It worked like a charm, and he slapped daemon's hand until the demon let her go.

Turning a smug kitty smile on Daemon, she settled into Kai's arms, licking at her furry lips and kneading his jacket.

"You're lucky this time," Daemon said, disgusted at her manipulation of the vampire.

Uzo and Jaia owned the other two pairs of legs that had followed her and she glared at the two of them as they approached.

"What happened to the shapeshifter?" Daemon asked.

"Dead. It seems like Etani is venomous."

She looked past them to the girl who had been lifted onto a stretcher and then at Nayishma who had spotted her and headed her way.

"Etani stop playing games," she scolded.

Etani glared at her, stubborn to the end.

"Don't scold her," Kai snapped and she was smug once more.

Nayishma glared at him, but he ignored her and instead turned to Uzo.

"Does she have to change back?"

"Not until we get to the next mythical," Uzo said, looking down at her and smirking when she yawned in his face. He gave her chin a scratch and suddenly she was purring, having no idea how it had started.

"She makes for a pretty cat at least."

Etani decided to ignore him and Nayishma sighed, motioning them all through to the dining room.

In order to give Kai freedom to eat, she had climbed her way up his shoulder and settled in close up his neck, glaring at Daemon whenever he threw her a disapproving glance.

She liked being a cat, so she was staying as one.

She rather liked being on Kai's shoulder, too; he smelt good and his height meant she could see more than she had ever seen before at her own height. It left her wondering what it might be like to be as tall as the dragon or Alaric.

Kai fed her bits of the strange bug meat when Daemon wasn't watching and it was really delicious, finally filling her, and she dozed against his neck. They had been talking, but she chose to ignore them.

It was only a few hours later when they decided to spend the night and Etani went with Kai after the Queen had bid them a fond farewell and kissed her head, staying close and exploring while he bathed. He used a comb to brush out her silky fur. Then she settled herself on his chest to sleep.

27

WATER SPIRITS AND THE NINE-TAILED FOX

When they woke the next morning, she yawned and walked up his chest to tap him on the nose, his eyes snapping open and she clung to his shirt as he sat upright, surprised by the touch.

Looking down at her, he laughed and curled his hand around her middle to lift her off him and onto the bed. "I wish I could become a cat," he said wistfully, and she tilted her head, thinking. He would make an interesting cat.

He changed after a while and she was scooped up into his arms as they headed out, finding Daemon and Uzo already up and preparing to leave.

Daemon glared at the sight of her and she hissed in response, calmed by Kai rubbing her ears.

It felt amazing and her eyes slid shut, enjoying the attention.

"It felt good to sleep in a real bed," Kai said gently, his clothes washed overnight and looking clean for the first time in ages.

Etani turned to Uzo and sniffed at his fingers as he scratched her head, leaning so far into it that she nearly fell out of Kai's arms when the Fae stopped and turned away.

Daemon snorted at her near fall and they returned to packing.

"Nayishma left you clothes for when you decide to join us again," Daemon said moodily and looked up as Jaia joined them, yawning and looking confused and rumpled.

"Are we leaving already?" he asked, scratching at his neck as he eyed her in Kai's arms, his lips pursed though she didn't know what he was thinking.

"As soon as Versalis decides to get his worthless arse out of bed," Daemon snapped.

"It's not worthless," Versalis said, looking disturbingly perky for that early in the day.

"As worthless as the rest of them," Daemon quipped.

Etani leapt down onto the table and stalked for a cloth wrapped hunk of some sort of meat, her mouth watering. She felt eyes on her, but she ignored them, nearly on it when someone caught her and she was lifted up with two hands under her forelegs.

"No more treats for you until you change back," Daemon said, looking at her.

She glared at him, hissing and then jerking when he hissed back at her. She turned to Kai and mewled pitifully. He came to her rescue, taking her from Daemon who gritted his teeth.

"You can't baby her forever," Daemon scolded, but Kai ignored him, his attention on petting her.

Etani turned smug eyes on the demon, enjoying his frustration.

"Don't you listen to that moody demon. I'll give you all the treats you want," he cooed, and she stretched up to butt her head against his chin.

Uzo laughed and shook his head. "She has him wrapped around her little paw."

"He's always been an avid cat lover," Jaia said, staring resentfully at his twin.

"Same with her," Daemon said and the two exchanged a look of shared misery at their plights.

She and Kai ignored them, instead spending their time together and only offering token assistance to help pack.

"So, the water spirit?" Uzo asked and Daemon nodded, picking up their bags. Kai took two and slung them over one shoulder, his free arm curled around her.

"Stop being so lazy," Daemon demanded, but she only curled deeper into Kai's arm, tucking her tail up over her little pink nose.

"Leave her alone," Kai said defensively, turning his body to hide her from the demon.

Daemon growled and took Jaia's wrist, the chain joining with her and Kai at the end and he pulled them through the tear in reality and back in Summer. "The next four should all be in Faerie," Daemon said as they broke apart in a clear meadow, the sound of water coming from a nearby stream.

"Where are we going to find a water spirit? They don't usually linger in the Courts," Uzo said.

"We should just follow the streams and we'll come across a pond sooner or later," Daemon said and nodded in the direction of the stream.

They followed along the bank for a good few hours, talking rarely until they came across a deep pond and Daemon picked up a rock, throwing it into the pond.

"Anyone home?" he yelled out and a woman's head popped out, looking at them irritably.

"What do you want, demon?" she snapped, sharp teeth flashing.

"Looking for a water spirit, any nearby?" he asked.

The woman looked at them all, considering, before she tilted her head down an offshoot.

"Claresha is down there," she said and then she vanished back under the water.

Etani wasn't sure what she had been, a kelpie perhaps. But they headed in the direction the woman had suggested.

They were discussing doubling back in case they had missed something when they found a large, deep pool and there was a watery figure sitting on the surface, watching them with interest.

She was made entirely of water that moved and rippled with her, but remained still when she did, a soft glow coming from her eyes and she was see-through for the most part.

She would have been pretty in life, but water spirits were all long dead and refused to pass on, allowing them to take form from the water in which they died.

"What have you come to see me for?" she asked in a high, youthful voice.

She had worn a long flowing dress when she died, the ends tattered and waving in a breeze that didn't blow, her long hair in tight ringlets and held back with a bow.

"We have come to ask for your magic to help us save the human world," Daemon said kindly.

"Is that so? You want to include me in your quest?" She stood and drifted closer, her feet touching the surface and allowing her to suck more water up into her form.

"Yes, Claresha, we would ask for your help."

"Who will I be blessing?" she asked and Kai sucked in a breath, holding her out.

Claresha looked a little taken aback by the cat sitting poised on his arm.

"That's a cat," the spirit said, looking to Daemon.

"Right now she is a cat, but normally she is a very stubborn woman who refuses to change out of her cat form to help us," Daemon snarled in her direction and she looked at him, yawning in his face.

She turned to look at the spirit and leant forward, her nose outstretched.

Claresha bent down and their noses touched, the spirit's form wavering slightly before solidifying once more.

A sense of coolness washed through her and her fur stood on end, making the spirit laugh with enjoyment.

"Why are you so willing to help?" Jaia asked, curious.

"I would like it remembered that I helped, later," she said cryptically and slowly sank back into the pond with a tinkling laugh.

"Creepy..." Daemon said, looking down at the pond, but he was content enough.

"Jiuwei Hu?" Uzo said and Daemon nodded, the group joining

hands and heading through the tear but then stepping out into Winter.

Etani leapt free of the vampire and found she could easily walk on the surface of the snow, her black fur a stark contrast against the white.

She leapt through the snow with ease, turning to look back at the group as they struggled to follow after her.

It quickly became a game for her, crouching down on the snow and then leaping away when Daemon got close, his swipes for her half-hearted. He struggled to keep a smile off his face at her fun.

Leaping ahead, she led the way deeper into Winter, waited, and then leapt off again, though she never strayed far from the group.

Their pace was slow with the demon melting his way through the snow and the others looking miserable, but they kept up the pace.

After a good hour, she had leapt away from a grab and then went still, her head cocked as she listened to the faintest breath of a sound.

Something lunged at her and she yowled as teeth sank into her side and she was tossed through the air, blood splattering the snow.

Landing less gracefully then she had intended, she turned to see an enormous snowy white fox with a black nose and nine huge, bushy tails prowling towards her, teeth bared and bloody.

She hissed, the sound of yelling coming from further back and she ran for the group, the fox cutting her off and snapping.

He caught her paw and she yowled again, dancing back and then turning, running away from the fox and the group.

He was faster, more experienced, and so she knew she had no other choice.

Mid-step, her shape changed and she spun, hair flying to grab the fox by the jaws and yank him off his feet, slamming him down into the snow and stepping over him, sitting on his shoulders and pressing his head hard into the snow.

She was naked but that didn't matter, the fox looking utterly baffled as he peered up at her, his black eye wide and flicking over her bloodied form.

He knew he had made a mistake when she bared her fangs at him, and he gave a yip of fear.

His transformation was neither as fast nor as graceful as hers, and she shifted to better hold him down as he became a man, a large red and white fox mask covering his face.

Lifting it, he stared up at her in wonder even as she stared at him.

He was snow white indeed, with long, black hair and equally black eyes, having no sclera at all, only a slight discolouration of brown in the black where the outer ring of his pupils would normally be.

"I thought you were a cat," he said in an accented voice.

"And I thought you were a fox," she said, blushing when his eyes flicked down to her bare chest and then back up.

He wasn't naked, instead dressed in a long white robe with black and crimson ties around his middle, a pretty flame pattern embroidered into the hem.

He had fox ears and they came out of the top of his head, but then he also had human shaped ears and she was curious to know if he heard with both or just the one set.

"Do both sets of ears work?" she asked, tugging at his earlobe and making him scowl.

"Yes, stop pulling on them," he growled and she let go, only after giving them another tug.

"That's what you get for trying to eat me."

The others joined them finally and the fox looked at them curiously, seemingly content with her sitting on him.

"Why did you try and eat me?" she asked, throwing the others a glance and Daemon looked back at her, happy she was in her normal form.

"You looked delicious and you were small enough to not put up much of a fight," he said honestly and she nodded her understanding.

He was like her, a predator. It was something she could understand.

"Why are you wandering around in Faerie?" he asked, looking at the group and then back up at her, or at least as far up her as her chest.

"Stop that," she snapped, accepting Kai's offered jacket and pulling it on backwards, her wings making it hard to wear it normally. "It's funny that you should find us, since we were looking for you."

His face immediately went wary, eyes narrowing and lips set in a grim line. "What for?"

"Magic. We need yours," she said, and he laughed.

"Oh, you're serious?" His eyes went wide as she nodded and he looked to the others who also nodded. "Why do you need my magic?" he asked curiously and she sighed, looking up at Daemon.

The demon frowned and then gave the speech on what would happen, and then what she would do in Faerie if she was forced to live there.

The fox looked only a little anxious by the end and glanced up at her, then back to the demon nervously.

"So it's not like I have that much of a choice, is it," he said, and she shook her head.

He frowned, looking irritable at his situation.

"We will just find another of your kind, after I eat you." She grinned, and he glared at her.

"You are a kitten."

"Wrong answer..." Uzo said gently, shaking his head.

She put her teeth against his shoulder, his sudden cry freezing her in place, that or it was his hands coming to land on her bare backside as he moved to throw her off.

She sat up and a resounding crack sounded as she slapped him, a welt forming on his face.

He howled in pain, clutching his face and staring at her in horror. "I didn't mean to grab you there!" he wailed and she lifted her hand to slap him again. His arms rose in surrender and she dropped her hand. "Fine, take the magic!" he said finally and she smiled, leaning down to press her lips hard against his.

He seemed surprised by the texture of her lips, but he flooded her senses and she shuddered at the rush of magic into her, the feeling of fur on her skin and the delicious taste of raw flesh under her teeth.

She broke the kiss and he grinned wickedly, enjoying the rush with her as they shared what he felt all the time.

"Careful you don't give in to that urge, little creature," he murmured, and she squinted down at him, getting off him without another word. He stood and brushed the snow off his robes, looking between them all.

"You should be more careful when walking through Faerie. Especially as a cat."

"She's not going to be a cat anymore," Daemon said as he grabbed her arm and pulled her closer to him.

She shook him off but remained close by as the fox grinned and shrugged.

With a slow change, he was the nine-tailed fox once more and then he was gone, leaving them alone in the snow.

"I didn't expect us to get here," she said slowly, watching the fox until his fur blended into the snow and he vanished.

"Neither did I," Uzo said and turned to Kai, digging through the bag and pulling out a pair of soft leather pants, boots and a vest.

She gave a happy cry and took them, pulling them on and feeling much more like herself in them, even without undergarments.

She kept the jacket, wearing it backwards, and she smiled at the group.

"Going to stay in your normal form now?" Uzo asked as he wrapped his arm around her and they turned back the way they had come.

"For now," she said playfully, all of them ignoring Daemon's warning growl. "I suppose I should be humanoid for Hades. I don't imagine he's going to be all that interested in a cat."

"I don't suppose he's going to be all that interested at all," Uzo muttered under his breath.

She glanced at him but said nothing, instead taking his hand in hers, and Kai's on the other side.

They joined together and were pulled into the tear, then dumped back out into Winter, though it was a part of Winter she had never seen before.

The whiteness had given in to a deep blackness of storm clouds and the snow had faded; it was too cold even for snow and everything was entirely frozen, hard and rocky.

"Welcome to the entrance to the underworld," Daemon said darkly, and they started forward.

28

HADES, THE GOD OF DEATH

She hadn't known what to expect, but a frozen wasteland of shattered boulders and skeletal trees hadn't been high on her list.

"Is this the only entrance?" she asked, not overly keen to go any further, though she was trying to hide it.

"No, Summer has one as well, but this is the side Hades likes."

Kai tugged on her hand and she looked at him, his eyes softening at her fear and he gave her another tug.

She set off reluctantly, her wings moving to encircle her though she didn't feel the cold as such.

They walked slowly, every crack in the ground glowing an ominous blue and when they looked down, they could see nothing but movement in a slow stream.

"Is this where the humans go?" she asked, peering down there.

"Yes, on their way to wherever it is they go after death," Uzo said gently.

"They aren't reborn?" she asked, looking up, and started; the Fae glowed an eerie blue in the dim light from below.

"No one knows; Hades won't tell us," he said and she bit her lip, following after him until they came to a set of stairs.

Daemon went first and she followed, the remainder of their party coming along behind her in an anxious line until they reached the bottom an hour or more later.

She couldn't gauge the time in Faerie, as time seemed to have no meaning.

At the bottom of the spiral stairs, they found themselves at a small dock, and without a word, Daemon held out six coins and dropped them into the glowing blue water.

Out of the water a large ship floated, guided by a figure in heavy black robes that covered them from head to toe aside from a single skeletal hand that held the ferry pole.

They piled onto the ship and the figure pushed off.

No one was brave enough to speak; instead they huddled together close to the middle of the ship, though she had inched away to peer over the side.

The water moved in strange ways and, with a shock of horror, she realised they were souls writhing under there, much like the souls she saw in the spirit world.

They had faces, but the rest of them was an amorphous mass that flowed out like a squid in motion.

Nearly throwing herself back into someone's chest, she sat there horrified, arms tight around her.

She didn't like this place. It was not the peaceful rest that the spirit world offered the dead Mythicals. This place was suffering and pain for the humans and she had to wonder how many of them she had sent down here. But most of her kills had been a result of her consuming their souls.

At least that was better than ending up down here with Hades.

It turned out to be Jaia who was holding her and she didn't care, just so long as she didn't have to be on her own, and she was the first off the ship when it docked again.

The ship didn't sink this time, waiting for their return, and she pressed herself into the rocky wall, as far away from the water as was physically possible to be.

Jaia reached for her hand and she took it willingly, clinging to him like a drowning person clung to scraps of wood. He kept her grounded and sane, at least for the time being.

She couldn't reconcile this world with the one she had known with the Mythical dead. It simply didn't mesh in any fashion and she didn't know why. She would have to find out when they were safely not in the underworld.

The path led them around in a slow curve and then down into a tunnel that branched off into small rooms and only marginally larger spaces that they didn't stop to explore; rather, they pressed on and everyone could feel her tension, her fingers trembling in Jaia's.

She understood her fear, the risk this place posed for her when she was not entirely immortal. She was feeling the fear of her possible death and she hated every second of it.

But the river was soon out of sight and the lack of its eerie blue glow allowed her to calm down slightly, though she still clung to the hand in hers.

At the end of the tunnel, they found a large cavern that glowed with the blue, and to her absolute terror, they came to a sheer edge and looked out into an enormous subterranean lake that moved constantly. The wail it made would give her night terrors for centuries.

It was absolutely brimming with the mortal dead.

She hyperventilated as she let go of Jaia, backing against the wall and staring at the edge as though it was going to collapse under them and they would all fall and be consumed.

Kai was at her side, cupping her face and forcing her to look up at him, his face serious as he tried to get her to calm down, yet the oppressive silence kept him from being able to speak a word, either.

The cavern pressed down on them, crushing their voices and yet there was so much noise that it made her ears hurt. Silent and screaming all at once.

Reaching into his pockets he fished around for something to offer her as she sank to the ground, her back against the wall and her head in her arms as she tried to breathe, but the pressure of the world above made her lungs feel tight.

A small metallic ball appeared before her face and she took it, the textured surface curious enough for her to focus on it, her fingers drawing out the pattern.

Finally she calmed down and looked up at Jaia, who had offered it to her.

He smiled grimly and stroked her hair, suffering from the oppressive weight that seemed to be crushing them all.

"You shouldn't wander into the land of the dead if you can't handle it," a booming voice said from above them, and they all looked up.

A man stood on another ridge, dressed entirely in black with waist-length black hair and dark eyes. His skin was an odd, pale purple colour and his mouth pulled into a sneer as he stared down at them.

"Or is it you can hear the screams of the dead?"

None of them spoke, too stunned by the appearance of the man.

He was obscenely attractive in a cold, malicious way with a pointed face and emotionless eyes. His attention flicked between them all one by one and then found her, and narrowed at her reaction to the cavern and the metal ball in her hands.

He looked away from them and then down again, considering, before he gave a cold, unfriendly smile.

"Might as well come in, then," he said, and the wall Etani had been leaning on suddenly vanished.

Kai caught her wrist before she could fall and he pulled her up, the small group shuffling into the new room that had opened up behind them.

The oppression left them like a cloak and they were all suddenly able to breathe, her panic seeming to fade as the light disappeared to be replaced by the warm red of flames.

The room was simple, a large fireplace with a well-tended fire, a table with twelve chairs that seemed to have been carved out of the rock itself.

The fire flared up and the man stepped out of it to reveal just how tall and skinny he was.

He likely stood at nine and a half feet and he was dressed in black armour.

He approached them and she tensed along with the rest, but he made no attempt to try and harm them. "So, little winged creature. You can hear the dead?" he asked coldly, those emotionless eyes locked on her.

She nodded and his lip curled.

"Who are you—" He cut off at the sight of Daemon and his mood seemed to sour even further. "Eros," he growled.

Daemon flashed a grin, but it lacked his usual attitude. "Hades, pleasure seeing you again,"

"Likewise," Hades replied, neither sounding like they meant it. "So this is the rag-tag group everyone has been whispering about. Some great quest to recover a Winter Princess." His eyes fell on her and she could only stare back at him, nervous about his presence.

"Yes and no," Daemon replied, looking a little nervous himself.

"It's more to keep the human world from being torn down."

Hades looked around at him, black brows lifting in interest. "I had heard the Creators were back in power. You prefer to live in the human world, don't you?"

Daemon nodded and Hades looked back at her, trying to figure out what they weren't telling him.

"So why come down here if you are looking to restore a Winter Princess, or whatever it is you are doing?"

"Because Etani needs your magic," Daemon said.

Hades's eyes locked on her then, narrowed as he contemplated her. "You cannot be the Winter Princess with my magic," he said to her.

"That's not the whole story of why I'm here," she said, finally speaking, and Hades flinched at her voice.

"What is it then?" he demanded.

"I..." she trailed off and looked at Daemon who was frowning at the lord of the underworld.

He met her eyes and gave a 'might as well' shrug and she sighed, jerking back as she realised Hades had moved way too close without anyone noticing.

"You?" he whispered, and she cringed, thoroughly creeped out.

"Thirty-eight generations ago you were with a woman named Minthe," she said, and his lips pulled back to reveal his teeth, canines long and sharp.

"Minthe is my distant grandmother and—"

Hades loomed over her, eyes flashing, and she shrank back as his hands curled around her face.

Forced to meet his eyes, her head tilted almost entirely back as cold metal touched her face and he bowed his head over her.

"Minthe had no children, little lying creature," he breathed, and his breath was cold on her face.

"She did," Daemon said, but Hades ignored him.

"Minthe had a daughter named Selbie, who had a daughter named Seloue and down and down until there was a man named Lutheral and then me," she said, wanting very much to run, but he held her captive with his eyes alone.

He seemed to be boring into her mind with those eyes and she swallowed, unable to look away or even move.

He made a soft, thoughtful sound as he seemed to find something inside her, and he finally smiled a real smile. It wasn't a friendly smile, but it was an actual smile.

"So, you're a descendant of mine, are you?" he asked, and at his question a sudden pang of self-preservation shot though her. She felt a sudden urge to be very careful then.

"Yes, and the Queen of Winter, once I have my magic back."

His eyes narrowed as he contemplated her and she felt the metal shifting, melting away to expose his long fingers.

He was freezing cold and she felt the coldness seeping through her skin and into her jaw to make it ache.

"You came here to beg me for my magic, because I am responsible for your existence?" he asked, his tone mean.

"I came here because when I was born I stole the magic of the Creators and now they are returned to power and they are going to destroy the human world," she whispered, his face a mere six inches from hers and the coldness spread, reaching tendrils for her brain.

"I see. So, you think I should give you my magic to save the humans?"

She had forgotten the others existed; nothing but him, those black, bottomless eyes and the cold reaching into her.

"I think you should," she said in barely a breath, her mind feeling foggy and tired.

"You realise that if the humans are gone I would not have to be here?" he asked, and she gasped as the first lick of cold touched her mind, the wolf inside her howling and the dragon rearing with flames, trying to heat away the cold.

"Then what would you do? Sit around and wait for several more million years before more humans are born that you can watch?"

Her breath escaped her in a mist, her lips numb.

"I could find my wife," he countered, and she laughed softly, the sound making him frown.

"Yes, because her mother would let you near her if you were free."

His lips pulled back in a snarl and the ice stabbed at her brain.

Her knees gave out and she dropped down to them, the God moving with her to keep a constant contact with her jaw.

"Give me one good reason why I should," he demanded, her vision darkening around the edges as her brain grew ice crystals.

"Because without the humans you are nothing. Not the God of the underworld, not a powerful being. Not even a husband; you will have no one and nothing."

The ice stabbed her again and she whimpered, his anger leaving her frozen and bleeding.

"Because the Queen of Winter will owe you a favour."

Again, it stabbed her and she felt herself fading fast.

"Because the descendant of the woman you loved is asking for your help," she barely whispered.

The coldness hesitated, lingering for a moment before it burrowed into her mind and she felt him there.

She felt him looming over her and her soul and she stood with her arms stretched, protecting the tattered, bleeding blue form.

He studied her for a long moment, a huge looming black figure with horns coming out of his head. "You aren't all you claim to be," he sneered, and she bared her teeth at him. "Come on, little girl, you can do better than that. You think some Lich can contain you? The child of Gods? Do it. Be who you really are."

She screamed at him, her body warping and changing. Wings burst out of her back and she grew taller, as tall as him. Her hand flung out and the scythe swirled into being, huge and lethal with a razor edge that seemed to sing as it moved through the air.

Red beat at her breast, her clothing becoming a tight leather and silk gown that flowed down around her, leaving one long leg open to view.

Her head felt heavy, weighed down by the headdress and she bared her teeth at him, at his shocked realisation of what she was.

"Impossible," he growled, and she advanced on him, her one goal to expel him from her soul.

"Begone, King of the Mortal Dead, or you will soon join your treasured wards," she snarled, not understanding the form she had taken, not knowing how she had taken it but accepting that it would force him out.

"We shall see," he crooned, and he was suddenly gone, leaving her alone with the dragon, wolf, and her soul.

Turning on them, she allowed herself to dissolve and her eyes snapped open.

Her entire body ached as Hades loomed over her, his nose a mere inch from hers, teeth bared. She glared back at him, her body refusing to move and ice freezing her veins.

"The one who is death shall rule the worlds and create more of her flesh," he growled, the ice tendrils drawing back from her, and she was finally able to breathe.

"Not if you do not help her," she murmured and he growled, his hand moving around behind her head and his lips came down on hers in a hard, disturbingly passionate kiss.

She didn't know how to react as his mouth moved against hers and hers moved against his in response, a part of her she didn't know reaching out to touch a part of him, kindred spirits, one and the same.

His being called to hers and she called to his, but then he broke the kiss and she felt herself singing all on her own as his magic flooded her. Then, she fell backwards onto the stone, the blissful silence of unconsciousness greeting her.

29

CATS, COWARDS AND CHIMERA

When she woke, she found herself held in someone's arms, her head lolling back on her neck with her arm hanging limply below her in a state of confusion as she tried to understand what had happened and what inside her had changed.

Nothing really, but then also everything. She could almost feel him there with a finger on her soul.

He had never left her, and she tried to shake him off, but still he held her down and kept her pinned.

They were moving slowly, the air warm and wet, the oppressive atmosphere telling of rain rather than death.

She clung to that difference and the smell of silk and vampire that lingered around her.

Her eyes opened slowly, and she found herself looking at a forest canopy, thick and heavy with rain that hadn't yet reached them so far below.

She had no idea where they were, but there was something weirdly familiar about the trees.

"Etani?" a soft voice murmured, and she turned her head to see Kai walking at her side, his face relieved.

A gasp sounded, and the gentle movement of walking came to a stop.

Kai's hand was gentle as he lifted her head, and she was able to see the group. Jaia was holding her. Daemon had a huge welt on the side of his face. Uzo was bloody and Versalis was missing his shirt and jacket, but otherwise they seemed to be relatively okay.

"What happened?" she asked warily, trying to reconcile the blood, missing clothes and welt that seemed to be stubbornly refusing to heal.

"Hades gave you his magic, but you looked barely alive, we were scared that he was going to kill you just for fun, so we attacked him. The sad part is that he could have killed any of us at any point during that meeting, he's obscenely powerful," Daemon said, touching his face.

Her eyes flicked between them, counting, but they were all there.

"He didn't try to kill us, he just wanted us to stop trying to attack him while he was working on you."

"What did he do to you, we couldn't hear half of the conversation," Uzo demanded and she frowned as she tried to piece it all together.

"I think he was freezing me, and he was demanding to know why he should bother helping. That without the humans he would be free. But I told him that without them he would be nothing. He would have no purpose." Daemon choked, indignant. "I told him that the humans needed him, but that didn't work. Then that the Queen of Winter would owe him and then finally that the descendant of the woman he loved was asking him for his help. That's when he stopped and he came into me and he was taunting me, telling me that no Lich could contain me. Then I changed and I was wearing a black gown and my scythe and my wings. He said..." she trailed off, trying to remember. "He said 'the one who is death shall rule the worlds and create more of her flesh,' but I don't know where he got that from."

She frowned at the exchanged glance between Daemon and Uzo.

"It was a prophecy made by one of the first oracles to be born. She predicted that death would be a Creator, but none ever were and so the Creators ignored it. But us who were there still remember."

A thought struck her, and she looked at Daemon. "You were creating this being, weren't you? You wanted to be the one to fulfil the prophecy." She was irate and his eyes went wide.

"I'm not the only one who tried. Most of us wanted to be the one. Hecate did it, Hades tried, Zeus tried, most of us tried but they all gave up, got bored or simply failed."

She gritted her teeth, glaring at him in resentment. "You *are* a demon," she growled, and he looked somewhat offended, given her tone.

"I am responsible for your entire existence little girl, show some respect."

She slapped him right on his welt and he howled in pain, but as he turned on her, Uzo stepped between them.

"Don't retaliate. We have work to do," the Fae said gently.

Daemon glared at her over Uzo's shoulder and she glared right back at him, furious that he had worked so hard, ruined so many lives, all because of a prophecy, and he was going to drag her along to make sure she fulfilled it.

Jaia shifted his weight and they set off again; she was fuming but she could do little to expend the energy.

"Where are we?" she asked finally, certain she had seen those trees before, yet she had no idea why. They weren't reconciling in her head.

"This is where the Cat Sidhe lives. He's been here for as long as anyone can remember," Uzo said and she squinted.

"I swear I have been here before."

"You have. This is where you first came out when you ran from Ceress," Daemon said and she blinked, looking around herself. Finally, she wriggled herself free of Jaia and her legs wobbled.

Staggering into Daemon, she growled but used him to hold her up as she looked around.

He was right, she never lingered long in the area, but it was her launching point into the human world.

"A Sidhe lives here?" she asked, curious as to why she had never met them.

"Cat Sidhe does. He's been here since before you were born. I thought you met him already." Daemon was frowning at her and then at Jaia for letting her go, but he kept a firm arm around her to keep her from falling.

"Catsit lives here-" She stopped, blinking as she realised her mistake all those years. "I thought he said his name was Catsit. He never corrected me."

A rumbling laugh sounded from under a rock and the black cat sauntered out, his white spot almost glowing in the dying light. "I thought it was cute, so I adopted the name whenever you visited," Catsit said as he approached.

He was a large black cat with golden green eyes, that one white spot on his chest the only thing keeping him from being a void of blackness.

Her arms stretched out for him and he leapt into them, content to be close to her. "Well, I'm not changing it. Did you know who I was?"

"Of course, Daemon and I have been watching. I always made sure the Fae couldn't find your tracks whenever you came through. That Cain fellow was sure I was helping but he could never prove it."

She hugged the cat and turned to Kai who had been making little squeaking and whining sounds under his breath and Catsit purred at the attention of the vampire who was almost giddy with the chance to pet the beautiful creature.

"You kept me safe?" she asked curiously.

"I knew what you were from that first day. Even before Daemon realised, he had succeeded. It radiated off you like a scent," Catsit said gently, revelling in the attention.

"So why did you help me?"

"Because you are of my blood. I will always protect my blood," he said, his luminous eyes turning on her even as he leapt to Kai, who gave him better attention than she did.

He was smug at her disappointment, but instead she scratched up under his chin and his eyes slid shut.

"I suppose you will be wanting magic?" he asked after a while of basking in the attention they gave him.

"Yes, we just left Hades."

"I heard Mara is talking about you all, too," Catsit said, licking his paw and cleaning his ears.

"I figured he wouldn't be able to resist. What news is going around?" Daemon asked.

"That the Queen of Winter is trying to reclaim her magic to take back her throne."

Etani frowned, looking to Daemon, but he seemed lost in thought.

"Will that help or hinder us?" Daemon asked.

"So long as you don't run into anyone who prefers Megara, you will get help. I think they are mostly just curious to see if you will succeed."

Chewing on her lower lip, she felt unsure. But there was no way of knowing who would be on her side or who would be on Megara's.

"I don't envy you," Catsit said lazily, basking in the attention.

"Will you give me your magic?" she asked, and his eyes opened to look at her.

"Yes, I will. I am curious to see how far you can go, little Winter Queen."

She bent her head, and he met her nose with his wet one and she felt the energy flood into her. She shivered as the sleek, smooth feel of it and smiled as the warmth moved around her, but something caught her attention and she looked at Daemon, her eyes settling on his chest.

"I can hear your heart," she said, and he laughed, the sound a little loud but it sounded wonderful in her ears.

She smiled at Catsit and he blinked at her slowly, his head dipping just slightly.

"Run along now, I'm sure I'll see you soon enough."

Leaping from Kai's arms, he lifted his tail and sauntered away from them and under a fallen log, vanishing from sight.

Taking advantage of their relatively easy success, she had eagerly taken Daemon's hand and Kai's, following the demon into the tear and out onto a steep cliff face. Moving automatically further from the edge, she pulled Kai with her and the group stepped back, looking down in confusion.

"Where are we?" Kai called, his words stolen by the strong wind and he looked down towards the ground so very, very, *very* far away.

She decided she wasn't going to look down again after gauging their height and instead locked her eyes on a cloud that was lazily moving along in the distance, doing her best not to imagine the impact.

The situation reminded her strongly of the waterfall and she was very aware that she was no longer immortal. Or was she? She didn't know and she wasn't keen to find out.

Kai gripped her hand like a vice and she clung to him in return, doing her utmost to keep calm and focused as Daemon led the way along the ledge, evidently not hearing the question or otherwise choosing to ignore it.

The path was only just wide enough for them to move single file and she crushed both hands in her grip as her tension mounted. The path wasn't in great condition and it made her exceptionally anxious.

It wasn't long however before they came across a large split in the side of the mountain and Daemon pulled them into it, finding steps had been carved into the natural stone. They looked both steep and slippery, but they were simply glad to be rid of the winding and narrow path.

"Sometimes I think you are doing this just to see how far you can push us before we finally break," she accused the demon, who flashed a grin at her.

"The Surale are reclusive creatures. They set up a home up atop this mountain and don't come down unless there is no other choice. Given how hard they are to find any other time, I figured we should go for the source."

"Why didn't we just step through, then?" Jaia demanded.

"I wasn't sure if the passage was still intact. It's safer not to try and tear realities into a rockslide," he said sarcastically, his irritation fading as he saw her terror at the mental image, their bodies being pummelled as they caused the rockslide to move and then throwing them out into oblivion.

He gave her a gentle tug and she swallowed as they headed up the passage, stepping carefully, but even then, they struggled on the slick, mossy steps.

Etani found herself staring down at the steps and was fascinated by what looked like hoof prints. She wondered if the Surale were sheep or goat herders.

They crested the passage and stepped out onto a large, weirdly green plateau that gave them all sudden pause as warm air washed over them.

The plateau was bigger than three Ayathians combined and it was a lush green, interjected with large clusters of boulders.

It took her a moment to realise that the boulders had been carved into little huts, and the clusters were small villages.

There were no trees, no cities, or anything that would make the area look inhabited at first glance, just an empty plateau with little fluffy creatures grazing on the grass.

Squinting, she tried to figure out what the creatures were, but they seemed to be sheep, the only problem was they weren't all white. Some were green, some were blue, and one was a spectacular rainbow colour that she was certain wasn't healthy for a sheep.

They looked up at them as the group started down the gentle slope into the lush valley, staring around in wonder.

It was not a natural state, leading her to think these Surale were magical creatures who had changed the weather to make it warm and sunny, with the low clouds adding enough moisture that the grass could grow thick.

As they approached one of the clusters of boulders, one of the sheep came trotting over, almost prancing before he stopped and to her utter surprise, he straightened.

He was definitely a sheep, but he had the face of a man, and while he looked stern, there was no way he could be considered anything but sweet. His features were soft and fuzzy, almost warm, with a round face and skin covered in a soft white fur.

Another sheep approached, much smaller, and his face was a deep black though they both had thick white wool.

"Greetings," Daemon said, and droopy ears flicked in his direction.

They looked curious more than anything, interested by the strangers and the second sheep man chewed slowly on a mouthful of grass, the slow roll of his jaw weirdly hypnotic. He was in no hurry to eat, or talk to them.

"What brings you to our lands, strangers?" the first Surale asked in a deep voice.

A black-wooled sheep approached and when he stood, they found he had a thick black beard that was filled with blades of grass and dirt.

"We have come to ask for your assistance in a delicate matter," Daemon said, and glanced to her.

She seemed to have drawn quite a lot of attention and she couldn't help but notice that there were no women in the valley. The fact made her slightly nervous and she had positioned herself deliberately between Kai and Jaia.

She didn't think they would hurt her, but she was reminded of the tactics of the dryads and their seduction of men in order to procreate.

Something sniffed at her ankle and she leapt away, squeaking. Kai was laughing at her; a little lamb had been sniffing around her ankle.

She almost leapt into Jaia's arms, staring down at the creature. He was one of the few young Surale in the field and he pranced back in shock.

Glancing at Jaia, who contained his smirk, she glared at him before she sank into a crouch and inched closer to the little creature, extending her hand to him and when he sniffed her fingers, she smiled and he butted his head into her hand.

Dropping onto her backside, she scooped him up into her arms and in a low voice, she started their story.

She tried to keep it short, but the more the Surale moved around them, the more she went into detail. She had to stress upon them the situation.

The little lamb had fallen asleep in her arms, his little ears twitching occasionally as he dreamt.

When she finished her story, she looked up to the group of Surale and they looked terrified, watching her and the men around her.

"Why did you bring this to us?" the eldest, bearded Surale demanded.

"She needs your magic," Kai said, and the old Surale scoffed.

"Surale magic cannot save this world."

"No, but it is needed in order to return my magic," she said gently, and felt his eyes boring into her side.

"You're a deluded witch," he snapped, meeting her eyes as she looked up at him.

"Are you so stubborn that you would see this entire world die rather than allow me a shred of magic?" She was genuinely curious, and his nostrils flared.

"Begone from our land and take your monsters with you. You are not welcome here."

She sighed and stood, offering the lamb to a man with blue wool and he accepted the little creature, his eyes wide and round face pale. "I'm afraid I cannot accept that. I had no desire to harm you or your people, however I will not take a 'no' answer." She picked a little fibre of wool off her vest and the wind whooshed it away.

Their eyes had followed it and she took advantage of the distraction, closing the distance to the old man.

Curling her fingers around his throat, she pressed her foot down on his backwards knee and he went down. Following him down, she smiled at his yell of fear and all eyes found her as he knelt before her.

The others in her group had moved instinctively to encircle her, protecting her back in case of retaliation.

"You have one of two choices, old man. Either you give me magic, or I kill you. Your cowardice will not be my downfall and I will not see this world ended just because of one old fool."

He glared up at her, jaw set, and eyes narrowed. "We will never give in to a witch. Kill me if you need, but we will not give in to fear," he said.

Sighing, she stepped behind him and slid her arm around his neck, her hand going to his jaw and she paused, giving the others a moment.

As expected, several called out and she looked up. Fear was a good motivator for them.

The man holding the lamb stepped forward and Versalis held out his hand to stop the approach, but the man was looking at her, not the vampire.

"I will give it, just don't kill him," he called, and the lamb had bleated awake, eyes wide and confused.

"Shut your mouth and do as you are told," the old man barked, and she tilted her head, her eyes on the blue sheep.

"You will give me what I need?" she asked, and he nodded.

Content with that, she let go of the old man and shoved him down, sweeping to the blue man and his eyes were huge in his fear. "I won't hurt you if you give me what I need. I don't intend to let this world fall," she said gently, her eyes going to the lamb and then back up to him.

He nodded once and set the lamb down before he approached her, and she noticed he only had three fingers. They were rough and hard as he touched her cheek and then bowed his head down to hers.

His lips were incredibly soft and furry, tickling hers as she accepted the kiss and his magic.

She had expected a change, yet nothing happened when she took in his magic, only a gentle softness settling into her mind and she found her tension melting into a calm that soothed her very soul.

As he parted from her, he smiled and nuzzled her cheek, his eyes soft and content.

It was an odd moment for her as she searched through herself for some change, but there was nothing, and she was unconcerned about that fact.

Stepping back from him, she gave him a quizzical smile before arms went around her waist and she was drawn back.

They did not linger after that, instead they stayed only long enough for her to pet the lamb again and then they were gone, the angry old man ignored even as he yelled obscenities at them.

They headed back down into the passage and then through the tear and into a new location.

They only paused after they were gone from the homeland of the Surale and then Daemon turned on her, his face livid and her calm indifference to his fury only seemed to enrage him further.

She wasn't listening to whatever he was yelling and after looking calmly into his face, she simply turned and walked away from him.

The scuffle was loud, and she knew someone was stopping him from coming after her, but she felt relaxed and warm as though the Surale had wrapped her up in a coat.

Looking around, she found they had stepped out into a rocky region and she approached the edge of an enormous cavern, looking down into the hole to find it weirdly circular with a flat bottom a very, very long way below.

Crouching down, she picked up a black clump of rock and examined it, turning to look at the mountain they appeared to be on.

It was a uniform black, until about halfway down where blackened trees merged into sparse grasses and flowers. They were on top of an active volcano and she looked down at the distant surface inside the hole. It had been a while since it erupted: a solid crust had formed on the lava.

Deciding the mouth of the volcano wasn't the best place to be, she placed the rock back down on the ground gently and backed away, bumping into someone.

Looking back, she found a smiling Uzo, his arms going around her.

"Good job," he whispered in her ear and turned her suddenly, her eyes going up to find that Daemon had lunged for her, staggered when she was suddenly gone and then turned.

"Now you cut that out," Uzo said calmly, his arms warm around her.

"Give her to me. You're going to get yourself killed!" Daemon yelled and she focused on him, curious.

"They were harmless, Daemon," she said and lifted a brow as he pulled a knife out of his pocket.

"He was armed, you stupid girl!" he yelled, and she looked up at Uzo, who shrugged.

"Nothing happened. We got the magic and now we have moved on."

Her calm only enraged him further and Jaia stepped between the raging demon and her, Kai coming up beside her, but Versalis wasn't paying attention.

A soft cough had them all looking around and freezing in place.

The beast was enormous; the huge wet nose of a lion sniffed at them, the sharp beak of an eagle came around to their right, sharp teeth of a dragon to their left and a long snake slithered around to encircle them.

"Morning..." Versalis said in false cheer as the chimera stared down at them, contemplating them as dinner.

She had never seen a fully grown chimera in person and was terrified at just how big it actually was. The eagle could have eaten her in one bite, and she found herself pressing into Uzo's chest as it peered down at them, seeming amused at their argument.

"What brings you up here, little creatures?" the snake asked, slithering around to hover before Versalis, who looked a little nervous.

"We've come to ask for your assistance," the vampire said, and the chimera looked between them, curious and haughty and hungry all at once.

"Assistance from me?" the lion asked, wondering.

"Yes, we have a favour to ask of you."

None of the rest of them dared open their mouths, leaving it to Versalis to tell the chimera whatever was needed to ensure they didn't get eaten.

"I don't think anyone has asked me for a favour before," the chimera said, and withdrew.

The body was enormous, front paws padding the ground while black talons shifted. Halfway down the long body golden fur transitioned smoothly into golden feathers and then to white, reptilian wings folded and the long, serpent tail swayed.

There was no denying it was a beautiful creature and yet absolutely terrible.

Versalis smiled charmingly and set off on a pieced-together story that the chimera listened to with polite interest, eight eyes settling on her and while six remained, the snake turned back to Versalis as his story continued.

She wanted very much to melt into Uzo's chest and vanish, but those eyes on her had her locked in place.

When Versalis had told his story, the chimera made a soft humming sound of thought and settled itself down, the great lion head resting atop giant paws.

"If I give you this, you will come back here and keep me company," the chimera said and Versalis looked taken aback.

"Me?" he asked, sounding shocked.

"Yes, you little vampire. I like you."

Versalis looked at them and they simply looked back at him, scared for him. "How often?" Versalis asked warily. "And can I send a substitute?"

The chimera smiled with all four heads, enjoying the game. "If you can find another who is as interesting as you, then yes. But I insist on you coming still. Shall we say twice a year, with one of those being a substitute if you can find one?"

Versalis nodded once, willing to take it on if it meant they would be able to leave quickly.

The lion eyes turned to her once more and grinned in a creepily human way. "Come then, little Goddess," the chimera said, and she sighed, stepping forward. She had intended to kiss the lion's great nose, but then suddenly hot arms had gone around her and she was tugged off balance, the arms holding her weight up as very human lips found hers in a disturbingly hot, deep kiss.

She was too shocked to respond, simply taking in the magic and then the arms were gone, and she dropped the last remaining foot to the hard ground.

The chimera grinned down at her, yellow hair and warm honey skin, feline eyes and two rows of dragon teeth. He had eagle talons and a long, serpentine tail with little patches of scales that were both dragon and snake.

She stared up at him, fascinated and terrified as his eyes bored into hers, a maniacal grin on his face.

"Run along now, little kitten," he said in a growling voice and she inched herself back from him, his eyes catching every tiny movement.

She had the disturbing feeling that he was resisting the urge to kill her and eat her corpse, his eyes snapping up to Versalis as the vampire helped her to her feet.

The two men stared at each other with an expression she couldn't understand, the vampire nodding once. The chimera laughed a high-pitched sound and then Daemon was on them.

The chimera returned, enormous teeth coming down and hot breath the last thing they felt as Daemon viciously ripped his way through realities an instant before they would have been consumed.

30

BOGEYMEN AND BASILISKS

hey fell through the opening and onto grass, panting and shaking as they tried to take in their new surroundings. They were at the entrance of a cave, on the outer edge of a large forest with a city not far away to the south and when she had decided that they were safe, she collapsed onto the grass.

"That bastard tried to eat us..." she whimpered, the feeling of his eyes on her making her skin crawl.

"Chimera aren't predictable creatures," Uzo said, flopping down at her side, and she huffed out a breath as his head found her stomach.

"I need a holiday," Kai complained as he sat down at her other side, taking her hand.

Jaia only grunted and plopped down at her head, lifting her head into his lap and she looked down to see Versalis drop at Uzo's other side. Daemon glared at them all.

"Come take a break, Daemon, we've been going nonstop for weeks," she coaxed and his eyes narrowed.

Deciding it was best to just give in, he stretched out over her legs and groaned as the angle made his back pop.

They stayed there for several hours, just trying to comprehend their adventures and their almost being eaten.

"Why do you do it?" Uzo's quiet voice reached her ears, low enough not to disturb the sleeping forms around her. Opening her eyes, she looked up at him to find he was studying her face.

"Do what?" she whispered, smiling as his fingers traced over her hair in a tender brush.

"Why do you let them hurt you? You could... you know. You could stop them all, but you just don't," he trailed off, face pinched as he studied her.

The question threw her, staring into those incredible blue eyes. Did she let them hurt her? She supposed one could look at it that way, and the more she thought about it, the more she had to agree. The reason though, filled her eyes with tears as the realisation burned into her soul.

"I want to belong..." she breathed, hating herself for her own weakness. Uzo's brows furrowed, but before he could reply, she continued, "I don't want to be alone any more, Uzo. I want to be happy."

"But they hurt you," he said, anger burning in his voice.

"Yes, but I'm not alone. I belong here, this is where I matter."

Smiling, she bit the inside of her cheek as his tender fingers brushed away a tear.

"You aren't weak, Etani. You are the strongest, bravest woman I've ever met, and you deserve better. One day, I will show you that."

His tenderness soothed her, but she wasn't entirely sure she believed him.

She fell asleep under the gentle stroking of her hair and it was just going on night time when she woke to a gentle touch on her forehead.

Her eyes met Jaia's and he froze, his kiss against her forehead meant to go unnoticed.

She smiled slightly and closed her eyes again, listening to the slow breathing of those around her.

It had been so long since they had stopped that they were simply glad for a chance to pause and relax.

"Did you hear that?" Uzo asked, sitting up and looking around in confusion.

She hadn't heard it, her attention focused on the feeling of fingers trailing through her hair and the purring snore of Kai at her side.

But when she focused, she could hear it and she opened her eyes and looked up at Jaia, who had stopped his combing of her hair to look in the direction of the cave.

Sitting up, she earned a grunt from Daemon, who had moved to use her stomach as a pillow much as Uzo had.

Twisting to look into the mouth of the cave, a weird dragging sound grew louder and then something stepped out of the mouth.

The shape of the creature was unnerving, because he seemed to be well over six feet tall, but his legs were only around two feet of that length. His arms reached his knees, only a good foot off the ground, and he had a wide upper body, giving him an almost teardrop shape with skinny legs and a huge chest with a mass of stringy, grey hair and a thick beard.

His face was covered in old blood, lips a disturbing pink colour with tiny, baggy eyes. He wore a coat, and his pants were baggy, both decorated with shrunken human skulls. His right leg seemed to be sideways, accounting for the dragging sound.

The sight of him sent terror through her at a speed she had never felt before and she froze, even as Daemon yelled out in greeting.

"Yril'Lysyr!" he boomed, and the disturbing creature looked up, squinting through the dim light before his face split into a grin with far, far too many little teeth.

"Eros!" the creature called out in a wizened old man's voice and hobbled in their direction.

Uzo looked at her curiously as she shrank back into Kai's chest, her fear drawing him and the vampire's attention to her, itching their hunting instincts.

"It's just the bogeyman," Uzo whispered to her as the demon and creature embraced roughly, seeming glad to see each other.

She shook her head, feeling only slightly relieved when Kai wrapped his arms around her. She did not want to kiss that creature; he seemed to have no real lips, anyway.

"I heard you were wandering around hunting old friends down," the bogeyman wheezed, and he joined Daemon as the demon led him back to the group.

"You appear to have quite the collection. I knew you liked all sorts, but do you really need so many?"

Uzo snorted and stood to shake the bogeyman's hand.

"We're not his consorts, just traveling companions," Uzo said cheerfully.

It seemed to her that she was the only one afraid of the creature and she had to wonder at her new fear, not understanding where it had come from.

"The rumours about us are spreading like wildfire," Daemon said with amusement and the bogeyman nodded.

"I heard three different stories in the last week alone," his almost-white eyes found her, and she shuddered, his smile fading slightly at the sight of her.

"This is your girl?" He seemed rather unimpressed by her.

Daemon frowned at her, unsure of her response to the bogeyman. "She's not normally so timid," the demon said, squinting in thought and then grunting. "Surale gift."

The bogeyman laughed and she shrank back at the sound.

"So, you *are* running around collecting magic, huh?"

The bogeyman extended one knobbly hand to her and she froze, staring up at him.

"Don't be rude, Etani," Daemon snapped, and she reluctantly took the offered hand.

His skin was dry and tough, but his touch was gentle as he took her hand and bumped his cheek against her knuckles.

The flood of magic into her made her jump and she sucked in a breath, her fear seeming to melt away and her eyes narrowed on him.

"Surale are timid creatures at the best of times," the bogeyman said cheerfully, patting her hand and letting her go.

"A healthy dose of evil should fix that," he said and laughed at the slow smile on her lips.

Daemon swore at him and the bogeyman laughed harder.

She found herself lounging in Kai's arms rather than cowering in fear, her eyes lingering on the bogeyman before turning on Jaia, who seemed to still be struggling somewhat with her previous fear.

She smiled at him, biting down on her lower lip, and his eyes locked on her lips. Releasing her bite, she slowly traced her tongue over the softness of her lips and his eyes widened slightly, his cheeks flushing, and he forced his eyes from her.

She laughed gently and Kai growled, but she ignored him.

They lingered there for several more hours, the demon and bogeyman talking about their travels and the others taking advantage of the break to take a swim in a nearby river and clean up.

The water was freezing, but it allowed them to get clean for the first time in what felt like forever though it had only been a few days.

Swimming under the water, she watched the fish avoiding the vampires and her like they were sharks, finally breaking the surface and turning when Daemon yelled for them to return.

Wading out of the water, she ignored the appreciative whistle of the bogeyman and bundled up her clothes, still damp, but there was nothing she could do about that.

Tearing some moss from the side of the tree, she used it to dry herself off and dressed, her hands making quick work of her dripping hair and she looked around, the others following her example to dry themselves off and get dressed.

"What are you lot after next?" the bogeyman asked, his eyes still on her and she smirked, making him blush.

"Basilisk and then Loki," she said, using the tree for balance as she pulled her boots back on.

She glanced up and frowned at the size of the moon, biting her lip.

"We still have a few days," Daemon said, catching her glance upwards.

She nodded her agreement, but wasn't sure how they were going to deal with her as a wolf.

"How are you handling all these different variations?" the bogeyman asked her, and she shrugged.

"Honestly, it's just confusing. I'll be glad when it's all over." She bent down to tie her boots and tapped the toes to settle her feet.

"I find it fascinating that you can be all these creatures and not simply be a blob."

She squinted at him. "It's strange at times. I do not always take on part of them. Sometimes it is just my mind that changes."

He nodded and glanced up at the sky, sighing at the passage of time.

"The sun will be up soon, not much point in going to the village. I'm going back to my cave and you all should be heading off."

Daemon and the bogeyman hugged tightly, and they watched as he shuffled his way back towards the cave and they glanced at each other.

"Where do we find a basilisk?" she asked

"That one should be fairly easy. They're a common creature," Daemon said as he bundled up their bags and he frowned at the low supply of blood for Jaia and Kai.

"We might have a problem," the demon said and she stepped to him, staring down at the almost empty bag and then looking at the twins.

"We can feed from humans if we need to," Jaia said dismissively.

"Will that work?" she asked.

Kai shook his head slightly. "Not really, but we have another month to worry about it."

"Can't you feed from Uzo?" she looked to the Fae, who shrugged.

"It doesn't usually work," Jaia said.

"What do we do?" she demanded of Daemon, who was frowning, trying to decide.

"We will have to think on it," he said and took her hand, drawing her close. "If we have to, we will drop them off in Ayathian and go on without them. They will be crazed but they will survive until we can get you back," he whispered in her ear and she nodded, worry settling low in her stomach.

"Speaking of which," Uzo said as he approached her and held his arms out to her.

She glanced at Daemon before going to Uzo and he drew her against him, her lips going to his throat eagerly.

His blood was sweet and delicious, filling her with a sense of him and leaving her tingling to the very tips of her fingers.

She didn't want to stop, but he forced her back and smiled sternly as she pouted, licking her lips.

"Come on, you lot," Daemon said gruffly as he threw the bag to Kai, who slung it onto his back, and she saw the look exchanged between the twins.

She understood their reaction to her fear then, realising they had been on starvation rations for long enough that they were both on edge and only barely clinging to sanity.

Taking Uzo's hand at the end of the line, she glanced back at the stream and frowned as she saw something moving towards them at a slow shuffle, its pace swaying and arms limp.

She watched it for a moment, but then Uzo pulled her and she followed him forward into the tear and they stepped out into a flat plain whose soil had been tilled and turned.

Glancing down, she turned in a slow circle to find they were on a farm of all places with a little house set off in the distance glowing with life.

Daemon pulled them in the opposite direction and as they walked, she watched as he pulled out a cloth bag and tore it into strips.

He passed out the strips and she followed his example, tying it around her forehead, and he smiled.

"A basilisk can kill with a look, so you aren't allowed to look at it. We will cover our eyes when we get to it and hopefully he will be willing to help."

The others were quick to follow suit and they all looked a little stupid with their headbands, but they weren't keen on death.

They had reached the edge of the farm when they heard a soft mumbled singing and Daemon made a gesture. Their blindfolds came down and a warm hand grasped hers, pulling her along towards the singing.

It was off key, growling and confused, but there was no denying it was a song, though it cut off when they approached.

"Who's there?" the voice demanded, and she felt it must belong to a young man going through puberty.

"Basilisk, we come to ask for your blessing," Daemon called out as they came to a stop, listening to footsteps followed by an entirely different dragging sound than they had known with the bogeyman.

"My blessing?" the basilisk asked and she shivered as she felt a breath against her back, the basilisk circling them and examining them all in turn.

"Yes, we come to beg for a trace of your magic."

And so it began, the demon telling their story and she felt the presence of the basilisk before her, his eyes boring into her.

She remained still, her chin lifted slightly, and she froze as she felt the brush of a feather against her cheek. Immediately she clamped her eyes shut and the blindfold was flicked off, leaving her terribly exposed.

"Won't you look at me, pretty creature?" he cooed and she shook her head, squeezing the hand as it made to let go of her, warning him not to react.

"Won't you give me your magic?" she countered and the basilisk laughed, the sound more like a crow than anything.

He took her hands and jerked her fingers free of Uzo's and lifted them to his face, her fingertips tracing over the oddest face she had ever felt. He was humanoid at the face, reptilian with scales, and instead of hair he had long feathers.

it felt like his eyes were covered and she frowned, her eyes snapping open at the realization.

They were indeed covered and she looked up at him, taking in his deep brown skin.

He had a snake-like cast to him, legs ending in chicken feet with a long, snake tail and large avian wings.

She stared at him in fascination and was left wondering how so many of these creatures had come to obtain humanoid forms.

Deciding not to ask him, she instead traced along his sharp face and he seemed to relax under her touch.

He smiled, his head tilted down towards her and he bowed his head to hers. His lips were burning hot and dry as he cupped her face to find her. He lingered far longer than he needed and she was forced to draw back from him, his grin wicked.

The silence seemed to be making the others distinctly nervous and she glanced at them and the odd sight they made, standing in a row with their eyes covered.

She looked back up at him and to her utter horror, he had removed the blindfold over his eyes.

They were an unusual golden colour, the iris slitted like a snake's, and she was certain she was about to be struck down.

Instead, he only studied her, just as she studied him warily. His flash of a grin was wide and he bent down until his eyes were a mere inch from hers, staring into them as though daring her to die.

She didn't, and she gave him a wicked smile in return.

His brows lifted and he laughed, making the others jump. "Strange little creature you are," he cooed.

"That's funny, coming from a basilisk," she countered, her eyes dragging down over the odd mixture of creatures that he was.

He smirked and when he reached for her, she danced back from him. "Come here, it's not often I get to be near a female who can look at me," he said, and she shook her head.

"You'll have to find another playmate," she said, his smile fading slightly.

"Another?" he asked, wondering.

"Another basilisk, I suppose. There are females of your kind," she responded and when he reached for her again, she jumped back. "Stop that, keep your hands to yourself."

He frowned at her, frustrated, and his eyes narrowed, the others struggling with their helplessness. "I have never seen another basilisk," he said and snagged her when he lunged again.

Caught, she huffed as he pulled her against his chest, his fingers going under her chin and tilting her head back. His mouth came down on hers again and she squirmed, this time there was no magic and his kiss was burning, rough and disturbingly possessive.

In retaliation, she bit his lower lip and he yelped, jerking back and causing his lip to tear.

He glared down at her. "Why did you bite me?" he demanded.

"I did not give you permission to kiss me again," she snapped and he looked a little surprised.

"So?" he asked, his arm tightening around her.

"You must have permission," she said, feeling like she was trying to teach a child.

"Why?" he demanded. "Why can't I just do what I want?"

Her brows lifted and she tilted her head at him, unsure if he was messing with her or if he really was that clueless. "Why can't I just kill you?"

"Because I don't want you, too," he countered, and she smiled.

"Why can't I just do what I want?" she repeated back at him, and his eyes narrowed.

"Touché, little creature," he said and let her go, allowing her to step back from him.

He looked irritated by her rejection, but he was polite enough to not try and force the issue a second time.

She watched as he covered his eyes again and stood with his arms crossed, sulking. She laughed at his moodiness. "If I see a female, I'll send her your way," she said and he seemed to perk up a little. He wasn't as young as she had originally assumed.

He gave her a wicked smile and as he turned from her and moved away, his form shrank until he was nothing more than a snake-tailed rooster, strutting off towards the henhouse.

"Let's go," she demanded of the demon and he nodded, his jaw set as he pulled them through the tear and into a plane with a small stream and large number of trees.

Ripping off the blindfold, he turned on her and raked his eyes down her, searching her for signs of injury.

She wiped a trace of blood from her lips and he seemed relieved, grabbing her and pulling her into a hard hug she wasn't expecting.

She hugged him back, understanding his fear and frustration. He hadn't been able to do much to protect her and she knew that impotence well.

Deciding they would take a day off to plan out the next few steps of their journey, they set up camp and agreed that Daemon would go in search of Loki.

He vanished through the tear and headed to Faerie to ask around for the God, leaving them alone and returning several hours later with a frustrated growl.

31

———

LOKI

The trickster God was not hard to find by any means, given he tended to seek out the most interesting thing around and when it had spread that they were looking for him, he had come to them. He appeared out of a cloud of smoke with a wicked grin and muddy red eyes. He had two horns sticking out of the sides of his forehead and had strung gold chains between them. He had blue-green skin and rich brown hair, his yellowish teeth all pointed and intimidating.

"I hear you've been looking for me," he said in a singsong voice, amused that the group had been so startled by his appearance in the human world. They had been planning to go into Faerie to look for him, but there he was, standing before them.

His eyes flicked between each of them and then settled on her, amused by her and their games.

"We were," Daemon said, but Loki lifted a finger and Kai squeaked as Daemon's mouth was suddenly gone.

Daemon glared, lifting a single finger of his own, to which Loki laughed at the rude gesture.

His long shoes had bells on them, otherwise he wore nothing but a simple pair of brown pants and a grey shirt that was open to the navel.

He offered his hand to her and she hesitated, uncertain, but allowed him to take it, to which he bowed over it and kissed it lightly. "Pleasure, little Queen," he sang and she lifted a brow, his sharp grin wide and amused.

"The pleasure is all mine, Loki," she said quietly, considering him and all that he represented. He was a trickster, dangerous and unpredictable. That meant they couldn't entirely trust him or anything he said. "You're a demon," she said, examining the horns that, it seemed, had been engraved with naked forms.

"I was before I became a God," he said cheerfully as he tugged her to her feet, pulling her playfully into a dance. She didn't intend to, but she found herself dancing with him, though she was very aware that he was moving her further away from her companions.

She pulled him to a stop only when she knew they would be out of earshot and she smiled at him, her eyes wicked and his own eyes widened slightly. "Tell me, Loki, what is it you hope to gain from finding us?" she purred, unsure if he would fall for the new ploy. He made her nervous and the quicker she could get the meeting over, the happier she would be.

"I was curious to know why you were hunting me. I hear things." He tapped his ears and grinned. "Hear little whispers of a Queen trying to reclaim her powers. Hear whispers of a Goddess trying to reclaim Faerie. Hear all things, I do."

She tilted her head slightly, this time pulling him into her and twirling him, his shoes jingling merrily. "And what do you think this woman is trying to do?" she asked, drawing him to her so that his back would be to her chest, their steps slow and careful though she no longer allowed him to draw her away.

"I? I think the little Fae brat is trying to gain power for another reason." He took control of the dance and pulled her hard against him, his grin wicked and knowing.

"And what reason would that be?" she asked innocently, allowing him to dip her back, his eyes following the long line of her throat to her shoulders and back up again.

"I think she is trying to reclaim the power of creation," he said, and she controlled her face, refusing to show her surprise.

"What kind of creation are we talking about?" she asked, her hand lifting over her head as he spun her out and then back against him, his arm curling around her waist and trapping her there, the dance ending suddenly as his smile melted.

"The power to create worlds on a whim. I am no fool, little girl, though I may act as one." His voice was no longer singing and her smile melted with his, wary and alert to his change of mood.

"Mara, Hades, the Jiuwei Hu, The Dragon King, Yril'Lysyr. You are working your way through the powerful one by one. And for what? What is the purpose other than to become stronger? What is the point if not to reclaim what was yours from birth?"

Her hands pressed to his chest in a request for him to release her, but he held her. The question demanded an answer. "I don't know what you're talking about," she lied, her eyes locked on his and his smile became cold.

"I am no fool, little Etania. I see and hear all, I saw what Eros was doing, I see everything. I know what you are, and I know why you have come to me."

"I believe it was you who came to us," she countered and hissed as he squeezed her waist.

"You cannot manipulate a trickster God with words, little girl. You want to be the Goddess of creation once more?" his tone was cold, his questions pointed, and she found herself frowning at him, trying to take in his question.

"One cannot become a God in that manner," she said slowly.

"Of course you can. Any being can become a God with enough magic, or enough worship. New Gods are born every day when just enough humans believe in them."

She frowned at him, her head tilting to the side. "Except that no humans believe in me."

He laughed then, taking her hand and spinning her out, drawing her back in and into another dance. "Ah, but they do. I believe you are referred to as 'The deadly sin' or something like that. The kiss of death that has men begging for it. Flesh eater, the mistress of desire."

She was certain he was teasing her and she laughed.

"No, that wasn't it. '*Pulchra Morte*,' it was." His words sent a shiver down her spine and she found her eyes going wide at the name.

She tried to translate it in her mind.

"The beautiful death," he supplied and she shook her head, smiling at his new game.

"Very funny, Loki. Humans do not think like that," she said finally, dismissing his teasing.

He smiled at her but let the subject go, making her anxious, but she pushed the thought to the back of her mind, instead focusing on the steps to the dance as he slowed.

"Do you have any more realistic theories on what it is I'm up to?" she asked, allowing herself to be drawn into him and when he dipped her this time, he held her there.

"Don't play coy with me, Etania, I have known your family since my Rose was taken from me by that wretched Eros and given to the doppelganger. I saw each and every step he took, I know what it is you are."

Her eyes met his and she lifted a brow in mock amusement. "I think you have an overactive imagination," she countered and he growled, irritated.

Pulling her up, he hooked his arm around her and much to her surprise, he yanked her off her feet and up over his shoulder, the sudden change from warm to cold telling her he had taken her from their location.

He dumped her in the snow of Winter and she looked up at him, confused and a little lost.

In Faerie, he looked rather different and she shrank back from the looming demon he was. He was massive, both in height and width, with markings all over his blue skin.

His horns had grown backwards behind his head, pointing towards large, bat-like wings. He wore nothing but a loincloth of tattered black fabric that revealed enormously muscled legs and an exceptionally well-maintained body, his eyes glowing a lethal red as he looked down at her.

Deciding right there was not the best place to be, she leapt to her feet and danced back from him, nearly tripping over a tree root hidden under the snow.

"How little you must respect us if you think we do not watch the goings on of a newling God," he growled as he stalked after her and she continued to back away, her hands up in a gesture of surrender. He looked big and strong enough to snap her in half and she wasn't keen to find out if he could.

"Loki, I don't think that at all," she said honestly, trying to quash her fear in light of her situation.

Without his returning her, or Daemon finding her quickly, she was trapped inside Faerie and she was very aware of that fact.

"And yet you still refuse to speak candidly with someone who might be able to help you."

She frowned, pausing in her retreat and cocking her head to the side.

"Why would you help me?" she asked, more curious than afraid and when he reached for her, his massive hand wrapping around her and lifting her bodily from the snow, she didn't struggle.

"You underestimate the depth of the truth in what you told Hades. Without the humans, we Gods are nothing," he growled, holding her up to his face.

She considered his words for a full minute before the realisation clicked into place like a puzzle.

He had said that the humans were beginning to believe in her, that if enough humans believed, a God could be born.

"What happens to a God who is forgotten?" she asked slowly, and he smiled. She had asked the right question.

Stooping, he scooped up a handful of snow and held it in his hand. They looked at it, watching as the snow melted under the heat of his body, and she swallowed.

"The Gods only exist so long as they are remembered and

worshiped?" she breathed. "Why are the Creators so keen to bring down the human world, then?"

"They believe the Gods will survive in their state of birth. Demons, witches, lightning kings, hydra, titan," he said, and she shook her head in disgust.

"If I fail, the Gods will no longer be Gods." She felt a sudden pang for Mara and Daemon, though she wasn't feeling all that much for Hades. But then her mind went to the other Gods she knew of. Hecate, Hera, Bastet, Odin, Anu, Zeus, Isis, Rid, Nuwa, Loki, Manat. So many names jumped to her mind and so many more she couldn't remember in that instant. So many lives changed by the humans, so many lost if the humans fell, and that didn't include the Gods who had been born since the rise of man's imaginings.

"Loki, this has to work," she breathed, and he nodded.

"Yes, it does, little Creator. You have to keep us all alive. Without us there is no order or control. The Courts will war, the dead will revolt, and Faerie will fall. There will be no future for any of us."

She stared into his crimson eyes, searching him for a hint of a lie, any desperate shred that she was being duped. But there was nothing. Not a single speck of a game.

"How many more do you have?" he asked and she bit her lip.

"After you, thirty."

"What about your Lich and vampires?" he asked, and she blinked, not understanding.

"Is it not only what I was born?" she asked, and he frowned, thinking.

"It is possible, but is it worth the risk?"

He had a point and she sighed, knowing she would have to deal with Epharis eventually.

"Thirty two."

"Then I suggest you get moving. You will have a lot of hunting to do. Mara is already smoothing your path, I will assist where I can."

She nodded and he set her down, his form changing back into that of the bell-shoe-wearing, smaller man with yellow teeth, and he laughed at her scowl.

"Now, now. You can't kiss all the pretty ones. Sometimes you have to kiss the ugly ones, too."

Sighing, she leant forward and he grabbed her, pulling her down and planting the wettest, slimiest, grossest kiss on her that she had ever experienced and he refused to let her go even after she had grown dizzy at his magic flooding into her.

She planted her hand against his face and pried him off her, much to his amusement.

Wiping her mouth on the back of her sleeve, she glared at him and he boomed with laughter.

"Tell me one final thing, little girl," he said, grinning as she scrubbed at her lips before finally nodding her acceptance. "Uzo, do you love him?"

Pausing, she considered the demon and the statement. "I do, but not in that way." Glancing in the direction of the man in question, she smiled just slightly. "He doesn't hurt or use me, he doesn't treat me like a toy or tool."

"Well, if there is one man for you to grow attached to, Uzo is the perfect one." Loki sighed, staring down into her face. "You have all these men to choose from, and Uzo is the one you chose."

"I'm not choosing. It's not like that."

"No, I suppose not. He at least doesn't want to sleep with you." Giving her a wicked grin and a wink, he yanked her close, laughing at the indignation on her face.

It wasn't like Uzo wasn't a handsome man. It was that he felt more like family. The father she hadn't had since she was a child. A brother, an uncle.

Biting her lip as her heart ached with the thought, she knew in that instant that she needed Uzo's love. She needed a friend, and he wanted to be that for her.

They loved each other, but it was a familial love. He was her family, and she loved him.

Loki remained silent as she worked out her thoughts, a grin flashing over his face when her eyes finally met his again. "Good, let him be that for you, Etani. You are powerful and dangerous. He will give you a reason to fight for us all. He is a good man, and he will do everything in his power to keep you safe. He will love you for an eternity, if you let him."

Before she could open her mouth to question him, he gave her a hard shove and she yelped.

She landed hard on grass, blinking up into a clear blue sky and completely baffled by how she had gotten there. Had he thrown her between realities?

A cry sounded and her head turned slightly to see Uzo running for her, waving to the others who had been searching in the distance.

She took his hand when he offered it and he pulled her to her feet, dusting off snow and scowling.

"No one ever said that Loki was not a trickster. We were sure he would have just dropped you off and left."

"No, he needed to talk to me in private and now I need to talk to you in private."

His brows lifted and she shook her head as the others approached, Kai reaching her first and nearly barrelling into her, instead sweeping her into a fierce hug.

"I thought for sure we were going to have to take a month to find you!" he cried as he spun her around, his arms around her middle and clutching her so tight she couldn't breathe.

"Did you get his magic?" Jaia called, reaching them next.

She nodded, smiling grimly at their relief.

"Where is Daemon?" she asked, and Jaia shrugged.

"He went after you as soon as we saw Loki take you."

"He'll be back soon enough."

32

SNAG IN THE PLAN

They were waiting for Daemon to return when the figure seemed to materialise out of the forest at their back and she caught the movement. Her cry of warning was the only thing that kept Versalis from taking a stake to the heart, as he turned to see what had startled her and the stake lodged under his shoulder blade instead.

The figure had shot the stake from a strange, horizontal bow and reloaded it even as Jaia was on him, trying to get his teeth into any inch of exposed skin.

He had white-silver hair and his face was three quarters covered by a black mask that crept down his neck and melded into black clothes that seemed almost like liquid.

The man threw the vampire off him and she watched as a red burst of liquid threw Jaia even further.

She leapt to her feet and he turned as she came upon him, Kai going immediately to Versalis.

Grabbing the end of the bow, she forced it upwards and it went off, the stake grazing her shoulder but missing them all and he slammed his fist into her chest, throwing her back.

She stumbled back and lunged forward again, driving her foot into his ribcage.

He staggered, dropped the bow, but instead she was suddenly frozen as his hand flung out towards her, blood dripping down it, and a drop landed against her jaw.

Screaming as every vein in her body contracted, she dropped to her knees, her brain feeling like it was going to explode as her blood was drawn towards him and his hand. Agony ripped through her, her skin turning first red and then blood began to ooze out of her pores, nose and eyes.

The sensation cut off as the man screamed and she heard Uzo's grunt of effort as he snapped the man's arm.

"Hunter!" Uzo yelled and Kai swore, grabbing the injured King and dragging him away from the silver haired man.

He hadn't spoken, instead he turned his attention on the Fae and she looked up through a smear of red as he withdrew a long black knife. Uzo retreated quickly as they all heard the whispers of the blade. It was a soul stealer.

"Run!" Uzo yelled and he turned, grabbing her by the arm, and they were all on the move, sprinting away from their belongings and the hunter.

They all knew better than to try and fight a hunter; their sort used blood magic and rarely ever lost. They were some of the most feared creatures in both worlds and no one knew how to kill them.

Her instincts had gone onto high alert and she was very aware of the other forms inside her, though she didn't know why.

She felt something inside her screaming a warning and, glancing back, she swore as she saw the bow rising for Kai and Versalis, and she grinned as she tapped viciously into the wolf.

She was not going to let them die because of some stupid blood flinger.

The wolf howled inside her and she felt fabric and skin tearing as she changed direction, her face elongating in the most delicious pain she had ever felt in her life.

Her muscles changed and fur sprouted over her flesh; suddenly she was no longer on two feet but four and the crimson eye of the hunter went wide.

She leapt for him and her jaws found his head, shaking him in the hopes of breaking his neck as she landed and skidded, her claws digging into the soil and grass.

He grabbed her jaw and she tasted his divine blood, letting go before he had the chance to rip her jaw apart.

Growling, she paced around him as he rolled to his feet. She had taken him off guard and the vampires were gone, leaving her alone with him.

Her ears flattened against her head as he found a new knife and the blade glittered silvery in the moonlight.

Her laugh came out as a bark and she licked her muzzle to clean it of his blood.

His one exposed eye narrowed at her and he lunged forward, swiping with the blade and she leapt back from him, the knife singing against her fur but missing her.

She went for his leg and her teeth cut through the leather of his boot, finding flesh and he groaned in pain, the sound muffled by his mask.

She yipped and backed away as the knife found her shoulder, but it wasn't a deep cut.

Growling at him, she slunk back and lowered herself onto the grass, ready.

He watched her, limping as he tried to decide what to do.

His blood magic would have to touch her flesh under the fur to make an impact on her and that was hard when she was a wolf.

She heard footsteps, but she ignored them, knowing someone had come back and she shouldn't draw attention to them. She barked and the man jumped, amusing her that he was so twitchy.

He lunged at her and she leapt back, but his fingers caught her fur and she howled as the knife drove deep into her back.

Turning on him, she caught his shoulder and chest, her teeth cutting into him like butter and he grunted, ripping the knife out and driving it into her again. She screamed, the sound a mangled humanoid-wolf cry of pain.

Her teeth found his throat and she shook him violently, ripping the knife free as she threw him from her. Staggering after him, blood coating her, she met his eye and bit down on his neck again, jerking him violently, and she felt his neck breaking but it was only a short-term fix.

Jaia appeared as she moved away from the hunter, pain pulling her down to the grass and she huffed, contemplating the stupidity of her actions but it had been better than Versalis or Kai being killed.

Jaia was on her, his face pale as he searched her, finding her fur wet with blood and the gashes not healing.

He swore and turned as the hunter moved, his arms flinging out to protect her from further harm.

Blood splashed over him as the hunter threw himself up and Jaia collapsed under the pain, the hunter using the same magic that had brought her down in the first moments of their fight.

A new player entered the scene and Daemon slammed into the hunter, the two going down in a roll.

"Get her out of here!" Daemon screamed at Jaia.

Jaia grabbed her, but she was too big. She focused on what she could do, the wolf stubbornly refusing to let go of her.

Instead, she and the wolf were satisfied with an alteration and her form changed to one of more humanoid shape, naked and bleeding heavily.

Jaia scooped her up into his arms and they were running again, the trees whipping past them as the demon did his best to rip the hunter apart, but again there was only so much they could do to incapacitate the hunter.

They ran for a good hour, finally skidding to a stop, and she found she had been staring up at the canopy as it whipped by, but they had stopped and Versalis was swearing under his breath as Kai tried to pry the wood free of his back.

Daemon was on them a few minutes later and he punched Jaia in the face. The vampire let go of her and she screamed as she hit the hard stones.

"You stupid vampire! You had one task, to keep her alive, and you almost got her killed!" Daemon was in full rage and she rolled onto her stomach, her head spinning wildly as the two screamed at each other.

Uzo joined them a few minutes later, panting. "I cleared up as much blood as I could, he shouldn't be able to find us."

He was on her as soon as he saw her, dragging her limp body from the ground and looking at her back. He swore and when the fighting pair seemed to not notice, he picked up a rock and threw it at them.

They broke apart and looked around, fuming and bloodied from their attempts to kill each other.

"What are you doing?! She's injured!" the Fae snarled, angry at them both.

Jaia looked down at her and his face went pale, his hands going to his shoulders, but his pack had been left behind.

Daemon swore and streaked from the clearing, returning a few minutes later with a large armful of the moss they had used to dry off. "What was that knife?" the demon demanded.

"Silver," Jaia snarled and his arms went around her ribs, easing her up against his chest. "We have to get them cleaned first, don't just bandage it."

With her cheek resting against Jaia's collarbone, she sighed at the scent of him and enjoyed the warmth of him against her while the others moved around behind her.

Water was poured onto her back and she whimpered as the wounds were held open to allow water to flush out the deep cuts.

Jaia murmured softly in her ear to help calm her and it worked well, her attention on his voice rather than the pain at her back.

"Is everyone okay?" she whispered and she flinched at the scream and weird sucking sound as the stake was pulled loose, Versalis immediately turning and crawling for her once he was free.

She took his hand and smiled, looking down at him over Jaia's shoulder.

"You have ears..." he said, blinking up at her.

"Didn't I always?" she asked, confused by his statement.

Kai joined them a moment later and he was staring at her head.

"You have dog ears..." Kai said, beginning to laugh.

"And a tail," Daemon said, his attention focused on his work and Kai tilted slightly to look.

"You have a tail! Your wings are gone, and you have a tail!" he laughed and she narrowed her eyes at him.

Something weird happened around the top of her head and she reached up to find that yes, she had a pair of ears on her head and they were furry.

"Stupid wolf..." she growled and she heard the panting laugh from inside her.

"You were a wolf," Jaia said and she nodded.

"She wouldn't go back down. So we compromised," she explained, flinching as the moss was pressed hard against her back.

Shifting, Jaia slid his arm down under her backside and she wrapped her legs around his middle, the angle stretching her back and she whined softly, but it made things easier for Daemon to wrap the moss around her and he used his belt to tie it in place around her waist.

"Stupid girl, you should have run," Daemon snarled.

"He was going to shoot Kai and Versalis," she said sleepily.

"Then you let them die. You're more important than them," the demon fumed as she shook her head.

"I'm not going to try and fix this world if they die. Any of them," she was mumbling, barely awake as her blood loss drew her into unconsciousness.

Kai made a soft choking sound and she nuzzled her face into Jaia's neck, dozing off against him.

33

DOPPELGANGERS AND PHOENIX

When she stirred, she found she had been drooling on Jaia for quite some time, his shirt soaked, but he didn't seem to care, his eyes alert and aware of their surroundings as the others slept and allowed time for her and Versalis to recover.

Her wounds had at least closed over and Versalis was back in full strength, asleep with Kai using his side as a pillow.

Lifting her head slowly, she wiped at her mouth and blinked sleepily, looking up at Jaia whose eyes found hers.

He smiled at her and she smiled back vaguely, jerking away suddenly as his lips found hers.

She hadn't expected him to kiss her, but he had, and she stared up at him in surprise before she closed the distance and kissed him back, tender and uncertain.

He sighed into her lips, but she broke away again at the murmuring of someone in their sleep.

She didn't know why she allowed the kiss, only the remembered image of him standing over her, protecting her from the hunter, and then carrying her from the scene when he could have gone with Kai to ensure his twin was safe. Instead he had come back for her.

She rested her forehead against his, staring up into his black eyes, unsure of him or what the kiss might mean. Deciding not to think into it too much, she lifted her jaw and met his mouth with her own once more and they lingered like that for several moments, exploring the possibilities that the other offered.

A grunt as someone stretched and yawned made them pull away and she looked around to find Daemon had begun to stir, sitting up and looking to her. He smiled slightly when he found her awake, though she was still exhausted.

"Glad to see you're not dead," he said gently and she smiled, amused by his jest.

"Get up, children. It's time to get moving," he called half an hour later. He removed his jacket and, after helping her to her feet, he wrapped it around her and buttoned it up, at least allowing her some semblance of privacy.

"Twenty-one," she breathed and he smiled, tapping her nose.

He leant down and had been about to kiss her forehead when he inhaled and his eyes narrowed. His attention went from her to Jaia and his jaw set, but he said nothing as he met her silent challenge, daring him to say anything, with a glare.

He didn't; instead, he turned away from her and she was left wrapped in his jacket, her fingertips only barely reaching out of the sleeves.

She turned to Uzo who had gotten up and he gave her a gentle hug. Kai lingered back with a small crease between his brows as he stared at her.

Something was bothering him but she didn't have time to ask before Daemon spoke.

"Doppelgangers are incredibly hard to find, given they look like normal humans. But I think our best bet is to go to Faerie. We might be able to find one in the Courts; if not, someone might be able to point us in the right direction. We will find the phoenix there anyway, I know one personally."

Kai was watching her still, and she frowned at him, totally baffled by his agitation, but he only shook his head and the group were silent as they passed through from the human world and into Summer.

Letting go of Uzo's hand, she stepped back and looked towards Ceress in the distance, half missing the stupid place even though she had hated it her whole life.

She turned back at a gentle touch on her shoulder to see Versalis, his eyes searching her face. Smiling up at him, she threw her arms around him and hugged him tightly, realising how little time they had actually interacted. It wasn't like they had a lot of time, but she still missed him.

He hugged her back as tightly as he dared and whispered a soft "Thank you" in her ear.

She only squeezed him tighter, not needing his thanks. She kissed his cheek and he smiled, letting her go, and they set off in the direction of the palace.

They had no intention of going to the palace, but they only needed to run into another group of people.

It really wasn't hard and they were more than disturbed when they came across a group of young men and women who all jumped up and rushed to them as they approached.

They were a mixture of elves, fairies, dryads, satyrs and others Etani couldn't place, but they seemed unusually excited to see the group.

"Don't suppose any of you are a doppelganger?" Daemon asked warily, but they seemed more interested in her than the others and she frowned as they crowded around her, talking all at once.

Looking to Uzo for help, he only shrugged and she looked back as someone placed a flower crown atop her head and she found herself being drawn away from the group.

"We're looking for a doppelganger," she said over the babble and they looked rather disappointed.

"Doppelganger?" the young brunette dryad asked, her wood-textured skin seeming to pale slightly.

"Yes, we are here to find one," she said and the group exchanged a look, concerned.

"Not for any of us?" she asked, very unhappy when Etani shook her head.

"No, I'll need a fairy later, but that's all."

"You're almost at the end of your journey?" the satyr asked, and she laughed.

"Oh mother, no, not even halfway."

The disappointment of the group lifted and she smiled faintly at their relief, not entirely sure what was going on.

"Well, I suppose we could go to the palace and ask around," the dryad said thoughtfully, but the fairy had already left, her graceful steps changing midway from a willowy, tall woman into a small butterfly-sized creature who was fluttering away at top speed.

"Why are you all out here?" she asked curiously, and the satyr laughed.

"Waiting for you, of course!" He laughed again at her confusion. "We are all rooting for you here in Summer. Megara is a horrible ruler and Winter isn't obeying her. We want you to take the throne."

Deciding not to enlighten them, she smiled but her smile vanished at a loud horn that sounded in the distance. "Uzo!" she cried, turning to see the Fae frozen in indecision.

"Daemon, take them and go, then come back for me."

Daemon moved, grabbing first one and then the next, forcefully shoving them through the tear as a horrible and yet entirely beautiful sight burst into view.

The wild hunt of Summer was massive; centaur, enormous dogs and boars, glowing felines, moving trees, smoking flames with human shapes, ogres and swamp monsters all moving along around an enormous gold chariot being pulled by two golden unicorns.

She knew that chariot would be pulling Queen Cecelia and she turned, seeing Uzo fighting to get to her but the demon dragged him through and the tear zipped shut.

Turning back, the group around her scattered and she was left alone as the hunt found her and the mass of mythical creatures moved around her in a circle.

She had never seen the wild hunt capture a victim before and she hoped to never see it again after that day. They were angry, fuming, and yet entirely overjoyed to have captured at least one of the trespassers.

The chariot came to a slow stop and the Queen stepped down, her bronze lips turned up in a smile that faltered as she saw who they had captured.

"Cecelia," she said conversationally, and the woman laughed, her beautifully high voice ringing.

"Etania, what are you doing in Summer? You can't possibly have triggered our alarms." The woman swept towards her, that beautiful black dress billowing around her slender form.

"Not I, but the others decided to vacate the scene," she hadn't moved, allowing the Queen to come to her.

"Look at you, I had heard the rumours but I didn't think them to be true." The Queen embraced her, smelling sweetly of wildflowers and warmth.

Etani hugged her back gently, surprised by the gesture.

"What happened to you? You have dog ears..." Cecelia sounded oddly like a mother and it bothered her for some reason.

"It's a long story, don't suppose you have a doppelganger handy?" she asked, glancing around, but none of those with her seemed like good candidates.

She found Barron and he was grinning hugely at her.

She gave him a little wave and he barked a laugh.

"A doppelganger? Not that I can think of. Do they still exist?" she asked of an ogre, who shrugged, looking bored by their catch.

"Shame. I'd hate to have to go to Winter. I don't imagine I'm going to be very welcome there."

Cecelia was looking at her jacket with a judgemental stare but Etani ignored her.

"Isn't that Bron fellow a doppelganger?" Barron asked and there was a general murmur of agreement.

"Could I borrow Bron for a few minutes?" she asked, her eyes on the centaur.

He shrugged, looking to Cecelia, who smiled widely.

"Why don't you join us back at the palace?"

Etani was immediately on edge and she shook her head, knowing she would never get back out if she went in there. "Thank you, but I'm afraid I'm on a time restraint today."

Cecelia's pale brows lifted and a commotion started; people drew back as Daemon approached.

"Eros!" Cecelia called, turning on the demon and hugging him tightly. He hugged her back and something he said made her titter. The thought of those two made her want to gag, so she turned to Barron.

"Bron?" she demanded, ignoring the giggling Queen and flirting demon.

Barron shrugged again and pointed over her head.

Turning, she saw that tiny flit of butterfly wings and a ghostly figure approaching.

In the human world, a doppelganger would look like whomever it was they were trying to destroy, but in Faerie they appeared as the spirits they were. They were terrifying-looking tricksters, with empty eyes, gaunt faces, and hair that seemed to be floating in water. Their flesh was in the process of rotting off and they had no lips or teeth, only a gaping hole for a mouth.

The pair moved quickly, the doppelganger's feet hovering only an inch above the grass.

Stepping past the Queen and the ring of growling dogs and angry boars, she approached the duo and the fairy was gone, leaving her alone with the ghostly figure.

"Did she fill you in?" she asked Bron and he nodded, looking down at her with empty eyes.

"Will you help?" she asked, and again he nodded.

He lifted a hand and touched her cheek, the colour of him changing to a pale cream as he began to shift, and then she was looking at herself.

She looked absolutely terrible, pale and sickly, with limp hair and faded blue eyes. She had lost much of her appearance when she lost her magic, odd with round ears and a spattering of freckles from their time in the sun.

Her lips were pale and she had a set of large black ears atop her head, fluffy and alert. She hated the sight of herself; the doppelganger only smiled and even his smile that was her smile looked tired.

"Shall we?" he asked in her voice, and she jerked back.

She had never heard herself talking and the sound of her voice was nothing like the same from a different mouth.

It was a low purr, but higher than what she heard in her head, making her realise why so many had been drawn to it. Even as a non-siren it was a voice that drew attention.

She sighed and shook her head, stepping forward, and so did he. She judged herself; her movements were far too sensual for her liking, and her lips dry and cracked as they met.

She felt sorry for Jaia when he had kissed her, having to deal with that.

The magic hit her like a breeze and she shivered, glad for there being no physical change, finding nothing much had gone on in her head, either.

It was odd how some did not affect her at all, and she had to wonder if there were changes she couldn't see.

When he drew back from her, he grinned and she was irritated at her own smile, white and perfect yet it formed creases around her eyes that made her feel terribly old.

"Thank you," she said gently and he nodded once, the colour of him draining to leave him that sickly green, terrible sight once more.

He drifted away and she chewed on her lip, watching him go, and turned at a touch on her shoulder to find Barron had joined her.

"Phoenix," she said, and he squeezed her shoulder.

Catching Daemon's eye, she lifted her brows in question as she accepted Barron's hand up onto his back. Daemon nodded and his eyes went back to the Queen, who he then pulled into a deep kiss, his hands around her and tugging at her dress demandingly.

The Queen laughed and there was a general sigh of frustration from the group.

Barron set off at a gallop and she clung to his back, unable to help but enjoy the speed as her hair whipped around her. He was massively powerful and he ate up the distance as though he was flying and she had to wonder if he was tapping into some magic to speed up their journey because they were slowing before she knew it.

Sliding off his back, she looked around in confusion at the small clearing and oddly, there was a tiny hut in the middle of it that looked like it had been burnt more than once.

She looked up at Barron and he motioned for her to go ahead. She sighed.

She didn't get time to knock at the blackened door before it was pulled open and she blinked; the man glaring at her was angry.

He was entirely naked, muscular with a set of magnificent black wings and crimson hair. His eyes were a bright yellow, but his iris was a deep blue instead of black, giving him an odd but incredible look.

He looked her over once and then growled and his hand shot out, grabbing the front of the jacket and pulling her inside.

The room was weirdly empty, having nothing but a metal bed, a metal desk with a metal chair, and a metal pot for cooking.

Turning to him, she was surprised to see she was almost the same height as him, which made her feel less weird about the tall monsters she lived around.

"What do you want, woman?" he demanded, irritable. "I don't have time for your games."

She had no idea what games she was supposed to be playing, but she studied his hard face for a moment and his eyes narrowed.

"Speak!" he yelled and she jumped, not expecting him to yell at her.

"I need a small amount of magic," she said and he went still, staring at her in confusion.

"What?" he demanded.

"Phoenix magic, I need it," she said slowly and he stalked forward a few steps, her cheeks flushing at his nudity.

"What for?" He seemed to calm down somewhat when he realised her reason for being there.

"Have you been following the rumours of the Court?" she asked, and he shook his head. "Well, I am going through Faerie and the human world in search of magic from specific creatures in order to turn my own magic back on. I'm the heir to Winter, and a Creator. I need my magic back."

He was indignant, staring at her as though she were insane and, she had to admit, it really sounded insane. "You can't be both," he countered, sliding another step forward, and she took one backwards.

"It's never been known that you can be both," she said and he frowned, considering that. "I'm also death, but I try not to lead with that."

He barked a laugh and she found the wall at her back with her next step and he closed the distance to her, pressing her against the wall with one arm against it beside her. He took in a deep breath and frowned at the scent of her. "What are you?" he demanded and she flushed.

"Well, I'm a lot of things: demon, vampire, God, faun, chimera, basilisk..." She trailed off as he stared into her eyes.

She felt his intrusion into her mind and she recoiled, his hands finding her shoulders and holding her in place. She hated the feeling of his hot mind inside hers and she retaliated, bringing her knee up between his legs.

He grunted, but when she made to slide out from under his arm, he gripped her hair and she gasped as he forced her forward over the metal table. "Stop fighting, girl. I wouldn't have to hurt you if you stayed still," he grunted.

"Let me go!" she cried, fear washing through her at her position. The coat did nothing to protect her from him and she was very aware of his nudity.

"Calm down, I'm not going to abuse you," he said soothingly and she calmed slightly, allowing him to pull her up and turn her around.

With movements so fast she couldn't see them, she found herself sitting on the table and he was between her knees, holding her hair with one hand, her jaw with the other.

"Look at me," he ordered and she met his eyes, feeling that invasion again.

She shuddered as the heat of him sank down through her protections and into the depths of her, exploring in a way that was a million times worse than if he had simply assaulted her.

"Stop..." she whimpered, pressing against his chest, but he refused to let her go and she felt him brushing against the wolf, the dragon, and all parts of herself, before he withdrew and she felt suddenly nauseous.

He let go of her and she bent forward, holding her stomach in an effort to keep from vomiting on his bare feet. "Interesting creature you are," he said slowly, thoughtful. "I'll make a deal with you. You give me the next generation and I'll give you magic."

She sat up and stared at him, horrified. "You said you weren't going to abuse me," she demanded, immediately thinking of her odds of getting to the door.

"A phoenix does not procreate like that. Sex is for pleasure, not breeding." His eyes went to her thighs and she immediately tugged the coat down, glaring at him.

"All I require is a drop of blood," he said.

"That's it?" she demanded. "No tricks?"

He nodded once and she bit her lip.

"Magic first," she bargained, and he laughed.

Without warning he gripped her knees and pulled her legs apart, stepping between them and his arms went around her, pulling her hard against him. His kiss was like a fire, soft and burning but not enough to heat her like the others.

Her body melted against his, his magic flooding into her and he pulled her even closer, the warmth of him irresistible.

She felt herself being lifted from the table by the backside and then lowered onto the hard bed as her lips moved against his and the deliciousness of his magic spilled into her.

Her legs went around his middle and the hem of her jacket was lifted.

Breaking the kiss, his lips traced down her jaw and to her neck, her soft gasp as the flood of magic stopped bringing her crashing back down even as his fingers left bruises on her hips and thighs.

He had felt her coming down like a falling house and still he took advantage of what seconds he had left, biting her shoulder gently and then he was flying across the room as her hand connected with the side of his face.

He was on his feet in a second, laughing at the game. "Should have kissed you longer," he said, making no effort to hide his erection as he stared at her.

Sitting up, she glared at him in both anger and a deep unsatisfied sexual need. "Yes, you should have," she growled.

"Maybe next time." He calmed himself and she shook her head, swiping at him when he approached with one hand out. He caught her wrist and pulled her up from the bed and into him, her head turning away as he made to kiss her again. "Ah, missed opportunities," he whispered in her ear, and she shivered as he bit her earlobe with one sharp canine.

"Stop that," she growled, but his laugh was low and suggestive, making something inside her clench in need. She shoved him back from her and he smirked. "Keep your hands to yourself," she snapped, and he obediently tucked them behind his back.

"Yes, ma'am. But now you have to hold up your end of the deal," he said, and she nodded.

Giving him a warning glare, she stepped away from him and followed as he moved for the fireplace. "What happened to your house?" she asked as she followed to kneel beside the empty hearth.

"Many failed attempts to do this," he growled, taking her hand and tugging her slightly closer. He leant forward and, to her surprise, he touched the wood with an index finger and it burst into flames. Smiling at her, he lifted his hand to her mouth and she lifted a brow before she bit into his palm.

His blood tasted like honey and she shivered, obediently following his direction to do the same to her own hand.

He grasped her bleeding palm and she felt his blood mingling with hers.

She watched in fascination; their blood refused to drip, instead, it built up between their palms though their hands didn't make a perfect seal.

The blood warmed up between their hands and she wanted to pull away, but he kept her there until she felt her skin beginning to blister and then he let her go.

Their blood hung in the air, slowly changing as the sparks of the fire flew up to it, the crimson darkening to black and it took its shape.

A small black egg hovered in place where their hands had been, sinking slowly into the flames and settling there.

She watched the egg with fascination, curious about it and after only a few moments, it began to twitch and crack.

Inside the flames sat a tiny puff of red and gold feathers, a little head and black eyes blinking up at them and she felt a sudden pang in her heart.

The phoenix baby had been created through her and the phoenix male at her side, making her realise with an ache that she now had a child, if only technically.

She drew back from the fire and turned, heading for the door before the tears could start but he caught her, pulling her back into his chest and his arms wrapped around her.

"Don't cry, it's okay," he said gently, and she knew he understood her pain; he had seen it all inside her.

She shook him off as her hands shook, the packet of grief she had bound up with six layers of rope giving a little shake and bursting open.

She screamed her anguish, unable to block it out any longer and she felt herself bursting into flames. Her body changed, her arms forming wings, her face shrinking into that of a bird and the door was blown out as she slammed through it, the house in flames as she flew.

She shot up like an arrow, a trail of flame behind her setting part of the forest on fire and Barron yelled his shock, his arms over his head, but he was unharmed.

She soared, her great wings outstretched as she burst through the clouds and rolled in the air. She wanted to shake off the pain and loss, wanted to throw it from her like an object but it clung to her and burned her just as she flames had done. She wanted to make the world burn with her and she wanted them to suffer just as she did.

Her mind went to seeing Summer aflame, the agony as all the creatures burned below her and she smiled in her mind, folding her wings and plummeting.

Something hit her from the side, and she struggled to catch herself as she streaked away from her attacker, glancing back to the most radiant, magnificent creature she had ever seen streaking after her.

He was bright like the sun, flames trailing after him and black eyes locked on her with an intelligence she would never expect from a bird.

Golden red and blue, he was a lot bigger than her and she folded her wings, streaking down, but his size and speed allowed him to catch up.

She screamed as he collided with her again and her wing buckled. She slammed into the ground and her flame extinguished, her body changing back without her permission.

Gasping for breath, she lay still in the centre of the burnt crater her body had created and he landed at her side, wings changing to human hands as he reached for her and pulled her up. She was naked, the coat burnt away to nothing, and she looked up at him through a cloud of red.

He shook her shoulders firmly, his jaw set as he stared down at her. "You can't burn the world. You have to get a hold of your grief." He shook her again and she whimpered, shoving him, but she felt weirdly disjointed as the bird inside her wanted to take flame again. It couldn't and she was horribly weak.

Something inside her was gone and her stomach roiled.

Throwing him off, she rolled onto her hands and knees and

vomited up a large amount of blood, her teeth on fire and her jaw burning.

Screaming, she felt the second set of fangs come loose and she pulled them free with blood splattered hands, throwing them onto the burnt ground. Blood filled her mouth as her teeth tore through the gums, aching as they grew. She still had the small canines, but they felt wrong; her entire mouth felt wrong.

The phoenix patted her back as she heaved, and she whimpered when the sound of feet joined them, and then silence.

Looking up, she found Daemon staring down at her, horrified. "Daemon..." she whimpered, and the phoenix caught her before she collapsed.

34

GIANTS AND JINN

She would have killed to lose consciousness that time, but instead it was only her body that gave out on her and Daemon slid down the side of the crater and threw the phoenix off her, pulling her against his chest.

She realised then that the cloud of red was her hair and she frowned, reaching up to pull a clump of the tangled mess in front of her face.

It was all a bright crimson and gold, the black entirely gone.

She grunted her disgust at the change and her eyes drifted up to Daemon. He looked terrified as a woman was screaming and he forced his way between realities and they stepped out into night.

Voices called out and he turned, the world spinning violently as he moved and she found herself looking up at a horrified-looking Uzo.

"Why is she covered in blood?" the Fae demanded as he scoured her for injuries.

"She threw it all up," Daemon yelled in a panic, almost throwing her into Uzo's arms and he grabbed her face, forcing her clenched jaw open to examine her teeth. He turned her head to his, searching her eyes.

He swore at top volume and turned; his profanity would have made even her blush had she the energy to do it, and she pondered his anger as Uzo held her, looking just as confused as she felt.

"Daemon, calm down, she's okay," Uzo demanded, but she was left wondering where the others were.

"She's not a damn vampire anymore!" Daemon raged and she watched as he kicked a boulder and the rock exploded outwards in a cloud of projectiles that felled a tree and shredded a few others.

Uzo looked down at her and he frowned, but while holding her up he couldn't check her teeth.

"All that blood is yours! She threw it all up!" Daemon had turned back to them, his eyes glowing a bright yellow-gold before he fell to his knees, screaming profanity again.

Lowering himself to his knees, Uzo set her legs and backside down on the grass and he gently lifted her lip, examining her teeth and then her body, frowning at the blood.

She wasn't injured in any way, even when she had crashed down to the ground.

"Kai! Get over here!" Uzo yelled but there was no answer. Uzo looked in the direction of her feet and cursed, hefting her into his arms once more.

"Daemon, go check on the vampires," Uzo called as he headed away from the raging demon.

He set her down in a stream and she jerked as the cold water shocked her body into movement and she frowned, blinking up at the Fae.

"Uzo?" she asked warily and he smiled, cupping water with one hand to rinse off her body while the other remained locked around her.

"You make for a pretty redhead," he quipped, and she laughed gently. The laugh suddenly turned to sobbing. He immediately pulled her against his chest, dropping down into the freezing water with her to keep her close.

He hushed her gently, but she gave in to her grief and clung to him, letting all that pain and loss out while she had the chance.

She felt weak, tired and drained, but her back had been healed in her transformation and her scars seemed to have melted away. The ears and tail were gone, her wings a presence inside her skin that was just waiting to burst free of her.

"Everything is going to be fine," he whispered, rocking her gently in his arms.

She calmed down after twenty minutes or so and she helped listlessly as Uzo finished cleaning her and raised her to her feet.

Her movements were slow, her legs not really wanting to work, and she paused to drink as much water as her stomach would hold, bringing most of it back up again.

Uzo stayed with her the whole time, holding her hair back and stroking her head while she struggled.

Finally straightening up, she went with Uzo back to Daemon, who was standing with the vampires, all of whom were lingering by the trees and looking sulky.

She ignored them for the time being and after several more minutes, Daemon approached.

"Etani, look at me," he said and she looked up at the demon and he was gentle as he cupped her face, his lips coming down on hers.

She felt him reaching into her and she shuddered at the intrusion.

He found her soul easily and he stood before her, her instincts sending her down to protect her soul from him. But he was looking at her soul and she glanced back to find it whole and blue, warm and alive with an odd golden glow.

"What you did is gone..." she breathed, and he growled, furious.

"Daemon, if I don't succeed all the Gods will be back to their birth state. What does this mean?" She turned to him and he stared at her, dumbstruck.

"Loki told me," she breathed, and he shook his head, unable to process.

"I tried to give you magic; it won't work. I can't give it to you again. But I don't know when the demon inside you vanished. We can only try, and if the Dragonkin fades with the giant, then we know you have reached your limit." He touched her face and she pressed her cheek into it, her eyes closed.

"I'm scared," she finally admitted, and he kissed her forehead.

"I'll keep you safe, I promise," he whispered, and she nodded.

He faded from her then, leaving her alone with the wolf, dragon, and her soul.

She looked into the round white eyes of her soul, who looked scared for her. She smiled slightly and allowed herself to rise up, falling back into herself.

Daemon broke the kiss just as she came to herself and she shivered at the sudden rush his touch gave her and she felt that twinge of need his species brought out of her. He jerked back and his grin was suddenly wolfish as he realised.

"Stay away from me, demon," she growled in a weak tone, and he laughed.

"My dear Etani, if I wanted you right now the only thing stopping me is your uncle and I think I could take him."

Uzo wrapped his arms around her protectively, baring his teeth.

"I prefer brunettes," the demon quipped, and he jumped back, dodging her weak kick.

Kai approached, but he stayed well back from her, eyes taking her in, and she frowned her confusion at his change.

"Kai?" she asked, a little hurt by his distance.

Daemon turned to keep an eye on the vampire as Kai fidgeted.

"I think we need to return to Ayathian."

His words cut her like a blade and she stared at him, not understanding. "Why?" she asked, unable to hide her disappointment.

"We are getting hungry," he said, but she knew that wasn't the full truth. He was avoiding her eyes and she looked up at Uzo.

"I think you should try feeding from her," Uzo said, making Kai flinch.

She felt as though her heart were being crushed and her eyes snapped to Jaia, who stared at the ground.

"What did I do?" she whispered, but Kai only shook his head.

"Go then, worthless vampire," Uzo snarled, turning her away

from him, and she found Versalis looking at her over Uzo's shoulder, his face pained.

Turning away from him and his pain, she buried her face in Uzo's chest and could do nothing but listen as Daemon unceremoniously threw the three vampires through to Ayathian, returning only a few seconds later.

"Let's go," she said, cutting Daemon off as he opened his mouth to speak. "We need to stop somewhere to get me some clothes."

Daemon nodded and squeezed her shoulder, pulling them through to a small village.

Dropping Uzo's hand, she moved ahead without a word and stole a pair of simple pants and a blouse. Pulling them on, she returned to the two and she noted that they had been talking and left her wondering if they were about to abandon her too.

"Ghatotkacha should at least be agreeable, he's a fairly nice guy. It's the next two I'm worried about. They're both in Winter and the Court is likely to be hunting for us. At least the rest should be in the human world after," Daemon said and she nodded, accepting a stolen water skin and a hunk of bread. She ate and drank quickly, the bread sitting heavy in her stomach but she thanked him.

Taking each man by the hand, she allowed Daemon to pull her through and they stepped out onto a village very similar to the one they had left though the buildings had weird slanted rooves and a curious amount of decoration with no glass in the windows.

The first human they came across made her stop suddenly, just as he did.

His skin was the same tone as Mara's and his eyes had that same shape. He stared back at them and then turned and pointed down the only street.

Daemon nodded and pulled her along but she turned to stare at the human in fascination.

Mara hadn't been lying; there were humans that looked like him and he was quite small, compact, and his eyes were dark.

She didn't know how to process the sight of a human that didn't have pale skin and she was left wondering what other types of humans there were. Sure, there were purple mythicals but that was a *human.*

Led by Daemon, he guided them into a small building with a blacksmith shed attached and another dark skinned man was working on a horseshoe. His eyes were the same as Mara's, hooded and dark.

"Daemon!" the man called out and the demon was yanked into a fierce hug.

She didn't know what to expect, but this massively muscled male was not it. The Ghatotkacha was supposed to be a giant, not a six foot nothing man who was almost as wide as he was tall.

His eyes turned on them and he beamed with very white teeth.

"Welcome to my smithy," he boomed and she too was pulled into a hug that had her bones aching, followed by Uzo. "What brings you here?" he asked.

"We need a bit of your magic," Daemon said, and the giant laughed.

"I love you, Daemon, but I'm not kissing you."

He was such a jolly fellow and she found his mood perked hers up a little.

"Oh damn, well how about you kiss her." He jerked his thumb at her and the blacksmith beamed.

"Her I will, certainly."

She swatted at him, smiling only a hint.

"Don't you even want to know why?" she asked, skirting his rough hands as he smiled at her.

"Daemon asks, I have no reason to doubt him." He caught her and he planted a sloppy, hot and rough kiss on her lips that made her almost laugh.

His magic was like a weight on her mind, pressing down on her before it recoiled up like a spring to leave her feeling dizzy.

"A big kiss for a pretty girl," the man said as he released her.

Glaring at him, she wiped her mouth and glanced down to find nothing had changed.

After the man had finished his work on the horseshoe, he invited them inside and they sat down at the low table with cushions instead of seats and he served them a juicy avian meat with a little white grain and a pot of the same red-brown liquid.

She ate eagerly, the fat off the meat satiating her and the white grain filling her up. After she ate, she flopped back onto the cushions and drifted to sleep, her belly full and her exhaustion pushing her down.

She dreamt of the time in the dungeon, Drizdan cutting her open and the horror she felt at her loss, the fury she felt for Alaric when she learnt he had ordered it, the pain in her body as he beat her again and again.

She woke suddenly and found Uzo curled around her back, his arms around her middle, and she felt infinitely safer with him.

Daemon had still been talking in a low voice, sipping from the pot of liquid.

Deciding not to wake up Uzo, she wriggled herself firmly into his chest and his arms tightened around her, allowing her to fall back asleep with the gentle murmur of male voices.

A cry brought her awake and she sat upright, Uzo moving with her as she found someone was standing by her feet, swaying slightly as he looked down at her.

He was very, very dead judging by the empty state of his eyes and the stab wound in his chest, but he seemed to be of similar origin as the men in that town.

"What is that?" she whimpered, scrambling back from the dead man.

"Ghoul?" Uzo asked; he didn't seem overly surprised, though.

"Don't ghouls eat flesh?" she asked, the ghoul stepping forward as she retreated.

"They eat the dead only, not the living. What is he doing here?"

Daemon approached, looking curious. "He came in an hour ago and had just been standing there, swaying and staring."

"You just let a ghoul walk in?" she demanded, and he shrugged.

"Like Uzo said, they don't eat the living. He seems to have taken an interest in you." He turned to the blacksmith. "Do you have a ghoul problem?"

"No, he's the first one I've seen. He seems overly interested in your girl though," the blacksmith said, and she frowned, recalling a similar shape, but she couldn't place when.

Pushing herself to her feet, she paced away from him and he followed, shuffling along and grunting softly. He didn't try to touch her, he only followed and stared.

"That's so creepy..." she whispered and her voice seemed to excite him, earning her a high pitched squeal sound from him.

She jerked back and he grunted, shuffling after her.

"He likes you." Uzo laughed, watching the ghoul.

"Take him with you," Ghatotkacha said and Daemon sighed, frustrated by the ghoul.

Deciding to test a theory, he opened a tear in reality and pushed her through; finding herself at the far end of the street, she watched as the ghoul started after her with that same soft grunting sound. Daemon laughed as he watched and shook his head.

"I wonder how many of these guys you have wandering around the human world trying to get to you," he called, and she lifted two fingers in response.

Her rude gesture made Ghatotkacha laugh and she watched the ghoul as he approached and came to a stop before her, swaying and silent.

"Go home," she told him and she swore he looked confused, staring at her before he started to shuffle away, stopping to look at her after only a few steps, then walking away, then stopping to look at her again. Over and over he did that, making her feel guilty until he was out of sight.

"What did you do?" Uzo asked as they reached her.

"Told him to go home," she replied.

"He looked like a scolded puppy," Daemon accused, and she shrugged. She couldn't have him following her.

"Come on, you two, we have to get into Faerie. We'll go to Winter to avoid the hunt."

He pulled them both through the tear and she waved to Ghatotkacha. His grin huge, he waved back as they vanished.

Winter sent a chill down her spine but she ignored the chill, instead focusing on where they were.

They were just outside the palace and she frowned up at the icy magnificence.

"We need to be careful," Daemon said gently, a sudden scream making them look around.

A young centaur stared at them excitedly, galloping up to them. She was stunned to see he had a horn growing out of his forehead. He was rare indeed.

"You're here! I can't believe I get to meet you!" He bubbled with excitement and shook their hands with great excitement. "I'm Tyna, who are you here for?"

They all looked to her and she blushed.

"A jinn and a fairy," she said, and she was stunned to see him prancing with excitement. She had never felt so welcome before in her life.

"Stay here!" he demanded, and fled the scene.

"That was weird," she said, and Uzo laughed.

"You're famous," he said, and she looked at him, shaking her head at his amusement.

They did as they were told, huddling around to stay warm, and the young centaur brought no less than six people with him.

Two centaurs, a young, brown skinned woman with a mass of curly brown hair, a young, willowy woman with pale white and blue skin, plus an elf and a young Naga.

They looked excited to see her and when she asked, the two nodded excitedly without needing an explanation.

She felt like she was taking advantage of them as the young jinn approached her shyly.

She was small, her full lips a soft pink and her big eyes a rich brown.

Her hair made her all of about five foot tall, wearing a pair of loose pants and a top that only covered her to her navel. The fairy was taller, willowy and her silvery hair and pale skin made it clear what Court she was from.

Bending down, the jinn gave her a gentle, quick kiss and then backed away quickly, the flood of strong magic hitting her like a slap.

The Fairy was a lot softer with the transfer, smiling warmly, and the kiss was lingering, feeding her a slow trickle that felt less abrasive and a shiver ran through her as the coldness of Winter seemed to fade into a comfortable coolness.

"Can we fix the loss?" Daemon asked, and the jinn shook her head.

"There is nothing to fix, it is all there but there is nothing to represent," she said, cutting off as Etani struggled, knowing what was coming. She yanked off her top until it covered only her chest and an instant later her wings burst out of her back with a spray of blood and gore.

As she bit hard on her tongue to keep from screaming, feathers flittered down around her as the wings disintegrated and she whimpered, nothing but bone left in a matter of minutes and those quickly scattered into dust in the breeze.

On her hands and knees, she heaved as the pain faded and she spat out blood from her bitten tongue.

"She still has those powers, but they are no longer dominant," the jinn said in a tiny voice, horrified by the sight.

"Thank you, Etani will owe all three of you a favour when she is Queen," he whispered and the jinn brightened, curtsying before they scattered, not wanting to get caught with felons.

"This is torture," she whimpered and the wolf inside her growled, very aware of how close she was to being lost.

Uzo pulled her shirt back over her and pried open her mouth to look at her abused tongue, but it was healed and he sighed in relief.

"Well, we have reached the halfway of your birth," he said, and she nodded. "Have you told Uzo?"

Uzo looked suspicious, and she shook her head.

"I was going to after Loki left, but so much has happened."

Daemon filled the Fae in, leaving her to try and control the wolf, the dragon sitting calm and relaxed as though it had expected it the whole time.

After Uzo had been told of the repercussions of their failure and she had filled them both in on Loki's thoughts on the Lich and vampire aspects, they decided to vacate Faerie and head back into the human world, hoping that the next stages would go well.

35

ADLET AND MERMAIDS

They decided to simply press on in the hopes that it would help keep them all distracted from grief. She didn't think Daemon and Uzo were as upset as she was, but she was in agony at the loss of the vampires. She couldn't understand why they would just leave her like that.

When she asked Uzo that night, he sighed and pulled her into his arms, cradling her against his chest.

"Your magic lost its hold on them, my love. They could run."

It took her a long time to figure out what he meant and when it did finally click, all she could do was cry at the dawning realisation that they had only loved her because they had been forced to by her magic.

Kai now would only love her because she was his mother, but Jaia and Versalis no longer loved her; her magic had bound them to her and that loss was destroying her.

He held her tightly, rocking her as she let her pain and misery out. She didn't know when Daemon joined them once more, but he took her hand and they sat in silence, the only two men she had left in her life listening to the quiet sobs of misery.

At least she still had them, but did they only love her because of her magic? She didn't know and the thought that they would soon be leaving her too was like nails down her back, leaving her dreading every started conversation and anxious any time they were left alone, fearing they would discuss abandoning her, too.

They set off the morning after their trip to Winter, giving them time to process and giving her time to wrap her head around everything.

It was decided that by then she would have lost the gifts of Mara and she had indeed; the strength she had come to enjoy was lost to her and made her more than a little moody, but they were kind enough to ignore her, at least until she decided that she didn't want to be a woman anymore and it was her turn to ignore them.

Licking her paws, she turned luminous blue eyes on the raging Daemon and simply looked at him with her best condescending stare until Uzo picked her up and settled her into his arms.

"Come on, if she wants to be a cat, let her be a cat," Uzo said, tired of the fighting when she was going to do whatever it was she wanted to do.

Being a cat was exceptionally easier; her needs were simple and she had dulled emotions that meant she didn't have to feel as strongly. She was small and fluffy, fast and sleek, so she felt safe inside herself for the time being.

"You had better change back just as soon as we get there, young lady," the demon shouted and she looked up at Uzo, who was trying not to laugh.

He scratched her ears and she flopped onto her side, basking in the pleasure of the touch.

They set off and only moved from the human world through to the human world again and after a while of not having any attention from Uzo, she leapt onto Daemon's shoulder and sat there, glaring haughtily at the Fae who only laughed at her attention seeking.

The demon caught her by the scruff and she hissed, curling herself into a little ball and looking at him pitifully as he held her out before him.

"You'll get no pity from me," he said, but the longer he looked at her, the more she saw him melting and after she gave a sad little mew, he sighed and tucked her into his arms.

Content there, she curled up and his sharp nails made for delicious scratches.

She purred loudly, making sure Uzo could hear her joy at the attention and the two exchanged a look, amused by her.

Within a few hours of steady walking, they came across a small hidden village in the middle of an unusually dense forest, the trees seemingly packed on top of each other and yet the smell of them told her that they simply grew like that.

It was odd enough that she stuck her little pink nose out from under his shirt and peered around curiously.

"Trees don't grow like that, do they?" Uzo asked and Daemon shook his head, all three on alert.

Etani had never seen an Adlet before, and so when she saw something flash across in the distance, she whipped her head around but it was already gone before she could get a lock on it.

She had the oddest sensation that they had been surrounded and when Daemon began to slow, she was certain he had felt it, too.

Without a peep, her nose retreated and she readied herself for the need to come bursting out, just in case she needed to defend her friends.

She had not been wrong in her thoughts that they had been surrounded and suddenly the mingled scent of man and dog was everywhere around them, warped and strange.

Daemon hissed his anger at being caught off guard and she had no idea what was going on, only that he was angry and tense.

"State your business," a deep voice said, and she felt Daemon turning, facing the one who spoke.

"We have come for magic," the demon said, and there was a very canine growl.

"A demon and a Fae coming into our land demanding magic?" The man scoffed, and Daemon snorted his amusement.

"It sounds like the opening of a bad joke," Uzo said, and Daemon laughed his agreement.

"This is no joking matter, Fae!" the man shouted and she jumped, making a soft squeak.

"What was that?" the man demanded and Daemon tightened his arm around her.

She slipped free of Daemon's grip and her small body leapt from the shirt, landing lightly on the ground and even as she set her paws down, she began to change before them, her body shifting outwards and drawing on the surroundings to return her mass.

Standing slowly, she found herself face to face with a small, slender man whose eyes looked like they were going to bug out of his head.

Of course she was naked, her long red hair shifting in the breeze as she studied him.

He was a man from head to waist, but below his hips there was nothing but a pair of strong canine legs and a long, fluffy tail that was still in his shock.

She smiled slightly at his shock and her eyes trailed down him just as his had trailed down her.

"It is me who is demanding magic," she said in a soft whisper that made the man swallow.

His fur was a deep brown, matching his hair and eyes while his skin was a softer shade of brown that she supposed would have blended into his fur had he been an actual dog.

"What business do you have here, witch?" he asked, and she smiled, the smile making him suck in a breath.

"I'm here for your magic. That's all." She stepped closer to him with a grace she had never felt before, her body moving in a way it was not used to and she wondered which creature had given that to her.

Her fingers lifted and she tugged at his shirt, amused that he was fully dressed aside from shoes.

"Won't you help me?" she whispered and she could feel his heart pounding. She was playing on the werewolf need to please the females and doing so relentlessly.

It worked like a charm and he stared around helplessly for assistance, but none of the others seemed to be able to move, either.

She laughed gently and the sound had him looking down at her, his eyes wide in panic.

"Please?" she breathed, drawing him in and her chin lifted, hovering a mere inch from his lips in a silent question.

His growl was low and pained as he bowed his head to meet her lips and magic flooded into her, but he didn't break away from the kiss after the supply was cut off.

Growling softly as pain ripped through her, she felt the wolf inside her howling in agony and when it vanished, so did the need of the Adlet.

He jerked back from her and she laughed, dancing back to join Daemon and Uzo. "You're not a wolf," the Adlet growled, and she grinned, shaking her head.

Daemon slid his arm around her and as spears were lifted, he pulled her and Uzo backwards through the tear and into coldness. "You're quite the little temptress," Daemon whispered and she shivered, looking back at him and his eyes were burning.

Uzo coughed; her eyes tore from the demon even as her cheeks flamed and she had no idea why she was suddenly reacting to him.

She could only assume it was because she was not a demon herself and as a result his desire had tainted her once more.

He seemed to be enjoying her response to him and she swatted at him, pulling herself free and moving away from him.

They seemed to have come out onto a small lake at night and it was eerie how dark it was as they stepped into the hard grass. Turning slowly, they could just make out the mountains in the distance and trees seemed to be dying.

"Is it winter?" she asked, and Daemon grunted a denial, pulling his jacket tight around him.

She hadn't noticed the cold, but the demon's breath was coming out in puffs of fog.

Exchanging a smirk with Uzo, the Fae grinned at her and they set off towards the water.

"Anyone home?" Uzo called out to the lake but there was no response, the water still and seemingly empty.

"Go out into the water, it might draw someone up," Daemon said, and gave her a shove.

Growling at the shove, she stepped forward into the chilly water and hissed as she stepped on something sharp.

Of course they would send her out, stark naked and with bare feet onto the spiny reeds.

She stepped out until she was knee deep in the water and she squirmed at the slimy feeling of the soil. The water rippled and she squeaked softly, only barely able to make out something very large heading her way.

She immediately thought of sharks and only managed to take two steps back before something curled around her ankle and she yelped as her leg was jerked out from under her and she was pulled down into the water.

She had nothing to keep her from being dragged down into the depths of the lake and she was already beginning to panic as she used her free foot to press down on the tight grip on her ankle.

Their descent slowed and a face loomed into view above her.

Mermaids were the pretty ones, mermen were not quite so pretty. In fact, they were generally terrifying and entirely yet beautifully hypnotising. He was pale white with short white hair and had a row of razor-sharp teeth, his eyes an odd silvery-grey colour. His tail was at least six feet long, if not almost seven, and his fingers were webbed.

No one liked to think about it, but they were carnivorous creatures who preferred humanoid meat, but would settle for fish if the opportunity didn't arise and she cursed the demon for setting her out as bait.

The sharp fingers clenched her in a grip that stung, clawing his way up her body until he had her by the arms and his too large mouth opened, showing her just how many teeth he had.

She jerked her arms up between them and curled her hands around his skinny throat, grinning viciously as her fingers clamped down on his gills and he jerked back from her, pointy fingers leaving long gouges on her arms and then her wrists as she choked him.

Her lungs were on fire and she desperately needed air, kicking hard, but his tail was far better at moving in the water and he kept her down, realising his advantage.

They were not stupid creatures and so long as he kept her down there, he was going to win.

She let go of his neck and swam up, her choking him giving her time while he recovered and she broke the surface, managing to suck in a breath before his fingers found her calf and she screamed as his teeth sank into her flesh.

She kicked him hard in the face, but the water made it difficult for her to move at full force and she was horrified to see the water rippling in her direction.

One was bad enough but two or three? She was dead, she was *so* dead.

Kicking him again to make him let go of her, she found herself being dragged down by her waist and her breath escaped as sharp teeth found her hip, tearing at her flesh and her blood was thick in the water.

A third found her and caught her wrists, his eyes wide and grin huge as he breathed in the scent of her blood.

Her mind reeled as she skimmed through what possible escape she had, and an idea ticked over in her head. She yanked the male closer to her and his smile faltered slightly, confused as she sank her teeth into his shoulder.

He jerked away from her and she screamed at a new bite against her thigh, knowing she was having chunks bitten out of her but there was little she could do.

The merman had released her and was swimming away in jerky, spastic movements as her venomous bite injected him and she smirked, surfacing again only long enough to suck in a hint of air before she was under again.

Cursing the stupidity of the demon and his stupid plan, she

reached down and grabbed a fistful of short dark hair. The male bared his teeth at her and she made a decision.

She allowed him to sink his teeth into her shoulder and screamed as his teeth grazed the bone, but while he was close, his tail wrapping around her legs and his arms around hers to trap her in place, she bit down on his shoulder in return.

He released her and she was suddenly entirely unsure of which way was up and which was down.

Panic filled her and she spun in the water, trying to see which way she needed to go. She was certain she would still be sinking and she looked to her hair, thinking the direction was likely going to be up.

Swimming up as fast as she was able, she turned just in time to see him coming for her and her eyes narrowed.

He hit her with enough force to knock the last of her air out of her and she wrapped her arms around his neck, gripping her own elbows. When he thrashed, she slid around and wrapped her legs around his waist and squeezed his neck to cut off his flow of water.

She pointed up and he screamed at her, but it was that or they would both drown and finally he shot them up. Sweet, cold air filled her lungs and she gasped it down, the male staring up at her but she only grinned maliciously and he realised his mistake.

He thrashed against her but she refused to let go until he went limp and she ducked him back under the water, forcing water back into him and he gurgled, flailing weakly.

She didn't have long and she slid her arm around his ribs and swam for the shore, dragging him up onto the mud with her as far as she could go with her injuries. "I let you live if you give me your magic," she hissed, and his pale eyes blinked at her weakly.

She shook him and he made an odd gurgling sound, his webbed fingers finding her hair and jerking her head down to his.

She met his lips with her own and they were slimy, wet and tasted of her blood and dirty water but even as he went limp, she dragged him into the water once more.

She cursed him as his gills pumped and after a moment of floating at her side, he flicked to life and was gone.

Panting, she crawled back up to the shore and flopped down onto it, her mood sour as she heard two sets of boots running for her from the far side of the lake.

And she heard her name being screamed as she gave willingly, eagerly into unconsciousness.

36

VODYANOY AND IFRIT

The first thing she was aware of when she came to was that she and her soul were again alone; the wolf and dragon gone and the dragon hadn't made a sound, simply accepting her banishment with a calm poise.

The second thing she noticed was someone was carrying her and her body felt sticky, though she was no longer in pain. Judging by the smell, it was Daemon carrying her and once that thought came into her head, she was furious.

She punched him in the jaw and he jerked, dropping her, and she hit soggy ground. She swore at him and he swore back at her, clutching his jaw and glaring down at her. "You almost got me killed, you bastard demon!" she yelled, and kicked the side of his knee.

He went down and she screamed as he landed on her, clawing his way up her body until he was sitting on her hips.

She slapped him and he bared his teeth at her, Uzo stepping back to let them fight it out.

He grabbed her arms and attempted to pin them down but she pulled her right free and punched him again, scoring a hard blow against his nose. He swore and grabbed her arms, pinning them down to the soft ground.

Leaning over her, his nose was an inch from hers as his eyes glowed a furious golden yellow, a threat more than anything he could say.

"Get off me!" she screamed, driving her knee up into his back but he only rocked back into position against her hips and growled.

Gripping both of her arms with one of his, he made to cover her mouth to keep her silent, but it was a bad move and she bit him hard, that satisfaction as venom was injected and he screamed in pain, using the hand to slap her hard across the face.

His body heated up and she cursed him for his magic that burnt off the venom before it could do any real harm.

Leaning down, he mashed his lips down on hers and she froze in place, stunned into confusion.

She considered biting his lips off, but instead she lifted her head into the kiss and he growled, his fingers curling in her hair. She knew it had been a ploy to distract her from her anger at him, but it worked and she gave into the need that flooded her body at the kiss.

He broke it and his eyes were smug, right up until she drove her forehead into his nose and he fell off her, screaming profanity.

Rolling away from him, she threw herself to her feet and glared at him, taking two steps forward but before she could kick him in the ribs, Uzo caught her around the middle and hoisted her backwards.

"That's enough, you two," Uzo demanded as Daemon leapt to his feet, equal parts furious and hungry for her body. She was in the same situation, wanting to hurt him and feel him inside her, preferably at the same time.

"Let me go, Uzo!" she snarled, her eyes burning on Daemon, and he grinned at her, his eyes raking down her to leave her skin tingling like a physical touch.

"Uzo won't always be there to protect you, girl, and when he's gone, you're mine," the demon growled and she growled back, furious that he thought she would be so easy for him.

She aimed a kick she knew would never land, he snarled and backed away anyway, just in case. "On the day he's not there to protect you I'm going to rip out your spleen and eat it," she hissed, and he grinned.

"Promises, promises," he purred and she glared in agitation, her body responding in ways her brain did not approve of.

"Come on, we're so close to reaching the end and we can all go home," Uzo said, and she continued to glare at Daemon, but finally she dropped her eyes and turned away from him.

Taking Uzo's hand, she allowed him to lead her on. She realised they were heading into a swamp and she tried to figure out where they were on the list.

The Vodyanoy were always male, but were capable of changing sex in order to reproduce, though it was only temporary and they didn't appear to change physically. They were very much like many breeds of fish, laying eggs that the male would then fertilise.

They always looked fairly similar to each other, elderly men with a lily pad or leaf on their heads; they liked to play the reed flute and were chatty. Much like the mermaids, they were carnivorous, but substituted low meat supplies with fish and insects or generally any animals that came to their swamp to drink.

When they approached the swamp she found the water to be disturbingly clean and clear under the carpet of lily pads. She watched frogs leaping around. She had to admit they were brave frogs if there was a Vodyanoy in the water.

"I'm not going in there this time," she snapped and Daemon glared at her, as he clearly had been planning to use her as bait again.

He growled and turned to look around, trying to decide what to use at bait and while he was distracted, she shoved him into the water.

The demon went down, tripping on some root or something under the surface and landing face-first in the water.

Exchanging a look with Uzo, she knew she was going to be in trouble but she only shrugged at his curious glance.

"I'll apologise if he survives," she said, watching as the demon flailed with the clawing lily pads and they watched as something moved under the water, heading for the demon.

"No you won't," Uzo said, and she smiled at him.

"No, I won't," she agreed and the demon went still as the thing reached for him and then suddenly he was flung out of the water, hit a tree, and landed hard on the ground several feet from them.

"I don't like demon," the old voice said and they looked back to the water. The elderly man looked at them, seemingly a perfectly normal old man with pale, waterlogged skin and white hair and beard. The leaf on his head was large and the point reached out long past his face.

He seemed more curious about them than anything and she supposed one would be if a demon had been dropped on you in offering for dinner.

"Afternoon, don't suppose you're up for sharing a bit of magic with me today?" she asked conversationally, and the man looked at her, his expression curious.

"Who are you, little creature?" he asked, and she smiled.

"Etania, Princess of Winter. If you give me some magic, I'll give you the Fae. Do you prefer Fae?"

Uzo looked at her and the old man laughed loudly, swimming closer, and the sight of him was disturbing.

He had a human body and he used his hands and feet to move along the shallow pool like some great bug in a skittering movement that triggered all sorts of creep warnings in her mind. "I like you. No, I don't eat Fae nor whatever you happen to be. I eat humans."

She snapped her fingers. Daemon was dragging himself to his feet, looking homicidal. "I'm afraid we're all out of humans today. How about we send you a human a couple of times a year when I get my magic back?" she offered and stepped forward just enough so that Uzo was blocking her from sight as the demon's eyes turned in their direction.

"You have yourself a deal, little Princess," he said, and she smiled. The Vodyanoy stood up in a liquid movement that irked her in a weird way. He approached her until he was only ankle deep in the water and she closed the distance.

He was slimy and smelt strongly of mud. The kiss was wet and gross, but the sense of peace that flooded through her was delicious.

It felt like water encircled her and held her aloft, warm and safe, even as someone breathed down her neck and fingers curled in her hair.

Those fingers yanked her back, she yelped, and the Vodyanoy tared at them as she staggered away.

"They married?" the Vodyanoy asked Uzo, who simply shook his head.

She elbowed the demon in the ribs, he let her go, and she set off at a sprint for the edge of the swamp with the demon streaking after her.

"Uzo!" she screamed, leaping out of the trees and running full speed north with pounding footsteps coming after her, gaining on her.

Changing tactics, she threw herself to her knees and skidded, her skin tearing, but he breezed past her with his arms outstretched and she was up, running back towards the Fae who was walking after them in a leisurely manner, his hands in his pockets as he watched them.

The demon turned, sliding in the grass, and was after her again and he tackled her a few feet from Uzo, their bodies rolling and she shrieked as he wrapped his arms and legs around her, trapping her against him.

"Let go!" she screamed but he refused, growling in her ear.

Uzo reached them and without a word, he kicked the demon in the ribs and Daemon was flung off her and she crawled her way up Uzo's body into a standing position and as the demon turned on them, she hid behind Uzo.

"That's enough, she got revenge for you making her mermaid bait and now you two are even."

Daemon looked ready to wring her neck the instant he got his hands on her and so she stayed safely behind the Fae, peeking at the demon from around his arm. "Just you wait..." Daemon growled, and she stuck out her tongue at him.

"If we are right, then we only have two more before we're in the final twenty, right?" Uzo asked only after Daemon had agreed to wait before he tried to kill her.

"Yes, if things stay even, we are in the final strip," the demon said moodily, his eyes on her.

"So the Ifrit and Sphynx?"

"They will both be in Summer. Aside from the siren, we should be able to get the next nine in Faerie."

"You don't think we will find a siren in Faerie?" she asked, and Daemon levelled a hostile glare on her.

"The siren can't enchant the mythical, they have no interest in being in Faerie," he said.

"At least they should be agreeable if they live in the human world," she said, looking to Uzo when she found Daemon's murderous intentions too much.

"Yes, they are likely to want to help, along with many of the others, but there are a few I don't think will be easy," Uzo said.

"The Gods will be easier now. I feel Mara and Loki would have made them all aware of the risk. It's the Strigoi I'm worried about."

"Is Mags still around?" Daemon asked and Uzo nodded.

"We should get a positive outcome from her. Hecate is generally not all that interested in her. But the witches will be hard to get to."

She chewed on her lip and she was glad for Daemon being there, given their list and maps had been lost in the hunter attack. "We should move on. We're running out of time," she said, and pushed herself to her feet.

Daemon stood quickly and she took a fast step back, but he made no move to hurt her. Instead, he removed his shirt and threw it at her and she blushed, pulling it on quickly.

"The Ifrit first, then the Sphynx," Uzo said as he stood, and she found herself examining Daemon's chest and stomach as he pulled his jacket back on. At least he was able to reproduce clothing while she hadn't gotten that power.

He smirked when he caught her studying him and she slunk

behind Uzo, taking his hand, and they were pulled through into an area very similar to where they had found the chimera.

It was a volcano and the heat mirage coming out of the crater was enough of a warning that this one was very active.

She was very nervous at the sight and she clutched at Uzo's hand, staring around.

The Ifrit found them only a few minutes later as he prowled around, picking up loose chunks of igneous rock and tossing them into the volcano. He was an interesting purple-black colour and had no hair. Instead he had smoke pouring up out of the top of his head. His movements opened creases in his hard flesh and caused red light to shine through, very much like lava that had a hard surface but still boiled underneath.

He looked up at them, then down to a rock and as he reached for it, their presence seemed to process in his head and he looked up again.

He was naked and the only thing that made her think he was male was the size of his shoulders and the triangular shape of him for he had no genitals to speak of. His eyes glowed a deep golden red and he looked around, confused by the sight of them and trying to tell if there were more.

"Hello!" Uzo called, and the Ifrit pointed to himself in question. Uzo nodded and the Ifrit came closer, curious as a puppy.

They moved forward to meet him and he stood before them, looking between them all and she noted with a pang of nervousness that he had no mouth.

Daemon shoved her forward; she glanced back at Daemon and extended her hand to the Ifrit.

He reached for her in turn and as their hands met, heat flamed out from him and the world seemed to explode.

Wind scolded and burnt her, her skin red and the shirt gone, her hair singed. She panted, glancing back to find both Daemon and Uzo gone.

Turning to the Ifrit, she jerked back as she realised he had changed.

His skin had become a warm brown and he wore a skirt of tattered, burnt fabric held around his hips by a heavy belt.

A sword was in his hand and he looked down at her through a mask made of stone that appeared oddly like a chunk of bark ripped from the side of a tree.

Several smooth stones had been embedded into a ring around his shoulders and chest, burning red.

"You come for my magic," he growled, and she nodded as he used the handle of his sword to lift the mask up. His eyes were still that eerie golden red and his lips turned up into a grin that showed sharp canines. "What do I get in return?" he asked, amused by her.

"A favour from the Queen of Winter," she said, and he laughed, the sound doing weird things to her stomach.

"No, kitten, I need no favours."

"Then what do you want?" she asked, frowning at him.

"I get to have you for the night." He grinned, and when her face paled, he laughed.

"That's out of the question," she said immediately, and he shrugged, stepping back from her.

"If you wish. Good luck on your journey, kitten." He turned away and she gasped, fear washing through her.

"Anything else," she said, going after him and catching his arm. His skin was incredibly hot and she let go, her fingers smarting from the heat.

"There is nothing else I want from you, kitten," he said slyly. "There aren't many of us left, so will you find another in time?"

The sound of growling came from behind her and she turned to see a very burnt Daemon dragging an unconscious Uzo behind him, looking furious.

"Daemon, is he all right?" she asked, and she jerked as the Ifrit slid his arm around her and her skin stung.

"Uzo is fine, what is going on?"

"Your kitten was just agreeing to stay with me tonight in exchange," the Ifrit said, and Daemon looked first stumped and then livid.

"Get your hands off her, we'll find another Ifrit."

The Ifrit was grinning, his chin resting atop her head, and she squirmed, the heat making her sweat. "Afraid you're running out of options and time, little demon. The Creators are getting impatient."

Daemon looked down at her and she bit her lip, begging him silently for an answer.

"There will be another way," he said and she exhaled in relief, prying the Ifrit's arm off her but he caught her again and smiled.

"Do you think you'll have enough time? You have a week at most," he whispered to her and she met his glowing eyes, panic filling her. "A week and all I want is a single night. Then you're free to run along on your quest."

He spoke low so that Daemon couldn't hear and she looked back at the demon as he crept forward, Uzo beginning to stir at the edge where Daemon had left him.

"Etani, come on, we can find another Ifrit," he called.

"Find one in time? I'm the only one in this range, perhaps you can find another volcano? But the chimera have taken over so many... oh, what shall you do?" he cooed, and she swallowed hard, trying to think through the conflicting information.

Daemon reached them and his hand was cool on her arm as he pulled her back, the Ifrit letting her go.

"Good luck then, I hope you can find another of us," he said, laughing at her fear.

Daemon drew her back and she stared at the Ifrit, fear making her reckless.

"How many are there?" she demanded of Daemon and he frowned, shaking his head.

"Not many, but we will find one. That is too high a price."

She pulled her arm free and turned to Uzo, staring down into his pained face.

"How long will it take to find one?" she asked as she stroked Uzo's cheek and he blinked up at her, his face relieved.

"A few days, a week at most," he said, and she looked up at him, fear ripping her heart.

"We don't have that long," she whispered, and Daemon froze, staring down at her.

"What do you mean?" he demanded.

"He's right, we're running out of time. We don't have a week to waste. The Creators are getting impatient."

"Etani? What is he asking?" Uzo asked and she realised he wasn't able to see her very well.

"For me, one night," she said and Uzo frowned, taking her hand.

They all knew the risk, and they knew time was running out; the question was, did she give in?

Without a word, she kissed Uzo's hand and pried his fingers off her, shoving Daemon with her shoulder to send him crashing to the ground and she threw herself away from them, running for the Ifrit who grinned massively, his arms outstretched for her.

He had been waiting for her and Daemon went after her, screaming her name as the arms enclosed her and the world exploded into flames.

37

LIES, RIDDLES AND LIGHTNING

The heat faded and she staggered back from the Ifrit, confused by the change in scenery and realising he had taken her elsewhere.

She turned and found they were in a large room that seemed to be a natural cavern, a bed and table set off to the side but there was nothing else in the room. She turned to see the Ifrit vanish and she was suddenly alone, confused and not sure where to go from there.

Making her way to the archway, she found the heat of the place was too much and she backed away, jumping when the Ifrit was suddenly behind her, his hand catching her hair and lifting it to his nose.

He made a soft sound of pleasure and she turned to him, seeing that he had collected a thick fur blanket of some sort and laid it out on the stone bed.

She didn't know what to do, didn't know how to respond to him or their agreement and she hated that she had to let him touch her at all.

Sensing her fear, he drew her back to the bed and he pulled her down onto the edge.

The mask was removed, and she found he had a mass of short, spiky, black hair that stuck out at all angles.

Without the mask he seemed less intimidating and more human, his face hard and strong with an exceptional rugged attractiveness to his features.

"I don't know how to do this," she breathed, causing his eyebrows to shoot up.

"You have before, though?" he demanded.

She nodded warily, unable to speak.

He seemed relieved by that and she wondered why her not being a virgin might have brought this reaction out, but she didn't linger on it for very long.

He drew her to him and his lips were hot on hers, scalding, and yet he seemed to be working to keep from actually burning her. "I will be gentle with you," he promised and she nodded, her stomach tight in her fear.

He pressed her down onto the fur and he moved to sit at her side, his fingers slow and soft as he traced them up and down her cheek, leaving a red line that faded quickly, but he seemed to enjoy the reaction. Leaning down over her, his lips met hers and she remained still, panicked. Unsatisfied, he moved back and glared down at her, irritated that she didn't respond.

"Try to relax," he said, and she nodded once.

He slid up onto the bed and he hooked his fingers around the backs of her knees and parted them to allow him between them. His hands trailed up her thighs and over her hips, up over her stomach and around the curves of her breasts until he traced them down over her shoulders and to her hands.

The warmth of his touch felt oddly good, like he was heating her up from the inside, and he lifted her hands to the belt at his hips.

He wanted her to undress him.

Her fingers trembled as she worked the foreign contraption that was his belt buckle, finally finding the lever and she pulled the hard leather free, sliding it off of him. She dropped the skirt and belt off the side of the bed, unable to look at him.

He seemed amused by her shyness as he leant forward and his hand rested on the bed at her shoulder, his other hand guiding hers to the small of his back.

Her fingers splayed against his hot, yet oddly soft, skin and he waited until she finally swallowed and gave him a gentle tug, encouraging him down.

He moved obediently, the heavy weight of him settling atop her and she bit her lip as he nuzzled into the side of her neck, inhaling the scent of her hair. He was gentle with her as he promised, his fingers exploring the length of her body and his lips exploring where his hands didn't and she surrendered to him.

The next morning she accepted his touch and the world around her exploded into flames, depositing her atop the mountain and she stood in silence, staring down at the stones beneath her feet.

She was still naked, though he had given her the fur blanket to wrap around her shoulders and she pulled it tight in the hopes of hiding from the world.

Uzo found her first and he didn't say a word as he pulled her into his arms, his fingers stroking her hair as she leant into him.

The sound of boots breaking into a run came a moment later and Daemon came to a stop, something warning him not to yell at her. Instead he slipped his arms tightly around her middle and she felt finally safe between the two of them, Daemon's lips rough on the top of her head.

They didn't speak as Daemon guided them through to Summer and she pulled herself free of the two.

The Sphinx was the last one they needed to get to before the final stretch and she was looking forward to it being over as she paced away in the direction of the palace.

Daemon and Uzo hurried to catch up to her and she looked up at Daemon who was again offering one of his shirts. She had to wonder how he was getting replacements as she pulled it on under her blanket and the fur dropped.

Uzo gasped at the sight of her and Daemon growled; her skin was red and raw, blisters forming around her hips, but she ignored them. The Ifrit had never intended to hurt her and he had been distressed at her burns, but she would heal soon enough. Buttoning up the shirt, she contemplated demanding a pair of pants, too, but she decided not to push her luck with Daemon already in that mood.

"There was a Sphinx in the palace, but I don't think we will be able to get to her," she said, and Daemon nodded, thinking.

"I can try and go in. We might be able to grab a handful like last time," he said, and she sighed, moving close to Uzo.

"Hurry back," she said and Daemon nodded, stepping through the tear and leaving them alone.

"Are you all right?" Uzo asked the second they were alone.

She looked up at him and shrugged but then nodded. She flinched as he lifted her chin.

"Did he hurt you?"

"No, not intentionally at least," she said, unable to look at the man she saw as her uncle.

"I'm sorry you had to do that," he whispered, and kissed the side of her head, pulling her against him and hugging her tightly.

"Me, too. But really we are lucky it took that long before the issue arose," she said and he growled at the thought of her forced to surrender multiple times.

"Never again," he whispered.

A thought popped into her mind, drawing her eyes up to him finally. "Did you like that I called you my uncle? I didn't really think about it. It's just... you're more than just my father's friend," she trailed off, unable to voice the thoughts and feelings she had for him.

"Of course I liked it. I have thought of you as more than just a ward since this whole endeavour started. You are incredibly precious to me, Etani. And I can't stand to see you hurt," he paused, touching her cheek gently. "I love you, very much."

"I love you, too, Uzo," she whimpered, tears swelling in her eyes at the thought. "I want you to be my uncle, even if it's not by blood. No one needs to know it's not by blood."

He smiled, wiping a tender finger against her cheek as the tear fell. "I am, my love. I'm your uncle, now and forever."

Wrapping her arms around his middle, she buried her face in his chest. Her world took an odd step sideways as she settled into a new reality. One where she was no longer alone, where she had someone to protect, and who could protect her. One where she could be loved in a way that was beautiful and perfect.

With that knowledge burning her heart, she found a new hope in their journey. They would make it, together.

They waited and waited, growing more anxious as the demon seemed to be gone for several hours before he finally burst back through with a Sphinx prowling along behind him.

Much to their surprise, he was recovering from rather severe burns and when asked, he refused to explain.

The Sphinx watched her curiously and she wanted very, very badly to go pet the ancient creature but she knew better.

The Sphinx was not the same one she had seen before, this one being almost purely white with a mass of black hair and red eyes; even her wings were white. She had black claws as well and she seemed to be curious more than anything.

"So you're the one everyone has been talking about," the Sphinx said in a calm, wise voice.

Etani smiled and nodded, bowing politely to the beautiful creature.

The Sphinx bowed her head in response and smiled at the group. "I will give you what you want, if you can answer my riddle," the Sphinx said, and Etani frowned. She didn't do well with riddles.

"Ask away," Daemon said, moving to her side.

"For now I must stay under the man who made me, but when he

dies I'll be as powerful as he. They will watch and listen to what I say, and some of their money to me they will pay. Who am I?"

Her mind instantly went blank as it always did when she was faced with a riddle and she immediately forgot the lines.

"I'm sorry, could you repeat that?" she asked, and the Sphinx sat down on her haunches and repeated the riddle.

"A wife perhaps?" Uzo asked, but Daemon was frowning, thinking hard.

"You don't become more powerful when your husband dies," Daemon said slowly.

"Who becomes more powerful when the man dies?"

Etani was thinking about her situation with Alaric and Epharis, the thought of Alaric dying making Epharis more powerful and her by association. It was not a magical power, but a human one and she had a suspicion that the Sphinx had made the riddle fit her own situation.

The last line had her thinking and she found herself staring into the crimson eyes as she thought it over.

'They will watch and listen to what I say...' People listened to royalty, the King. 'And some of their money to me they will pay...' Taxes. 'For now I must stay under the man who made me...' That caught her up, but then she realised.

"A Princess," she said, and the Sphinx laughed.

"How did you get that?" Uzo demanded.

"For now I must stay under the man who made me, a Princess to her father, the King. But when he dies I'll be as powerful as he, ascending the throne. They will watch and listen to what I say, royal subjects, and some of their money to me they will pay, taxes," she explained, and the Sphinx nodded, amused.

Stepping forward, the Sphinx pushed herself up and their lips met, the Sphinx was warm and soft, the magic flooding into her making her feel odd and ancient.

The Sphinx moved away and her long tail swayed as she left them alone and Etani glanced back to the two men.

"Why are you all burnt?" she demanded, but Daemon was still watching her with a slight frown.

"How did you guess that?" he demanded.

"The line 'when he dies I'll be as powerful as he' reminded me of Epharis and Alaric. Why are you burnt?"

He scowled at her and shook his head. "Come on, smarty pants, we're in the home stretch," he said and she looked to Uzo, who only shrugged.

Pulling her into his arms, Uzo took her by the hand and they stepped through from Summer and into Winter, shocking her by the transition.

"It's safer for Uzo," he said, and she nodded.

She had to admit she was getting excited by the prospect of going home, though she wasn't as keen to be going back to the vampires and Epharis. "Do you think we can try and rid me of the holds they have on me when we get back?" she asked Daemon as she released his hand and he looked at her.

"I will do whatever it takes to rid you of them all," he growled, and she smiled.

Stepping away from him, her mind went to the phoenix and then to the Jiuwei Hu. She smiled as she tapped into that part of herself that would have her changing but then she staggered and she spun, indignant, on the demon.

"I can't change form!" she cried, and he laughed.

"No more kitty for Etani," he said mockingly, and she glared at him, blaming him though it was irrational.

"When this is all over... I'm going to kill you a hundred times over," she growled and he laughed, ruffling her hair and leading the way into Winter.

They found the bird sleeping with its head under his wing several hours later, the tree he perched on scorched black and badly abused, but the bird himself was magnificent.

He was a hypnotic black shot through with blues and greens that gave him a magical look. He was an eagle shape, huge and haughty-looking, with two long flexible feathers at the tail that moved like a cat's as they approached, his head lifting at a scuff one of them made.

He gazed down at them and, as she stepped forward, the bird cocked his head to the side.

Considering her, he made a deep squawking sound and his massive wings spread.

The wind of his wings was enormous as he fluttered down to the ground and she covered her face to protect it from twigs and snow.

As she lowered her hands, the bird was gone, replaced by the most beautiful woman Etani had ever seen, all the more shocking as she'd expected to see a man.

Her skin was a stunning black, and her eyes were the eyes she herself had once owned.

Markings covered her perfect flesh in strange spirals and spots in the same blue and green that her feathers had held only a moment later.

Her hair was black, streaked with that same blue and green.

"Hello, Etania," the woman said in a voice that was like silk, and Etani swallowed, closing the distance to the woman. "It has been some time since I saw you," she said and Etani frowned, surprised.

"You have seen me?" she asked.

The woman laughed softly, the sound high and warm. "Of course, Gabriela was the love of my life. But alas she did not return my love and so I watched and ensured no harm came to her daughters," the woman said gently.

She swallowed, unsure of the woman but when the beauty embraced her, she hugged her back tightly.

"I have been monitoring your progress; you are a braver woman than any I have ever seen," the woman whispered in her ear.

"Thank you," she said gently, that kindness and softness digging into her heart.

Breaking away, the dark beauty tucked her fingers under Etani's jaw, and their lips met.

The kiss was soft and deep, not entirely for the magic they shared; it was one of love and admiration and she found herself melting into it, desperate for that kindness and affection.

Tears stung her eyes as the woman held her tight, squeezing her, and the kiss deepened.

Daemon growled and the woman smiled against her lips, drawing away.

"Ah, there they are," she whispered and Etani blinked. "Those are the eyes I fell in love with."

Whether she was referring to Gabriela or herself, she didn't know, but she longed to feel that warmth again. It was selfish and she felt cruel for wanting to abuse that love, but part of her was so desperately lonely and craving affection that the kindness of the woman had settled into her heart like acid.

"When you are ready, my beloved, come find me again," the woman said and smiled. Her startling blue eyes were warm and Etani wanted nothing more than to go to her right then and there, but the woman had turned away and with a heavy gust of wind, she was a bird once more.

Turning back to Daemon and Uzo, Daemon cheered and Uzo looked relieved.

"You're starting to look like your old self," Uzo said, and she smiled sadly, looking back to the bird who had settled herself down on the branch.

She allowed Uzo to pull her into his arms, he took her by the chin, staring into her eyes and she could see them reflected in his.

They were her eyes, the lightning blue ones that seemed to glow from within, giving her an eerie magic about her.

He kissed her forehead gently and she smiled, relieved by his presence. "Not long now," Daemon said and she nodded, her cheek resting against Uzo's collarbone.

"I want to rest for a while before we go on," she said and Daemon looked around, trying to decide where to take her.

"Come on, we should go back to the human world. I'll come here and see if I can round some of them up," he said and they agreed silently.

Taking them back to the human world, they set up camp beside a river and the moment Uzo sat down, she crawled into his lap and began to doze with the steady sound of his heartbeat in her ear.

"So why are you all burnt?" Uzo asked, the deep rumble of his voice soothing her.

"The Ifrit lied to manipulate her. We don't have a week, Megara and Cecelia are holding them off for now. I killed him," Daemon growled and Uzo swore, clutching her tighter to him.

"We can't tell her," he said, and Daemon growled his agreement.

"The Ifrit play the helpless but they are more demonic than even I. He used her compassion and fear against her."

She lingered just above sleep, content in her little bubble of warmth that throbbed in time with Uzo's heart and she considered the spark of fire that was the phoenix inside her as she drifted down and fell asleep.

When she woke, she was confused by their moving again and she squinted into the darkness of night, her body encased in the warmth of Uzo's arms. "Where are we?" she asked and Uzo looked down at her, fear on his face.

"Try to stay calm, we've been arrested," he whispered, and she jerked awake.

Her hands had been encased and she looked around to find they had been surrounded by guards and were being taken to the most dreaded thing she knew, a ship.

An armoured face appeared before her and the group was called to a halt, the man gripping her by the cuffed arms and yanking her from Uzo's hold.

"She's awake!" the man called and she stumbled, looking around in confusion.

They appeared to be elves and similar humanoids, but she was totally lost on why they would have been arrested.

"Good morning, Princess, it's a pleasure to finally meet you," a hissing voice whispered, and she turned to see a Naga slithering towards her.

"Where are you taking us?" she demanded, and he smiled.

"Well, since your demon refuses to help, we're taking you to the Under Dark so we can get you back to Winter," he said, and for one terrible moment, all she could do was laugh.

It was so completely ridiculous that they had just left Winter and there Winter was, following after them, and then Daemon refused to transport them.

Her laughter was only a little manic and the Naga exchanged a look with his companion. "Really? Winter is transporting us by *ship* to Faerie? Are you fresh out of gate keepers?" she asked.

"Most of the gate keepers are dead," he growled, and that shut her up.

She blinked at him, shocked by the news.

"The Creators are closing down all access to the human world in preparation. The Under Dark is the only remaining gate in this area."

She stared at him in horror, unable to wrap her mind around the news that the Creators had come so far already. She turned to Uzo who looked pained and she realised they had cuffed him in iron.

Daemon was unconscious on the back of a horse, limp and helpless.

Yanking the chain to get her attention, the Naga smiled at her, but something odd about the men kept her attention.

Several of the men wore unusual clothing, covering them from neck to feet, while the rest were dressed in more casual armour, and there was something about it that bothered her.

The slap sent her staggering and she gasped, pain shooting through her body.

"Pay attention when you are being spoken to!" the Naga screamed at her and she looked up at him, her cheek blazing red. "Hurry up, we have a ship to catch and Megara is impatient," he snapped and yanked on her chain.

Scuffles behind her told her that Uzo had gone furious at the blow but she let it slide that time.

The ship was enormous and the size of it made her feel only slightly less anxious at the prospect of sea travel. When they had been loaded, the oddly dressed men joined them while the remainder of the men left and it made her even more suspicious of them.

But her suspicions were put on hold as she was taken to her room and she screamed in delight at the sight of a steaming bath. She ignored the guard and ripped the shirt from her arms, jumping into the soapy heat and moaning at the feeling of finally getting clean.

He stayed with her, trying not to watch as she doused herself in oils and thick creams that left her smelling like lavender.

Only once the water had gone cold did she get out and dry herself off, the chain long enough that she could do most of it on her own.

The clothes that had been left were suitable for her hands being cuffed, too, and she pulled on a long black dress with no frills or layers. It was little more than a skirt with two strips of fabric that crossed over her breasts and tied at the back of her neck and she demanded the guard help her with the tie.

He did and she smiled up at him, finally feeling clean.

"Am I allowed to explore?" she asked, and he nodded.

38

WINTER

Several hours of travel later she stood at the bow of the ship, anxious and wanting to be anywhere but onboard with so many men. She did not suspect they would try and harm her in any way, but they still made her nervous and she found herself looking down into the water, wondering if any sharks prowled below.

Daemon was still unconscious and Uzo had been bound below deck, and as such it came as a surprise when she heard footsteps approaching her. She ignored them at first, trying to place the pace, but then realised that firstly the steps did not belong to either of her companions and, secondly, they were getting faster.

Her eyes narrowed as the figure came upon her and she exhaled a slow breath, hearing the singing of metal on leather.

Had he wanted to sneak up on her, he should have drawn the sword before reaching her, not when her delicate hearing could catch it.

The sword screamed as the air rushed past it and she turned, dodging an upward thrust that had been intended to impale her.

She glimpsed silver hair, pale skin, and white tattoos as she caught the wrist and slid her foot in under his lunge, tripping him.

With a tug she shoved him unceremoniously off the bow of the ship and he hit the water with a splash, and then a thud as the ship struck him.

Peering down, she lifted her fingers to her nose and inhaled the scent of male elf.

Turning at the soft scuff, she came face to face with four men, all of them smiling grimly at her, all having similar white tattoos that gave off a soft glow. They all had silver hair and wore nothing but pants, skirts, or cloths tied with belts.

The man in the forefront had tattoos on his face as well, his long hair catching in the breeze and his left arm covered by dragon scale and bone armour. He had a trident; the rest had long, thick, curved swords.

Setting her backside against the railing of the ship, she watched them calmly as they advanced, more curious than anything else.

Two of the others had gauntlets, but the fourth was unprotected and that was what made her more concerned than all the swords in the world combined. He either didn't need a weapon, or his body created weapons.

At least the sight of the four had calmed her of her fear of the ocean below.

"Don't suppose we can all go back to our cabins and pretend this never happened?" she asked, and the smallest of the men grinned. He had a rather large scar running down his face, his tattoos mostly lines and large dots.

The leader had a circle on his chest and the unguarded man seemed to be covered almost entirely in them. Man number three had circles and spirals, allowing her to easily identify them, and she found herself deciding what each headstone should have marked on it.

"Winter sends its regards," the leader said, and her brows lifted.

"Well, I know where I'm heading next," she said, and pushed herself off the railing, stooping to press down the tops of her boots and revealing six knives she had stolen from the galley.

Spirals seemed surprised, but the leader did not.

Scarface only seemed amused by her intention to fight them.

"All at once or one at a time?" she asked, reaching behind her and sliding two long blades from the small of her back and settling them in her palms.

Something moved behind her and she tilted her head back, finding a fifth, very wet, and very angry looking man looming over her, his hair a pale brown and his markings mostly circles within circles. It reminded her somewhat of an arrow target.

She knew which parts of him to aim for.

Turning, her knife lifted and she drove it deep into one of the targets on his thigh, earning her a satisfying scream as she leapt back and spun, her knife lifting to defend herself from the trident that had been aimed for her side.

It gave him quite the reach and she stepped into it, her next step driving her foot into his ribcage and throwing him into the railing.

Dropping her free hand, she hooked three fingers into the loops of her knives and flung her hand out towards the unarmed man, but he dove out of the way, leaving two of her knives in the wood of the ship and the third in the water.

Disappointed that she had only scored one blow, the remaining two were on her and she blocked a heavy overhead blow with her knife thrust upwards, her body bending backwards to absorb the impact of his strength and then recoiling to throw his arms backwards.

Lifting her foot, she slammed her heel into his solar plexus and he fell back, gasping.

She hissed as pain sliced through her side and she spun, back-handing Scarface as his sword flashed and blood splattered onto the wood.

It was not a deep cut, but she was still annoyed. Five on one was not good odds.

The leader came for her again, trident thrusting, and she blocked again, her defence attempting to get his trident lodged in the wood of the ship, but he seemed very aware of her plan and was prepared for it, though he pressed her back towards two of his men.

He was disturbingly fast, and as his trident recoiled, he swiped at her with his guarded hand and the fingers were pointed, tearing the clothes of her stomach and catching skin.

Dropping her hand to her other boot, she drew one knife and as he recoiled from the successful strike, she stepped into him and drove the small knife into his side, grinning as she snapped off the blade and threw the handle at the unarmed man, causing him to duck again.

The leader clutched his side and she turned to Targets, struggling with her knife. She was kind enough to rip it out of his leg for him, causing him to howl and aim a punch at her face, which she dodged with an easy step to the side.

He was not a major threat at that moment with his leg wound and she turned into the seemingly nondescript attacker, unable to decide what about him that made him unique but then deciding that his being so un-unique made him unique.

He lunged for her, timing his attack with Scarface, and she threw herself backwards into Targets and he fell off the railing, nearly ending up in the water again, grabbing a rope to save himself.

Mentally thanking him for the idea, she turned and caught the tail of one of the ropes and stepped into Nondescript's lunge and looped the rope twice around his head and neck. Spinning and turning to step around behind him, she heaved forward and his back slammed into hers, the rope pulled tight around his neck.

To keep Scarface and the leader busy, she plucked out her last remaining knives and threw first one, then the other.

Scarface seemed to have trouble with his scarred eye and he took the knife to the shoulder, the leader deflecting it easily. She didn't mind all that much, given she was only trying to keep them busy.

The man at her back choked and she scanned for the unarmed man in her peripheral while keeping her eyes on the leader as Scarface worked the knife free of his shoulder.

The fight thus far had only taken a minute and yet she had heard no cries of alarm; that fact alone making her realise they had been duped into going on the stupid ship.

She had to wonder how much fun her friends were having below the deck, if she was up there with the five of them. It was somewhat flattering that they had sent five after her.

Facing the unarmed man, a shiver rolled down her spine as she found his eyes to be glowing, his tattoos radiant, and frost starting out from around his feet and his hand where he held the railing.

Cursing, she turned and shoved Nondescript off the side of the ship, the rope pulling tight as he hung there struggling for breath and Targets rushed to save him from choking to death, leaving her Scarface and the leader to deal with.

Scarface grinned and she glanced down only long enough to see that the frost was reaching for her boots.

She took two running steps and leapt off the deck and onto the thick pillar of one of the masts, allowing her to climb up the ropes and metal bands that held it together.

The leader called something and she looked down to find Scarface running for the mast, beginning to scale it like a monkey, and she growled, placing one knife between her teeth and one in the back of her belt, and she climbed faster, the nimble bastard gaining on her.

Pulling herself up onto the horizontal beam, she skipped across and used the rope for balance, watching the slow creeping of the frost as it worked its way down the steps to the platform they had been standing on. She spit the bloodied knife from her mouth.

"Come on, you know that's cheating," she called out, and the leader laughed, staring up at her with a wolfish grin.

"Come down and we'll play fair," he called back. She lifted two fingers in a rude salute to his lie, turning at a grunt to find Scarface had joined her on the beam.

"Five against one, you lot must be good," she taunted, and he grinned, pulling his sword from his teeth.

"Got to send the best to beat the best," he said, and she laughed.

"Flattery will get you everywhere," she purred, and he returned her laugh, stepping along like the monkey he was.

He swung at her and she ducked, her knife flashing up, but he knew it was coming, jumping back and slapping away the blade, returning with an overarm parry that she barely caught, her fingers tight around his.

"Can you fly?" he asked as he pressed down on her and she bared her teeth at him.

"Sometimes. Can you?" she retorted, pressing upwards and then taking the cheat's way out. She punched him in the groin.

His eyes watered and he staggered back, toppling from the beam, but caught himself in the shroud before he could end up in the water.

"Now who's cheating?" the leader called out and she looked down at him, offering a sweet smile.

"All's fair in love and war," she called back, turning to look at the second of the three masts. Sighing, she gauged the distance and leapt from the beam, catching the rope that she supposed was meant to be a safeguard to keep the mast from falling over, and slid down it, much to her hand's resentment.

Her boots hit the deck and she smiled as she heard the leader following her, leading him up onto the stern deck and turning to watch his approach and observe the others.

Scarface was climbing down and, unarmed, had pulled Nondescript up from the side of the ship. Targets was still unable to walk, trying to encourage his healing to seal up the wound.

That gave her time to deal with the leader and she waited patiently for him to join her.

"Having fun?" he asked as he approached, and she grinned.

"Nothing like a good assassination attempt to get the blood flowing," she replied, making a note of Scarface's recovery as he clutched himself and wheezed. The frost seemed to have stopped while its maker was trying to help Targets with Nondescript.

"Why elves?" she asked as the leader's pace slowed at her waiting for him, taking him in with his long skirt that had been tied at his right hip, trailing to the ground and leaving one leg exposed. It had been bunched around his left ankle and bound there, making it look more like half a pair of green pants than a skirt.

"We work for Megara," he said conversationally, and she nodded.

"Megara sent you?" she asked, her eyes lingering on the circular pattern on his chest, partially covered by the strap that held his arm guard in place.

"No, we came on our own. But we don't feel she would disapprove."

She laughed gently, making him frown. "No, I'm sure she'd be thrilled to find out her band of assassins went and tried to assassinate the rightful Queen. I'm sure that news will go down really well,"

His smile was angry; they both knew she was right.

"Unless the rightful Queen just suddenly vanishes without a trace."

They both stopped at an enormous boom from below the decks and she smiled slightly, amused at the mental image of Daemon losing his cool.

"But that doesn't tend to happen," she said and turned back to him, watching his slow approach out of the corner of her eye while he thought she was distracted.

Scarface seemed to have recovered as well and was making an attempt to come up behind her.

"It will this time. A tragic accident with their ship going down at sea."

"That's not very nice. I really don't like the ocean and would prefer if you didn't try and drown me."

"I wasn't going to drown you. You'll be dead before you reach the water."

"Are you trying to scare me or turn me on?" she quipped, making him pause, confused.

She was amused when he glanced down at her, the same reaction most men had when she reminded them that she was a woman. When it came to fighting, one often forgot the sex of their foe. He took in the dress and ripped fabric that revealed the tops of her hips and the bottom of her ribcage, her long hair lifting in the breeze.

He shook his head, meeting her eyes and her wicked smile, and glared at her.

She took advantage of his momentary distraction and lunged for him, a heavy overarm blow, and her free hand reached behind her for the second knife, using it to slice cleanly across his gut.

Spinning, she threw the bloodied knife at Scarface and it caught him in the side.

Both men went down, and as the leader did; she bounced back up and drove her knee into his face, throwing him backwards onto the ground.

Stepping over him, she kicked his side and then ducked as something came whizzing towards her, flying past and then exploding in the ocean several metres behind the ship.

Straightening, she looked to the bow of the ship and the unarmed man had geared up for another ball of whatever magic he was throwing.

Lifting her knife, she glanced down at the leader and cursed as he grabbed her ankle, yanking her leg out from under her.

She landed hard on her knee and rolled, swearing at herself for becoming distracted, only to find his grip was tight on her.

Flipping over onto her back, she growled as he crawled up towards her, bloody and grinning. At least he had been until she smashed her boot into his face and she felt his nose break.

He let go of her and she rolled to avoid Scarface's boot aimed for her side.

Looking up, she found Nondescript looming over her, a very large and angry-looking bruise forming around his neck. "Nice necklace," she said, earning her a boot to the ribcage and she felt all the air leave her lungs.

She ignored it, instead rolling with the kick and throwing herself up onto her feet only to lift one hand up in a gesture for them to wait and then bending forward, heaving in a breath.

They waited, oddly enough, until she got her breath back and she straightened, only to duck again when another ball of something flew over her head.

Scarface moved as she straightened a second time and his fist found her sternum, throwing her back into the railing and knocking the air out of her a second time.

He followed after her, sword raised, and brought it down, the blade lodging in the wood of the railing as she threw herself sideways and into the leader. He grinned as his sharp fingers curled around her throat and she went for the cheap shot, though he was prepared, using his trident handle to block her attempt to kick his groin.

His fingers clenched around her throat and she hissed, her empty hand reaching for his fingers to try and pry them off her.

Laughing, Nondescript appeared at her side, then darted back again when she tried to stick her knife in his stomach.

Her eyes locked with the leader's and she offered him a faint smile as she tapped into the flame that was buried deep inside her and screamed for it, her body erupting into golden flames.

It lasted only a second, but it was enough to get him to let her go and she turned, not expecting the next magical attack from the unarmed man, and it hit her squarely in the chest.

Landing hard on her back, she gasped as cold flooded through her and she rolled to avoid another boot, finding her hands empty and having no idea where her knife had gone.

She could barely breathe, clutching at her chest. Again she rolled, not sure of who was coming after her.

Flinging herself to her feet, she staggered and sucked in a breath through her teeth, the coldness burning through her flesh to leave a large black mark that spread out in tiny veins as coldness inched its way out from the strike point.

The unarmed man whooped in triumph as she staggered backwards, holding onto the railing for support.

Her racing heart sent the ice faster through her and she cursed, realising she had tapped into the flame too early and would have to hope that it was able to heat her up before the cold spread too far.

The leader had been burnt in her flame, but it only seemed to make him angry and he stomped after her, followed closely by Scarface and Nondescript. It appeared that Targets had been forced to retreat, his bleeding leg making him weak.

Backing slightly, she pressed her hand to her chest and found the skin there to be freezing cold, burning her hand, and she hissed.

"Don't suppose you'll take a surrender?" she asked, her breath escaping her in a little cloud of mist.

The leader only smiled at her grimly, the three men spreading out around her to guard her retreat.

39

NO SURRENDERS

Deciding that their silence was enough of an answer, she considered her situation and how convenient her past abilities would have been had she managed to keep the dragon or werewolf traits; even the Naga would have helped.

But she was no longer a demon or vampire, no longer a chimera. Instead she was mostly harmless creatures and that was more than a little annoying to her in that moment. What good was a sphynx against assassins? Was she going to riddle them to death?

If push came to shove, she would take her chances in the water, but that was going to be a last ditch effort. She wasn't sure if she could outswim a shark.

"What was the flame?" Scarface asked.

"Fire magic," she replied, not knowing why she answered, but he had been polite at least.

He grunted and she realised they were waiting. Looking down, she found the blackness had spread another inch in the moments of their conversation and she pressed at the fire, pleading for it to hurry up.

"I'll give you three wishes if you go away," she offered, the men exchanging amused looks and shaking their heads. "Worth a try," she breathed, and decided she needed one of their swords. She aimed for Scarface, his two wounds and seeming visual difficulties making him the best target in her eyes.

She drove her foot into his raised arm, he deflected it, but hadn't prepared for her to spin and throw her elbow into his temple. Her elbow screamed and he went down.

"Thank you," she quipped as she took the sword from his hand and spun it, aiming it downwards and driving it into the join of his shoulder and neck.

It only took a second and the man collapsed onto the deck, his collapse allowing her to drag the sword free and turn on Nondescript, who came for her.

His anger made him erratic and she was easily able to deflect his overhead blow, using the sword to push it up and then to his side. She took advantage and drove her fist into his face, causing him to stagger back.

Turning to the leader, she found his hand coming for her and she turned, not fast enough for his backhand that sent her crashing to the ground.

He was on her in an instant, dropping his knee into her gut and curling his fingers around her throat.

Gasping, she reached out but found the sword to be missing from her side, only barely able to reach it, not enough to grab it. Her free hand pulled at his fingers and her knee to his back did nothing to dislodge him.

His teeth were bared, furious that she had killed one of his men and his unarmoured fist rose, driving down onto the side of her face.

She was unable to draw in enough breath to scream in pain, his armoured fingers crushing her throat and allowing not a single shred of air to enter or escape her body.

She reached for the sword, the handle taunting her fingertips with bare hints of a touch, her head beginning to spin.

Grasping it, she drove the handle into the leader's jaw and he fell off her. Gasping in a breath, she rolled onto her side and shoved herself onto her feet, staggering away from Targets, Nondescript, and the leader as they made to follow her.

Someone's fingers curled in her hair as she reached the stairs, dragging her back and drawing up her head to expose her throat.

The blade against her skin was cold and she went still, panting as she realised it was the unarmed man, holding one of her knives.

"Slit her throat," Targets snarled from across the deck, but the leader growled his fury.

"Not yet; I want revenge," the leader hissed.

He stumbled into view and she looked up at him, a small bead of crimson forming where the knife bit into her skin.

The unarmed man, whom she now dubbed the Magic Man, given he was no longer unarmed, eased the pressure on her throat so that when the leader drove his fist into her gut, he wouldn't accidentally kill her.

She crumpled under the strong blow, managing to hold down her stomach contents as they all threatened to come up and it was the man's grip on her that kept her off the deck.

"You killed my man," the leader snarled, his armoured fist landing on her cheek and tearing the soft skin to leave shreds of it on the guard.

"To be fair, you tried to kill me first," she wheezed, her retort earning her another blow to the stomach and she whimpered, collapsing to the ground as the Magic Man let her go. Curling into a ball to protect her stomach, she could see them out of the corner of her eye.

"She'll be dead in the next ten minutes," the Magic Man said, ignored as Nondescript stepped up behind her and drove his foot into her back, her voice ringing out in a cry of pain.

"She deserves a slow, painful death. Not one by your magic," the leader snarled, using his foot to roll her onto her back and she looked up at them, smiling weakly though she felt like vomiting on their feet.

"Either way, she will be dead."

She touched against the flame and laughed inside her head, focusing it and in an instant she engulfed herself in flames once more, the fire burning off the ice inside her and she took advantage of their distraction to roll and throw herself away from them, towards the stairs.

They swore and came after her as the flame died and she leapt down onto the main deck, knowing she wasn't as fast as she needed to be but neither were they.

She took them on a merry chase around the ship as she found herself back on the bow and cursed as Targets came up before her, Nondescript leapt over the railing, and the leader and Magic Man approached behind her.

She looked between them, frowning, and then backwards at the water. There was always that option but she really didn't want to have to go swimming.

The leader had lost his trident somewhere, and that left him as the only one unarmed. It didn't make for great odds on her side.

Deciding her best chance was to throw another one of them overboard, she turned to the leader and offered him a smile.

"Shame about your friend," she said tauntingly, and he gritted his jaw. "Close, were you?"

"He was my brother," the leader snarled and she laughed, looking between them all.

"Sorry about that."

Targets lost his cool and she found it rather fitting that he would be the one to end up back in the water. So when he came for her, she drove her foot into his shin, grabbed his head as he staggered and pulled it down, guiding him face first into the railing and then scooping her arm under his gut and heaving him up and over the railing.

There was a splash and she was down to three.

"Do you think he'll stay down this time?" she asked, smiling at the livid leader and his two remaining men.

"I'm going to make you regret the day you were born," Nondescript said, and she laughed.

"I do that on a regular basis," she quipped.

A boom rocked the ship and all eyes turned for the disturbing buckling of the deck, the wood seeming to bend outwards in a way that was both terrifying and enthralling.

Taking advantage, she drove the sword into Nondescript's stomach, his grunt drawing the attention of the last remaining men and she calmly plucked his sword from his limp hand as he fell against her, eyes wide.

"Three down, two to go," she said and smiled, now having two swords.

"I wonder how many of yours we killed," the Magic Man said and she flicked her attention to him, eyes narrowing.

"If it's less than yours, then it will be worth it," she growled, and he smiled in response.

The leader seemed to be beside himself and while he was having his meltdown, she went for the Magic Man, swinging for him and her knives were deflected by the same blue balls of magic he had been throwing at her. The swords were growing cold, but she ignored them as she drove him back and then around, an idea forming in the back of her mind.

She pressed him, keeping an eye on the leader and when the Magic Man tripped, she took full advantage.

He tripped over Nondescript and as he fell, she stepped forward and both swords found his chest even as his back found the boards.

They lodged in the wood beneath him and then froze over. Immediately she let go and danced back, right into the waiting arms of the leader.

She yelped, trying to jump away, but he caught her, his gloved hand curling around her face, the other wrapping tight around her middle and trapping one arm against her body.

She lifted her free arm, clutching at the armoured hand even as the sharp guards bit into her skin and he strained.

Horrified, she realised he intended to rip her head off her shoulders and she let go of his fingers, driving her elbow once and then twice into his ribcage. Her neck burned, her blood running down her face, but still he refused to let go.

Stamping down on his bare toes with her bootheel worked only after she ground down, one of his toes breaking, and he threw her from him, her body colliding with the wheel.

Turning, she found him coming for her, blood blinding her left eye and his fist flying for her gut.

She doubled over, allowing him to drive his knee up into her face and her back hit the deck with a loud thump.

He dropped onto her stomach and his fist rose high above her, driving down and barely missing her as she tilted her head to the side, merely clipping her ear.

Throwing her foot off the boards, she hooked her ankle around the front of his neck and pulled, dragging him down into an arch and then hooking her other foot around his throat, locking him in place.

His sharp gauntlets tore through the leather of her boots and her skin, but she ignored it as she turned her foot and squeezed, cutting off circulation.

He strained, his body bent backwards, and he changed tactic, instead going for her calf and his fingers dug into her flesh.

She screamed, his fingers finding the tendon and ripping it free, her foot releasing, and he sat up, grinning maniacally at his success even as he licked her blood from his guard.

His fingers curled around her throat and she gasped, her nails digging into his wrist but she didn't have the sharp nails that she needed. No, that was still four away from where they were, and she was being choked out.

He leant his weight into it, crouching over her, and she gasped for air, unable to suck any down.

He was so close she could have kissed him if she was still a Celestrial. Instead she went for the only other idea she had and bit the tip of his nose.

He screamed, his jerk allowing her teeth to rip the tip of his nose off and she spat it out, shoving him off her and turning for the Magic Man. Crawling for him, she ripped the knife free of his frozen fingers and screamed as the leader caught her ankle and dragged her back.

Flipping onto her back, he loomed over her, dripping blood onto her and as his eyes flashed murderous rage, she drove the knife into the side of his neck and he slumped on top of her, the knife cutting vital nerves.

She whimpered as his weight crushed her, feeling his breathing slow and then stop as he died and she relaxed in sudden relief that they were all dead. She had taken out five royal assassins.

Rolling him off her, she pushed herself up onto her knees and screamed her triumph, knowing it was stupid, but she needed to voice her win.

Hearing footsteps, she ripped the knife free of the man's neck and turned, finding Daemon standing before her, his face livid and covered from head to toe in blood.

He took her in and then he was on her, clutching her to him and she clung to him in relief.

"Where's Uzo?" she demanded, and he cocked his head towards the deck.

Without thinking, she turned her head and her lips found his. The kiss shocked him for an instant, but then he was kissing her back and she pulled herself harder against him, relieved that he was okay, and they had all survived.

He pressed her back into the mast and she sighed into his lips, the sound making him shudder in delight. His fingers dug into her back and she traced her tongue along his lower lip, the motion forcing his lips to part and he groaned as she slid the smooth muscle past his teeth and he met it with his own.

Suddenly going rigid, he threw himself back from her, panting with eyes glowing that same golden yellow she knew all too well. "You stop that," he demanded and she shook her head, trying to clear her thoughts.

"Don't you want me?" she asked, her voice sounding small, and he growled, his need almost radiating out of him.

"You know I do, but not now. Not yet." He was struggling with himself and she smiled, stepping closer, and she saw him waver, the need inside him and his demonic tendencies driving him wild.

"Don't you want me to be loved even once?" she asked, and his eyes went wide at her implication.

She wanted him to be the first man she was with willingly, her body screaming for him, and he swallowed hard to try and clear the dark thoughts from his mind.

"Not yet, not until I can't accidentally kill you," he whispered, and she considered him, finally nodding once in understanding.

He had once told her that mortals never survived him, and she was still mortal.

"But after? Once I'm not mortal?" she asked, and he nodded, his hunger touching her like a physical finger on her soul. "Do you promise?" she asked, and he shivered.

"I promise," he whispered, and she smiled, the tingle of his magic entwining them. He went to her then and enclosed her in his arms, warm and safe as Uzo came out onto the deck and saw the carnage.

"I suppose you don't need to be a Fae to be an assassin," he said in wonder, and she snorted, pulling him into the embrace.

"Daemon, the Creators are moving to close the gateways and shut off the human world, we are running out of time," she said, and the demon cringed, exchanging a look with Uzo that she didn't understand.

"There is only one gateway left," Uzo confirmed and Daemon nodded.

"They might be aware of what we are doing. They might be hurrying," Daemon said, and without a word, he pulled them through to Winter.

They stepped out into a small clearing where someone waited, looking bored though he smiled when he saw them.

"I was starting to think I was going to miss the party," the dark skinned man said, looking bored and amused by the sight of them. "I thought she was a brunette?"

"She normally is, but the phoenix got to her," Daemon said, the man nodding his understanding.

"Nice to meet you, your majesty," the man said, making her start at the title.

"This is the Genii Loci," Daemon said, and she frowned, thinking the name had been a species, not a specific being.

"Pleasure," she said warily.

"I'm afraid I am running out of time, so we will have to make this quick. You might consider joining me, a lot of big names will be there," the Genii said as he took her hand and his kiss was brief but wonderfully cool and dry.

The magic he spilled into her made her feel odd, like she needed to be sure they were both alone and safe. Glancing around, she made note of her surroundings in a way she had forgotten to do in the months since she had become a human.

"Thank you," she said gently, the Genii smiling warmly in response.

"Perhaps you would be so kind as to allow us to accompany you to this party?" Daemon asked. The Genii beamed at them.

With a wave of his hand she felt magic swirling around her and her torn dress changed to one that was whole, longer, with a train with the front filled in with fabric, becoming a front sheath instead of a cross.

It left her arms and back bare, but it curled up her throat and covered her far better. Long gloves snaked up her arms and her hair pulled up into a pile atop her head set in with a silver tiara.

Turning, she saw both men changing as well, Daemon's clothes becoming whole again with the chains around his neck, his hair a tousled mess that triggered all the right things in her.

He caught her stare and smirked, the rings in his ears and lip returning, dark kohl lining his golden eyes. His coat was long, patterned with silver, with a thick lining of black fur around his neck.

Uzo's clothing melted into a black jacket and pants, simple and elegant, that suited him very well, tight without being too tight and revealing in a way that made her only slightly uncomfortable, his hair ruffled and shortening. The colouring of the blue marks on his cheeks seemed to brighten sharply and he grinned at his new clothes.

"Let's go see Sobek," he said, and her stomach clenched as Daemon slid his arm around her. In the next breath they were pulled through to a massive foyer, the Genii getting there on his own.

40

GODS, WITCHES AND PIXIES

he room was empty, but the sound of footsteps told them someone had only recently vacated the room and they were quick to follow the steps, the doors swinging open on their own, leading out onto a small balcony.

Looking down at the floor below, she smiled at the sight of the dancers. They moved in perfect synchronicity as though they had choreographed the entire thing. It was an absolute sight to behold, their cold blacks, blues, silvers and greens blending into beauty.

Turning to the announcer who cleared his throat at their dawdling, Daemon leant closer and the man's black eyes turned to her.

He had a mask in the shape of a crocodile and she found herself staring back at him, fascinated by what Sobek might look like. "Announcing Eros, Lord Uzo Ernin of Winter, and the Princess Etania of Winter," the man called and the room went silent, faces turning upwards to them, and she shivered at the sight of so many predatory eyes finding her.

She was indeed famous; a man stood at the back of the room— much to her surprise he did indeed have the head of a crocodile, his eyes were black and his long mouth pulled up into a smile as he spotted her.

He wore a white skirt that seemed to be bunched up around his navel in a loop around his hips, a large strip of blue and black fabric hanging down the front and a wide, gold belt holding it all in place. Around his chest and upper arms were more gold and he wore an enormous gold and blue headdress.

Finally tearing her eyes off him, she found other unusual faces in the crowd: the jackal; the cat whose white eyes had locked on her, contrasting sharply with beautiful black fur and silver jewellery; the ram; the falcon. She froze in fear at the sheer number of Gods who had congregated at the party. Not only them, but Loki grinned in the back of the room, the dragon sat with hungry eyes on her. The spiked and feathered headdress depicting a half moon that was Hecate, and the white-haired giant with a belt loaded down with lightning that was Zeus.

Their eyes bored into her and without a word, she accepted Daemon's hand and they descended the stairs into absolute silence, Uzo moving at her side.

Many more whom she didn't know by name stood around her, judging her in ways she had never expected to be judged.

The crowd parted as they approached the dais upon which Sobek sat once more and he grinned, his bronze hand lifting. To her surprise, he shoved up the crocodile face to show a wild, excited, and dark-eyed humanoid face. As the crocodile head lifted, it became still, stiffening into a mask.

He stepped down with bare feet to greet her, his teeth sharply white against his dark skin. "Etania!" he boomed into the silence. Loki laughed in a high giggle that broke the silence.

The music kicked up but no one was dancing, they were still watching her as the warmth of Sobek embraced her.

"Don't suppose you're here for me?" he asked.

She shook her head, smiling at his warm welcome. "Not yet, but we aren't far from you," she whispered while he nodded, looking mildly disappointed.

He was incredibly good looking with black paint around his eyes and a little curl of a beard on his pointed chin. Smiling, he kissed both of her cheeks warmly. "Who is the lucky chump?" he asked, and she laughed softly, the sound seeming to catch far too many eyes.

"Theseus," she said, making the God look up, his black eyes scanning the room.

"Hey, hero boy!" Sobek called out, and a man turned.

He looked both entirely normal and incredibly abnormal in the same instant, naked and incredibly muscled, with nothing covering his bronzed body except a tall helmet on his head with a spray of crimson bristles.

He beamed as he approached, taking her into his arms and laughing at her furious blush at the sight of his nudity up close. He was not the only naked one in the room, but none of them were pulling her into a tight embrace.

"I had hoped I would be included in all this," he said happily, his soft brown hair forming curls close to his head. His eyes were a deep, warm brown that wrinkled at the corners when he smiled.

"Lucky you, you're first," Daemon said.

Theseus grinned widely, clapping Daemon on the back. "You old dog, how did you manage to get the Queen on your side?" he asked, but Daemon only shook his head.

"One day you will have to tell me," Theseus said as he turned his eyes to her.

He was considerably taller than her and he stooped, his hot fingers finding the underside of her jaw, lifting her chin to meet his lips.

Her mind did a disturbing warp and she was certain she was going to throw up, but when it settled, she felt suddenly like she could actually think again, clear and rational. It was the oddest feeling and she found herself frowning up at him.

"You're a hero, aren't you?" she asked, the man beaming.

"Close enough to a God," he said.

She nodded her agreement, though she wasn't entirely sure of the difference.

"You and I will have to have a long talk soon, little fledgling Goddess."

"I'm not a Goddess," she retorted, but he boomed out a laugh.

"Not yet, but you will be before much longer."

With that, he tapped her nose to make her jerk back, and he swept away, bellowing at someone and tackling a newcomer who vanished into a crowd, screaming a battle cry.

"Gods are strange creatures..." she said, and Daemon snorted his agreement.

"This is why I don't come to these things."

"Is it not strange that there just *happens* to be a party with all of them in one place?" she asked, looking to Daemon, but it was Sobek who spoke.

"I knew you were getting close, so we called everyone together who was anyone. Most of us have been watching your progress and many have been monitoring your family for some time. We knew when you would be coming for us."

She looked at the God and he smiled, amused by her confusion.

"We want you to succeed," he said, and when she smiled, his smile faltered and he swallowed, looking at Daemon. "Is it always like that when she smiles?" he demanded. Daemon nodded. "Try living with her for a year. She enchants everyone she comes across," he quipped, ignoring her as she glared at him.

"Did anyone think to invite Mags?" Daemon asked

"She's around here somewhere, lurking as she does," Sobek said, and he looked around the crowd, finally pointing to the underside of the stairs.

Following his gesture, she met the silvery eyes of a blind woman who frowned and then scurried away.

"Stay here," she said to Daemon, who growled his response but she was after the old woman, hitching up her skirt and leaping off the dais, her bare feet light on the marble only to skid to a stop and look up into the black face and white eyes of Bast, unable to bring herself to walk past the Goddess.

"I love you," she breathed hurriedly and curtsied, then was off again, leaving the beautiful Goddess utterly baffled, long fingers stretched out for her retreating back.

The crowd parted for her, people staring down as she streaked through them and she found the corridor that the old witch had scuttled down.

Skidding on the marble, she changed direction and sprinted after the witch, the crowd chuckling behind her at the chase. The woman came to a sudden stop and spun on her, throwing something. Etani ducked, and a scream came from the room behind her as green light shot out in beams.

She was on the woman, grabbing her arms and holding them out.

Her eyes went to the woman's nails and she found they were her own.

"Why come if you weren't going to give me what I want?" she demanded, and the old woman hissed like an angry cat.

She was skinny, with huge ears and saggy breasts, a long chin and big nose. She had stiff white hair tied back with a kerchief and she wore nothing but rags, a little bottle with a fairy in it hanging from her hip and a pouch overflowing with blue petals bumping against it.

She was covered in beads and bones that made up her jewellery and she glared up, making Etani certain she was not at all blind.

"Curiosity killed the cat," the woman growled.

"But satisfaction brought it back," Etani countered, making the woman cackle at the proverb.

"Clever little beast, aren't you," the witch cooed.

Etani frowned, glaring down at her. "Will you give me your magic?" she demanded. The witch pursed her thin lips.

"If, after all this, you use your magic to make me eternally young and beautiful."

Etani paused, frowning at the witch before she tilted her head, curious. "You would ask for something so simple?" she asked, and the witch nodded. "Very well, after I have returned from the dragon, I will make you so. When you are ready, come to me," she said, to which the witch grinned, flashing yellowed teeth.

The kiss was short, rough, and weirdly hairy, the magic abrasive, and she let go of the witch as her fingers began to burn.

Crying out in pain, she clenched her fingers, and when she released them again, her palms were bloody, her nails a deep silver and razor-sharp once more. "Bloody demon…" she whispered, the witch cackling her agreement.

"He was very careful with his breeding of your ancestors," she crooned, and Etani looked to her, shaking her head in disgust. "Run along, little witch, you have others to see and your time is short. The Creators know what you are up to, someone spilled the beans on your secret." The witch burst into green flames and was gone, leaving her alone.

She stepped back from the spot the witch had been, still looking down at her hands when she bumped into someone. Spinning, she came face to chest with the Goddess. "Sorry!" she gasped, jumping back in horror.

"What are you up to, little fledgling Goddess?" the Goddess asked, her feline lips turned up into a smile of amusement.

Her voice was a soft purr that made Etani want nothing more than to listen to every word, her movements so incredibly graceful that she felt like a toddler with a backwards foot.

Etani was so completely starstruck that she could only stare, hypnotised by the animated beauty of the ancient Goddess of Cats.

"You should be more careful running after people, you'll get yourself hurt," the Goddess said when it was clear Etani was incapable of rational speech.

Bast reached for her, the black skin of her hands smooth and soft, her long nails black and sharp, but she was intent on her work.

Pulling Etani into a room, she considered it before she went to a closet and ripped apart an expensive-looking garment, returning to mop up the blood, and examined the healed wounds.

"Why did you say you loved me?" the Goddess asked. Etani finally swallowed.

"I have an affinity for felines. They're the only creatures not afraid of me. One of my ancestors was a werecat and I always felt... I don't know, like I belonged to you."

Bast considered her with those luminous white eyes and she bent forward, pressing her nose gently to Etani's.

The zap of energy between them made her jump and the Goddess laughed softly, straightening up.

"My blessing for a fledgling Goddess. May you know love and joy in music, dance, and the love of a feline to call your own," the Goddess whispered while Etani almost melted.

The Goddess's slender fingers lingered on her cheek as she moved away. "Oh, also may your lineage be eternally strong, with the man of your choosing. Never with a man to whom you do not desire it."

The tall Goddess swept from the room and Etani stared after her, entirely baffled by the blessing. Did that mean she would be unable to procreate unless it was her own wish?

Collecting herself, she moved to head out the door when it was flung open and four men piled in, followed by a small fluttering creature.

The Snake God looked down at her irritably, Sobek looked amused, and Daemon looked flustered.

The pixie flitted around in a state of manic excitement while Uzo appeared worn out.

"Get to work, Apophis," Sobek demanded, and the bronze-skinned man stepped forward, his lips pressed into a hard line.

"I do not approve of your existence," Apophis said abruptly. She took a step back from him, affronted by his tone.

"Well good thing you'll never have to see her again after this," Daemon snapped, and Sobek gave the God a shove in the back.

"Eros, this is entirely your doing from start to finish and you should be punished," Apophis said as he approached her.

He looked quite similar to Sobek, except that he had a snake atop his tall crown and another around his throat, even one as a belt, and they made her exceptionally anxious.

Without a word, he caught her around the wrist and his hot, hard lips came down on hers in a rough kiss that forced his magic into her with no concern for the damage the sudden force would cause.

She staggered back from him and he let her go immediately, his lips curling in disgust at her weakness.

"You should have bred a stronger God," Apophis hissed at Daemon. Daemon snarled back, moving for her, but Sobek had already reached her.

She didn't have time to process before his lips came down on hers and she shuddered against him. His magic was slow and sensual, brushing against her senses like a lover until it settled low and then lower, somewhere below her stomach and into the region of her groin.

She was confused by that until she remembered that he was the God of Fertility. She jerked back from him and he grinned, amused by her retreat.

"I was always impressed by your fighting tactics and the fact that you got pregnant by a Lich," Sobek purred while she glared at him.

"A Lich?" Apophis demanded, staring at her and then Sobek before turning on Daemon.

"She did. Her husband is the Lich in Ayathian," Daemon said, and Apophis looked at her again.

"Well, if nothing else, Sobek has opened us up to a whole new era of mixed species," he said dryly before stalking from the room.

Sobek grinned wickedly. "You could always give me a child you know," he cooed, and she slapped him.

He jerked back, holding his cheek, but he was laughing as he left the room, almost bouncing in his retreat.

"Gods… think they own everything," Uzo said and the pixie tittered, fluttering down. With a burst of sparkles, a tiny woman was standing before them.

She had a round, cheerful face and small, pointed ears, her transparent wings tight against her back and wearing nothing but shreds of colourful fabric. "I'm so glad it got to be me!" she squealed in a voice that made Etani's ears sting.

"Me, too," Etani lied smoothly, the pixie seeming even more excited by the lie. It didn't hurt her any to lie to the creature but it made the pixie happy. When she started to care about what others thought she didn't know, but it seemed to be working.

Her hair was a spectacular shade of purple, short and stuck up in a little curl above her head, and her eyes matched in a softer shade of violet.

As she smiled at the pixie, the tiny woman approached and it was Etani who bent down for once; the kiss was soft and sweet. The pixie smelt of water and fresh air, her skin cool and smooth as silk.

The magic that flowed into her was slow and warm, curling around her like a blanket that left her shivering, but there was no obvious change in herself.

She cupped the pixie's cheeks and rested her forehead against the smooth, small head of the pixie. The tiny woman quivered in excitement as though she were going to explode.

"I won't ever forget you," she whispered. The pixie squealed, exploding into a cloud of sparkles and zipping from the room.

Etani snorted, looking after the glittering light, amused.

"You're cruel," Uzo said. When she looked up at him with wide, innocent eyes, he met her gaze with one of disbelief. "And I'm not falling for that. You're as devious as Apophis."

"I am perfectly kind and nice," she said, giving him a mock glare.

He tapped her nose and Daemon grinned, pulling her into his arms.

"So close now, only twelve left!" he crowed. She couldn't help but grin at his enthusiasm, allowing him to pull her from the room.

41

SIREN AND STRIGOI

The remainder of the party was a whirl of dance, delicious food, and laughter as she was passed from hand to hand in some sort of celebration she didn't understand, but enjoyed nonetheless. Male or female, humanoid or animal, she didn't care.

She knew she was being sucked into the magic of the dance, but she gave in wholeheartedly and revelled in it, the hours melting away until finally the party broke up.

Bast found her before she left, tracing black fingers against her jaw and kissing her forehead before sweeping gracefully from the room, leaving Etani to watch her go longingly, before being pulled into a slow dance with Daemon.

"Welcome to the club," he purred, and she lifted her brows in question.

"What club would that be?" she asked curiously as he drew her up against him, their movements slow and careful.

"The club of Gods of course. Do you think they would celebrate like that for just anyone?" he was amused by her lack of understanding.

"I keep saying I'm not a God," she countered and when he dipped her back, he held her there, his golden eyes hooded.

"You are, though, at least once you get back to your magic. The newest Goddess of Faerie." His lips found hers and she shivered, her arms snaking up around his neck. She met his kiss with her own, not caring if they were the centre of attention.

A delicate cough made him draw back from her and they looked up at Sobek who smirked slyly, his hand on his mask.

"You're welcome to stay and recover from your travels. We have baths and clean clothes prepared for you all," the God said.

Shoving Daemon off her, she took Sobek by the hand and pulled him into a tight, hard hug. "You are the most wonderful creature in all the worlds!" she gasped and he threw a smug smile at Daemon before leading her away, his warm arm wrapped around her middle. She went eagerly, leaving Daemon and Uzo to follow after them.

She stripped out of her dress and undergarments the moment she hit the steamy room, ignoring the men behind her as they struggled to strip.

The bathing room was enormous and there was only one giant tub that one could easily swim in, but she didn't care. Pulling the pins out of her hair, she was finally forced to give up, turning on Sobek, who looked like he was about to faint.

"Help me, would you?" she asked, and glared at Uzo and Daemon, who had already streaked past her and into the water.

Sobek's long fingers made quick work of the pins and she smiled her thanks before jumping into the bath. She melted into it, fully submerged in the hot water and revelling in it. She popped back up and looked around at the God who settled himself down by the bath on a bench.

"So how many do you have left?" he asked, offering them bottles when asked for them.

"The pixie was what? Thirty-seven?" she looked to Daemon, who nodded as he scrubbed his hair, eyes clenched shut before he dunked his head forward into the water.

She waded across to Sobek, who squinted down at her before picking out a bottle. She took it, opening it to smell an oddly spicy scent that reminded her of Nayishma.

"So that leaves twelve of the birth species plus the Lich and the vampires. I think there are only three left from Faerie."

"Which ones are those?" he asked as he handed her a pot of sand that she accepted politely, using the sand to scrub her skin raw.

"Aswang, Dominick, and the Strigoi."

Sobek looked like he was choking and she looked up at him, concerned.

"Are you all right?"

"The Strigoi aren't going to help you," he said, sounding horrified. Daemon looked up, frowning.

"Why not?" Uzo demanded as he moved up beside her.

"Surely they will if the loss of the humans is at risk," she demanded, fear washing through her.

"The Strigoi don't feed off humans, they feed off the immortal, it's what makes them Strigoi," the golden God lamented.

She looked at Daemon who was frowning, chewing on his inner cheek as he thought. "Is there anything we can offer them?" she asked, doing her best to ignore her anxiety.

"Likely they will want you," Sobek said as he motioned to her.

"Why does everyone want me all of a sudden?" she demanded.

Daemon snorted in amusement. "They've always wanted you, now it's just more important. To have a young Goddess and Creator on their side?"

She squinted at him and lowered herself into the water until only her eyes were above it, refusing to listen to him.

"You can't hide from this, little one. We need them."

"I'm sure you can try and bargain with them," Sobek said, but he didn't sound overly certain, increasing her anxiety.

"Do you think we could reason with them? A lot of us will die off if there are no humans," she said finally as she surfaced.

"It will make it easier for them to return to power," Sobek countered, shocking her by the news.

"The Strigoi were in power?" she demanded, both Daemon and Sobek nodding.

"Before the human world was created and the Fae became more

powerful, the Strigoi were the leaders. There were always the Courts, but the Queens were controlled by the Strigoi. They will do whatever it takes to get their hands on a Queen they might be able to control again."

Frowning, she shook her head and poured a healthy amount of oil into her hand. Using it to scrub her hair, she ducked her head under the water. She wasn't about to let herself become the tool of the Strigoi, or any of them. But she didn't know what to expect from them and so she would just have to wait and see.

"Is Stacius still alive?" Daemon asked, looking relieved when Sobek nodded. "Well, we will go directly to him, he might help us."

They finished their bathing and dried off without much more being said between them, everyone lost in their thoughts.

The clothes they were given were sturdy leathers and soft fabrics in various shades of black. She was delighted to see she had been given pants and a comfortable-looking top that covered her entirely.

Braiding her hair back from her face, she looked around at Sobek, then swept the God into a tight hug.

His arms wrapped around her in return and he squeezed her, his lips firm on the top of her head.

"If nothing else, you are welcome to come live with me," he said, and laughed as she aimed a punch for his ribs that he leapt back from.

He reached up and pulled down the mask, the stiff visage coming back to life as his handsome face was hidden and he grinned, sharp teeth flashing.

"We'll see you soon, I hope," Daemon said and Sobek nodded, watching as they left through the tear in realities that dumped them out into a large cave with a waterfall opening the egg shaped space to the sky above.

It was stunning, warm and green, with moss everywhere. The water was so incredibly clear and blue that she could see the forms below moving.

The sirens were very similar to mermaids, except they looked less like fish and more like eels with long tails ending in sharp fins. They were various shades of purples, blues and even some greens but they were radiantly beautiful, even with their large webbed ears and red eyes.

They didn't seem to have noticed the intruders into their cave and Etani smiled as she watched the beautiful dance.

Sirens, unlike mermaids, were capable of becoming humanoid on a whim while the mermaids had to go through a whole ritual to have legs and it took a great sacrifice, as it meant they were unlikely to ever be a mermaid again if they did not genuinely wish for it.

It was the main reason why the mermaids and sirens hated each other and why one would never find them in the same body of water.

There were about five down there and they were eating something, or perhaps it was a someone, so when she crouched down and stirred the surface of the water, all eyes snapped up and what appeared to be a human leg was between them, torn and shredded by shark-like teeth.

They stared up at her for a second and then moved like she had never seen before. Speed and grace weren't enough to describe the way they cut through the water like it was air and the first siren was on her, gripping her wrist.

She smiled at the siren, who while underwater was hairless and eerily beautiful, but when her head broke the surface, long black hair sprouted from her scalp in the wake of the falling water.

She was a rich purple colour with violet tones, her forehead and chest a deep green along with stripes over her arms.

"Hello, sister, I'm afraid I'm not up for dinner tonight," she said and the siren looked first amused, then confused by the sight of the two men.

Realisation dawned on her beautiful face and she looked down, making an odd whistling, squealing sound.

The other four shot up like arrows and they were all exquisite; the body of what had once been a man sinking to the bottom of the pool, forgotten.

"You're the one everyone is talking about?" a silvery beauty whispered, looking stunned when Etani nodded.

"I remember you," a blue and silvery-toned siren said, looking at Daemon, and Etani turned to see him blushing.

"I um... like their singing," he said nervously, and the blue siren giggled.

"You like more than that, you perv," she purred at him, her sharp teeth flashing as she licked her lips.

"We didn't think you would make it this long," the purple beauty said and Etani looked back to the siren and found that her hand had been dipped into the water.

"Stop trying to pull me under; I'm not going to let you eat me."

The siren pouted and let go of her wrist, wading back to join her sisters.

"Well, then we aren't going to help you," she said petulantly, but Etani only smiled at her and straightened.

"Well, that's fine," she said, turning to look at Daemon and Uzo. "Do you suppose someone will come and get them before this world is pulled down? I imagine the rivers in Faerie will fill up quickly. The mermaids will probably get first dibs." She looked at Daemon, her tone conversational, but she knew how the siren would react.

Their hiss was low and angry and the sirens shoved the purple siren back towards the shore.

"Go do it."

"We don't want to share with the mermaids."

"They smell."

They seemed rather eager to get the task done and Etani smirked, the purple siren looking irritated, but she shrugged.

"If it means we get to stay here..." she said finally, not wanting to cooperate at all.

"You will, I'll even have the occasional human sent your way," she bargained, and the siren's lovely face lit up.

"Male," she said and Etani nodded.

The siren's tail split and she stood, naked and lovely in her unashamed nudity.

The siren took her hands and her lips were wet but not slimy, smooth and clean with just a hint of blood.

The magic moved through her like a whisper and she shivered as her throat began to itch, her vocal cords tightening and then releasing again to make her feel like she needed to cough.

"Thank you," she said gently and the siren laughed, looking over her shoulder. Her voice had caught the attention of both men and Uzo smirked, Daemon looked as though he was going to pop like a soap bubble.

"You're welcome. Watch out for that one, he is devious," she said with a gesture towards Daemon.

Etani smiled and nodded, watching as she dove into the water and her tail returned seamlessly. "Stop staring at me," she said, not needing to look at Daemon to know he was staring at her and the effects of her voice were turning on all sorts of needs in his brain.

His hand was tight on hers as he drew her from the beautiful cave and she desperately wanted to go back and join her sisters in the water, but she was not foolish.

They stepped out into Winter, but only the chilly air told her that it was Winter.

They were inside a massive foyer and their appearance sent a small man scurrying from the room.

Daemon glanced at her and Uzo before he let out a slow breath and followed after the small man into a long corridor lined with doors.

The floor was tiled in black and white, the walls were black and the doors were a dark wood that gave everything a dark, creepy feel to it.

At the end of the corridor, they stepped out into a large living room where three men stood around the cowering small man who had fled.

Turning at their intrusion, she froze in place at the sight of them.

She had never seen anyone so incredibly terrible and attractive at the same time and their eyes seemed to dig into her very soul as they looked in her direction. Uzo froze in place as well, his breathing seemed to have stopped just as hers had.

Daemon was the only one who wasn't affected and he approached the group. "Friends, how are you?" he called, trying to break the cold silence, but it wasn't working.

The Strigoi embraced him nonetheless, their eyes lingering on her and Uzo with a keen interest.

"Have you brought us dinner?" one of the beautiful men asked, smirking.

They all looked very similar, black-eyed and black-haired with snow white skin and long nails. They wore the same black robes and black hoods, but no two looked exactly the same and she found herself studying them with intense interest, trying to find what was different about them.

"Not exactly," Daemon was saying and the tallest of the three turned his eyes directly on her.

Her breath froze in her chest as he gave her his attention and everything seemed to melt away to leave her with nothing but those black eyes and his lips turning up into a smile.

He was so incredibly beautiful that it was painful to look at him, like she needed to cut out her eyes so she could never see anything but him again, the most perfect creature to ever exist.

He crept closer to her without her noticing and it was only when his fingers touched her cheek that she realised the danger she was in.

It was the exact same response her body had gone through when Versalis turned his attention on her human body, but this was a million times stronger and she was in his arms, not having a clue when or how she got there.

Distantly, she was aware of the second Strigoi at her side, his attention on Uzo and she frowned, something about that bothering her.

"Don't you want to join me?" the Strigoi whispered in her ear and she shivered, his fingers gentle as he tilted her head back and to the side, exposing the smooth line of her throat to him.

Daemon was speaking, getting angry, but it didn't matter to her.

She was trembling in a burning need to feel the Strigoi's teeth sliding into her skin, desperate for it to happen and still he teased her, refusing to give her what she so desperately needed.

"Stacius, listen to me. You can't let them hurt her, she's Etania." Daemon sounded frantic and she gasped as a hot tongue touched her throat, his breath cooling the moisture and her legs gave out.

His breathy laugh was like nothing she had ever heard before, his arms the only thing keeping her from hitting the floor.

Uzo seemed to be faring better than her, the Strigoi shoved back from him.

Teeth grazed her throat and she whimpered, needing it like she had never needed anything in her life.

He gave her what she wanted and she cried out as two sets of fangs pierced her throat. Several things happened very fast then at the sound of her pain and bliss.

Daemon flew into a rage and Stacius suddenly leapt back from him. Uzo grabbed the Strigoi by the hair and dragged him back from her and the flame inside her woke up.

Her body burst into flames spontaneously and the Strigoi was thrown back from her, leaving her to sink back onto the ground with the oddest sensation settling low in her stomach.

The wall behind her was aflame and she looked at the beautiful flames and the way they called for her to dance with them, to move and sing and destroy, but she couldn't, her legs weren't working.

She looked up as Uzo tried to reach her, but he was unable to get any closer to her flames and she smiled at him softly, content in her fire.

Daemon grabbed the Fae and pulled him back; they were shouting and the Strigoi were screaming. The one who had bitten her was gone, left as nothing but a humanoid shape of ashes on the ground.

The remaining two screamed in rage at the loss and she looked up at the four men, fighting over something that she couldn't really hear through the roaring flames that were her.

She was going to miss the phoenix when it left her, it had saved her more than once now, and she gasped as the flame found her throat, digging into the bites and down into her. She realised then that the saliva of the Strigoi had paralysed her legs, leaving her unable to stand, but the fire had found the traces and was burning it off.

Only once she was able to move again did the fire around her die down and she pulled herself to her feet using a chair that was only half on fire.

"Get that witch out!" the Strigoi screamed and she looked at him, curious, then at the ash body, and then back at the Strigoi as a darkly amused thought trickled into her mind.

"Give me your magic or I do that to you," she said, and the Strigoi froze in place, staring at her.

"We will not be threatened, witch Queen!" Stacius screamed, and she smiled at him, stepping forward, and she lifted her hand to touch him.

She had no way of calling the phoenix to help her again so soon, but he didn't know that.

They moved back from her and she followed after them, forcing them to have to deal with her.

"Who are you, witch?" Stacius demanded, and she smiled.

"Mattie and Jeanne are my ancestors. I'm Tatialia's granddaughter. I'm your great to the tenth-degree granddaughter."

He went still, searching her face, and she realised he hadn't actually looked at her properly until that moment. His eyes locked on hers and his lips pressed down into a hard line as he realised she wasn't lying.

"I didn't know Jeanne had any children," he said slowly, and she shrugged.

"One girl, every one of them, until Lutheral."

The Strigoi stared at her before he turned his attention to Daemon and growled. "You are responsible for this? You kept up with your stupid game with the Gods?"

Daemon grinned, amused. "Sure did, and she is my success,"

Daemon quipped. "I suggest you give her what she wants before she kills you."

"You're my blood, you belong here with me," Stacius demanded, and she laughed.

"No, Stacius, I belong in the human world, but it's nice to know you care."

Her fingers touched his cheek and he flinched, but she kept the pressure light and persistent.

"You would kill your own blood?" he growled, and she tilted her head, curious about him.

"If you refuse to give me what I want, yes," she said simply, and he glared at her, furious.

"Fine, but this isn't over," he growled and his fingers were sharp on her arm as he brushed her hand away. He caught her by the back of the neck and pulled her against him, his lips dry and warm, rougher and older than she expected.

His magic slid into her like a shadow, flooding down into her and bringing cold to the tips of her fingers.

He released her and his face showed his triumph. "Maybe now you'll be more willing to listen to your family," he said and she lifted a brow, her face blank.

"Perhaps so," she replied calmly, as she stepped back from him. She ignored the flames as she swept from the room and his laughter followed her after what he had seen in her eyes, the coldness that dripped its way through her and left her feeling finally secure in her distance to those around her.

42

WITCHES AND ELVES

They left the burning house to the Strigoi and Uzo and Daemon hurried to catch up to her as she left and then turned on them, stretching out her hand for Daemon to take.

He hesitated, then took it, searching her face, but she kept her expression calm and blank.

The two men exchanged a look and then Daemon guided her through the tear in reality to a different but equally large house. It was as bright and friendly as the Strigoi house had been dark and foreboding, leaving her somewhat shocked by the difference, but they were back in the human world, at least.

Their arrival seemed to have set off an alarm, because the door burst open and a tall, slender young woman stalked out.

She had dirty blonde hair and bright green eyes, pale skin. She was wearing a dark purple and black, corseted dress that ended in tatters around her booted feet. A cloak with a tall hood covered her head and she wore a star around her neck on a long chain. She stared down at the three of them, her lips pursed as she considered them all.

"Her only," the woman said, and she immediately started forward, leaving them behind her without a word.

It was not uncommon for men to be refused entry to a coven,

given the witches tended to believe men were little more than animals if they weren't also witches, and mythical men were the worst of the worst. She was glad that her clothes hadn't been burnt off in the flame this time, though. The magic had been expelled outwards, leaving her skin and clothing singed but unharmed.

Her boots thudded on the steps as she followed the swishing skirt of the woman directly into a crowded sitting room.

It was filled with couches, large cushions, bird cages and hanging herbs, plants in pots, and it was packed with women of every shape, size, and description.

She froze at the sight of so many hostile faces and contemplated leaving, but the door shut behind her before she could turn to it.

"Come in," the blonde witch said and she stepped forward slowly, nervous as the air positively vibrated with the restrained magic of so many witches.

"Hecate told us you would be coming,"

Etani looked at her and nodded. "Yes, I saw her," she said slowly, unsure of what to say.

"You saw Hecate?" a tall, buxom redhead demanded.

"Yes, she was attending a party," Etani said warily, unsure how to speak to the women.

Witches were usually quite peaceful creatures, but she was a dangerous intruder and that made them wary and hostile towards her. She didn't blame them at all, but it made her very aware of how many there were and how few she could take down if she had to try and fight. It wasn't a good number.

"I'm Naile," the blonde said and offered her hand. Etani took it and did her best not to jump at the spark of energy that leapt between them. Naile only smiled at the exchange.

"Why are you here?" a small, dark-skinned brunette demanded, and Etani turned to her, taking in the chocolate colour of her skin, eyes and hair, and leaving her wondering again about the possibilities of the humans. The girl was not human, but still.

"I have come to ask for the blessing of your magic in order to return to my own powers."

"We know exactly who you are, Pulchra Morte, you'll not have us."

The name sent a shiver down her spine and she gritted her teeth, frustrated by the stupid title. "I am neither interested in witch souls, nor capable of taking them even if I did want them," she replied, knowing it sounded rude.

"Too good for you, demon?" the redhead snarled, and Etani snorted.

"I enjoy life, no one messes with the witches if they want to live," Etani said, and they exchanged looks. "You thought we left you alone because we don't want to eat you? Please, witches are rumoured to be delicious. But no one wants to cross Hecate, if they survive the magic you lot throw out," she crossed her arms under her chest, staring the redhead down. "Witches have been off limits for as long as anyone can remember," she said when none of the witches said a word.

"What if we refuse?" the redhead demanded, and Etani looked up at her, frowning slightly.

"Then we'll keep going until we find a witch who will help. But we are running out of time. The Creators have closed most of the gates and will be coming here to bring down this world in less than a week," she said.

The news made the witches anxious and she could feel the change of mood in the air. They were no longer angry, they were scared.

"How do you know that?" Naile demanded, and Etani turned to her.

"We were being taken to the Under Dark in order to take us through the only remaining gate in this area, the Ifrit even said it," she said slowly and watched as they grew even more afraid.

"Surely Hecate told you?" she demanded, not understanding.

"Hecate will take us to Faerie if things turn bad," the small dark woman said.

"All of the witches?" Etani frowned, highly doubting it.

"All of us," Naile said and Etani laughed gently.

"There is no way all of the mythicals who can get to Faerie, plus whatever creature they can drag along, and then all of the Gods bringing their people, will fit in Faerie," she said, and the witches exchanged another look.

"Faerie isn't that big and there are a lot of us. That's why this world was created, because Faerie isn't big enough. Not only that but how do you expect to eat? You're modified humans, you can't eat Faerie food." She shook her head at the naiveté of the witches.

"No, that's impossible. Assuming we all fit shoulder to shoulder, Faerie could never sustain that many lives, that many hungry mouths. So they either have to start a new human world straightaway, or else start removing the less vital creatures," It was cruel, but it was logical. "Or, we can avoid all of this by you agreeing to give me magic and I take back the power of the Creators."

"What's to stop you from doing what they are doing?" a heavy-set, blonde woman demanded and Etani glanced at her, smiling faintly.

"I don't like Faerie all that much. I'd like to stay here," she said.

"And if we give you our magic?" Naile demanded, and Etani looked at her, head cocked to the side.

"If what? There is no catch. I need a trace amount, then I leave you in peace. Or I leave you in peace and find someone else. As I said, I'm not stupid enough to mess with witches."

She folded herself down into a crossed-legged position on the carpet, tugging at a spot in her hair that was pulling.

"Honestly I can take it or leave it. I'm quite content to stay as I am without the rest of you. It's not like I enjoy running all over the world trying to convince creatures to give me magic and I could use a real break. We've been at this for far too long." She undid the braid and redid it, her eyes on her work. "In all honesty, I simply prefer this world, but I could live in Faerie just as easily and I'm quite good at adapting to new surroundings." She looked at the ends of her hair and frowned at the tattered look of the red strands. She had never had that issue before and she wasn't sure what to do about it. "But I tend to think it's all of you who care about this world given you have always been here. I was born in Faerie, so it's not like I don't know it."

Her eyes lifted from her braid as she tied it off again and they all stared at her in horrified silence.

"So it's up to all of you, we can go hand in hand into Faerie and damned be this world, or you can give me what I need and I go on my merry way hunting down the rest of these creatures and we all get to stay here."

She smiled at them, her hands on her knees as she looked from face to face.

"What'll it be, ladies?"

Naile stared at her, her face pale, before she finally shook her head. "No, you're right, we can't all fit in Faerie. Creatures will be left behind and how can we live with ourselves if we took a place and left another to die?"

"Vanish," Etani corrected, and Naile frowned in confusion. "You wouldn't die, you would simply cease to be. It's quite different and death is pretty easy going, but I don't imagine we would enjoy being vanished. At least with death you get to go around again. Vanishing is simply that, you are gone and that's the end of your story."

"How many times have you died?" the redhead snarled, and Etani looked at her, chewing on the edge of her nail.

"This century? Seven or eight, I think. I stopped keeping track a long time ago." Her tone was casual but her words made the redhead look like she had eaten a lemon.

Looking down at her nail, she frowned at the sharp edge and bit it again, trying to dull it down but her teeth weren't strong enough yet.

"As much fun as this conversation is, I have a demon and a vampire out there getting bored and I have nine more creatures to get through before this world goes down." She pushed herself up and tossed the heavy braid behind her, hands going to her pockets, and she smiled at them all.

"If you're really looking for a catch, I could owe you a favour."

That caught the redhead's attention and she bit her full lower lip. "Why would that matter?" she asked curiously.

"It's not often that I have to explain things lately, but I'm the heir to Winter and I will be Queen when the time comes." All eyes lifted to her hair and she grinned. "A temporary side effect of a phoenix. Should be two more and I'll have my hair back. I'm not liking the curly thing." She threw the redhead a sympathetic look and she snorted.

"Very well, I'll give you some magic, and you will owe us a favour. Each of us," Naile said, and it was Etani's turn to snort.

"No chance, little witch. Your coven gets the favour and you can argue it out between you. If it's within my power, I'll do it."

A general murmur went up and Naile looked to the redhead who seemed to be a fellow leader.

Finally the two seemed to come to an answer and Naile stepped to her.

Leaning down to meet the witch, she felt the magic sliding into her like silk, teasing around her skin and mind until she tingled deliciously with it.

She didn't feel any different, leaving her a little disappointed that she couldn't suddenly make things fly.

Without a word, she grinned and then licked the tip of Naile's nose, making the witch jerk back in surprise. "Careful, witch, one might think you enjoy kissing me," she teased and Naile blushed, making Etani laugh.

Ruffling the girl's hair, she gave the witches a wave and left the house to find Daemon and Uzo sitting on the grass outside the gate, looking bored.

They stood up as she approached and she smiled at them, turning to look back at Naile who had come to see them off.

She took Daemon's hand and he pulled them through the tear and... into Ayathian...

Etani pulled her hand free and turned slowly, staring around at the familiar hallway she had paced a hundred times before. "What are we doing here?" she asked, and a soft curse made them all look up to see Aelen glaring down at them.

"Hey, elf boy, come down here," Uzo said, and Aelen only looked even more annoyed.

"You brought us here for Aelen? Out of all the elves in both worlds, you pick Aelen?" she demanded, and a thump had her turning back to the elf.

"I'm not good enough for you?" Aelen growled, his eyes narrowed.

"Oh please, don't act all hurt now," she snapped back, and he grinned at her.

"How I've missed your attitude. How's the adventure going? I did make a note that I wasn't invited." He was teasing her and she glared at him, recalling when he had tied her to a chair and injected her with iron to keep her weak and unable to heal.

"That's because I don't like you," she quipped, and he put on a hurt face, but then smirked and his hand shot out.

He caught her by the back of the head and jerked her forward, his lips mashing down on hers in a fierce, unexpectedly passionate kiss that flooded his magic into her in a way that baffled her as though he had dripped ink into water, the cloud of it spreading out into her.

She jerked back from him and was about to yell at him when her ears stung and she gasped, gripping them.

In a matter of seconds they were on fire and she felt them moving, the cartilage tearing and ripping apart, the skin moving and pushing her fingers out of the way as they stretched.

At some point she had fallen to her knees, curled in on herself as pain radiated out from the sides of her head and it was over as suddenly as it had started.

Her fingers trembled as she felt along her ears, long and tapered as she had always known them to be.

"You look better with those ears," Aelen said, smirking down at her as she glared up at him, trailing her fingers along them. They were, indeed, her old ears back.

Taking the elf's offered hand, she pushed herself back to her feet and then kicked his shin.

He yelped and jumped back, her boot getting a good solid blow on his skin. "Why are you incapable of being nice to me?" he demanded, indignant.

"You poisoned me," she said, but it wasn't entirely the truth, or at least it wasn't the whole truth.

Daemon took her hand and she stepped back, being pulled by the two men. "That was business," he complained, and she narrowed her eyes at him.

"I'll show you business when I get back," she snarled, and his face split into a wide grin.

"I look forward to it, Princess," he purred, and they were through the tear in realities.

43

ABARIMON AND WERECATS

If nothing else, she looked forward to the end of their journey and a good year off duty, though she doubted she would be given that.

The thought got her through the day and it took that long just to find the village of Abarimon as they seemed to have moved from where Daemon recalled.

The Abarimon didn't seem to have gone all that far and they came across the village by nightfall.

The Abarimon were not generally that easy to spot, given they looked like perfectly ordinary humans with one difference: their feet were on backwards.

Regardless of that fact, they were some of the fastest creatures in either world and that was proven when they were suddenly surrounded.

One second they had been approaching the village and the next they had been stopped by no less than ten spears and Etani was getting more than a little tired of it.

"Can we just cut out the games? I want your magic because this world is going to die if I don't and I really don't want to keep this up for another month. We have one week and I'll kill you all if you refuse," she said it all in one breath, feeling very tired.

The Abarimon seemed more than a little taken aback by her and her speech, but she wanted nothing more than to take a nap. Was it really so hard for her to just get a break? More than just a few hours? For a year? Just a break for one year?

She was ranting to herself and she forced herself to focus, as the male and female couple before her looked at her like she was a crazy person. But it seemed that her threat was effective, if nothing else.

The spears lowered and they moved away from the trio, whispering softly.

"You know, something dawned on me just now," she said, watching them.

"What's that?" Daemon asked, watching the discussion.

"How lucky we are that there isn't a language barrier," she said and Daemon snorted.

"Luck has nothing to do with it, unless you count your bad luck. The average Faerie creature can understand all languages, you're one of the few who can't."

She looked up at him, indignant. "Well that's just not fair," she said moodily.

"You might gain it if you become Queen," Uzo said and she sighed, frustrated by her massive amount of magic, and yet her lack of it in the areas where it mattered.

"You'll just have to learn them the hard way," Daemon said and threw his arm around her shoulders.

She elbowed him in the ribs and he grunted, letting go of her. She offered him a sweet smile and stepped away from him, the Abarimon turning back to them and approaching.

Etani smiled slightly at the approaching male and he nodded to her, looking confused and wary, but it seemed they had no real reason to doubt her. Or maybe they simply didn't want to run the risk of her being correct and their being the cause of her failure.

Whatever the reason, she didn't bother to ask and she was just glad for a chance to have an easy win.

His kiss was tender and brief, but not so brief that he forced his magic into her; it was gentle, like the brush of a mother's hand against her cheek

She was eternally glad her feet didn't turn backwards, but she felt the burning in her lower muscles from her abdomen down, hardening and strengthening in a way she had never expected. Having never paid any attention to her muscles before, she didn't realise just how much they had to change in order for her to be as fast as she was.

He looked pleased when he parted and she grinned at him, grabbing the man and kissing him hard on the cheek to make him blush.

"Thank you," she breathed, and he nodded.

Her ability to run at such speeds was one of the things she had missed the most, the freedom and power that made her feel like a mythical creature, her ability to fly across the land.

Looking at Daemon, she grinned wickedly and his eyes immediately narrowed on her.

"Should have held onto her..." Uzo said, and Daemon lunged for her, but she was already gone, screaming her pleasure as she flew.

The Abarimon had scattered and their hoots were loud as she was able to finally run again.

Her legs burned in the best way and she knew that if anyone tried to take that from her again, she would kill them without a second thought.

For over an hour she simply ran, keeping in a relatively close circle around the vampire and demon, but she wasn't about to let them catch her.

Only after she got tired did she fly back to them and come to a skidding stop before the two, her hair a wild mess and her skin littered in tiny scratches as she'd zipped through the underbrush without a care.

"Better?" Uzo asked, and she nodded, her smile sheepish as she looked to Daemon. He looked angry, but not likely to try and tie her down and she took his hand willingly.

"Thank you," she said as she kissed his knuckles and he grunted in disgust.

Uzo only chuckled and took her free hand in both of his, the three stepping through the tear and out into a dense forest.

The air was thick and humid and she sucked in a breath, though it seemed to require two breaths to get the same amount she was used to.

Daemon paused to give her and Uzo time to adjust, the Fae seemed to be having the same trouble.

"Lightweights." Daemon sniffed, and she glared at him from her position bent over with her hands on her knees, trying to get in enough air.

"Where are we?" Uzo demanded, his hands on his hips and his head back in an attempt to expand his lungs as much as possible.

"I recall you made friends with one of the jungle tribe cats. Hopefully we can get him to help," Daemon said and she looked up at him, frowning.

"How do you know that?" she demanded, but Uzo looked guilty.

"That was my fault. We were discussing the war and I may have mentioned your fans and how angry Epharis got whenever the soldiers paid attention to you."

Sighing, she straightened up, but she still felt starved for oxygen. "Jagum lives here?" she asked, turning in a slow circle to examine the massive trees and the thick canopy. Staring up, she studied the weird cracks that formed in the canopy; no two trees were actually touching and it gave the ceiling of leaves a weird, dry earth look that she found fascinating, when she heard the sound of a puff and Uzo yelped.

Looking down, a second puff made Daemon jerk in alarm.

Uzo pulled a dart from his lower back and swore, his voice covering the third puff, but she threw herself backwards, just in case.

"What is it?" she demanded, as Uzo lifted the dart to his tongue and then spat it out.

"Sleep toxin," he snarled and turned on the spot.

Scanning the trees, she could see nothing and when a new puff came, she dove for the ground and rolled, flicking back to her feet and circling the two men, trying to find where the darts were coming from.

"I'm going down..." Uzo warned, his body swaying and she swore as he dropped to his knees and then his hands.

Wanting nothing more than to go to him, she growled as her impotent fury bubbled, hating that she couldn't or her pause would end with a dart in her.

A rustle made her look up and she saw a flash of movement.

Turning to Daemon, he was glaring at her, grabbing her arm and pulling her closer. "Go to Faerie and wait. I'll get Uzo there," he hissed, but he seemed to be struggling to focus on her.

"No, I'll stay nearby and get to you," she whispered and he nodded, the movement making him sway. She pulled her arm free and jumped back from a double puff; they were playing with her, seeing how long they could make her move.

Turning, she threw one last glance to Daemon and streaked into the forest.

A yell went out and she cursed as movements above her were no longer subtle; they were coming after her.

A massive body landed beside her and she threw herself sideways, claws missing her by a breath as she changed tactics and got a brief flash of huge teeth and orange-brown fur covered in mud and leaves.

Sneaky cats knew how to camouflage well in their surroundings and they were as fast as her when running, but she had the stamina they lacked.

Why couldn't the cats be as friendly as some of the others? Just willing to listen? No, they had to try and dart her, which was exceptionally rude.

Cutting off her mental criticism of the werecats, she changed direction again and headed back the way she had come, forcing her pursuers to change direction with her.

She saw him coming and threw herself to her knees, her boots being the only thing keeping her skin from being shredded on the rough ground, and he flew over her.

Rolling, she leapt back to her feet and was off again, unable to help but enjoy the chase.

She was on him before she even knew he was there and her sudden momentum change had her curling around his fist as it found her stomach. She whimpered, feeling something very long and very rough sinking far too deep into her.

Her scream cut off sharply as the claws sank into her and she looked up at the sound of a roar. Daemon seemed to still be awake.

She looked up from bone armour and feathers, to his leather arm strap covered in little darts, to his pierced flesh, and to his face. She smiled slightly as his bared fangs disappeared behind fuzzy lips and his golden eyes went from rage-fuelled to confused.

"Hi Jagum," she breathed, blood dripping from the corner of her mouth.

She had wondered what it would be like to have those six-inch claws sinking into her and now she knew it wasn't a good feeling.

He stared at her, horror crossing his face as he tried to figure out if he should rip out the claws or leave them in her.

So long as he didn't move it wasn't quite as bad as she'd expected.

"Princess?" he asked, seemingly unable to comprehend the situation and his tribemates were around them, triumphant that she had been stopped.

"Could you not move?" she asked as his hands shook and the tiny vibrations sent pain rippling through her body.

He quickly disengaged the claw from his wrist and curled his arm around her, his giant paw catching her around her chest while being careful not to bump the claws.

"How is she not dead?" one of them demanded, and a general growl went up.

"I'll finish the job," someone else said behind her and she clenched her jaw, ready for the blow that would end her life, but

Jagum caught the descending weapon and she shivered at the rush of air over her.

"You can't kill her, she's the Lich's wife. Princess of Ayathian," Jagum snarled, throwing the weapon away from whomever had been about to kill her.

At that point she was pretty disappointed that he hadn't killed her, all things considered, and she poked the bone claw that was sticking out of her stomach.

She wasn't entirely sure she was going to survive it anyway, so a quick death might have been nice.

Jagum lifted her easily off the ground and into his arms, earning a hiss of pain as the movement made the claws cut into her further.

"I should have beaten your face in when I had the chance," she wheezed and he snorted.

She found six oversized men looming over her, all wearing various designs of bone, horn, and leather armour. They all had different patterns of fur in various shades of browns, oranges, and even one soft grey.

They looked down at her in concern now that they knew who she was.

"Didn't you say she had dark hair?" a black-furred male asked, sounding sceptical.

"She did," Jagum growled, and she smiled up at him, causing more blood to bubble out of her mouth.

"I will," she said, and his eyes narrowed at her.

They moved and she looked up at Jagum, his jaw set and eyes hard as he led the streak of tigers and she noticed something above them. There were rope bridges everywhere, the trees set with large huts, and she realised the cats had set their home up in the canopy.

Fascinated, she followed the lines that crisscrossed the empty air and joined homes and businesses together in a tangled web that made no sense from below.

Coming to a small platform, Jagum shifted his weight on her and she tilted her head back to watch one of the tigers pulling on a rope, the platform rising.

Lifting her brows, she watched his tail swaying and found it to be a little hypnotic, swaying back and forth, back and forth.

She shook her head hard, refusing to give in to blood loss. Lifting her head, she looked down at the damage and made a silent note of just how much blood there was.

A scream made her look up once more and she found Daemon had been locked in a little hanging cage that was far, far too small for him.

He was furious, his legs dangling free from a little gap in the bars, staring down at her with furious glowing eyes.

She gave him a little wave and she was certain he would have set that cage on fire had he been able to.

Uzo was in a cage nearby, his poor face mashed against the bars and drooling as he slept. But Daemon seemed to be fighting it with every ounce of energy he had.

When they reached the canopy, Jagum turned and came to a sudden stop, an ancient-looking tiger standing before him, grey streaking his face and chest.

His eyes were cloudy, but they still locked onto her with eerie certainty.

"Kill her and the other two," the man said and Daemon growled, his eyes searching the cage.

"We can't kill her, she belongs to Prince Epharis," Jagum said, clutching her tighter to himself.

"The prince?" the old man said, his face thoughtful. "That's interesting, what might he do to get her back?"

"Not a whole lot, we're not talking right now," she wheezed, her head spinning and the old tiger looked down at her, smiling coldly.

"Get her help, if she survives we will decide what to do with her."

Jagum nodded and she felt a terrible moment of vertigo as the bridge swayed under him and she knew full well a fall from that height would kill them both. She didn't like being that high up when she couldn't be certain of her own safety.

She soon found out that the cats had cut away at the bark of the trees so that the trees wouldn't die but it gave them more room to work with.

The huts themselves were larger than they had appeared from the ground, a healthy ten paces between the outer wall and the trunk allowing plenty of room, with the walls covered in storage and the trunk carved into bunk beds.

The cat who approached her was a woman, though it wasn't overly easy to tell the difference between the men and women.

She was smaller, without a narrower chest, and she had six nipples running down her abdomen. She wore a short skirt that was split at the sides, much like a loincloth only wider. She had no skin piercings and her face was kinder. Otherwise she looked almost exactly like the males.

It was her smell that spoke of her sex though, the men being quite musky, but she had a sweeter, softer scent accented with jasmine.

She looked down at the wound and frowned, then back to Jagum, who gave a guilty shrug. "Why don't you just kill her and put her out of her misery?" the female asked, eyeing the wound.

"She's important, we need to keep her alive," Jagum growled and the woman sighed, shaking her head.

"Put her down then, I'll do what I can."

The removal of the claws was considerably worse than their going in and her screams echoed through the trees, muffled by Jagum's heavy paw on her face, but she made no effort to try and be quiet.

With a final, horrible sucking sound the claws were removed and the female pressed down hard on the wound with a cloth pad.

"You heal, right?" Jagum demanded, horrified by the large holes the claws had left in her.

She could only nod, her head spinning terribly, and she motioned for a bucket.

Jagum gave it to her and she emptied her stomach of blood and what little food she had eaten, heaving that made blood flow freely off the bed and onto the floorboards.

The woman cursed, working quickly to dig out any splinters of bone, and Jagum was quick to silence her new screams of pain as the metal tool dug around inside her.

Blissfully, she found the world darkening and she eagerly welcomed the darkness, wanting to be free of the pain.

44

———

PRISONERS

She woke slowly, groggy and exhausted, to find herself lying on the bottom bunk still, her body sticky with blood and her mouth feeling like she had stuffed it with cotton.

Rolling her head, she found Jagum had fallen asleep at her side, his lanky body stretched out on the floorboards. His head tilted back to rest against her thigh.

He was such a pretty specimen and she smiled as she lifted her hand and rested it atop his head, her fingers light on the stiff fur.

His eyes snapped open and he looked at her, relief showing on his face.

"Killing me would have been less punishment," she croaked and he snorted, shaking his head as he got up and vanished from sight for a moment. "Your butt is covered in blood," she said and he swore, returning to her side with a large mug.

She snatched it from him and downed the sweet, cool water with a loud moan of pleasure.

"You bleed more than a stuck pig," he complained, and she lifted her two fingered salute to him, making him chuckle as she drained the mug and held it out to him. "No more until you eat, or you'll be sick," he said, and his brows lifted at her glare. "Don't test me, woman."

She flopped back onto the bed and groaned at the hardness of it. "No wonder you're all so angry all the time. Don't you believe in mattresses?" she complained, her back complaining even louder.

"I have one in my house, but they're hard to clean so the hospital gets none," he said and vanished again.

A smell hit her and her mouth was watering before he rounded the corner. He carried a plate of meat that was big enough to hold almost a whole animal and he laughed at her intent stare.

There was a fork, but she ignored it, instead rolling up the strips of animal flesh and biting into them eagerly, the herbs and spices making her jaw ache from the sudden flavour.

Sitting down at her side, he held the plate out until she had scoffed almost half of it and groaned, belly full. "You don't eat much," he said, eyeing the plate.

"Have the rest, my stomach is smaller than yours."

He made a happy sound and started eating, freezing at a growl from the door.

Looking up, she found the female in the doorway.

"She said I could," he said, and she nodded quickly.

There was something about nurses that made them feel like disobedient children; they made most soldiers feel like that.

"Did you give her any of it?" the woman demanded and he looked at her, eyes wide.

"I ate half of it," she said, meeting his scared eyes with her own.

"Good, you get out, I need to check her wounds."

Jagum slipped from the room, his tail low, and she remained still, allowing the woman to check the wounds.

They were pink and angry-looking, but they had sealed over. Inside, she knew they hadn't knitted together and her stomach wasn't happy with the amount of food she had forced into it, but she was no longer at risk of dying.

"Good, you heal fast," the woman said, and Etani smiled slightly.

"Not as fast as normal."

The woman's brows lifted and Etani shrugged, pushing herself up into a sitting position and groaning as her spine popped angrily.

"Where are my friends?" she asked, trying to move as little as possible now that the bandages were removed. The skin felt like wet parchment and she didn't want to tear it open.

"The Fae and demon?" she asked, and Etani nodded. "Out in the cages. They've been asking for you."

Etani sighed, rubbing her eyes and frowning at the blood coating her hands.

"You can see them later, after you've had time to heal and bathe," the woman said, and Etani nodded obediently.

It was another several hours before she was allowed to get up and bathe, Jagum standing with his back to her as her guard while she turned the bath water crimson and then got dressed in a simple grey dress that had been provided for her. Her clothes had vanished while she bathed.

Following Jagum out, her eyes went to the cage and Daemon looked up from his intense conversation with Uzo.

"Etani!" he called, and she waved to them, smiling slightly. Uzo whipped around and his eyes burned with fury, but she didn't think it was at her. "Are you okay?" he called out, and she nodded.

"Healing," she called back, following along behind Jagum to get closer to the cages.

"Are you both all right?" she asked, several feet still separating them, but she didn't have to yell as loud to be heard.

"Better now. They underestimated the dosage and Uzo woke up soon after they took you to the surgery," Daemon said, his eyes lingering on her stomach.

Jagum shuffled and she looked up at him, the movement catching the attention of both men. They both stared at Jagum with murderous intent in their glares.

"This is Jagum, the one we were looking for," she said, and

Daemon's face spasmed as though she had slapped him, unsure of how to react.

"You were looking for me?" Jagum asked, shocked.

"We didn't come here for the fun of it. We came to get your help," she said. Daemon growled, and Uzo stared daggers at the tiger.

"What kind of help could I offer?" Jagum asked, but she didn't have time to answer.

Her conversation with the caged men had brought the elderly tiger out and he stared down at her, smiling grimly.

"So, you're all better. That was quicker than expected."

"Not better—" she started to say, and then she staggered back, his paw coming out of nowhere and she tasted blood. His claws had raked her face and pierced right through her cheek and into her mouth.

She nearly went over the railing under the force of his blow and she gasped, clutching her face that poured blood.

"You weren't given permission to speak," he snarled and she whimpered, clinging to the railing.

Daemon and Uzo had gone entirely silent, but she could almost feel the fury radiating off them in waves.

Looking down at her blood-soaked hand, she spat out the blood pooling in her mouth and tested the area as it healed over.

"What worth is she?" the old man was saying to Jagum, who shrugged.

"She might not be worth anything to them," he said, and she yelped as the old man gripped her by the front of her dress and she was suddenly being bent backwards over the railing. She clutched at his paw, very aware of how lethal that fall would be.

"What worth are you, girl?" he demanded while she clung to him, terrified that he was going to let her go and she would be ended.

"I'm valuable to Summer, and Winter wants me dead, but if you kill me you're going to regret it in a week when this world is brought down," she gasped, glancing behind her and whimpering as the ground seemed to be further away than she remembered.

"What are you talking about?" he snarled, pulling her up a tiny bit.

She wrapped both arms around his paw, knowing he could shake her off if he wanted to be free of her.

"I'm the reason the world wasn't brought down nine hundred years ago. When I lost my magic the creators got theirs back and they're coming to bring down the human world. They want Faerie to be at full magic again so they can try again. If you kill me you'll be killing everything in this world including yourself. You will be responsible for the entire world being ended."

He stared into her face and jerked her away from the edge, clean off her feet. He was strong for an old man and she hung from his grip, his face mere inches from hers. "How do we know if you're lying?" he growled, and she laughed, a dark sound that made his ears flatten.

"In a matter of days you'll find out, an instant before you get vanished," she said, and he bared his teeth at her. He shoved her forward, and she screamed as he held her out over the abyss. She clutched at his paw, entirely at his mercy.

"Why did you come here, then, if you're so important?" he demanded, and she glanced at Jagum, his eyes glowing in anger, but he refused to move.

"I need magic and we hoped we could get to Jagum without coming to a fight." Her dress made an ominous ripping sound and her face went pale, terror filling her. "I have been going around collecting magic from various species who I need to return me to my powers. I knew Jagum from the war, we thought he might be willing to help, but we didn't expect the ambush. We wanted to get in and out quickly!" She saw the tear in the fabric, slowly growing bigger the longer she hung there.

"And I suppose this means you want us to let you go free?" he demanded, and she nodded.

"Staying here would make it difficult to get to the others. After you we still have seven and then we need to get back to Ayathian for Epharis. You have to believe me!" Her body jerked as the fabric tore, and she whimpered loudly, clinging to his fist.

He considered her, what she was saying while in danger, and then the two in the cages, before he finally pulled her in and let go.

She slumped to the ground and clutched at her dress, torn down the front.

"We will have someone sent to Winter to confirm this," he said, and she looked up at him, her eyes wide.

"They want me dead, they don't care about the human world, they just don't want me taking the throne."

His eyes snapped down to her and she thought back over what she had said, realising she had told him too much. "Is that right?" he breathed, and she cursed; even Jagum was watching her with more interest.

"You can't keep me here," she said, but he was no longer listening. He motioned for someone and she was jerked to her feet.

Rope was bound around her arms and she whimpered as it pulled tight. Looking up, she found her rope attached to a pulley and as it pulled tighter, she was dragged backwards towards the edge of the platform.

"You have to let me go or we're all dead! I'm not dragging you to Faerie!" she snarled, and he only smiled. Glaring at him, she swore and drove her foot into his shin, making him howl, but then she was yanked backwards and she shrieked as her feet left the balcony and her shoulders burned.

She swung several times before settling a few feet from Uzo's cage, hanging painfully by her wrists. "I hate this world and everyone in it," she said to Uzo, who snorted.

"Could always shut it down when you're in power," he said, and she glanced at him, her shoulders settling into a steady burn.

"Tempting... very tempting," she sighed.

The hours passed and the sun set, leaving them in darkness. Her hands had gone numb, leaving her fairly sure she wasn't going to ever get her arms back down.

Someone had been sent from the camp but she knew they wouldn't be back in time, the portal to Faerie was too far away and they were fast running out of time.

Deciding she was going to make a try for the platform, she let out a breath and tucked her legs up behind her, thrusting them down, and she grinned as her body swayed.

Within a minute, she was swinging in long arches, growing closer and closer to the platform, straining to reach it, and she felt the eyes of the others on her, intent on her progress.

She reached the balcony and caught the edge with the ball of her foot, but then began to fall backwards and cursed quietly, trying again a second time and then a third time, able to barely touch the platform but not reach it fully.

Something caught her attention as she made her fourth attempt and she watched as the shadowy figure slunk along the bridge in silent intent, seemingly not having noticed her.

He made his way up to the platform and she cursed, unable to slow her progress, but she had an idea.

She planned to wrap her legs around the figure and either drag them out with her, or use them to keep her from falling back again.

But the figure had other plans and when she swung into them, arms went around her even as her legs went around them.

The low grunt was male and she looked up to see the dim face of Jagum looking down at her, smiling slightly.

"Clever little thing, aren't you," he purred, and she laughed softly.

"Don't suppose you're going to let us go?" she whispered, and to her surprise, he nodded.

He reached up and cut her down with a knife, his free hand on her back to keep her from falling. He turned and she let go of him, her arms screaming as she finally lowered them and she muffled a groan of pain.

Turning to the others, Jagum pointed and she looked up, barely able to follow the rope up and to the pulley system.

Jagum led the way and she followed after him, her bare feet only a whisper on the wooden boards.

They scaled up to the branch that held the rope and Jagum worked to feed the end of the rope through the two pulleys that added tension and allowed them to easily lower the cages, but the ropes shrieked in the pulleys and a shout came from somewhere.

Swearing, she looked to Daemon and Uzo, giving them a silent apology, and let go of the rope.

The descent was fast, but not a freefall, and Uzo's cage hit the ground, splintering open, and he cursed. Looking to Jagum, she frowned at his pulley that seemed to be a lot slower and she decided to take the risk.

Turning, she backed up and then took a running leap for the cage.

Daemon screamed her name, but she caught the side of the cage just as his fingers caught the sides of her dress.

The cage fell faster, but it wasn't until a second jerk had them both looking to Jagum as he hung by his fingertips.

She wrapped her legs around his torso and they went down quicker, their feet touching the ground and Jagum cut the rope to keep Daemon from being pulled back up.

With a strain of Jagum's muscles, the cage door was ripped off and Daemon climbed out, groaning at the pain in his muscles.

She went to Uzo, who was dazed but unharmed, and she grabbed him, heaving him to his feet, and they ran as arrows came down on them.

Daemon grabbed her hand and Jagum gripped her shoulder as she dragged Uzo and they fell through the tear and into a field thick with flowers and blinding sunlight.

Four voices cried out in unison at the sudden brightness and they staggered apart, hands over eyes and trying not to go blind.

"A bit of warning might be nice!" she snarled at Daemon, and he growled his response.

"I thought it would be night, I was in a hurry so you'll have to excuse me if I didn't consider your *precious eyes!*" he yelled back.

She squinted at him through streaming eyes and found him squinting back at her, his face angry but relieved.

Without a word, he pulled her into a tight hug and she hugged him back, glad they had managed to escape. "Anyone shot?" he asked over her shoulder and Jagum shook his head. Uzo was still a bit dazed, but a quick examination told her he had not been. "Good," he said, his arms tight around her.

"I guess you're joining us on this adventure?" Daemon asked, and Jagum shrugged, his eyes barely open and his fur wet from the tears.

"I hadn't intended to, but they know I helped you escape so I can't go back for a while. At least not until after this is done. You weren't lying about the world ending, were you?"

She shook her head and he sighed, looking a little disappointed by that.

"And the part about you taking the throne?"

Again she shook her head and he scratched at his cheek.

"We don't have time for this, give her magic and let's go," Daemon snapped.

Jagum nodded once and stepped to her, bowing his head, and his mouth met hers gently.

His magic filled her with warmth and the feeling of rough fur on the inside of her mind, warming her to the tips of her fingers.

Her eyes stung and she felt an odd tingling that started at her scalp and she shivered at the sensation of movement against her back, the curls falling free and the length extending down against her backside.

As he stepped back, he jerked at the change in her and she lifted a brow. "You changed," he accused and she looked down, picking up several long strands of black hair and let them fall free. "And your eyes," Daemon said, smirking. "Look more like a cat's now."

Her pupils were more oval-shaped than a human's and she preferred them that way. Without her eyes being like that, she struggled to see in the dark, but now she would be able to see quite well again.

"Phoenix is gone," Uzo said, and she looked to him, his face pained, but he was back to his old self.

"Sorry for dropping you, we were out of time," she said, and he nodded.

"Better that than leaving me behind," he said, his hand touching her cheek where the tiger had clawed her.

She would have scars, but she didn't really care. It seemed to bother him, though, and he pulled her closer, his arms around her in a tight embrace.

"We're so close," Daemon sighed, and she understood his relief. They had been going for so long that she was exhausted and she knew they must feel the same.

"How many have you been through?" Jagum asked, and she looked up at him.

"You make forty-three," she said, and he blinked at her, shocked.

"I didn't expect it to be so many," he said, and she laughed.

"It hasn't been easy, we've had to make a lot of deals and do some pretty bad stuff," Daemon said, and she twitched, remembering the Ifrit.

Jagum caught the reaction but said nothing, their grim silence enough of a warning for him not to press the matter. "What's left then?" he asked.

"Dziwozona, Asrai, Aswang, banshee, Dominick, the Fae, and the Celestrials."

Etani went still at that last one, having not really thought about it until that moment.

"How are we going to get the Celestrials?" she asked in a whisper that had Uzo and Daemon looking at her.

"Oh I didn't even think about that..." Uzo said, and they both looked to Daemon who frowned.

"We may have to get violent," he said, and she nodded.

"I can get us into the city, but finding someone to cooperate will be difficult," she said, and the idea of trying to sneak *into* Ceress had her shivering in terror. Cain was not the only assassin and while he was a good fighter, he might not be their best. He wasn't ever part of the elite. It would be exceptionally dangerous.

"We'll deal with it when we get to them. After all that we have Epharis and the twins."

Etani looked at Daemon and frowned, not liking the idea one bit. "We don't need to get the twins in particular," she said.

His face was dispassionate as he looked back at her. "Do you really want to risk it after all this?"

"Can we find another set of twins?" she demanded, but he shook his head.

"We don't have enough time to find another set of twins on short notice. We're scraping the limit as is."

"Fuck you, whore," she snapped, trying to come up with a suitable insult but coming up short.

Jagum looked shocked by her language, but Daemon burst out laughing.

"I love you, too," he purred and she growled. "Come on, you three, let's get moving. We're down to the single digits!" he sounded excited and his excitement affected her, making her mood lift with it.

45

DZIWOZONA AND ASRAI

They stepped through the tear after Daemon gave them time to get used to their new position. They took time to stretch and get the blood flowing again, tired and sore, but everyone was alive and that was what counted.

When they passed through the portal, they were prepared and the swamp they stepped into was cool and dim.

Looking around, she frowned as she tried to figure out where they were, but it was no good. They had travelled all over the human world and she had no idea which part they were now in and so she let it go, taking in the murky water and fallen, rotting logs.

This one wasn't anywhere near as pretty as the one with the Vodyanoy, but the woman made up for it.

She was absolutely radiant with long, deep green hair and pale skin. She was dressed in what looked like weeds wrapped around her, layered to hide her flesh and a dress. Her face was smooth and calm as she picked up long strands of weed and draped them over a fallen log with precise care. She hadn't noticed them and they simply watched her as she worked, calm and peaceful.

When she turned, she was shocked to see them and her eyes were pure white, no pupil breaking up the white.

"Hello," she said, confused by their appearance.

Dziwozona were omnivores and one of the few peaceful water-dwelling creatures. They tended to only eat fish and bugs to subsidise their tree bark and water plant diets and they had a deep love for decorating everything around them in whatever happened to float into their swamp.

They were not fighters, but if angered them they would drown someone in a heartbeat, though that was no easy feat. Generally a person had to be actively trying to destroy their swamp to earn their anger.

"Hello, what a lovely swamp you have," Etani said, and the Dziwozona beamed, genuinely happy with the compliment.

Pausing to find something, she picked up a long-fallen streamer of vines and approached the Dziwozona, offering it to her.

The Dziwozona studied it and then smiled brightly, taking it and tossing it into the water. It wasn't soggy and rotten enough for her, but it would make a very nice decoration in a few days.

"What have you come for?" the green haired woman asked, offering Etani a handful of rotting sticks and a torn lily pad in return for the vine, which she accepted happily.

"I have come to ask for a shred of your magic, if you are willing to give it," Etani said, affecting an overly happy expression at the gift and taking the time to carefully examine every twig she had been given before piling them very neatly on the lily pad. The Dziwozona looked on in pride, approving of the little pile.

"Will it make you happy?" the Dziwozona asked and Etani nodded.

"Like finding a new patch of brown moss," she said, and the Dziwozona's white eyes widened.

"Then of course!" she gasped, and Etani smiled brightly, sliding down to sit on an undecorated patch of the log and the Dziwozona approached her.

The kiss was surprisingly dry and soft, more like that of a human than a water-dwelling creature and the magic was as slippery and wet as water weeds in her mind.

She didn't feel any different after the exchange, wondering why Daemon had been so insistent on a second and third water-dweller.

"Thank you," Etani said, affecting a blissful smile that the Dziwozona returned, simply glad to help. "If you ever need anything, I will come to you," she said and the Dziwozona tilted her head, but then nodded.

"How will you know?" the Dziwozona asked, and Etani smiled.

"I'll know. Your magic will call to the magic you gave me," she said, having no idea how she knew that, but it was correct in her mind.

"I will do so, then. Farewell, strangers," the Dziwozona said, and her attention was back on her work, politely waiting for Etani to move before she could slap a pile of mud down as a base for her decorations to stick to.

Etani left the Dziwozona and returned to the men, her little pile of twigs and plant matter clutched protectively in her hands.

Daemon said nothing as he took them and wrapped them carefully in a cloth before he slipped it safely into his pocket, patting it gently when he saw her watching it anxiously.

"I'll keep them safe until we return," he said, and she nodded. She didn't know why she cared about them, but they were important.

Neither of the other two spoke as they stepped back through the tear in reality and onto a beach, of all places.

The sound of crashing waves made them all turn, but Daemon kept his hand in hers to keep her from running off. She pouted, wanting nothing more than to run into the water, but then she remembered the last time and her joy sank to the bottom of her stomach at the memories of the twins and her conversation with Uzo.

When she turned, she found the Fae watching her with a pained expression, but she only shook her head. "Why so many water creatures?" she asked Daemon, and he blinked.

"I lost the eyes back at the Strigoi and had been trying to get them back, so I kept going back to creatures likely to return them. I got them back after the Asrai," he said, and she nodded slowly.

She felt sure he had mentioned that before, but it eluded her. She frowned and shook her head as they headed away from the beach and into a small cave with a shallow pond and a magnificent waterfall that trickled out into the ocean.

It was a lovely little cave and the tiny woman basked in the waterfall.

She had bright green hair that reached to her knees and iridescent butterfly-shaped wings that shone a bright blue and purple. She was naked entirely and quite curvy for such a tiny woman, making Daemon grin and Jagum blush. Uzo only stared and when she nudged him in the ribs, he looked away and blushed.

She had to admit that the sight of the naked woman was enthralling and she wondered about her own attraction to the woman.

Letting it go, she cleared her throat and the little woman squeaked, jumping and turning.

She was covered in softly glowing blue markings in smooth waves that looked remarkably like water. Her lips were a bright pink and her eyes the soft, green-blue of the ocean.

"Lovely cave you have," Etani said, but that was all she got to say before the woman started screaming and she was hit in the middle by something surprisingly heavy.

The Asrai tackled her and she sprawled in the sand, pain from her scars telling her she had torn something.

"Oh, mother, you came for me! I can't believe you picked me! I was hoping it would be me, but I had no idea it would actually be me!" She spoke in a high pitched, rapid voice that was hard to follow with the speed and lilting accent.

The Asrai was pulled off her and she looked down to find a few spots of blood on her dress, but nothing serious.

"Oh no, I hurt you!" the Asrai wailed, but Etani only shook her head.

"Not your fault. I had already been hurt." She accepted Uzo's hand and he helped her to her feet, but when he reached for the hem of her dress to check her wound, she slapped at his hands. "I'm fine, don't worry," she blushed, knowing she was wearing nothing under the dress.

The Asrai stepped back from them and her lips formed a soft pout, looking upset but still happy to have them there.

"I take it you were aware of our going around?" she asked, and the Asrai nodded quickly.

"Everyone knows and everyone is hoping you'll come to them. The whole of Faerie is watching to see if you can do it," she said happily, but Etani frowned, looking to Daemon, who was also frowning.

"That's concerning," she said, dusting sand off her dress.

"Why's that? Surely they are helping?" the Asrai said, looking more like a young girl if only her body wasn't so developed.

"Well, we have only been threatened a few times, so I suppose that's a start," Etani said, and the Asrai looked shocked.

"What's your name?" Etani asked.

"Tilly!" The Asrai piped up, looking elated to have been asked.

"Well, Tilly, I'm sure you know why we have come to you, are you willing to help?"

Tilly squealed again happily and it was clear she wanted to tackle Etani again, but she resisted the urge. Putting on an air of maturity, she lifted her pointy chin and smiled, stepping up onto the tips of her toes even as Etani bent down.

The magic was odd, liquid and cool, but it made her lungs ache and tasted like salt. None of the others had tasted like anything, but this time it did and when she drew back, Tilly was crying and smiling widely at the same time.

She didn't have any trouble with her breathing after the salt taste left her and she was left wondering why her lungs were burning in the first place. She could only assume it had something to do with her not needing air when under water; something she would have been glad for when facing the mermen.

"I don't think we've ever gotten a warm welcome like that," Daemon said, his eyes still on Tilly's chest, appreciatively.

Etani slapped his arm and he looked at her, shocked and offended, but when he saw her glare, he grinned.

"Jealous?" he asked, and her eyes narrowed. Was she? She didn't know, and she didn't want to think about what feelings she had for the demon.

She shook her head but he smirked as she looked away from him, watching as Tilly danced away to her waterfall, waving to them. Etani waved back and shook her head at the excitement of the Asrai. At least they had gotten two easy ones.

She doubted the rest were going to be that easy; they were into the more dangerous areas and a thought occurred to her, turning to Uzo. "I just realised that we all assume you would agree to giving me some of your magic," she said, and his brows lifted, amused by the realisation.

Daemon tilted his head, seeming to come to the same conclusion as her. "I'll consider your request when the time comes," he said haughtily, and laughed as Daemon swiped at him, running from the cave as the demon went after him.

Looking to Jagum, she shrugged and he sighed.

"How you have managed to do this so many times is astounding," he said, and accepted her hand when she offered it to him.

Waving a farewell to Tilly, they left the coolness of the cave and headed out after the pair.

"I'm not looking forward to the last five, Jagum. It's going to be really dangerous. I won't blame you if you want to leave, we can drop you off somewhere."

He looked down at her when she looked up, his frown stern. "I'm no coward," he growled and she shook her head.

"It's not that I think you are a coward, it's just that this isn't your fight and I don't want your blood on my hands. The Aswang and the banshee, then the Celestrials at the end, it's going to be a miracle if we get out of this in one piece."

He squeezed her hand and his paw found her cheek, stroking

446

along the scars there. "I will do whatever it takes to ensure you survive, if no one else," he growled, and she bit her lip, hating the idea of him dying simply because he had been pulled into their troubles.

"Just promise you won't get yourself killed," she demanded, and he nodded, though they both knew it wasn't something he could guarantee.

"I'll do my best," he said, and she could only nod.

"Come on!" Daemon called, having Uzo in a headlock and grinding his knuckles into the top of the Fae's head, making him howl.

They set off at a jog for the two and Daemon released the Fae, who aimed a kick for his stomach, sending him flying.

He landed with an explosion of sand and his grin was feral, but she stepped between them and he skidded to a stop, looking irritated that she stopped the fight.

"You can settle this later, I need you both in one piece," she demanded, and the two glared.

It seemed like they had been arguing about more than just whether Uzo would give her his magic or not, but she decided it was better not to ask. "We have the Aswang next and I need you both to stay on guard; this is going to get ugly. If we make it out of that alive we're up against a banshee who could kill us all in a second. Stop messing around."

That sobered them both and they nodded obediently, the four joining hands and heading through the tear into the darkness of night.

46

ASWANG AND BANSHEE

They stepped out onto the outskirts of a small, rough village and it only took a moment for them to realise that there was something very odd about the village. The windows were all boarded over, the doors fortified, and the chimneys covered with metal grates.

It had all the hallmarks of a village at the mercy of a predator, and they knew why. The Aswang were demonic creatures who ate humans, so the sight of the boards, fortification, and absolute desertion of the village streets was understandable. There weren't even any animals in the streets.

An odd keening sound drew their eyes in the direction of the only source of light that the village possessed and a feeling of dread settled in her heart. There was a reason the village was so dark: light drew attention.

As they approached, they found the house had been boarded up, but the door had been flung open and warm golden light flooded out into the street.

Daemon led the way towards the house, moving slowly and carefully to see what was going on. He peeked in, then jerked back and grabbed hold of her, forcing her to back up with him. Affronted, she watched as the two men got to look but then turned away, both pale, and Uzo stared at her in horror. She frowned, unsure of their reaction, and jerked herself free of Daemon, peeking around the door.

She wished she hadn't. She wished a million times over that she had obeyed Daemon that one time and had never seen that.

A woman lay on her back, her massive belly gnawed open, and the creature was devouring whatever had once occupied that belly.

She jerked back into Daemon's chest and he wrapped his arms around her, one hand going over her mouth. It was a good thing, for she had let out a sob unconsciously at the sight of the dead pregnant woman whose child was being eaten by the Aswang, digging and clawing it out of her womb.

The sight cut her like a sword and she found herself shaking, Daemon clutched her to him like a vice as he stared at the other two, silently demanding they do something to fix the problem.

Her fingers clutched at his hand over her mouth, tears streaming freely down her face as she struggled with the sight, trying to crush it down so it couldn't burn itself into her mind, but it already had. She would never be able to forget that.

Tasting blood, she realised she had dug her nails into Daemon's hand, but he didn't make a sound or move, his fury that the others were still there keeping her from screaming.

Uzo and Jagum exchanged a look and Jagum gave a signal that made Uzo nod grimly. Jagum grabbed Daemon by the collar, dragging him and her back behind the side of the house.

Uzo was still out by the door and a second later, a loud banging clatter sounded and then a screech.

Something thudded against the inside of the hut and then the sound of the door closing.

Further away came another screech and Uzo was at their side, holding up three fingers and motioning down the street.

Jagum and Daemon nodded and Daemon turned her to him, staring into her face.

"We're going to catch it. You stay here until we whistle. Do you understand me?" he demanded, and she nodded, his hand slowly leaving her mouth. He bent his head and kissed her lightly on the lips before the three of them left her there alone.

She didn't want to be involved in that fight, she was glad for the chance to be left out of it with that picture scalding her brain. She would listen to Daemon next time; she wouldn't go unless he said so.

Dragging fingers through her hair, she looked at her trembling hands and clenched her eyes shut, leaning back against the wall of the hut.

The sounds coming from down the street were confusing and she tried to piece them together, but it was impossible.

Tilting her head back, she looked up at the sky and found that it was lightening, and she realised what the plan was. They were going to contain it until dawn, when it would become human again.

They seemed to be having trouble with the thing, though, and she found herself chewing her nail in anxiety, a habit she had never had before, but she didn't try to stop it.

The whistle came finally and she hesitated, really not wanting to go around the corner to see the thing. But a glance up told her they were only an hour or so from dawn.

Sighing, she stepped around the corner and headed in the direction of the group that had the thing pinned between two trees by its massive wings.

The sight of the Aswang made her very much want to run in the other direction and she forced herself to not flee but to continue on towards the three men and the monster.

It was little more than skin and bones, with sparse white hair and glowing white eyes. It had the unnaturally long limbs that Aswang used to scuttle around like a bug and massive bat-like wings that they regularly left in shredded tatters when they fought.

The Aswang watched her with animalistic curiosity and she looked at Daemon, his fear only adding to her own. If Daemon was afraid then what chances did they have?

"How did you do this last time?" she whispered, and the Aswang jerked at the sound of her voice, looking to her with an intelligence she didn't expect.

He was male, entirely naked, and it was hard not to look at him by the way he moved, dragging his genitals on the ground in a way that made even her cringe.

"Laurentius took to Lizbeth, she was beautiful and so long as he only saw her in the daytime she was fine," Daemon said, and she nodded.

He had a human face and his teeth were long, sharp and bloody, as was his chest and most of his face.

Looking to his wings, she found two knives had been stuck through the flesh rather than the thin membrane, keeping the creature trapped. His hands remained free, however, so they all kept well clear of him.

He leant forward as far as his position would allow him, sniffing at her, and his lips pulled back from his teeth. She refused to move back or closer, remaining still as she imagined where that blood had come from. The distention of his belly made it clear he had eaten well that night.

"They are normally more robust and harder to catch, but he was weak. The villagers here are good at locking themselves down when they needed to," Daemon said softly as he moved to her side, and she nodded slowly, not wanting to think about the exception to the norm.

"Can we keep him contained until morning?" she asked, and Daemon frowned, looking up.

"It's only an hour or two, we just have to get this done quickly."

She looked at Daemon and then the others, noting that they had multiple scratches and claw marks, but no one had been bitten or really hurt. It was a relief, but she was still frustrated that they had been injured at all and that she had been forced to stay behind. Not because Daemon had told her to, but because of her own weakness.

He slipped his arm around her and after a while, the group settled in to wait out the night that seemed to take an eternity to pass.

As soon as the sun crested the horizon, the Aswang groaned and sagged, his hair going grey and filling out, and the glow of his eyes fading to nothing and then deepening to a washed-out brown. He slumped to the ground as his wings vanished.

Uzo and Jagum were on him the instant he was down, pinning him to the ground and glaring at him.

"Morning," Daemon said angrily, and the man looked up at him in fear.

"Please don't kill me, I didn't mean to. I thought I had more time!" he whimpered and squeaked as she stepped up between the two men and dropped down hard onto his gut.

Daemon pulled the knife free and slipped it to her and she pressed the knife against the man's throat.

"You have two choices, Aswang: you can give me your magic or I can slit you from ear to ear and we get a prize from the villagers for killing the monster that murders people," she purred, and he whimpered, squirming to escape her.

"Please, it was an accident," he squealed, and she smiled, digging the knife into his throat until blood spilled.

"Magic or death?" she demanded, and he nodded feverishly.

"Magic, magic!" he gasped, and she bent down, her stomach rebelling at the taste of blood on his lips and she smiled at the rush of magic that felt like wind on her face.

As the magic faded to nothing, she slid the knife between his ribs and into his heart, the blade vibrating with his heartbeat.

He cried out as she jerked the knife down and his heartbeat stopped, his eyes huge in his terror.

Without a word, his arms were released and she slid the knife free of his corpse.

They didn't dare say a word to her in that instant, not when she was still armed, and she doubted they would have said anything anyway. They had all seen what he did and knew what he was; it went against everything all of them respected to kill children or the unborn and the Aswang targeted those particularly.

It made them the lowest of the low in their eyes, in the eyes of everyone from Faerie. Like with the witches, children were considered untouchable when it came to feeding.

She stood and offered the knife to Jagum, who took it silently and slid it into its sheath, padding away to collect the second.

Taking his hand, she was the last in the line stepping through the tear and she glanced back to the hut, knowing no one would be waking from that place this time.

Stepping out, they were greeted by an absolutely magical sight. They had come out onto a cliff that stretched on for an eternity, jagged and beautiful, with bright green grass covering the hills. The water was a deep, dark blue and as they turned, they found an enormous castle not too far in the distance behind them, broken and fractured.

Lifting her brows, she looked to daemon, who smiled, but didn't speak. Instead he clutched her hand and pulled her along while the others straggled behind, staring around in wonder.

She had never seen a place that was so perfectly green, never seen water so beautifully dark, and she wanted to stay there for a time and simply admire it.

How could the creators want to bring down something so lovely? She didn't know, but it was beautiful.

The castle would have been magnificent when it stood and she was fascinated by the destruction, which didn't make a whole lot of sense as the destruction had blown out in the direction of land, leading her to think that the attackers had been on the water.

She didn't know how that would be possible, but she let it go for the time being.

They found access to the castle from a wall that had exploded outwards and they climbed over the boulders, dropping down into a cobbled yard that had been damaged by fire though it appeared to have been a training yard.

A skittering sound made them all spin sharply and the fluffy white animal froze, his long face as surprised as they were.

"Sheep," Daemon said in shock, and she snorted her amusement.

"Shoo home," Uzo said but her attention had turned to Jagum, whose eyes were intent on the sheep.

"You're not allowed to eat him," she snapped, slapping the giant cat's arm. He looked down at her, appearing offended and hurt, but she knew he wanted to eat the poor thing. He didn't try and deny he had been thinking about it either.

They had a few moments of amusement while Uzo tried to get the sheep to leave, the sheep was unimpressed by him and his antics.

Finally giving up, he threw up his arms and returned to them, looking irritated by his failure.

"I don't think you can get stubborn animals to do what you want," she said, and smirked as Daemon looked at her, knowing she was talking about him.

"Very funny, go on and find yourself a banshee," he snapped, and she grinned, stalking away from him.

It was not hard to find her as she glowed a bright green. Etani saw her through the remains of a window once she had entered the castle itself, or at least what was left of it.

Hurrying to catch up with the dangerous creature, she made enough noise that she wouldn't startle the woman. But as she came across the banshee, she found the banshee had stopped to wait for her, looking curious.

She had knee-length white hair that flowed around her in a constant cloud, her dress was beautiful in a solid black with a large, white belt over her stomach that protected her from breasts to groin. She wore a crown that floated several inches above her head and large shoulder guards.

She looked like a warrior queen, a shawl drifting eerily behind her as she moved. Her arms seemed to be too long for her and her fingers were three times too long, giving her an even creepier look, but she had a soft face, gentle and with a soft smile. Her eyes were white and glowed gently in the dim light. Etani hadn't expected her to look so soft and gentle; she had expected a monster.

"Hello, I'm sorry to bother you," Etani said warily, ready to cover her ears in an instant if the need arose.

"I don't get visitors often," the woman said gently, her voice sounding weirdly far away as though she were speaking from the other end of the hall.

The banshee were not physically capable of hurting others; they were ghosts in that sense, but their screams could kill, and they were rumoured to use them for seemingly no reason.

"I suppose people are wary," Etani said slowly, unsure of how to respond to the idea of a lonely banshee.

"Wary of me? Why?" the banshee asked, sounding almost hurt.

"Well.... you're a banshee," Etani said and the woman looked shocked by the news.

"Pardon?" she demanded, and Etani took a step back. The retreat confused the woman, who glanced down at herself as though startled by something.

"Why do you fear me child?" she asked.

"Banshee kill," Etani said, and the woman's pale brows lifted.

"I have no interest in killing you. I have killed no one," she said.

Etani frowned, tilting her head in her confusion, trying to piece it together. "But banshee kill all the time," she said slowly, but then she frowned, trying to think of a single case in which she had actually heard of a banshee killing that wasn't herself. "Your scream can kill."

"My scream only warns of death; I cannot kill," the woman said slowly, patient while Etani tried to wrap her brain around the new concept.

"I..." Etani was lost for words, staring at the beautiful, ghostly figure who floated back in her direction, her hair, dress and shawl shifting slowly in her wake.

"Why did you come here, strange girl?" the banshee asked, and as she got closer, Etani realised she was older than she first appeared. She had small creases at the corners of her eyes and laugh lines.

"I came to ask for your magic," she said slowly, and the banshee laughed gently.

"Whatever for?"

"So I can stop this world from being destroyed," she said, still lost in her wondering over the banshee and reprocessing everything she knew.

"I see, well I will give you my magic under one condition: you ensure we banshee are no longer feared," the banshee said, and Etani smiled, nodding.

"You have a deal, banshee," Etani said.

"Medb," the banshee said and Etani frowned, recalling the name from somewhere but unable to place it.

"Thank you, Mebd, I'll be sure it is known," Etani agreed, and Mebd smiled warmly.

Etani didn't expect to feel the kiss, but the pressure was like a whisper of silk on her lips and a soft chill washed through her, catching at her throat. Again her vocal cords burned, though this time it was joined with her lungs burning, both changing and expanding to allow this new change.

She sucked in a breath and found she could take in more air than she remembered, but she wasn't going to complain.

"You're welcome, young one," the banshee said gently, her long fingers tender on Etani's cheek before she smiled and started down the hall, leaving her alone with the tingling feeling of silk on her skin.

Relief washed through her as she realised she was so near to the end of her journey. She hurried to leave the broken castle, her relief bubbling out of her.

Joining the others, she threw herself into Daemon's arms and hugged him tightly to her, his surprise lasting only a second before he hugged her back.

"We're so close," she breathed, and he nodded, his jaw against the top of her head.

"Three more and we can go home," he murmured.

It sounded wonderful, the thought of going home so long as it was with him, and the thought startled her.

"Let's go, we have to find Dominick," he said and she nodded.

47

______

NEPHILIM

The only case of a Nephilim was Dominick and they were glad that he was still around, though it was likely impossible for him to die, given what he was.

"Dominick had been one of the Protectors of Faerie and at some point it was rumoured he had fallen in love, though no one knew who he was in love with. Due to his emotions, he had inadvertently chosen a side, so he was no longer impartial. As a result, he lost his wings and he fell long before the others fell. He never sought out the one he had loved and he lives in shame," Daemon explained as they walked through the long grass of Summer in the direction of the palace where the man was likely to be.

They had drawn a lot of attention and a crowd of followers were trying to sneak along unnoticed, but they were all terrible at it and the group was very aware of the attention.

It took some time to explain things fully to Jagum, who had taken the news of the four Courts fairly well, all things considered.

He simply nodded, but he had taken to staring at her when he thought she wasn't watching. She chose to ignore it and let him ask his questions when he was ready.

Approaching the palace, she looked up and was anxious to see the occasional glimpse of the Protectors above, dark purple wings and glowing crowns. "Do you think the Protectors will try and stop us? It will leave them unable to fly again," she said, fear pulling through her.

"I don't know," Daemon said softly, his hand still tight in hers.

"Will Dominick help us?" she asked, and Daemon avoided her eyes.

"I can only hope so," he replied, their eyes lifting to the roiling clouds that covered all of Faerie in a mass that was unnatural, even for Faerie.

"We are running out of time," she breathed, and he picked up the pace.

They reached the palace and the guards didn't even try to stop them all from barging in, watching them curiously, and the throne room was packed, though Cecelia was absent from the dais.

Nyrellia was present, though, and her lovely face lit up at the sight of them, trying to shove her way over. Daemon saw her coming and dragged her along, Uzo keeping his head bowed and trying to go by unnoticed.

She had wanted him to stay behind, but Daemon said he needed to be there, just in case.

They hurried through the milling, whispering crowd in search of the Nephilim, but he didn't seem to be there and Daemon cursed, looking back at her and a terrified Uzo.

"This was a bad idea," she whispered and Daemon clenched his jaw, knowing she was right.

A massive hand came down on her shoulder, the other on Uzo's, and they looked up to see Toro standing over them, his black helmet pulled up to reveal a mass of red hair, a beard, and a wicked, gleeful grin.

"Fancy this, a Winter Fae in the Summer palace..." he purred, and she felt panic going through her.

Turning, she drove her clenched fist up into Toro's face, the giant of a man stumbling back. "Go, Uzo! Ayathian!" she cried, and the Fae slipped sideways out of that reality.

Daemon hooked his arm around her waist and they were running, Jagum slinking easily along beside them as Toro screamed profanity and the guards moved. They were fine so long as there was no aggression, but they had attacked first and now they were all in trouble.

The crowd parted to allow them access as they ran, ducking down empty corridors with the pounding boots of Toro barrelling down on them.

"Where would he be?" she gasped as they skidded down another corridor and Daemon scowled, unsure where to go.

"Dominick!?" he yelled, and the name was repeated, whispered, and spread along the halls and the search for the Nephilim was on with half of Summer calling for him while they dodged guards.

Caught up in a crowd, a fist came down on her shoulder and she yelped as she was jerked back from Daemon who spun, teeth bared.

"Stop, demon," Toro snarled, a long blade held against her throat and she looked to Daemon, his eyes locked on hers.

"Let her go and I won't rip you apart, Toro," Daemon growled, unable to take his eyes off her.

"Leave and I won't cut her pretty head off," Toro countered, and finally Daemon looked up from her.

"Why do you care about what happens?" Daemon demanded.

"You brought Winter into the Summer Court, you're a traitor," Toro said angrily, the blade firm against her throat but not yet drawing blood.

"I'm neutral, I can't be a traitor," Daemon countered and Toro growled, unsure and angry.

Her eyes slid from Daemon to a figure who was walking towards them, the man looking confused and frustrated. There was no denying who that man was even if his wings had gone. He wore a mask similar to that of Galad, only it had been broken apart, the left side missing from the horn to the edge, leaving him around three quarters of it.

He was still a muscular God-like beauty and his eyes shone a shocking shade of violet that she found painfully captivating.

He wore black pants but nothing else aside from the headdress.

"What are you doing, Toro?" Dominick demanded, and Daemon spun to the man.

"I've captured the Winter Princess," Toro snarled.

"She's not the Winter Princess, she's not even Fae," Daemon snapped, unsure where to look.

"Let her go, she's not Fae and too old to be a changeling, unless you're looking for a sex toy," Dominick spoke with a dispassionate tone that had her even more horrified by his casual suggestion that Toro keep her for sexual needs. Daemon seemed to have the same thought pattern, his eyes glowing a soft golden yellow in his anger.

The suggestion made Toro look down at her, his free hand going up under her jaw and jerking her head back.

"Good looking enough," he grunted, and when his hand started to drop down her chest, she growled. Toro laughed and shoved her away from him, the sword nicking her throat but doing no real harm.

Daemon caught her and she was pulled into his arms, Jagum stepping to protect her back from Dominick.

"What are you doing here?" Dominick demanded and Daemon turned on him.

"We need to talk to you," Daemon snapped back. Dominick's brows lifted in surprise.

Toro didn't look overly impressed to have to let them go, glaring at her as she lifted two fingers in a rude salute that made his jaw clench in anger.

Dominick led them away from the giant in black, guiding them into a small sitting room and pulling the door shut behind them.

"I take it you're the girl everyone is so keen on?" Dominick asked, and she nodded, unable to take her eyes off him. It was odd, but he was the only close living relative she had left, and she wasn't sure what to think about it. He was so incredibly attractive and yet he was her great-grandfather.

"Don't suppose you remember Tephania," Daemon said, and Dominick's eyes snapped to him, narrowing in anger.

"What about her?" he demanded.

"Well, she never told you, but she had a child," Daemon said slowly, unsure about how to broach the subject, and Etani was stunned by the fact that he was capable of having children. His genitals must have formed when he fell in love.

"Tephania and I never married," Dominick said, and Daemon laughed.

"Reproduction doesn't require marriage. Trust me, I know she had a child because she asked me to take that child and hide her away. That child was named Tatialia and she was chosen by Winter."

Dominick looked at her again and she stared back at him, curious to know what he might be thinking.

"I'm sure you know who Etani here is. Tatialia's granddaughter and the heir of Winter," Daemon said, and Dominick jerked, realising the connection.

"That's impossible, Lutheral had no children," Dominick snapped.

"He had two, to a Celestrial woman named Belladonna. Twins, in fact," she explained. Dominick glared at her, trying to find the lie in her words, but the longer he looked at her, the more his anger seemed to fade.

"His eyes," Dominick finally grunted. Daemon nodded in agreement.

"So why did you bring her here?" Dominick asked, unable to look away from her.

"Well, the rumours are true, we are running through the family tree to return her magic but it's not for her to become the Queen of Winter. It's so she can become a Creator again."

The silence that followed was absolute as Dominick stared at her and she shrugged, forcing her eyes from him to study the sparse room.

Letting the Nephilim process the news, she went about his room studying the various objects, coming across a small glass bird that reflected the light of the sun coming in the window.

Placing it back, she jumped as she found Dominick right behind her, his hands going to her jaw as he lifted her face to his. His expression was stern as he looked into her face, forcing her to look up at him.

"How did I not know I had a child?" Dominick asked, but he wasn't speaking to her.

"Tephania asked me to hide her pregnancy from everyone, so I did. And when the girl was born, I took her to Winter to be raised. She was not aligned with Summer, so there was no issue with her integrating and Titania raised her."

"Where is Tephania now?" Dominick asked, but Daemon didn't reply straight away. Their eyes turned to him in unison.

"She's dead, Dominick. She killed herself," Daemon said slowly.

"Why?" Dominick didn't seem overly hurt by the news, but she saw the shift in his eyes.

"She realised you would never have her, so she said she wanted to go see her mother's grave. I took her, but she jumped off the cliff before I could stop her."

Dominick's fingers pinched her jaw painfully and she clenched her jaw to keep from making a sound, his eyes back on her with a burning fury.

"And you killed my child," he said slowly, her jaw aching under his grip.

"She had no choice," Daemon said, but it was a lie; Etani had the choice not to kill her, she simply chose to do it anyway.

"Yes, I killed her," she whispered. He pressed her into the wall, fury burning in him.

"Why shouldn't I just kill you?" he whispered. Daemon moved but she held up her hand to stop him, her eyes locked on Dominick's.

"Because I'm the only thing keeping the Creators from destroying the human world, and then what? They try to create another one? What are the odds of that working?" His grip was so tight she was sure he was going to break her jaw, but she refused to flinch. "What happens if they fail again? Will Faerie survive another attempt? What if they bring down Faerie?"

Tears sprang to her eyes at his grip and he finally let go, trailing his fingers down her jaw to her throat, clenching it instead.

She refused to try and pull his fingers off her, her chin lifted and staring up into his eyes in a silent dare for him to answer her.

"What do I care if Faerie falls?" he asked, and she frowned, not understanding.

"You are a Protector," she whispered.

"I was a Protector, not anymore." His nose was only an inch from hers and she swallowed, thinking fast.

"What if I can find a way to make you one again?"

Daemon hissed and Dominick's eyes widened for an instant before narrowing. "How?" he demanded, his fingers clenching painfully.

"I don't know yet, I'll find a way," she said, her voice strained. She was running out of options and she glanced at Daemon, his face stricken, though she didn't know why.

He jerked her neck when she looked away and her eyes snapped back to his, finding him close enough that his nose brushed hers. "Tell me, little witch," he whispered in a lethal voice.

"I'll find a way."

"Not good enough."

She felt something between them and shivered at the whisper of metal against her side and she knew Daemon hadn't noticed. He could kill her in an instant and there was nothing Daemon could do about it.

"I can't give you that answer right now," she whispered, and flinched as the knife dug into her side, blood trickling down to drip off the handle. "But I promise I will find a way. I'll be the Queen of Winter, death, and a Creator, I'm even supposed to be a Goddess," she whimpered as the knife dug deeper.

He paused at that, his eyes narrowed at her in confusion. "That's not possible," he said slowly, unsure suddenly.

"Daemon made it possible," she whispered.

"Why did you come to find me?" he demanded, and she smiled very slightly.

"You're my great grandfather, and the only Nephilim known to exist, I need your magic."

His eyes were hard on her but she saw them wavering, unsure of if he should believe her or not.

"You've seen what the Creators are doing, you've seen the sky. It's going to happen in only a matter of days, if we even have that long," she whispered.

He swallowed. "You have five," he breathed, and her eyes widened.

"Five?" she asked.

He nodded. The knife slid free of her and she breathed a sigh of relief.

"They are waiting for the equinox. That's in five days," he said, and her eyes turned to Daemon, hope filling her that they might have just enough time to get it done.

"We can do it," he whispered, and she turned back to Dominick.

She opened her mouth to speak, but his lips were on hers and she gasped at the sudden flood of magic that left her tingling all over.

He broke from her as her head spun and he let go, leaving her to wobble to Daemon, who caught her.

"You're not to touch my great-granddaughter, lust demon," Dominick growled. She felt Daemon moving, glanced up to see him staring at the Nephilim in surprise. "I see the way she looks at you and you watch her. I know what you are going to do. If you touch her, I'll kill you."

Daemon could only nod, clutching her to him as her world spun in the most enjoyable way.

Dominick's breath sucked in at the sight of her, Daemon grinning at the response.

"Sucks being on the receiving end of that pull, doesn't it?" Dominick said, and Daemon nodded slowly.

"Where will you go now?" Dominick asked after a short pause.

"We have to get Uzo, then it's to the Celestrials."

Dominick snorted and shook his head. "Good luck with that last."

Daemon could only sigh his agreement and reached for Jagum, who allowed the demon to grasp his arm.

"We'll no doubt see you again soon," Daemon said, and Dominick growled in response.

"I will be coming for my kin, Daemon, and if you try to hide her, I will find her." The threat made her shiver and she looked to Dominick, who was glaring at her. "Don't forget your promise, little girl."

She nodded her agreement as they stepped backwards through the tear and into the rain.

She gasped at the sudden cold, looked up at the sky resentfully. She frowned in concern; the clouds were an eerie green colour. The Courtyard was empty and filled with water, it seemed to have been raining for quite some time.

"That's not normal," Daemon said.

She couldn't help but agree, shaking her head slowly in wonder.

Splashing sounded and they turned to find Uzo running towards them, soaked to the skin and looking cranky as a result.

"Let's go inside and get a hot bath, then we can go to Ceress," he called over a boom of thunder, the trio nodding their agreement.

Deciding to skip dealing with anyone else, they headed straight for her rooms beside Alaric's and they all piled into the bathroom, arguing over who got to bathe first, when Alaric stomped in after them.

"She's not here, you dense git!" he boomed, then froze at the sight of them, looking stunned. "I did not expect to see you here," he said, looking between them all and the puddle of water they had brought in with them.

There was a very awkward silence that she took advantage of, elbowing Daemon in the ribs, stomping on Uzo's foot, and ducking under Jagum's grab only to slam the door in their faces and shove a chair under the handle.

Daemon swore at her and she laughed, backing away from the door and immediately starting the water. Daemon wasn't having any of it, though, stepping through the tear beside her, making her shriek in surprise.

"Get out!" she yelled, but he was already stripping.

"The least you can do is share!" he snarled back, and Uzo shouted his agreement from the door.

"I have a bath in my room," Alaric said and then shouted as the Fae and werecat broke into a fight over who got to go first.

Finally, Alaric was forced to separate them and sent them off to their own baths. By then she was in the water, glaring at a smug Daemon, who had already filled it with his favourite oils.

Ignoring him, she set to cleaning herself and soaking in the heat for as long as possible. Her hair needed a good wash.

"Need help washing your back?" Daemon purred, jerking back as she threw a cloth at his face and dunked her head under the water to rinse out her hair.

Surfacing, she found him watching her and frowned at the creepiness of it. "What are you looking at?" she demanded, but his hand was gentle as he touched the large scar on her cheek.

"You have no idea how angry I was when he did that to you," he growled, but she shrugged.

"It's not the first scar I've gotten from this trip," she said gently, the demon grunting his agreement. "It's almost over, though, and then what are we going to do? It'll be boring after that," she teased.

His eyes narrowed and without warning, he leant forward and kissed her hard. She went still at the kiss for a moment and then she was kissing him back, her fingers tracing up over his shoulder to curl around the back of his neck. He pulled her into his lap and she settled against him, enjoying the warmth of him pressing so close to her.

He broke the kiss reluctantly, his forehead resting against hers as he ran his fingers through her hair. "I love you more than you could ever imagine," he breathed, and she jerked back from him, her mind instantly shutting down the idea.

"No you don't," she breathed, but he tugged on the long strand of hair to draw her back to him.

"I think I should know my own feelings," he said playfully as she moved back to him.

Straddling his lap, she stared up into his eyes in confusion. "People who love me tend to end up dead, or just leave," she said slowly, uncertain of him.

"I'm immortal and I'm not going to leave," he countered, but he could see her hesitation. She was scared to get hurt again. "Just because that vampire boy wasn't brave or man enough to love you doesn't mean I'm not," he said darkly.

She bit her lip and rested her head against his chest, his arms going around her in a tight embrace. "I love you, too, Daemon," she breathed, but she didn't know what kind of love it was, it was all too much to think about just yet. She would figure it out later, when they were all out of danger.

He growled softly as he clutched her to him, his voice a low murmur. "If we all survive this, I'll spend the rest of my life proving to you that I love you and that I am worthy of your love."

She clenched her eyes to keep the tears in, her arms sliding around his middle and hugging him tighter to her, wishing it were true.

They stayed like that until the water cooled and finally got out, Etani pulling on a pair of her black pants and a vest.

Padding from the bathroom after removing the chair, she found Alaric still in the room. She ignored him as she headed into the bedroom to pick a pair of boots out of the closet.

"How long are you staying?" Alaric asked, but she ignored the question.

"How long has the rain been going on like that?"

"It started two days ago," he said, the news making her frown.

"The week mark," she said, looking up at Daemon as he was fully dressed and she cursed his magic as she dried her toes in order to get her boots on without issues.

"A week?" Alaric asked, watching her.

"A week until this world comes down," she elaborated, and Alaric choked.

"We had a week two days ago?" he demanded. "How many have you met?"

"The Fae and the Celestrials are left. Then we need Epharis to do his thing and the twins. If we get the Celestrials today, we will have two days spare with how long the last two take," she said, tying up her boots.

"Is that likely?" Alaric demanded, and she exchanged a glance with Daemon.

"We're going to have to rush it," she explained. "We may need you to give a royal command if either party refuses," she added, and Alaric nodded slowly. "Where's Uzo?"

"He's in my bathroom but I heard the drain not long ago."

Uzo walked in just as Alaric finished speaking and he, too, was fully dressed in his usual black.

"How is it you two can magically grow clothing but I can't?" she demanded.

"Have you ever tried?" Uzo asked. Stumped, she only stared at him, her fingers frozen on her boots, then swore at him.

"Language, young lady, I'll show you if we survive," he said, grinning.

Grumbling about unfair magical abilities, she tied up her boots and tapped her toes to settle her feet.

"Will you give me your magic?" she demanded of the man, his grin turning into a sly smirk.

"I will, in exchange for a future favour," he said, her brows lifting in surprise.

"What could I possibly offer you?" she asked.

"You never know, having a Queen, Goddess, death, and world creator's favour might be useful in the future," he said, and she shrugged.

Alaric looked surprised by the titles, but she shook her head.

"I'll explain when we get back," she told him. The giant man let out a breath.

Jagum joined them shortly after, dressed in only a pair of pants that she suspected might have belonged to Alaric at some point, his armour hanging over his arm to dry.

"Good, I think your husband is heading up this way," Jagum said, and she looked at Daemon.

"Let's go!" he grabbed her arm, Uzo gripping her shoulder, Jagum taking the other and the door slammed open right as they left, hearing the furious snarl of her name, but they were already gone.

48

CELESTRIALS

They stepped out onto the green grass in the shadow of the giant spiral city and Jagum was looking up at it, but Etani was looking at the clouds, roiling and angry above them. The wind was heavy and she frowned as lightning cracked down somewhere.

"This is bad," she yelled over the wind and Daemon nodded, hurrying them along towards the side of the city.

"Let's get this done before we go in," Uzo called. She accepted his hand, he pulled her closer, and his free hand touched the underside of her chin.

His kiss was light, gentle, and brief but the sheer amount of magic that he poured into her buckled her knees and only his arm around her kept her from hitting the ground.

He lingered as long as he dared, and she felt like she might pop from the energy singing in her.

She looked up at him, tingling, and she wondered at how much magic the man was capable of holding if he could feed that much into her.

He grinned wickedly and tapped her nose before she was able to get her feet under her again. She felt like she was going to fly away, but she remained solidly on the ground.

"How powerful are you?" she breathed, the man laughing gently.

"You don't ask a gentleman that question, my dear girl, it's impolite." Winking at her, he grew serious as their eyes went to the city above them and the smooth, sheer wall they were pressed against.

"The only way in is the gates," she said, biting her lip, refusing to give into fear. "I guess it's my turn to lead."

They followed along the wall in single file, making it harder for them to be spotted from above. Then they came to the gates and she frowned at the sight of it going unguarded.

That was seriously abnormal and she paused, searching for a hint of a trap.

The gates were elaborately tooled in spirals and arcs made of solid gold and inlaid with massive precious and semi-precious stones, offsetting the sheer blankness that was the city itself.

"Why are there no guards?" she whispered as Daemon leant forward to peek around her shoulder.

The lack of guards had thrown her off entirely and it was raising all sorts of alarms in her head. But they had no choice and so she set off at a run, crossing the inner curve to the flat line that started the spiral shell shape.

The others followed along behind her and they found the gates to be open just enough for someone to walk inside.

Daemon pulled her back and he went in first, frowning as he found no ambush on the other side, and he shrugged, motioning for them to come in.

Stepping inside, she cursed silently under her breath as she saw the solid flatness that was the inner walls. "They closed the doors," she said slowly. "They knew we were coming."

The gates slammed shut behind them and she grabbed the two closest to her, yanking them forward on instinct as arrows rained down.

Jagum already had the reflexes to avoid it and she pulled them as more and more figures stood up along the walls.

"Go! Up the spiral!" she snarled; the two men sprinted ahead, Jagum keeping pace with her.

"This whole city is designed to trap you," he said and she nodded, her legs burning on the incline.

She noted that the arrows never were aimed directly for them, only trying to push them upwards, and she clenched her jaw, realising they were being herded.

Reaching the top of the spiral, they skidded to a stop and found the circular flat meeting place to be filled with people.

They were all pale. Pale hair, pale skin, pale eyes, and pale clothing that had always made her stick out like a sore thumb with her black hair and vivid eyes.

There were weapons everywhere and she felt a sudden dread that she had led her friends to their deaths. She should have gone alone.

"Get them out," she whispered to Daemon, barely audible, and his body tensed. Jagum growled and Uzo twitched, but none of them responded as a woman moved into view from a balcony set into the largest white-walled building that was the palace.

She had white-blonde hair and pale skin, her eyes a soft grey-green that Etani knew all too well.

Wearing nothing but a sheer gauzy dress that did nothing to hide her figure and a crown made of five large crystals sticking up, her pale lips turned up into a smile as she observed the group. "How nice of you to return home, Etania," Illia said, her amusement cold.

"Illia, you're as bitchy as usual," Etani retorted, and Illia glared.

"Insolent girl, you'd think the humans would have taught you some manners by now."

Glancing behind her, she found the passage back had been enclosed by more pale figures, and she noted a few of them from her childhood, all cold and angry. "Don't suppose we can all go our separate ways and pretend this never happened?" she called out, the Queen's malicious laugh echoing through the meeting place.

"No, I'm afraid not. The cat can go, but I need a new husband and you have two very delicious looking men with you."

Snorting, she glanced at Daemon, who looked revolted, and Uzo smiled politely, but she could see the anger in his face. "Sorry, Illia, I don't think they're keen, and he's an incubus. Imagine that, being so unappealing that an incubus wouldn't even want you," she taunted, the Queen's face flushing with rage.

"Kill her," Illia snarled, and her stomach dropped out in fear.

"Do you really want to try and kill the Queen of Winter?" Daemon called out, and Illia froze along with several of those around her who had started moving forward.

Etani looked at him curiously and he looked back at her, grinning.

"You're Fae now," he explained. It took her an instant to realise what that meant. She could tap into Faerie and claim the throne. "Do it..."

She looked from him up to Illia, who was glaring down at her, and she grinned savagely. "I am Etania Daewen, Queen of Winter."

The magic hit her like a physical blow and she gasped, her breath escaping in a cloud of mist.

Her skin tingled and burned as markings engraved themselves into her flesh, leaving her marked with sharp angles and smooth lines down to her fingertips. Her scalp stung and she looked down to see her black hair turning silver starting from the roots and flowing down to the tips before it all lifted under a gust of frigid air and she felt it winding into a tight braid that clung close to the back of her head.

Something tickled her ear and she touched it to find a string of tiny gems trailing from her earlobe up over her head and hung down loose, more in her hair.

Her clothes melted away to be transformed from her pants into a long, slender, flowing gown that started in a heart shape at her chest, leaving her shoulders and arms bare, the fabric of her dress inlaid with small white gems and embroidered with a pattern similar to that of her skin.

She could feel Faerie whispering to her, loving her for what and who she was. It wanted to please her, and it would do anything she asked, anything to make her happy.

Her eyelashes felt longer and thicker as she looked up at Illia, who looked utterly terrified.

"Kill her!" she screamed, but Etani knew instinctively what to do.

She pulled viciously on the magic and a barrier of thick ice shot up out of the ground, buckling the stone as she forced water up out of the mountain below.

Turning her eyes to the door to the palace, she lifted her hand and the ice flew in a line for the door, expanding out to form a passage.

Her friends were frozen in place, their mouths hanging open as they stared at the ice she had created and she left them where they were, going for the palace.

Walking calmly, she smiled as she felt absolutely invincible, high on the magic and wanting more. She understood then why Faerie needed more magic; her pulling on it so hard was making things waver and she wanted more, she wanted Faerie to be bigger even though her draw on the magic didn't actually deplete it, only moved it to where she needed it to be. In that case, she was drawing it from the water below and changing it, but it was not spent.

She stepped inside the palace, smiled at the familiar place with its mass of colour that the outside didn't hint at. Illia liked greens and purples and so the decorations were those colours, long strips of fabric and cushions.

People scattered at the sight of her and she paused at a mirror, frowning at the sight of the crown on her head that was spiked ice, glowing a soft white and looking like a weapon in and of itself.

Her eyes were lined in kohl and decorated with violet powder, merging into little crystals stuck to her skin, and her lips were a deep mauve.

She looked very odd with silver hair, but it worked.

Turning from the mirror, she saw the flash of the Queen as she fled. Etani hitched up her skirt, her bare feet adorned with silvery chains like her hair.

Rounding the corner, she cut Illia off and the woman screamed, skidding to a stop and almost crashing into her.

Etani smiled as she curled her long fingers around the woman's throat and, for the first time, realised she was taller than the Queen. It was unusual, given the Celestrials were all tall with the shortest being just over six feet, but this woman was shorter.

"Oh, Illia, I'll bet you never imagined this happening," she purred, delighted at the sight of the terrified woman in her grasp. "For decades you punished me for being born, you had your soldiers torture my sister and me. And likely you were responsible for the death of my mother, if not directly, then as a result of your choices. You punished us for being different, but that wasn't why you actually did it, is it? You were punishing us for what we could possibly become."

As she spoke, she pressed down on the woman, forcing her to her knees, and the Queen whimpered.

"No, never," Illia whispered, and Etani grinned.

"You shouldn't lie, Illia," she purred, squeezing that delicate throat.

"I'll make a deal with you, Illia, give me your magic, and I will consider sparing your life," she said, her nails cutting easily through the delicate skin and leaving rivulets of blood to roll down her pale skin.

"Yes, anything you want," she gasped, and Etani grinned.

"Do you promise?" she pressed, and Illia nodded.

"Yes, yes, yes!"

Etani leant forward and pressed her lips gently against the Queen's, knowing full well the promise meant the woman wasn't capable of trying to consume her soul until after.

The magic that slid into her was all barbs and she let go of Illia as she gasped, pain ripping through every inch of her as her heart slowed and her body changed. Her skin paled and the scars she had accumulated smoothed over, her teeth sharpening into fine, razor points and her mind roiled, revolting against the change in the various parts of her.

Her eyes watered and she touched them, finding the black of tears she had always known. She had done it; she was herself again, and her body vibrated with the remembered feeling of being what she was.

Looking up, her eyes focused on the fleeing form of Illia and she laughed softly, going after her, but someone reached the Queen first and Jagum slammed into her, smashing her small frame into the wall.

He turned as she approached and his eyes widened at the sight of her, her liquid movements calling to his primitive mind and that magic pull made him want to go to her and make her his.

She trailed her fingers gently down his spine and he shivered under the touch, her lips a gentle brush against his cheek before her eyes turned to Illia.

Pressing Jagum away from the Queen, she stared down with hungry eyes, her fingers curling around the slender throat she had always dreamt of crushing.

"You promised to let me go!" she gasped, terrified.

"No, Illia, I only promised to consider it," she said with a satisfied grin.

Clutching the woman by the jaw, she kissed her and delved into her mind with ferocious abandon, tearing through all of the defences and ripping her soul free.

She sucked it into herself, shivered and groaned at the rush of energy as something collided with the side of her mind, and then an internal scream as she felt Letari's presence flood her with relief.

Letting go of the corpse, she frowned as she looked down at her hands, finding guards forming over the tips of her middle fingers and creeping up her fingers to form gauntlets around her wrists in a lace pattern that she recognised with a moment of panic.

"Well shit... I shouldn't have done that," she said slowly as the body of Illia disintegrated into dust before their eyes.

She had murdered the Queen of Ceress and that meant that she was now the Queen.

She had become the first dual Court Queen of Faerie.

Turning to see Daemon and Uzo staring at her, she could only shake her head in frustration, unsure what this meant. There had never been a time when one Queen ruled over two parts of Faerie and she didn't want to know what was going to happen to it if that lasted.

"What are you going to do?" Uzo asked in a low voice, something in his face telling her their relationship had changed in some way but she didn't want to deal with that at the moment.

"I'll deal with it after. Probably make Megara Queen regent," she said, and the two nodded slowly.

"You are incredible," Daemon whispered and then blushed, realising he had spoken aloud, and she grinned, curling her fingers in the front of his shirt and pulling him against her.

Her lips found his in an instant and he melted into her, revelling in the possessive gesture. She pulled back from him after a moment and her teeth caught his lower lip, pulling it slowly to leave a small cut that made his eyes flash to golden yellow in an instant.

Amused by the sight, she pressed him back and she knew she was teasing him, getting him worked up only to make him wait, but it was fun. "When we get there, we have to make sure Epharis and the twins are willing to help. We can't take no for an answer this time," she said.

"Did we ever?" Uzo asked, and he grinned at her glare.

"You're so pretty when you're angry," he said as he wiped at her lower eyelid, removing the dark lines that had formed with her tears.

"Don't look at me like that, you're still my uncle," she said, and she caught the slight sadness in his expression.

"Yes, but now you're my Queen," he said.

"I'm your niece first and always," she said, and he seemed to brighten at that. She didn't care that they didn't share blood; he was her uncle and that was all that mattered. "I acknowledge all pre-existing deals," she said gently and shivered at the sudden feeling of those promises and deals she had made, knowing she wouldn't be able to ignore the ones she had with Alaric and Epharis.

"We have to go," she said, and Daemon nodded, but when he was about to take her hand, he grinned and bowed to her.

"After you," he said playfully and she shook her head.

Biting on the tip of her finger, she drew the line in the air and the door opened, revealing the throne room of Ayathian.

They stepped through and the door closed behind them with a soft pop.

49

LICH

They had been gone so long that she had partially forgotten what the hall looked like when they stepped through, her finger smarting but healing over quickly with a tingle of magic inside her that made her feel deliciously normal.

The hush that came over the room as the doorway opened and they stepped through was loud, and they were met with an audible intake of breath.

Glancing around the room, her eyes found Alaric and then Epharis, whose eyes had locked onto her in an instant.

Her eyes moved from him and she found Versalis, his intensity drawing her attention.

His jaw was set and she caught a glimpse of his disappointment when she turned her attention from him.

"Where are the twins?" she asked into the silence, and Alaric cleared his throat.

"Welcome back, Princess."

"Where are the twins, Alaric?" she repeated, and his jaw clenched.

"Dungeons," he said moodily, very aware that she had been rude in front of half of the Court.

Turning her back on him, she swept from the room with the three men following along with faces like marble, cold and determined.

When the door turned out to be locked, she simply ripped it off the hinges and stepped inside to find the two vampires shackled to the walls and looking pitiful, unnaturally skinny and hollow.

They keened as she approached and she lowered herself to her knees between them, her arms lifting to them.

She didn't so much as flinch as they bit and ravaged her forearms, digging for her blood that spilled the moment they bit her.

She let them feed until they were satiated, and Kai looked up at her as she stood, his face pale as he saw her indifference.

"Release them," she ordered, Epharis having followed them though she had not seen him. When she turned, she found him breathing down her neck.

"You and I are going to talk, just as soon as you release them."

He seemed taken aback by her demand and his curiosity got the better of him, nodding.

She ignored the cry of her name from Kai, sweeping from the cell and back upstairs to find Alaric stomping towards her looking agitated.

"You, who do you think you are speaking to me like that?" he snarled.

"I'm the Queen of Winter, Alaric, and I will speak to you how I wish," she said coldly, causing the man to stop and stare at her.

"Move, or I will move you."

He blocked the hall and, without a word, he stepped aside to allow her to pass. She swept past him, her companions following along behind, with new additions being the twins and Versalis.

She ignored them all as she moved through the halls and up to her rooms beside Alaric's, finally turning to observe the group of stragglers.

Uzo, Jagum and Daemon moved to flank her immediately as the various men moved into her room.

"You, Epharis, and you two," she indicated the Lich and twins, "will perform the same methods you performed before in order to return me to my natural state. We have four days and I'm not in the mood to play games with any of you. I came to you three only as a courtesy; if you refuse, I will find others."

Her coldness was met with silence and she turned away from them, drawing Daemon down, and he bowed to her immediately.

"Incapacitate them if required," she murmured in his ear and he nodded once, his golden eyes going to the group as she swept from the room and into the bathroom.

The door didn't close as she had intended it to and she looked up in the mirror as she began tugging at the silver strands of her braid but then she realised that it was black once more and she wondered when that had happened. The Lich looked ready to breathe flames as he stalked towards her.

"I don't recall inviting you in," she said calmly. "If you touch me, I will remove your arm."

He paused an inch from her, his breath warm against her back as she began to run a comb through her hair. "What are you thinking, coming back here and making demands?" he hissed. She turned to him, pressing two fingers against his chest and pushing him back from her. He took one half step back and she knew that was the best she was going to get out of him.

"I no longer belong to you, Epharis, keep in mind that I rule over two quarters of Faerie and can obliterate you with a thought."

He bared his teeth at her and she smiled; a cold smile, but it was a smile.

"I require your attempt to change me, Epharis. That is all."

"You are my wife and still you speak to me like that?" he growled, and her cold smile melted.

"Do not for an instant think I will not kill you and find another Lich. You are important only so long as you do as I ask."

His hand flung out to strike her, stopping dead an inch from her skin as she called magic to her and it flowed out of her in an aura.

He stared at his hand and she smiled at him, a cruel smile. His eyes widened just as she drove her fist into his chest and he was flung out through the bathroom wall, and then through the brick wall of her bedroom and into the hallway.

"Apologies Alaric, I'll have that fixed," she said as she stepped out through the wall and they heard Epharis groaning in pain.

The vampires stared at her in horror, their faces smeared with her blood, and Kai moved to block her.

"Move," she said, her voice a low growl of warning. Something in her wouldn't allow her to strike him, not Kai. It didn't matter what he did to her, how many times he abandoned her or lied to her or broke her heart, he was still her love and her child.

Uzo took the vampire by the arm but he refused to move, staring down into her eyes. "Etani, what happened to you?" he whispered, afraid for her.

"You lost the right to ask me about my state when you and your brother decided to run away from the fight," she said coldly, and his face paled.

Jaia growled and Versalis sucked in a breath at her implied accusation of cowardice on their part.

"How could you say that?" Kai whispered, and she met his eyes, indifferent to his pain.

"Winter is driving her anger," Epharis growled as he dragged himself back through the hole in the stone, looking like she had broken his spine by the hunched way he moved.

Her attention turned to the Lich and he glared at her.

"She is drawing on Winter like a leech," he growled, her eyes narrowing at his choice of words.

"Either agree to my task or we will find others who can," she said and Kai whimpered, grabbing her arms and giving her a little shake. Her eyes lowered to his hands on her, then rose to his face, and he looked terrified at her expression as anger pulsed through her that he would dare touch her.

"Etani, please stop, we love you," he pleaded. She pulled on Faerie and his hands were suddenly thrown off her, howling as his fingers blistered under the sudden drop in temperature that left him holding ice.

"You're up, Lich," Uzo said, and Epharis swore at him, turning his eyes to her.

"I'll turn you over my cold, dead body," he snarled.

"Very well," she replied calmly, and lifted her hand, her index and middle finger pointed at his chest. His eyes went wide and Kai grabbed her arm, forcing it up.

The magic hit the ceiling and rubble exploded down on them in a cloud of dust and stone.

Someone grabbed her and their body covered her; the smell of Jagum told her who had protected her from the rubble.

When the rubble stopped falling, she straightened and looked up at the hole in the ceiling; her magic had blown a hole clean through two floors. Movement caught her attention and she turned to Epharis as he lunged for her, his arms going around her middle, and he tore her apart.

Landing hard on the frozen grass, she heaved at the sensation and her body rejected the teleportation as it did every time.

He reached down and curled his fingers in her hair, pulling her up and glaring down into her face. "You tried to kill me..." he growled, but then let go of her as his fingers suddenly burned with the cold.

She pushed herself up and dusted off her gown, looking to the Lich. "Epharis, why do you have to be so difficult? If I wanted to kill you, you'd already be dead," she demanded, frustrated finally by his antics. "You are fully aware that we are on a time constraint and you decide now to be difficult?"

"I want something in return," he snapped, and she paused, curious at the revelation.

"What do you want?" she asked, her cold indifference fading slightly in the new situation.

"You agree to help me depose Alaric, then I'll give you my magic."

She was completely floored by that turn of events, staring at him with lips slightly parted.

"You want me to help remove Alaric from the throne?" she demanded, and he nodded. "Why?"

"He needs to be punished for what he did to our child. For what he did to you, and his instability. He is not fit to rule."

"And you think you are fit for the throne?" she asked, genuinely wondering.

"I am more suitable than he is. If I have you at my side."

There was the catch, and she narrowed her eyes at him, suspicious. "What does that entail?"

"You are my side, my Queen and confidant, adviser. You at my side, and in my bed."

She snorted at his words and shook her head, turning her eyes to the city in the distance. "I'm not going to be your plaything again, Epharis," she said, heading back in the direction of the city.

He gripped her wrist and immediately let go when she looked down at his hand. "I will not touch you until you are ready. But I will require an heir."

"Find yourself a consort, it matters none to me. Have a whole harem for all I care."

He gritted his teeth, moving to block her path. "I would have no woman but you."

She might have been flattered, had she not been contemplating blowing him into Lich bits.

"You will not touch me if I do not wish it?" she clarified, and he nodded.

"Should you desire it, we will have an heir," he said calmly.

She contemplated that, the fact that she could refuse him forever and throw women in his path for him to hopefully latch onto. But then she recalled what Sobek had said and she was irritated to know that she was the only reason a Lich could procreate, but Bast had blessed her that even if he did try to force her, she would not bear him a child again.

"Very well, Epharis. I will help you, but you must perform your magic today."

He extended his hand and she took it, his smile wide while she felt frustrated that he had entwined her in his life once more.

It was she who opened the gate back to the room and as she stepped through, Daemon let out a breath and Epharis stepped through after her, still entirely intact.

"He has agreed," she said simply, her protectors exchanging a relieved sigh.

Her eyes turned to the twins, Jaia staring hard at her and Kai looking like he was going to cry.

"What is your answer?" she demanded, and the twins exchanged a look.

"Etani, please just let us explain," Kai whimpered, but her cold stare silenced him.

Jaia nodded once and she looked back to him, his stern expression faltering under her cold glare.

It was the second time that man had ripped out her heart, but now her heart was frozen. She would never give him a third chance.

"Where is my gem?" she asked Versalis.

He stepped forward; the thing still lay lifeless around his throat.

She turned her eyes to Daemon, who studied it and then looked to her with a significant glance. Loki had been right, they needed the Lich and vampires.

"Come to my rooms, we will do this there," Epharis said, glancing at the gem.

She swept across the room and Epharis growled at the demon who made follow her.

"Shut up, Lich, I'm not leaving you alone with her," the demon growled, but she waved him down.

"Calm, my love, I will be safe."

Daemon looked doubtful but he accepted her words and stepped back to Uzo and Jagum, his smirk blatant on Jaia at her choice of endearment.

Jaia looked like he had swallowed glass and his eye twitched, Kai gripped his arm to keep him from making any stupid moves.

"I'll be back for you two tomorrow," she told the twins and left the room, the Lich taking her arm and guiding her regardless of the fact that she knew where to go.

"You shouldn't torture them," Epharis scolded gently, and she looked to him.

"I never thought you would be one to defend them, especially with my past relationship with Jaia."

"The key word there is 'past.' That vampire has as much chance of being with you as I do."

She snorted her agreement and he squeezed her arm, guiding her into his cluttered room where he stopped to have three, then five, humans brought up.

In silence they set to work removing the books and papers from his table and he motioned to her chest.

Without a word she tugged down the heart neckline and his eyes lingered on the curves of her breasts in the brassiere, adding spectacular new heights to their plumpness.

Sitting on the edge of the table, he moved in front of her and stared down at her hungrily, but her returned stare was indifferent. He sighed and hitched her back on the table, allowing her to lie down on it, and she stretched her arms up in the air above her, her silver nails glistening in the light. "Will you fill me in on everything that happened since the twins returned?" he asked, and she glanced at him, shrugging.

She filled him in while they waited, reaching down to itch at the spot around the golden anklet, and she smiled at his sucked in breath when she hitched up the skirt to her knee to better reach her ankle and the fabric slid down to expose the length of her thigh.

She had to admit she was enjoying the attention of the man who should have no sexual desires, but there he was wanting her like a hormonal teenager.

She hadn't bothered to tug her skirt down when the humans were brought in and the guard's eyes almost bugged out of his head at the sight. Her eyes turned to him with her breasts partially exposed, her bared thigh, and those eyes that could seduce any man.

"Run along now," she purred at the guard and he backed from the room, unable to tear his eyes off her until the door closed.

"You're going to make their heads explode," the Lich said jealously, and she laughed, the sound low and slightly sexual as she slid the fabric with deliberate slowness back down towards her knee.

All eyes were on the hiss of fabric over skin and the Lich shivered, growling at her before he set to work.

She had his promise, regardless of how much she teased him and rubbed it in that he was capable of sexual need. She knew it would drive him crazy with lust and she enjoyed the scent of his desire.

He forced himself to focus on his task and he took her hand, his lips touching her wrist and she flinched as his nail cut along the crease in her skin. He caught the blood in his cupped hand and when the healing made the blood stop, he licked her skin clean.

Without a word, he picked up the amulet and placed it over the first human's head. The man looked terrified and she smiled at the remembered course of events.

One by one the men dropped, one by one the amulet began to glow, and then he was at her head, using the last of the blood to trace the rune on her skin.

He placed the leather strip between her teeth and she exhaled slowly, preparing herself mentally for what was to come. The amulet felt heavy against her breast and he closed his eyes, his fingers splayed against her head.

The pain dug into her and she gasped, her eyes clenching shut, but she didn't fight it this time, letting the teasing coldness creep into her.

It burned like acid and she screamed through the pain as it reached down through her body and encircled her racing heart.

She was ready for it, not wanting to risk her success against it being what had allowed her to stay mostly herself. She swiped at the tendrils, but they seemed oddly more aggressive and her screams cut off into a terrible silence as they ripped through her.

Throwing herself downwards, she found herself standing before that strange, childlike figure.

"We no play with Fae," it said, and it was he who shoved her down, landing lightly at the door of her soul home.

The demon was waiting for her, his grin wide.

"So you're the one Daemon has been so obsessed with?" he asked.

She only smiled slightly. "And you're the reason he found me?" she asked, and his grin grew wider. She had suspected that this demon was how her demon had found her, but he had clarified her suspicions. "I hope you don't plan to fight me again," she said, the demon shaking his head.

"No, little Faerie Queen. I will not waste time trying to fight you, I only came to repeat the process and let you move on. We are all counting on you to stop the Creators."

She lifted her brows and he approached her, his fingers light on her jaw.

He stepped past her, her soul moving forward to meet him, his hands going into her core, and she sank to her knees, pain ripping through her. He withdrew his hands, smiling at her before he vanished, leaving her alone with her soul.

Letari seemed to melt into focus beside her, the pale beauty smiling down at her and helping her to her feet.

Immediately she pulled her twin into her arms and the two embraced tightly.

"I'm so glad you're back," Etani whispered, and Letari laughed gently, clinging to her.

"Me, too E, I missed you so much."

They hadn't had time to be together and even then she felt her body pulling at her.

"Go and kick the Lich for me," Letari said and she laughed, kissing her twin's cheek before allowing herself to be drawn up.

She gasped as she sat up, her body humming with the energy of the dead humans, and she turned to look at an exhausted Epharis.

She moved to him, he inched over to give her room in his seat, and she kissed his cheek gently.

"The demons are rooting for me," she said, and he laughed softly, slipping his arm around her, and she settled into his side until he recovered.

50

THE TWINS

It was close to morning when she finally drew away from the sleeping Lich and she covered him with a blanket, ordering the humans be taken away. She swept through the halls, catching sight of her pale grey-blue skin in the reflections of the dark window.

She huffed at the change, having hoped it would stay her snowy white colour, but no such luck.

When she opened the door, she found the twins had almost completely drained themselves and were both looking pale, Versalis monitoring the situation, and Alaric snoring like a waterfall on the end seat.

Daemon leapt to his feet as she swept in and came to her side, cupping her face and staring into her eyes.

To her surprise, he leant in and kissed her firmly, deepening it until he was nearly throwing her to the floor. She smirked at the furious growl coming from Jaia, but she allowed the kiss, breaking it finally and pressing him back.

"You stop that, now isn't the time for a tryst," she scolded, and his grin was wicked. She knew what the demon was doing and she wanted Jaia to suffer as much as she had when he abandoned her.

Stepping to Versalis's side, she looked to the crystal that had come to life, a soft glow emanating from its core, but it wasn't the brightness she remembered. "It must take them both," she said to Daemon, who had followed her and was looking at the gem.

He grunted his agreement and she turned to Uzo, who slept on the floor by the balcony, and then to Jagum, who had propped himself up in the corner, his long legs stretched out. They were all so exhausted and she wanted them to rest as much as possible.

"You should sleep, too," she said to Daemon, who looked frustrated, but agreed.

"We might as well get this started," she said gently, and Versalis looked up at her.

The twins pulled the needles from their arms and stood, Kai looking exhausted and Jaia looking ready to rip her apart, but they followed her into her room in a moody silence.

Without a word, she settled herself on the bed and watched the two vampires as they brought in the stands and carefully inserted new needles into her arms, their fingers oddly warm on her as they worked but no blood flooded into her system yet.

Kai bit into her wrist but Jaia stared at her, angry and hurt, but she only met his eyes in a silent dare for him to say a word.

Dropping his eyes to her wrist, he bit down hard and gnawed at her skin in retaliation. She smiled slightly, knowing she was hurting him, but it made her feel better about their situation.

It felt good to have their teeth digging into her and she shivered, her eyes shut as they drew as much blood from her as they dared before they moved away, both flushed with it.

Silently the twins moved and both pins were pulled in unison, ensuring the same amount of blood from each of them filled her system.

She hissed in a breath as the blood hit her veins, her body singing at the changes it tried to make in her, slow at first, but it would speed up before too much longer.

The first day didn't feel like much to her, just exhaustion and sleep, waking to find the angry Jaia staring at her as she slept and watching her for the minute changes that took place on her physical form.

"Stop staring at me like that," she breathed halfway through the second day, too tired to care much after her body first fought to replenish her blood, and then switched to fight off the change the new blood caused in her.

"Why him?" he demanded, and she frowned at him, barely able to stay awake. "Why the demon?"

She smiled slightly at the remembered argument in the forest, but her smile only seemed to enrage him further. "He never abandoned me," she said quietly and jumped as the bed shifted, finding herself face to face with the furious vampire.

"You think we left on a whim?" he growled, a mere inch from her face.

"I don't know, Jaia, you never bothered to explain why you simply abandoned us. One might see that as desertion if one chose to look at it that way. You're a soldier, you should have known better."

His eyes burned with fury and she met them with calm indifference. "We left to save your life, stupid woman," he snarled, and she lifted her brows.

"Oh, please do tell me why your abandoning me was for my own good. Was it also for my own good when you manipulated me into taking on this quest to begin with?"

His eyes narrowed and before he could start yelling, Versalis came in and Jaia seemed to vanish into nothing.

"I'll go today," the vampire King said, pretending not to notice the tension. He sat down at her side and gently turned her head to the side, his teeth cutting cleanly through her skin.

Her eyes found Jaia, who glared at her, but she turned her eyes away and before long she fell asleep as her body was drained of what little blood had been produced.

Waking the next morning, she looked around blearily and found Kai sitting at her side, his feet bare and legs crossed as he stared at nothing on the wall, his head in his hands. He was deep in thought and it took him a few minutes to see she was awake.

His face lit up but then faded again and she felt a pang of pain at his sadness, but she refused to give in to him. "How are you feeling?" he asked, stroking her hair back from her face.

"Like three vampires are trying to turn me," she quipped and he laughed gently, his eyes greedily taking in her pale face.

"It should be done by morning," he said and she nodded, feeling the strength inside her as their blood rushed into her muscles, enhancing them and leaving her deliciously warm. "I'm sorry we left," he said, and her calm turned icy.

"Let's not discuss that right now, Kai," she said.

How did he manage to make her feel like she had kicked a puppy with the pitiful face he gave her? She didn't know but she felt guilty for hurting him and the guilt made her angry.

"Won't you at least let us explain?" he asked in a small voice.

"What is there to explain? You left, not even halfway through. You refused to try and take my blood, instead you tucked your tails and bolted. We needed you and you weren't there."

Kai's eyes dropped to the bed and he pulled at a thread from the naked mattress. "When you stopped being a vampire we felt suddenly free of your hold."

His words stabbed her over and over and she gritted her teeth to hold down her sudden pain. "So you only came because you had to," she growled. "Get out, Kai."

He looked hurt, fear in his eyes as she ordered him out. "Etani, please don't say that. It's not like that, we wanted to help you. But when the bond was broken, we wanted to run. We knew it was only a matter of time before we started getting really hungry and we didn't want to kill you. We had no reason to stay."

She planted her foot against his side and shoved him off the edge of the bed, his grunt of pain satisfying to her. "Once this is over, I never want to see you or your brother again. Get out."

His words ripped her heart in half and there was no stopping the tears as the vampire fled the room, his sobs quiet.

Reaching up, she pulled down the two bags, clutching them both tight between her fingers and squeezed, hissing as the pressure forced their blood deeper into her at a rate that she knew was dangerous but she didn't care. She wanted it over and she wanted them gone.

"Versalis I need the rest of the blood," she called out.

He appeared at the door in an instant, confused, with the bags in his hand.

Seeing what she had done, he growled but she motioned him forward, squeezing the last of the blood into her system until her cheeks flushed and her body screamed in pain.

She took the remaining two bags from him and hooked them up, her eyes shut at the pain as she squeezed them, and she felt blood oozing down her upper lip but she ignored it.

Pausing only when she felt like she was going to pop, she looked up at Versalis and he stared at her in horror.

"Etani you're going to kill yourself," he pleaded, unsure of what to do.

"Does it matter at this point?" she snapped, the man flinching at her tone. Her body was on fire and sweat broke out over her skin. She pulled her dress off and shoved it away, leaving her in her undergarments and she only felt slightly cooler.

Versalis fled the room and returned a short while later, ignoring the enquiries as he moved to cover her skin with cold clothes and then rushing from the room again and returning with ice from the kitchens.

It cooled her and she smiled slightly, the bed soon soaked with water dripping onto the floor.

He didn't ask why she had done it, seeing Kai's distress shortly beforehand and knowing what she had done.

Within the hour the giant chunks of ice had melted and she was burning, her body flaming, and Versalis had thrown open the window to let cold air in.

Panting at the heat, she could feel her body changing at a rate faster than anybody had ever been designed to go through it, her mind warping and leaving her confused before snapping into a clarity that was like a slap to the face.

Blood dripped almost constantly from her nose and she looked up as Epharis came into the room, catching a glimpse of Jaia and Kai, who looked at each other in fear.

"Stupid woman, you can't speed this up," the Lich snarled as he approached her, gripping her elbow and his nail raked down her forearm.

She screamed both in pain and relief as blood spilled, the pressure in her veins easing.

He swore at her, curling his fingers around the cut to help it seal as he took the bags and examined how much she had left. "How much did she force down?" he asked, and Versalis swallowed.

"A whole bag and then some."

"How did she get that much?" Epharis demanded, and the vampire looked guilty. "Get out," Epharis snarled, and Versalis fled the room. "If you were that keen on killing yourself you could have given in to the demon," he said, pulling the needles from her arms and throwing the half bags onto the table.

When she made a sound of protest, he took her hands and lifted her chin to better examine her eyes.

"They use so much because your body will fight it, with this much inside you there is no need to use as much. You're in for a lot of pain, my darling."

He wasn't wrong; she had never experienced pain like that and he endured her screaming, her profanity, and her clawing his chest as she struggled to get free of him, but he refused to let go, even when she cried and begged him to.

He endured it all in stony silence, his eyes set on the distance and finally, after four long and terrible hours, she felt the final snap inside her and found herself looking around the room, the particles of dust and the grain of the wood clear to her vision as it had been before.

She breathed slowly, her pain and agony switching off like a blown out candle.

He looked down at her and sucked in a breath, his pupils dilating as he took her in and she smiled slyly at his sudden desire.

She slipped herself free of his arms and swept from the room, eyes opening to take her in as she wiped still-wet blood from her lower face, her sweat keeping it liquid.

She made a soft sound and took Epharis by the front of his shirt, pulling him into the bathroom with her, and ignored Jaia's fury.

Lifting up the lank mass of her hair, she showed him the complexity of the brassiere and he understood, immediately setting to work on the clasps and laces until the heavy metal came free.

She tossed it to him and he caught it, almost dropping it as his eyes caught her bare chest as she hooked her thumbs in her undergarments and pushed them down, too focused on her bath to notice him burning behind her.

She ran the bath and stepped into it before it had managed to even fill the bottom, sitting down with her head under the stream and she moaned at the warmth washing away her sweat.

Her moan seemed to be too much for Jaia and the door burst in, his fury fizzling out as he took in the scene, the Lich's face red and clutching the metallic garment and her sitting under the tap, the water steaming the room.

Her brow lifted as he looked first at her, then the Lich, and back again.

"Etani and I need to talk," the vampire said angrily, and Epharis snorted his amusement.

"Good luck," the Lich said as he left, taking her brassiere with him.

She was around knee-deep in the water when she decided to add oil and a soapy substance that was new; she was immediately delighted to find a thick carpet of white bubbles forming and she grinned, ignoring the furious vampire as he approached the bath.

She looked up when she heard his boots hitting the marble and she stared at him in surprise as he stripped out of his jacket and he stepped into the bath, still mostly clothed.

"You're going to listen to me," he snarled and she was immediately wary, not trusting him as he sat down across from her, stubbornly set on staying in her bath, clothed.

She said nothing, instead scooping up a handful of bubbles and blowing them at him.

He jerked back, glaring at her and her stubborn refusal to speak.

The water was up around her ribs when he joined her and it was up around her underarms when she finally turned off the water and looked at him, neither of them willing to be the first one to talk.

Deciding he was just as stubborn as she was, she crawled on her knees to the side of the bath and pulled down a few bottles, ignoring him until the water moved and she felt him beside her.

He gripped her wrist painfully tight and she went still, refusing to look at him. "You made Kai upset," he breathed in her ear. She frowned, giving her arm a little tug, but it only made him grip her tighter. "You both made me upset when you left," she said finally and he growled softly, yanking her arm and forcing her around to look at him.

"You know why we had to leave," he hissed, his free arm going around her waist.

She didn't want to use her magic on him, but he was becoming aggressive and she would if she needed to defend herself, though the thought of actually hurting him stung her.

"You had no reason to stay once the bond was broken. I was not enough of a reason for you to stay," she hissed and pushed at his arm, trying to pry it off her.

"You have been an addiction to us both since the instant we laid eyes on you. We finally had a chance to be free and we took it," Jaia snarled, refusing to let her go.

"Yes, you did. You realised that there was nothing there for you except your addiction to me and you would rather take death over being around me when you don't have to be," she pressed her hand against his chest, trying to push herself back from him.

"Yes, we did. He is my brother and if I could rid him of the addiction that is you, I will always take it. But it only made us realise that your magic isn't the addiction. *You* are the addiction and we had no way to get back to you."

She huffed when he refused to budge and she glared up at him in anger. "Talk in circles all you want, Jaia, it means nothing. Let me go." She dug her nails into his chest in warning but it only made him pull her closer.

He bared his teeth at her and pressed her back into the side of the tub, trapping her in place between him and the tiles. His hand moved from her back to her throat and he held her still, not enough to choke her but enough so that she was forced to pay attention to him.

Anger that he would dare touch her mounted and her hand flew, connecting with his face.

The sound of her hand meeting his cheek was loud in the silent room and his eyes flashed a dangerous red that sent a thrill of terror down her spine

His grin was feral as he leant over her, his fingertips leaving bruises in the delicate skin of her throat and she was torn between the need to fight and her need to never hurt him. She didn't know what to do.

Keeping her pinned there, his free hand rose between them and she watched with a certain fascination as the buttons of his soaked shirt slipped free and he jerked her forward until she was pressed into his bare chest.

All of her instincts were telling her to run or to fight and yet she struggled with it, her need to protect the twins burning out her anger and leaving her feeling hopelessly confused.

She could feel in him that his anger was setting him off and the part of him that was rational Jaia was being lost under his own fear and grief at losing her, but she wanted him to release her and finally she pressed her hand against his chest.

Tapping into Winter, she sent a pulse of cold into him that made him freeze in place, his eyes wide that she would dare.

"Let me go," she whispered, her eyes meeting his and she felt that thrill of terror. Jaia was no longer in control; it was the vampire who had taken over and her fear made him smile slowly.

It was not often that the vampire in any of them managed to gain control and she knew that while it was not him, it was still him in a way.

His fingers crushed her throat and she whimpered, her hand finding his chest once more, but he retaliated.

He slammed her against the wall of the bath, and she hissed in a breath and the connection to Faerie was lost in her distraction, his teeth bared and eyes flaming crimson.

"You are mine," he growled, and she shivered at the words, shaking her head as much as she could with his grip on her throat.

"Jaia, stop," she gasped, struggling with him, but his grip only tightened and his fury mounted.

Without a word, he dragged her out of the water and onto the tiles, following after her, and he settled atop her with his free hand going to her thigh and prying her leg away for him to settle between them.

"Stop!" she cried as she felt his hand moving between them, her cry cut off as his grip around her throat released her only to cover her mouth and he squeezed her face, leaving her mostly silenced.

"No, Etani, you aren't allowed to leave me," he whispered, staring down at her and his fingers clenched on her inner thigh, terrifying her all the more. "You belong to me; you are mine."

Shaking her head, she whimpered as he considered her face, then smiled faintly, his eyes going down her body.

"You can be mine willingly, or I can simply *make* you mine," he hissed, jerking at her and forcing her legs further apart to allow him to grind his groin against hers.

Her mind went blank as she stared up into his eyes, trying to wrap her mind around what he was saying. Was he threatening her? Threatening to force himself on her? Fear flooded her system and she shook her head quickly, her eyes wide as she stared up into his, a new feeling beginning to grow inside her that she couldn't understand.

"You can deny it all you like, my precious love. But you have belonged to me for a long time, and I'm not going to let you go. I will not allow you to leave me, you are my mate."

What could she do? She could only stare up at him, torn.

Part of her was terrified of him, but a new part of herself revelled in his dominance, in his demands that she remain his, and she contemplated that part of herself, contemplated what Mara had said.

Finally she gave a slow, barely-there hint of a nod, and Jaia's tension eased, his lips parting as he stared down at her and slowly his hand left her mouth, uncertain.

When she didn't immediately scream, his face showed his dark joy and his mouth came down on hers in a hard, demanding kiss that she returned somewhat hesitantly at first.

They had both hurt her terribly, had left her broken and bleeding, but Jaia was not going to let go of her and his demand for her to remain his was doing all sorts of things to her body and mind.

Returning the kiss as roughly as he gave it, she shivered as his hand left her to move to himself, his lips moving with wild abandon against hers and she realised belatedly what he was intending as she felt him tugging the ties of his pants free.

Breaking the kiss, she shook her head, his eyes immediately narrowing on her.

"We can't..." she whispered, fear swelling as he seemed intent on ignoring her refusal.

"Why not?" he demanded, the hiss of the ties coming free leaving her trembling at the thought of his simply taking what he wanted whether she wanted it or not.

"Epharis will kill us both. He'll kill Kai and everyone," she whispered urgently, trying to think of how best to disengage herself from him.

"Then we kill him," he said, slowing in his attempt to get his pants down.

"Yes, we have to kill him first," she agreed, trying to hide her relief when he stopped undressing himself.

His forehead rested against hers and she bit her lip gently, staring up into those hungry, glowing crimson eyes.

"You are mine," he growled, his possessive stare heavy on her.

"I'm yours," she whispered, trembling her.

Finally he released her and straightened up, kneeling between her legs and staring down at her.

51

THE END

*S*he flushed as his eyes raked down her, embarrassed by the thought of what he was seeing in that moment, naked and exposed, but her attempts to cover herself and close her legs were met with a growl.

He looked glorious kneeling over her, his pants hanging so far down his hips that his erection alone kept them from falling to his knees, his tight muscles and anger giving him the look of a God.

He was triumphant at finally getting what he wanted, even if it wasn't to physically have her body. She belonged to him and he almost vibrated with that knowledge, staring down at what was his.

Leaning down, he pulled her up into a sitting position and his arms wrapped tightly around her shoulders, holding her to him and stroking her hair tenderly, his lips pressing hard against the top of her head as he clung to her.

When his fingers curled under her chin and tilted her head back, she met his lips without hesitation, the realisation that she and Jaia were... whatever it was they were, making her feel oddly warm regardless of how it had come about. But still she was scared of him and what he might expect from their relationship.

Without a word, they decided to finish bathing but no real answer had come from their encounter and his actions only further confused her, although he seemed calmer now that he had her agreement. She didn't know what she was going to do about him and the threat he represented. Vampires were exceptionally possessive creatures and she knew his claim on her would complicate things with Epharis, but that would have to wait until later.

She felt his eyes on her as she slipped from the bathroom, clean and dressed, and he followed after her, his eyes alert to the other men around her but none seemed to pose any real threat to what was his. Glancing around, she noted that Daemon was gone along with Jagum and she was very glad for that. What was she going to tell Daemon?

She felt her stomach clench at the thought and swallowed hard, realising that Daemon's response would be the worst part. She couldn't let him kill Jaia, but he would be fully within his right to kill the vampire for the threats.

She was lost in thought, trying to decide what to do, when she noticed Kai watching her.

Kai had noticed the intense stare from his twin and tilted his head in confusion, unsure of their new tension, nor how she felt about either of them, and she felt odd, as though Kai would be able to sense his twin's mark on her or what he had done.

Jaia was smug, however, dropping onto the couch and lounging back as though all of his problems had been washed away in the instant he forced her down onto the tiles. But to her it had only made more problems and these were bigger than the ones she had known before.

When Kai tried to speak to her, she fled the room and heard him turn on Jaia and demand to know what had happened, but Jaia only laughed in a low, growling sound that rolled shivers down her spine.

Slipping into the lab, she looked over the dusty instruments and tools of her trade and made a mental note that she had a lot of work to do if she was going to replenish all the supplies that had been lost on their trip.

After a few minutes of collecting things she would need, she looked up to see Versalis sliding into the room. Her eyes immediately went to the warm crimson glow at his chest and that need to take it from him was enough to make her fingers twitch, but she kept her hands to herself. "I don't want to fight, Versalis," she said gently, in a tired voice.

"I'm not here to fight. I make no excuses for my leaving, only to beg for your forgiveness," he said, and her lips turned down into a frown as she studied him.

He was as handsome as ever, his pale lavender eyes boring into hers in a silent demand.

"Why should I forgive you?" she asked finally, the silence between them stretching on too long.

"Because you're angry right now but you still love us, Kai especially. And your punishing Jaia isn't going to end well. He is strong and as stubborn as you, one of you will get hurt."

She stayed silent as her mind went to the bathroom and his near-loss of control. "I could always just leave," she said, and she saw the flash of panic in his eyes before he controlled himself.

"You know full well no one would let you leave. Epharis, Alaric, the twins." His eyes were hard and the 'me' was a clear threat between them.

"You're assuming that you can contain me," she growled, and his grin was a flash of white.

"How's that bell going for you?"

Unconsciously shifting her foot, the bell tinkled into the silence. "None of you deserve forgiveness, you're deserters," she snapped, and anger flashed over his face.

"Don't call us that," he growled, a warning in his voice.

Setting down the empty bottle she had been about to crush in her fist, she approached him and stood only a few inches from his face. "You and the two of them are deserters. You abandoned the mission and fled. Like cowards."

His eyes flashed to crimson and she moved on instinct, her hand landing on his chest before his hands left his sides and she pulled viciously on Faerie, forcing the energy into him and throwing him backwards. The door slammed to the floor as he struck it, landing hard on his back and rolling back to land on his feet.

She followed him out, ignoring both Kai and Jaia as they stood frozen in place, shocked by the projectile vampire. Her skin tingled at the use of the magic and she turned on the twins, both taking a step back from her in unison. Deciding they were not the threat, she turned to Versalis only to have him slam into her and they both went down hard.

His fingers dug into her shoulders to try and hold her down but her hand found his chest and she pushed energy into him. She threw him hard enough that he hit the repaired ceiling and landed back where she had been only a second before.

Rolling to her feet, she took advantage of him being down to drive her foot into his side and he grunted, hitting the wall under the force of the blow.

He was on his feet in a second and she bared her teeth at him.

She paused as a keening sound started up somewhere in the back of her mind and she tilted her head, listening to the sound.

Versalis hit her and landed hard on top of her, his fingers curling around her throat.

Hissing, she reached up, and he froze as her fingers closed around the gem under his shirt and power rocked through her body, screaming inside her like the winds of a tornado.

Destruction and desire were her world and she wanted it, but someone grabbed her hands and her fingers were pried off the gem, her arms forced down to the ground.

The power left her in an instant and she felt its loss like a physical blow, looking up into the crimson eyes of the vampire King.

Kai and Jaia joined him in helping to hold her down and she glared up at them all.

"Get off me!" she snarled, her eye beginning to twitch as the keening grew louder. "What is that noise?"

They all looked confused by the question and Versalis's eyes dulled back to violet in his confusion.

The door burst open and Uzo froze at the scene, totally confused, but his eyes found hers and she knew he could hear it, too. "It's happening!" he screamed. "The Creators are here! Why are they here, Etani? You should have taken their magic!"

She could only stare up at him in confusion. "But that doesn't make any sense," she said, not understanding it at all.

"You, boy, give her the gem," Uzo demanded, and Versalis hesitated, unsure of if he should obey the order. Kai and Jaia let go of her arms and she shoved the vampire away from her.

Without a word, she held out her hand in a silent demand. "You don't get to control death anymore," she snapped, but his eyes narrowed on her.

"You can have it only if you promise to return it after. You are too dangerous to be running around like that all the time," he demanded. She didn't want to admit that he was right, and so she bared her teeth at him in anger.

"Promise!" he yelled, and she jumped, finally nodding, but he refused to hand it over.

"I promise. I promise, I promise," she finally snapped, and he lifted the chain over his head.

The gem was deliciously warm in her grip as she took it from him and the tornado of power filled her mind, screaming for release.

Slipping the gem over her head, it settled between her breasts and she felt the brand on her wrist burning into life. Looking at it, she smiled warmly at the sight of her weapon at her call once more.

Turning to the window, she saw that the day had darkened under the heavy clouds. "Where are you..." she whispered, her voice taking on an eerie echo in her mind.

The sky stopped crying and the suddenness of the change was jarring, like someone had turned off a tap, and she looked out over the darkened field.

An enormous tear in reality had formed and the air itself warped as hundreds of figures stepped out, each causing light to flash like lightning.

She heard the others joining her and they stood in utter silence as they watched, terrified and enthralled by the sight of so many beings who had come to destroy their world.

"Well shit..." Uzo said, and she had to agree, that was the exact right thing to say.

ABOUT THE AUTHOR

Born in Mackay, North Queensland in Australia, N. Malone's writing journey started at the age of nine. It wasn't until the age of twenty-nine that the career began.
The story of Etani had been building for nearly ten years, daydreams and forums until the character became a reality when book one had begun. Now, with nine books in the works, the story can continue.

"If you like writing, then write."

nmalone.net

 facebook.com/Author.N.Malone
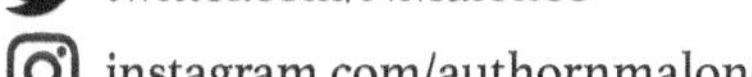 twitter.com/NMalone8
instagram.com/authornmalone

AFTERWORD

If you enjoyed Always a Fan, you can continue the adventure in book four "Goddess of Death", available on pre-order: https://books2read.com/u/b6ZZQJ

Your opinions are valuable, please take a few moments to leave a rating.

www.ingramcontent.com/pod-product-compliance
Lightning Source LLC
Chambersburg PA
CBHW020538120726
47903CB00001B/23